Stealing Symbols & Souls

Jerry
Hope you enjoy the whole piece
Like you did the chapters!
DT Sanders

D T Sanders

This is a work of fiction. All the characters and events portrayed in this story are fictional, and any resemblance to real people or incidents is purely coincidental.

ISBN 13: 978-1514663493
ISBN 10: 151466349X

Cover Illustration by S. C. Watson

Table of Contents

Chapter 1

"Somebody broke into my lab."

"Somebody," the campus police officer echoed. The officer was over six feet tall, towering over her. Other than his height, he wasn't remarkable: brown hair, brown eyes, brown clothes, brown gun holster, he even had a brown name tag with Brown on it.

"Yes, somebody broke into my lab, again, and destroyed my printer and desktop." The smallish raven-haired woman had drawn herself up to her full wrathful height of about five three and crossed her arms under her ample chest.

The officer noticed the chest part. She glanced down to see herself showing too much cleavage. She hadn't buttoned her flannel shirt up all the way, again, and the tee was scoop necked. "My eyes are up here," she said forcefully.

"Yes ma'am." He drew a deeper breath and scribbled his stubby pencil on his wrinkled notebook. "Someone broke into your magic lab and broke some stuff."

"It is not a magic lab. It is a lab for conducting comparative symbolic studies." She sighed again. "I am comparing symbols from cultures, old and new, and creating patterns of similarities." He gave her a blank, uncomprehending look.

"Look." She picked up a No. 2 wood pencil from the bench and showed him the eraser on the end. He was trying not to smile and failing.

She turned away from him and gestured with the pencil. "This pencil has no magic or power to it. It is non-conductive, won't channel electricity, but use it for the right symbol …" Her voice trailed off as she concentrated. Slowly, she began tracing something in midair. As she moved the pencil in the air, it left the slight residue of a faint light trail. Slowly, a complete, precise, complex geometric symbol, dimly glowing, took form and hovered in the air. With a mumbled word and a poking gesture from the pencil, a photoflash lit the lab.

The officer jerked back from her. "Wow."

"Yeah, not magic! Science!" She emphasized this by poking the now blackened eraser at him.

"Whatever," he seemed to be paying more attention. "Who are you again?"

Her shoulders slumped in frustration. "Stephanie Blackraven. I'm a PhD candidate in the Applied Physics department, Mystology section. I am working here on a fellowship."

"Oh yeah, one of the wizards." His stubby pencil did more damage to the notebook.

"I am not a wizard. I'm an engineer." She realized getting angry wasn't helping, but for just a moment, she wanted to stab him with the pencil. "Look, this is the third time in four months that someone has broken into my lab and melted down my printers. This is interfering with my research. It has to stop."

"Take it easy, doctor; I am just trying to get the facts down."

"I'm not a doctor yet. I am a PhD candidate." She wondered how Barney Fife, here, got this job and whether he had the bullet today or not. "So facts, you want facts." She turned and marched over to the door to do a Vanna White. "Fact one; here is the door to the lab, one of two, and as you can see, there is no sign of forced entry. The door assembly is still in an unblemished state. No scratches or gouges. The other door," she pointed across the lab to the far wall, "is closed and locked at all times. There is no sign of damage there as well." She marched back to officer who was smiling at her again.

"Fact two; I left the lab last night at 11:30 and locked," she turned and did a double hand point at the door she had just walked from, "that door. Fact three; I show up here this morning at 9:30 and the door was ajar, that means open a little bit, to find the lab a complete mess and my equipment melted." She gave him a smiling ta-da pose. He was smiling at her still.

"You think this is funny?"

His smile faded, "No ma'am."

"Margret's lab got broken into two months ago. She's just across the hall. Across campus, Sylvia Bloomerton's lab got ransacked five months ago. Haven't you guys been investigating or something? Aren't you supposed to look for clues or something?"

He looked like a deer in the headlights, mouth open, eyes vacant, then something else slid across his eyes.

Officer Brown was a different person when he asked, "Margret Vanderhousen?"

"Yeah."

"Did you know Miss Vanderhousen?"

Stephanie frowned, "A little, she and I shared equipment sometimes. Chatted in the hallway. Her research isn't the same as mine. So, now you're interested?"

"Do you know where Miss Vanderhousen is?"

"No! I haven't seen her the last few days." She thought about it a moment. "No, make that a week. I spoke with her a week ago, last Tuesday. Why?"

"No reason." His pencil punished the paper again.

"Oh, you've got to be kidding. Don't give me that no reason thing. What is going on?"

"Hey Steph, oohh shit! Not again!" A male voice exclaimed from across the room. They both turned to look. A dapper, handsome, tallish guy was framed by the doorway. Sharp creased chinos, starched turquoise shirt with a cardigan sweater that just seemed to make it work, and a hat with a feather. He had forgotten more about dressing well than she ever knew which was really odd for a handsome white guy. She was more the hiking boots, jeans, and flannel shirt type.

"Bruce, thank God!" She waved around the lab. "They hit us again."

"Oh, girlfriend," he said, moving quickly over to give her a little hug. "How do they keep getting in?"

"A key," she blurted out. "They must have a key."

"This your boyfriend?" The officer asked.

"Lab assistant, Bruce Richardson," Stephanie provided.

Bruce was just good looking, about as straight as a circle, and didn't care who knew. He smiled big for the cop, offering his hand for a shake. "And you are?"

The officer eyed him coolly. "Investigating this break-in."

"Steph, hun, aren't you supposed to be teaching Rosemary's class right now?"

Stephanie jerked and looked at her watch. "Shit, I was supposed to be there five minutes ago. I have to go." She darted back to a desk in the corner to grab a backpack. "Bruce, talk to Barney Fife here, and see if you can get him to understand there is a pattern in this."

"Barney Fife, like from *The Andy Griffith Show?*" the officer said with no smile.

Bruce had bent down and snagged a lab coat out of drawer. Stephanie winced as she realized she had said that out loud.

"You mean the one they wouldn't give the bullets to?" the officer asked.

"Ah, yeah," she said as she darted by to grab the offered coat and made a beeline for the door.

"Put it on. Look professional, and, girl, cover up that shirt. My God, flannel should be outlawed."

She darted out the door just as Bruce said, "Don't mind her. She gets a little preoccupied sometimes, you know, anal. Now, what about those question? Would you like to get a cappuccino?"

She hated being late, but this time it wasn't her fault. She knew the route to class by heart: down the hall, through the door, up stairs to ground level, more doors, through the trees, cross the common's courtyard. Dodge slow students hanging out there, down more stairs, another courtyard, grass, cut through the trees, and into the Cramer building to the basement classroom. She was only ten minutes late, so she hadn't hit the magic number of fifteen. That was when the students figured that the prof wasn't going to make it so they scattered. They were grad students, so they might give the prof until twenty past.

She was helping teach Professor Stein's class on Applied Symbology. Rosemary Stein was also her doctorial advisor and mentor. She had only the slightest hint of "the gift," but it was enough to demonstrate some simple symbols. Stephanie had the knack; the expression for a huge amount of the gift, or being an anal-retentive engineer, both applied in her case. Her gift allowed the more complex symbols to light up and sometimes even do other things. Truth-be-told, she taught this class more than Rosemary did.

Slamming through the door, she slowly stopped. There was a mountain standing inside the door, wearing a suit. He had short, well-groomed, dark hair, wore Old Spice aftershave and leather shoes, and big just didn't begin to explain it. She wasn't sure he had a neck. His hand dwarfed the spiral notebook he held, like it would make him look like a student.

"Excuse me," she said.

The mountain turned carefully. She saw a craggy, tough, clean-shaven face, deep-set, steely colored expressive eyes, and a slowly breaking smile. "Sorry. Is this Applied Symbology?" His voice probably set off the seismic sensors.

"Yeah, I'm a little late, but we'll get started shortly. You a grad student?"

"No." His eyes sparkled with amusement. "My name's Joe Bremer. I'm just monitoring. I'd like …"

"Sorry Joe, I'm running a little late, and I need to …" That was when she noticed all the grad students were sitting in their chairs. Normally, they milled about or gathered around up front so they can see the symbols as she drew them, it made it easier to discuss what was going on. But now, they were all sitting quietly in their seats. It was weird.

She saw the cause and it made her day --just-- worse.

Standing up front in his oh-so-typical, calculated casual posture was Professor Rhinebolt, her least favorite member of the faculty, mainly because he took every possible opportunity to discredit her work. He was thin and seemed tall, but wasn't. Not particularly handsome and had this god-awful handlebar mustache. However, on second look, he seemed to be a little beefier and his thinning hair was thicker. He had like five PhD's, none of them really technical, boatloads of tenure, and made sure everyone knew it.

He was also standing on the Solomon circle they had been creating. He had been demonstrating something, but her entry or Joe's had caused his concentration to waiver, and the faintly glowing symbol was fading away. He didn't have much of the gift, either.

"Ah, there she is." He looked down his nose at her, criticizing her … everything, and obviously annoyed with her arrival.

"Hi, everybody, sorry I'm late." She moved over to the demonstration table in front to drop her backpack and fish out her notes. "Someone broke into my lab again, and I had to deal with the police." She pulled her lab coat on the rest of the way.

"So, what brings you here, professor?" she asked while moving to the podium with her notes.

"Two things actually, but they can wait." He said it as if it was some great sacrifice. "You shouldn't keep your students waiting any longer."

She gritted her teeth and gestured. "You're standing on my lecture."

He glanced down and then back at her. "Oh, sorry."

She could tell he wasn't really.

"Isn't that supposed to be hanging on the wall?" He sharply asked.

"Normally, but we are in the process of correcting it," she blurted out.

"What do you mean 'correcting'?" His tone was less than pleasant.

She winced inwardly. She had forgotten that he was the one who had originally created it.

"There are inaccuracies in the outer ring symbols and on the inner dual spokes." Pete, one of the students, helpfully supplied.

"Yeah, and the middle ring has those little squiggles that are supposed to be the other way," Andy added.

"Who has …"

"It's right here in Professor Stein's notes." The ever-helpful Tom chimed in. Apparently, they didn't like Rhinebolt, either.

"Let me see that." He snatched the notes from Tom's hand. He studied it for a moment and then turned to Stephanie. "These are your notes. This is part of your doctoral thesis." There was venom in his tone.

"Yes, they are. But …" she started.

"This is strictly against the rules. You can't use your thesis material until is approved by the curriculum board. You're just a student like these here." His voice dripped with scorn as his hand waved dismissively at the class.

"Professor Stein had it approved. This is her lecture. I just help out as her teaching assistant."

"I don't care about Professor Stein's opinion. Show me! Prove to me these are correct!" he yelled, waving the notes toward the circle.

It just pissed her off. She didn't like him, anyway, and then to belittle her like this in front of the class. "All right, Tom, help me move this." Tom leaped up, smiling to help her lift the hanging off the floor. Under it was another series of symbols that were subtly different. It was three concentric rings with symbols laid out and aligned in a precise pattern. Stephanie snatched a chisel point Sharpie out of her backpack. "All right guys gather round. Consider this a pop quiz. I draw them, you name them." Using a compass, protractor, triangle, and a piece of string attached at the exact center, she started filling in the remaining symbols to the drawing on the floor. As she added one, the students would either name it or look it up. She lost herself in the symmetry and motion.

A while later, Stephanie knelt in the center of the concentric circles and wiped a drop of blood off the inner ring line. She had poked herself with the compass. There was still blood in the dark part of the ring, but nothing broke the lines. She checked everything. It was perfect. Just the way her mind's eye had pictured it.

"That doesn't prove anything." The snide tone of Professor Rhinebolt just made her madder.

"It's ready. It would ignite with a trigger word." She glanced back down at the tracing. "No one's been able to energize these types of circles yet."

"Do it Steph," Tom called out. "Light it up."

"You can do it, Steph," Andy yelled.

"Yes, Ms. Blackraven, show us all how it's done," Rhinebolt added with a singsong, condescending, snide lilt. He just wouldn't let up.

She was so mad she didn't stop to think about what she was doing. She took all the anger she was feeling at Rhinebolt and directed it at the circles. With a small pushing gesture from the Sharpie, she said, "Orce-Fay Ield-Fay." A bright flash and the smell of burnt Sharpie filled the room.

All the rings were shining on the floor, and the fiery symbols between the rings glowed hotly, then faded out, leaving nothing behind.

Applause sounded in the classroom. "Holy shit, Steph!" another student yelled.

"Well," she started, feeling a little vindicated and embarrassed. "Now, you can see how the symbols interact and would appear if the circle was truly functional." She tried to take a step and ran into an invisible wall. "What?" Everyone jerked to their feet and were staring now.

Professor Rhinebolt stepped forward and poked his finger into an invisible wall. "No," he said with complete incredulity. "It can't be a functioning containment circle." He swept a book off the podium to see it bounce off the invisible wall.

"I told you she was doctoral material, Dean Rogers." Rosemary Stein's voice sounded very smug from the back of the room. "And that, my good sir, is definitely a solid thesis defense."

Chapter 2

Joe stood back and watched the room devolve into chaos. Some of the students threw things at the circle to watch them bounce off. Others started texting as fast as their fingers could fly. One was taking a video with his phone. The dean and two professors were arguing about the significance of something. In the midst of it all was the buxom, raven-haired little gal standing wide-eyed, startled, and speculative in the middle of the impossibility.

Joe guessed she was about five foot two, black hair, dark blue eyes, heart-shaped face, slightly tanned skin, blue jeans, hiking boots, big chest, and nice hips. Lots of cleavage, in an unintended display. He realized suddenly she was beautiful in a down-home, girl-next-door kind of way. She was hot; he liked her. A deep kind of burning started low in his abdomen.

He snorted and shook himself. She was a person of interest, and he was here gathering data, not looking for a girlfriend. Well, maybe not a POI, but at least a source. He needed to treat her with some respect. And based on everyone else's reaction, she had just done the impossible.

More official-looking persons, probably professors, arrived and started clucking with the others off to the side. Lots of pointing, arm waving, book shaking, all talking at once, but no one listening to anything anyone else had to say. Most of the grad students packed up and headed off, probably to their next class.

Joe made his way around the edge of the room until he was standing behind the circles. "Hi. You okay?" he asked.

"Yeah. Just surprised." She sighed and crossed her arms under her breasts, which just highlighted everything.

"Ah, can we chat, since it doesn't seem like anyone else wants to talk to you?"

She gave him a puzzled look. "I'm trapped in a Solomon Circle. It's not like I can walk away."

Joe smiled. "True. I'm a Bellevue police officer, and I would like your input on something." He hesitated. "I don't need to talk right now. Maybe after you extract yourself from this, we could grab a coffee?"

She smiled slowly. "I'm trapped in a circle, and you're hitting on me?"

"No! No! It's ah ..." Joe was really nervous now. "It's business, police business," he added lamely.

She smiled in a mischievous way, "So, police officers don't go out?"

"No! Yes." Joe smiled. "Yes, we do, but this is business."

"So, this is official police business?"

"Yes, well sort of."

"So, you are hitting on me?" Her smile deepened.

"No, no, no, it just that ..."

"So, I'm not worth hitting on, or this isn't police business?"

This girl is too smart and cute, Joe thought. "I'm exploring this on my own time," Joe admitted. "I'm following a hunch. I've taken some classes here on magic stuff, and well, I heard that you were really good at this applied symbology magic, so ..." He trailed off with a shrug.

"It's not magic. It's science." Her statement was immediate and with an edge.

"Right."

She eyed him suspiciously and then said, "So, Joe Bremer, the Bellevue police officer, who isn't hitting on me, even though I am trapped and helpless, ask away. I'm not going anywhere and they don't have a clue yet." She gestured at the noisy academics. "And I don't, either. However, you are going to have to pull a chair over, cause you're just too tall. My neck's starting to hurt having to look up at you. How tall are you?"

"Not helpless, too smart," Joe muttered, pulling out a picture from his spiral notebook. "I'm six foot ten," he said as he pushed the paper against the invisible wall. "This is a partial symbol we found at the scene of a robbery. Have you ever seen this before or know what it should look like when it's completed?"

She studied it for a moment, "Yes, I think I have," then pointed at one of the books on the floor. "Would you grab that, hold it up so I can see it, and page through it slowly? Start about a third of the way through."

Joe pulled a chair over and picked up the book she pointed at, held it up, and starting flipping pages. "What was the surface this thing was on?" Stephanie asked.

"Wood, painted wood."

"It looks porous, dimpled, not a smooth surface." She was glancing between the image and the book.

"Okay, why does that matter?"

"Well, it makes it harder to put down the symbol. You have to fill in all the imperfections, the little dimples; otherwise, your symbol wouldn't be complete. I'll bet that's why it didn't work."

"How do you know it didn't work?"

She gave him a look like his mother use to when he said something stupid. "Cause you could get a picture of it." She gestured at the floor around her, "If it worked, the symbol would've faded."

He glanced at the floor to see that all the carefully scribed symbols were gone. "Oh, good point."

"I assume, since you are here, there was a robbery or some type of crime, and that they still got into wherever this was scribed?"

Joe nodded.

"Hmmm, look for another spot that has the paint warped or heat warped or really smooth stone or metal."

"Nice thought." Joe scribbled down the notes in his notebook. He pulled another picture out and turned it to face her. It showed a black scorch-marked plastic box that had little keys on it and LEDs spaced around. Over one part of the case was a yellowed gummy label. It looked like it had gotten almost hot enough to catch fire. Stephanie snorted and nodded, "Security box, right?"

Joe frowned. "Yes, it is the control panel for the security system. There were no signs of it being tampered with, and the owner stated that that label wasn't there before."

"Probably another symbol. Let's try that book." She pointed at another textbook peeking out of her backpack. "What symbol would short out an electrical box?" she mused to herself. "Lightning, perhaps, Norse. Thunder Walker?"

Joe decided she was talking to herself, so didn't comment; instead, he grabbed her backpack and came back to the chair. "So, how does it work?" he asked while pulling out the book.

"How does what work?"

"The mag, … ah, science of symbols?"

She smiled at him, in a kind of predatory way. "I'm not really sure how it works. I have a theory, well, several actually. That is part of the research I'm doing. The proper symbol seems to contain energy, which with the right stimulus, is released with an effect. Some of the really old grimoires call it "the Will, the Word, and the Way," which really has to do with a mental visualization of what effect you want. Then a word to trigger the symbol into the visualization or bring the symbol to the mind's eye, and a wave to direct the effect or energy, but that's not really right, either."

Joe frowned, trying to take it in. "Hmmm, I'm not sure if I understand completely."

"That's okay." She smiled. "Not many can. I try to teach it in class with minimal success; it's how I did this." Her hand patted the invisible barrier.

"So, you have taught others to do the three W thing?"

"Yeah, I have several grad students that can light up a symbol. Most of them were in this class." Glancing up, she waved and called out, "Hey Andy, come here." The student in question waved back, pointed to his wrist, shrugged, and hurried out of the room.

"Do you have a roster of students?" Joe had watched the whole thing. Andy look scared, not busy.

"Yeah, it should be in that three-ring binder … Hold it." Her brows knit together. "You don't think …?"

Joe pulled out the three-ring binder. "I checked around. Yours is the only class on applied symbology in a three-state region. You are one of a handful of wiz ... ah ... scientists that has successfully gotten measureable effects from symbols. And yours is the only class that has reportedly been able to teach others to power symbols. We have three robberies in Bellevue that has these kinds of indications, and there are more in Seattle proper and the surrounding area."

"Am I a suspect?" She was pale, looked stunned.

Joe smiled his reassuring smile. "Probably. We call them persons of interest. I haven't really shared my finding with the detective sergeant. However, all I need are your locations for the three dates, and I think we can clear that part up."

"Sneaky, Joe, the Bellevue policeman, catch me in circle, and get me talking." She didn't sound pleased, but she did relax.

The smile must've worked, Joe thought. "It wasn't my intention, the circle part. If you remember, I did ask if we could meet over coffee." He continued the reasonable reassuring tone.

She smiled her impish smile. "That's right, you asked me out, hitting on a person of interest." Her smile turned wicked. "I'll bet that could be construed as sexual harassment."

"Good thing you're trapped in there then," Joe shot back. *I should've kept her scared,* he thought while holding up the binder with the list of names in a column. "This the one?" She nodded. "There aren't many students, eleven." He carefully extracted the page. "I'll return this after I make a copy."

"Don't bother; I'll just print another one out. It's a graduate class. Most of them have undergraduate degrees already, and the ones that don't are taking it for an easy *A*."

Joe smiled a knowing smile. "I'll bet that isn't the only reason," he muttered as he slipped the roster into his notebook.

"What?" She eyed him, speculating. "What do you think the reason is?"

"You're kidding, right?" He saw the puzzlement in her eyes. "You're beautiful, smart, really smart, single, or at least no known boyfriend." He couldn't believe he had said that out loud and froze. Everything just locked up.

She blinked and blushed. "Wow," just kind of popped out of her, then she got the wicked smile again. "You've been checking me out." Joe blushed and choked a little, which made her laugh. "You really are pushing for the sexual harassment angle, aren't you?"

Joe didn't know what to say or do. He couldn't believe that his mouth just had run off like that, even if he was thinking it. He needed to change the subject and quick. His eyes focused on a page in her three-ring binder. *Job, focus on the job.*

"Is this your schedule?" He flipped the book to show her the page.

She was very pretty when she smiled. "Yes, that's my weekly schedule. Changing the subject, huh?"

Joe felt his face heat up and focused. "You work every day and have labs into the evening four days a week?"

"That's what it says. I know. I need to get a life. All work, no … Ah, why?"

"How long has your schedule been like this?"

"Months."

"Is there anyone that can validate that you are working this schedule?"

"Sure. Students, faculty, most of which are over there arguing. Ah, Bruce."

"Yo, girl, I got a text. You did it!" Bruce came up front, pushing a cart of equipment. "Who's your big friend?"

Joe instantly didn't like this guy. "This your boyfriend?" There was something else about him.

She laughed teasingly, "Not Bruce. He swings a different way. Anyway, I thought you'd already checked me out?"

Joe decided not to answer. No matter what he said, she would use it against him.

"Steph, ease up on the man," Bruce said, laughing. He offered Joe his hand. "Bruce Richardson. I am her lab assistant and partner in crime."

"He's a cop, Bruce, and investigating a crime." She smiled weakly at Joe. "He didn't mean the crime part."

Joe studied him. "Can you power a symbol, Mr. Richardson?"

"Nope, not even a little bit." Bruce turned and started moving equipment around. "She's the one with the knack. I'm just her prop man." He reached down and pulled a thirty-two inch flat screen monitor up. It clicked when it locked into position. He fished a power cord out and held it out to Joe. "Plug me in, would you, Joe?" Bruce said with a smile.

Joe frowned at his innuendo, looked around, and saw an outlet. "You don't seem to be too concerned about being involved in a crime, Mr. Richardson?"

"Well, you are hitting on the girl when she's trapped in some kind of way cool invisible force field." Bruce smiled and Joe noticed Stephanie blushing. "And she is flirting with you, so I gather you aren't all that serious about arresting anyone here." Bruce pushed some buttons, and the screen came to life with a boot-up theme. "She is also trapped in a Solomon Circle, which we don't know how to get her out of yet, so we have time." Bruce turned back to Joe. "So, what do you say, Joe the policeman, maybe you cut us some slack?"

Joe noticed a different look in Bruce's eye. He might be gay and joking around with them both, but there was steel in his spine. Joe would also bet that Bruce was worried about Stephanie. He rose a notch in Joe's judgment. "Do you think she's in danger, Bruce?"

Bruce glanced at Stephanie and then looked back at Joe. More of his jocularity faded away. "I don't know, but one thing for certain, we shouldn't scare her any worse than she already is. Don't ya think?"

Bruce rose another couple of notches on Joe's approval meter. "Anything I can do to help?" Joe asked quietly.

Bruce started to say something, but Stephanie cut him off. "I'm not scared."

"So, why were you flirting with a guy you didn't know then?" Bruce glanced back at Joe. "Although, he is quite a hunk, and you do need a boyfriend." He winked at Joe.

And down a notch.

"Okay," the little woman said. "Let's figure out how to get me out."

Chapter 3

"So," Joe said. "You were waiting for him to show up?"

She smiled at him. "You must be a police officer, maybe a detective." She turned back to Bruce, no smiles now. "State the problem."

"You are in a Solomon Circle of your design. How did you trigger it?" Bruce was bringing up software tools on the screen as they talked. Joe thought it had the sound of a process or ritual. She was a wizard after all.

"I used the process outlined in version seven of my thesis. Bring it up." Bruce's hands flashed, and a document appeared on the big screen. "Page eight or maybe seven." Pages flashed by on the document. "Bring up the circle design on a separate window." Another window blossomed with a familiar pattern displayed with three concentric rings. "Restate the problem."

"Did the triggering function as designed?"

"Yes."

Joe could see Bruce's eyes scanning down the page. "How was it visualized?"

"Visualization." Her eyes closed and fingertips went to her temples. "A bell jar, I was thinking of a bell jar. No specification of permeability. I was thinking of it as a glass bell jar." Her eyes popped open. "No air. How long have I got before my air runs out?"

"Focus," Bruce said without inflection. "Stay focused. You have time."

Her eyes were a little wild as she repeated, "State the problem?"

"You triggered the circle as specified in," Bruce glanced up, "page seven of your thesis." Bruce looked at Joe, "Would you reach up and tap above her? Let's see how it formed."

Joe did as asked, running his hands up the smooth invisible surface and over the top. He nodded to Bruce.

"The circle triggered as a bell jar exactly as hypothesized," Bruce stated and typed. "Problem, how do you cancel it out?"

"Deviation." Stephanie put her lip between her teeth as she tapped her fingertips on her temple. "I bled on the innermost circle. I put my blood on the innermost circle."

Bruce's hands flashed as he added a note to the open document. "Brilliant, how did you think of that? It matches the Fourth Dynasty grimoire."

Stephanie giggled briefly. "I stabbed myself by accident with a compass and didn't want to risk smudging the circle by wiping it off. Corollary, there was a book that mentioned how adding blood made the summoned effect personal to the blood owner. Dark ages, Europe, Italy, I think, someone nefarious."

Bruce's hands flashed as he started a search engine. "Problem: you are in a circle designed as a bell jar that you triggered. How do you take it down?"

"Joe," Stephanie said.

"What? I didn't do anything." He had been studying her, well, anatomy. He couldn't help himself. She was like a fascinating creature trapped in a jar.

She flashed a brief smile at his instant guilty denial. "Joe has a partial symbol. The hypothesis is that the complete one was used to open a locked door into a house. Bruce, would you please scan his partial and start a compare with our symbol library? Let's see if we have anything on record? I know I've seen it before. Egyptian, I think, P'Tah maybe or one of the temple symbols."

"P'Tah, like Egyptian god, 'opener of the ways,' kind of thing?" Joe blurted out.

"Yeah, you study Egyptian lore?" Bruce asked.

"No, well, not exactly. Dungeons and Dragons, by TSR hobbies, you know Gary Gygax's invention. I had a cleric to P'Tah. Never mind." Joe held out the picture. Bruce grabbed it, shook his head, and put the picture into a scanner on the bottom of the tool tray.

"Don't let him buffalo you, Joe. Bruce runs one of the hottest D&D worlds on campus. Old school." Stephanie had the wicked look again.

"That's some collection of equipment." Joe nodded toward the mobile tool stand, changing the subject. Cops were not supposed to play D&D or stare at cute girls while working.

"Lecture stand, Steph gets asked to guest a lot, so I rigged this up for her," Bruce explained.

"Guest?"

"Guest lecture, she's been all over the Northwest, pretty much the whole coast, talking her symbol theory." Bruce sounded very proud of her.

Joe groaned and put his face in his hands. "Shit!" His list had just grown.

Bruce looked shocked and stepped closer to defend her. "What? She's damn good."

"Bruce." Stephanie waved to get his attention. When Bruce finally turned his scowl to her, she added, "Joe thinks someone has figured out how to adapt my symbol theory into crime tools. He has indications that they are being used for breaking and entering all over the Puget Sound, and now you told him it might be the West Coast."

"Oh," Bruce grimaced. "That would be bad. Let's work his problem after we get you out. We need to focus."

"I guess I'm not the only one worried about her?" Joe muttered so only Bruce could hear.

"Well, at least I'm not staring at her ass." Bruce turned back to the screen. "We have fourteen partial matches," Bruce stated much louder.

"Flash through 'em," Stephanie commanded.

Joe hoped she hadn't heard the staring comment.

Bruce typed, another window opened, and a symbol appeared. The symbols flashed at fifteen-second intervals as the slideshow proceeded. "Stop, bring that last one back." Stephanie studied it for a moment. "We did a paper on that one."

Bruce's fingers flashed on the keyboard, and a document window appeared. "Yep, but it had nothing to do with opening. It was an example about powering the symbols."

"That's what we thought. Who knows what it actually does?" Stephanie mumbled.

Joe watched as her brow crinkled. He thought she was thinking hard, at least it looked to him like she was. She was really cute when she did that. He couldn't believe how she was affecting him, totally unprofessional.

"What are you doing here?" A harsh voice broke in.

"I am assisting my partner." Bruce added with obvious disdain.

The pompous professor, Joe thought his name was Rhinebolt, drew himself up to his full height, literally with his nose in the air. "This is no time for some graduate student falderal. The senior staff is assisting Ms. Blackraven. Pack up your technological items and take them back to your lab space," he commanded, pointing dramatically.

"Not likely," Joe found himself saying.

"What?"

Joe stepped forward to put himself between Professor Rhinebolt and Bruce. "I said it was not likely that you would be helping Ms. Blackraven." He was holding his anger in check, just as they had taught him, using crowd control techniques. What he really wanted to do was pop the little weasel's head off his shoulders. Joe was furious and didn't know why.

"How dare you! I would like you to know ..."

Joe cut him off. "You are the one who was trying to sabotage her thesis. What I observed was," he flipped open his notebook like he had noted it down, "you belittling her work, condescending to her methods, and trying to take credit for her success, even as you goaded her into doing what you thought was impossible, only so you could shame her in front of her class." Joe was trying his calm, detective delivery tone used to intimidate suspects. "So far, all I have observed is you interfering with a doctoral student's education, interfering with her efforts to do a difficult job under stressful conditions, even life threatening. You just want to get in her way." Joe paused to regain some control. "Stephanie Blackraven is something you are obviously not, professor, she's competent." He was also slowly moving Rhinebolt away from Stephanie, using his body as a ram.

Rhinebolt paled as he backed away. "Who do you think you are talking to me like that? I could have you expelled for threatening a professor this way!"

Joe snorted in total denial of his threat, "I am Joe Bremer, a Bellevue police office, here investigating several crimes." He used his coldest tone, reaching for that low bass in a calm, reasoning voice. "Now, don't you have to be somewhere else?"

Professor Rhinebolt turned white and scurried from the room.

Joe turned to see Stephanie staring at him with some type of approval on her face. Joe had this warm feeling and then got embarrassed by his display of anger.

"My hero," Bruce said, then turned to see the look on Stephanie's face. "No, your hero."

Stephanie glanced at Bruce and then blushed deep red. "Thanks, Joe," Stephanie said in a quiet voice. "I ... ah ... I ... thanks." She held out her hand to him.

Without really thinking about it he reached out and took her hand to shake it, reminding himself not to crush it. It was more like she was shaking his fingers than hand. "Hey, how did ..." He realized she wasn't trapped anymore.

"I figured it out while you were keeping Rhinebolt off us," she answered shyly. "It wasn't hard. You gave me the clue."

"Wow, you are good!" Joe was amazed.

"She does symbols, too," Bruce added with a laugh, making them both blush like teenagers while stepping apart.

And then the professors noticed she was out of the field.

They circled in, clucking, gesturing, questioning. Joe backed away to leave her as the center of attention. Unlike Rhinebolt, they all seemed to be excited about her success.

"Officer Bremer, what are you doing here?" The cool voice of his boss, Detective Sergeant Grayson asked.

Sergeant Grayson was about six foot, cold eyed, with dark hair graying at the temples, and distinguished looking. They kidded him about being a politician.

"I am following a hunch about the burglaries you assigned to me."

"Do tell?" Grayson turned to observe the professor spectacle.

"You remember the partial symbol we found at the first robbery. I brought it to Ms. Stephanie Blackraven; she's the cute, black-haired girl they're all talking to." Joe gestured toward the collection of professors. "She identified it as a subject of one of her papers and confirmed that it was possibly a magic implement for opening doors."

"Hmmm," was all Grayson said.

"She is a practitioner and has been teaching her symbol theory to classes here and in other parts of the Northwest. My theory is that some of the gangbangers have picked up on the capability and turned it into breaking and entering tools. It fits the pattern of mysterious break-ins and other robberies in the region." He glanced back at Stephanie as she demonstrated setting the circle again and then dropping it. Bruce had set up a laser to measure something. "She's really smart, just had a major breakthrough in her area. I got to watch. She trapped herself inside that containment circle and then figured out how to get herself out. She's pretty amazing." Joe glanced over at the detective sergeant who was looking at him.

"Joe, are you hitting on a person of interest? Is she your girlfriend?"

"Ah, she's not a POI, sir, and not my girlfriend. She is a potential expert source on this magic or science as she calls it. Sir."

The sergeant harrumphed and turned back to the group of academics.

"Sergeant," Joe had to change the subject. He couldn't believe that his sergeant had figured out he had the hots for Stephanie. "Why are you here?"

"Murder, Officer Bremer, I am here to talk about murder. Somehow, your not-a-girlfriend is involved."

Chapter 4

She had her doctorate. Stephanie couldn't believe it. They had been stonewalling her for months, and now in a single evening, they had agreed. She would feel better when the paperwork was done, and everything was posted and released, but right now it felt great.

It had been kind of cool, scary, but cool, with the circle and all. The look on Rhinebolt's face when he realized she had triggered the circle; it was priceless.

They had kept her there for hours, reenacting setting the circle, analyzing the process, demonstrating setting it, and then taking it down, reviewing her thesis. It was tiring. She was taking the well-worn path back to her lab. It was dark, but not that late. Puget Sound in November, it got dark at five PM. Her mind kept jumping topics.

And then there was Joe, the mountain, she mused. It made her smile to think about him. So big, so careful, he really was worried about accidently knocking other people down. He had been there through the whole thing. She blushed again when she thought about his concern for her when she had trapped herself. He was the only one who actually asked her how she was doing. Bruce liked him, as a matter-of-fact, Bruce hadn't stopped teasing her about him. Then when he had gone off on Rhinebolt, wow! Bruce had pestered her into accepting Joe's invite to coffee. She smiled again when she remembered the look on his face when she had walked up to him and the other policeman to accept his invitation. He had actually stuttered when he confirmed it.

Something smacked into the side of her head, setting the world spinning.

She hit the dirt, getting it in her mouth and eye. It was a dry, sunny, shiny day outside the barn as Uncle Raymond smashed her into the sand practice square. She burst into tears. "Uncle Raymond that isn't fair!" She sobbed, "That hurt!"

"Life isn't fair, Princess," his harsh whisky voice rasped out. "Get used to it. There are bad people out there, and when they have you down, they just kick you again." And he did, right in her stomach. She cried out, sobbing harder. "Get up. You can't just lay there. They'll just keep kicking you 'til you die. The animals love it when you just lay there." He prodded her again. Tears were really streaming now, making mud on her face. "You said you were a big girl. You could take care of yourself. You weren't afraid of those boys. Well, this is what they can do to you. How do you like it?"

She launched herself up and at him.

"Uncle Raymond, you rat bastard," she screamed as he foot swept her back to the dirt.

"They're waiting for the weak. This is what you can expect." He smoothly stepped away as she tried to kick him in the knee. "You want to date some cock, then fight me. Show me how tough you are, little girl," he growled out at her. "Sixteen is, oh, so old," he scoffed.

She shot up off the ground with rage giving her strength. He had made her go to martial arts classes since she was eight, and she hated it. Now she was going to show him. No miss nice girl this time. He was old and slow; God, he had to be close to a hundred. She warily circled him, careful, measuring, and then shot in with a front kick as a fake, followed it with a knife hand to the collarbone, and a palm strike to the nose. She wasn't pulling anything. She was going to hurt him bad if she could. She had been taking his male shit for eight years, and she had had enough. She would date whoever the hell she wanted to. The flurry was fast and furious. She didn't know how many times she hit him, but it was several, and they weren't tournament shots, either. She had gotten him in the groin once and smashed his nose with another. He had only hit her once, and it had sent her to the ground again, sucking for air.

"Nice try, Princess, but I'm bigger 'n you …" pant, pant, pant, "and tougher." Pant, pant. "You better get used to it, every guy will be stronger and bigger than you." He spit blood onto the ground. "You're only going to get one shot at them. You better make it count." His voice was a whisper. "Then run like hell for a weapon."

She was struggling to get up. Maybe pissing off her uncle hadn't been such a good idea after all. She continued to struggle when she noticed the pine smell. There had been no pines on the ranch, at least not in the barn. The left side of her face was numb, but pulsing like it would really hurt in a minute. Ten years of martial arts had taught her that. She cracked one eye open to see a pinecone and needles. *Hadn't I been on campus?* she thought.

"You fuckup," a rough male voice harshly whispered. "You didn't have to hit her that hard. We want answers." Hands reached down to grab her shoulders and lifted her off the ground, shaking her a little.

"These bitches talk best when you hurt 'em," another man said. "Slap the bitch. I haven't even started to hurt her yet."

She hated it when Uncle Raymond was right. Through her teary blurry eyes, she made out a ski mask on some guy, way bigger than she was, and another one next to him. Her right hand flashed upward in a palm strike, smashing his nose flat. He dropped her back to the ground.

"Ahhh," ski mask one yelled.

"Wait for it," she mumbled to herself. "I'm only going to get one shot at it. Wait for him to ..." She brought her legs up under her like she was trying to stand, but couldn't.

Ski mask two was just starting to swear and bending over to grab her or hit her.

Now, she thought. She powered up off the ground to put her knee on the inside of his knee and her elbow in his throat. She heard the knee pop when it dislocated.

"Aaaahhhh," the second ski mask screamed.

Stephanie ran -- right into a tree, glanced off it, and stumbled out into the grass. She still couldn't see very well, and the side of her face hurt like hell. But she remembered Uncle Raymond's lesson well, "you only get one shot, then run like hell." She was hurt bad, that one shot had rung her bell.

They had caught her in one of the places where she always cut through the trees. She could hear Uncle Raymond again. "Don't be predictable, they can track that and plan for it. You don't want to give them any edge."

She stumbled to the sidewalk, but couldn't really make out where she was. The side of her head was starting to throb, her eye wasn't working well, and the other side of her head was burning. She stumbled around on the lighted sidewalks until she spotted a RAPE pole. The campus had set them up all over for women to use in case of rape, well, attempted rape. From the pole, she saw her lab building down the block.

"There she is," she heard behind her.

Fear lent her strength; she smashed the red button down on the pole and put on a burst of speed to the door. She knew it would take at least five minutes and more like fifteen for the campus cops to respond. The bad guys weren't going to give her that much time. She pushed through the doors to face a long flight of stairs, there was no way she would be able to stumble down the stairs and keep ahead of the muggers. "Problem," she mused to herself, "how do I get to the bottom quickly?" The stairs were separated by a center handrail, rubbed smooth by countless students. "Ha, gravity," she announced. Pulling the rayon-nylon fiber lab coat tight over her front, she bent over the rail on her stomach and hopped up a little to clear the ground and start her sliding down the rail. She built up speed pretty quickly, as they were steep stairs, and there were a lot of them. "Aw shit." Reality intruded into her neat plan. "I forgot about safely getting to the bottom." About then, she reached the end of the rail, was flung off, momentarily airborne, and landed on her butt to roll into the closed doors with a great deal of force.

She loved the country kitchen in the afternoon, quiet, comfortable, peaceful. It was several days after the barn slap down. They hadn't been talking, just moving around each other, going through life, she at school and Uncle Raymond doing whatever it was he did. She hadn't had the guts to ask him about dating again. There had been questions at school about her bruises, black eyes, and cut lip. She had told everyone it had been a martial arts tournament in Billings. Far enough away from Uncle Raymond's place near Cascade that they wouldn't really know what was going on, but not too far that she couldn't have gotten there and back over the weekend.

Uncle Raymond stepped into the kitchen looking like he always did, pissed at something. "Come here, I got something for you." He turned and went out the door.

Arguing wouldn't get her anywhere, so she got up reluctantly and sort of shuffled toward the door. Sitting outside was a red Ford Ranger 4x4 with flair sides. It looked brand new and had the special off-road tires. Uncle Raymond was leaning against the porch railing, doing his long, lean cowboy act, with a set of keys dangling from his finger.

"Here's the deal. I pay for the truck, gas, and insurance. You go to school and do the best damn job you can. Forget this stupid ass, afterschool, working thing. Your job is school. You're smart, too damn smart, so make something of yourself. Find something that smart mouth of yours can make you money at." He gave her that look that scared her to her toes as he tossed her the keys. "You wreck the truck, your fault, their fault, nobody's fault, and it's gone. You're going to have to earn another. You are not a taxi, so don't let your friends talk you into hauling their sorry asses around." He nodded with his chin towards her. "You got it?" She dumbly nodded her head. "No, I want to hear you say it."

God, she hated this game, too. "Yes, Uncle Raymond. You give me a truck, and I go to school. No afterschool job. I wreck it, and it's gone. My job is school. I'm not a taxi."

He nodded and did his almost smile. "Got something else for you, since you are soo damned stubborn about dating, being as how you are all grown up and know everything." He reached behind his back and came up with a pistol. It wasn't one she had ever seen before. With a practiced ease he had with all weapons, he safed the gun: removing the magazine, pulling back and locking the slide, while catching the ejected bullet in the air. "This should fit your hand. A Taurus Millennium Pro, .380, ten-shot magazine, reliable. I would've got you a .45, but with your little hand and the light frame, one shot is all you would get." He held it out to her butt first.

She took the weapon and checked it out, even though he had just unloaded it in front of her.

"You use that," he said, pointing at the gun. "Some guy starts knocking you around, like I did the other day, you put two in his chest and one in his head just like I taught you."

"Uncle Raymond, I don't need …"

"Goddamn it to hell, girl," He exploded off the rail like he was going to hit her, but instead, just turned to gaze out on the pasture. "You got a body guys will kill for. You're gorgeous, and that's not just some dirty old man talking. Princess …" His voice trailed off as he shook his head in some internal argument. "It's just … You don't know the world like I … Damn it! Why can't you just believe me and do what I tell you for once? Damn it, you're all the kin I've got, and I'm not going to be around forever."

The gun was stupid, but she was really excited about the truck. It looked brand new. She also regretted having called him a dirty old man when he was trying to explain something to her. "Thanks for the truck. I'll try to remember what you're saying."

He huffed, "Sure you will, Princess." He turned around toward her, wiping at his eyes. "Here, let me show you where the gun goes. Don't go flashing it around; it's illegal for you to have it." He had shown her the specially designed place for it with the electronic combination lock. She could get to it in seconds, while still keeping it safely locked away.

Stephanie opened her eyes to see tile and an industrial doorjamb. Her flashback faded away, and the recent event came crashing in. *Where's my gun?* Crap, it was locked in her safe at the apartment.

They were coming after her, she remembered. Groaning, she struggled to her feet and through the door. Her lab was only halfway down the hall. She hugged the left wall because she couldn't stand on her own while limping that way.

The door to her lab was ajar.

She eased forward as quiet as she could to peek around the doorjamb into her lab. There was another ski-masked guy in the process of burning up another printer and desktop. She heard him quietly swearing to himself. She started to ease back, and her backpack caught on something. She shrugged it off, letting it swing around in front of her. Grabbing it, she turned back to the outside doors. Ski Mask One, she could tell because he wasn't limping, but blood was running out around his neck from under the mask, stepped through the door.

Rage rose in her again. *These bastards just won't give up.* "What in hell do you want with me?" she screamed at him while backing down the hallway with her backpack held in front of her.

"You busted my nose, bitch!" His voice was nasal as he hissed at her. "First, I get some pay back. You'll tell me what I want to know."

"Yeah, that worked well the first time. How's the other guy's knee?" She was yelling at the top of her lungs and trying every door she came to. Maybe someone would hear her.

"We'll see, bitch."

"Is that the only word you know? Not much of a vocabulary, dickhead." He growled at her and started down the hall faster. *Damn*, she thought, *Maybe Uncle Raymond was right about the smart mouth thing, too.* As she turned to run to the other stairs, Ski Mask Three, or was it four, stepped out of the other stairway. He was holding a gun. There was a pssst sound, and something struck her backpack. It was a dart, like they used to tranquilize animals. They were going to kidnap her. She threw herself across the hall at another door. The knob moved, opening the door and spilling her onto the floor. She saw her cell phone go sliding under one of the benches.

She started crawling after it for all she was worth. She fumbled with it, sending it under another set of tables. Finally, she grabbed the phone and snapped it open. Punching 911, she made her way further into the lab. It was an applied physics lab, high-energy section.

"This is 911, what is your emergency?"

"Shhhh. Talk quieter. I'm Stephanie Blackraven, there's a man in the lab and three more outside. They attacked me. Beat the crap out of me. I think he's trying to kidnap me." She was holding her hand around the phone, trying to make as little noise as possible while continuing to crawl away from the door. She knocked over a stool that made all sorts of noise.

"Where are you now?" The 911 woman shouted out, at least it seemed that way.

"I'm in one of the labs, applied physics building. He's got a dart gun that shoots those tranquilizer darts." Her head came up as she heard a muffled curse as the man stumbled over an overturned stool. "Oh damn, Bosh-Gates Pacific University, Bellevue campus, building 405, room 115 and 116 in the basement." She stumbled up from behind a bench and shuffled for the door into the lab resource room.

She heard a grunt, and something heavy hit her in the back, pushing her into the doorjamb. She hit it hard and spun through the doorway into the room and onto the floor, her cell phone spinning off another way. She scrambled away from the door in the dark. Her head, back, and chest hurt, bad, but this was a bad guy, he would just kick her while she was down. She scrambled around equipment until she got caught on something and had to stop to pull her skin off a nail. The new sharp pain of a puncture wound and tear cleared her head a little.

She looked around, and in the dim light made out what some of the equipment was; lightning-strike simulation, DC plasma torch, DC ultra-high voltage transmit tester. She got up and limped over to the bench, and by the illumination of the power-indicating lights, she located a switch. A noise from over by the door brought her up short, and she held her breath to hear another sound. She instinctively grabbed a thick heavy rod off the bench. Having a weapon in her hands was better than not having one. A scrape sounded closer, she threw the switch. Nothing happened.

Something snapped in her, she got furious. This wasn't supposed to be happening. People weren't supposed to be treating her this way. Women just didn't get beat up in her school. She whirled around, waving the rod in front of her. "Come on, goddamn it. You think you can take me, then bring it on!" She wasn't seeing real well, but she could make out a shadowy form on the other side of the room. "This is a lightning lab, and I just turned it on. So, in a moment you're going to eat lightning."

She heard a soft laugh from across the room. "I think not," a man whispered. "I believe the main breaker is off."

Panic set in, her mind started jumping around, looking for an answer. Norse, symbol, thunder, flashed into her mind, and the symbol formed in her mind's eye. "IGHTNING-LIE." She screamed, thrusting the rod at the shadows. There was a blinding flash. She felt herself flying backward.

Chapter 5

Joe was standing, staring out a window in the Evergreen Hospital waiting room. He had been home asleep when he got a call from a friend on duty about the report of a strange explosion at Bosh-Gates Pacific University, Bellevue campus, building 405, Applied Physics building. There had been one subject found at the scene, a Stephanie Blackraven, POI in a case related to one of his investigations. He had dressed in record time and gotten to the hospital only to be told to cool his heels in the waiting room. Then he called into his office and found out about a 911 call correlating to the time of explosion. Now he was wondering whether he had brought this down on her. Was it a coincidence that the same day he came to question her about the symbols related to gangbanger breaking and entering, she got mugged, possibly raped, and hunted into a lab?

"Bremer, what are you doing here?" Detective Sergeant Grayson asked.

Joe's head snapped up and stopped Grayson in his tracks. "I flagged a person as a POI earlier in the day. Something happened to her, and I got called. I came down to collect information. I'm wondering if I brought this down on her." He ended up gazing out the window again, thinking dark thoughts.

Joe could see Grayson's reflection looking him up and down. "Why are you here in tactical fatigues?"

Joe looked down and noticed he was wearing his SWAT clothes, with his badge on his belt and gun on his thigh. "Got dressed in the dark, in a hurry, and they were the closest."

Grayson nodded his head slowly. "You see her yet?"

"No sir."

"Why?"

"They won't let me up to her room."

"Why?"

"No idea, sir."

"Hmmm," Grayson said, then walked toward the desk with his detective badge out. After a moment of polite, but intense conversation, Grayson turned back to him and gestured with his head. Joe came over and they started walking. "Next time, tell them you are a police detective and the person is under investigation."

"But I'm not a police detective, . . . yet."

"You are assigned to my office, undergoing evaluation for becoming a police detective. That makes you part of the detective branch." He walked on a few more steps. "They won't know the difference." Joe snorted, and Grayson smiled briefly.

When they reached the right floor, Grayson grabbed Joe's arm to stop him walking. "I've reviewed the preliminary report." Joe was confused, and it must've showed on his face because Grayson added, "She got beaten up pretty bad. Her face swollen, one eye shut, scratch marks on her face and neck, bruises on neck, back, butt, and legs. They must've taken a hose to her and then stuck her hand in a light socket . . . Ahh, . . . explosively. She has extensive burns on her right hand, lost a finger, and may lose another. It's bad."

"What?"

"I know she's not-a-girlfriend, but she is a cute girl, and bad guys beat her up. Any of us would be pissed off."

"Was she raped?" Joe asked quietly.

"No indications." Joe sagged a little in relief of that while Grayson looked at him intently. "Now is not the time to get the hurt out."

Joe blinked a few times and fought back his anger. "I'm good."

Grayson looked at him for a moment and then started walking again. "It's always seems worst when it's the cute ones," Joe heard Grayson mumble to himself.

They walked down the hall to a desk. The nurse was not happy to see them, but pointed them to her room. As they approached, they heard a female voice talking. "Try this one. What do you get with a low-jumping bull?"

"I don't know," a male voice stated.

"A steer." Muffled laughter came out with a few "ow, ow."

"I told you not to laugh. The ice packs and stitches," the male voice said.

They walked into the lit room. The male nurse was taking a needle out of the IV bag when he noticed them. He fumbled the syringe, dropping it to the floor, left it, and came over. "Stephanie, you stay there. I've got to talk to your visitors."

"Vissithorss," she said. Now that Joe was closer, he could hear a slight lisp or slur in her speech. "How would vissithors . . . oh, missth be police. It iss way after vissithing hours, mussth've been the 911 call. Hey Joe, di' ya bring coffee?"

"Way too smart," Joe mumbled as he moved into the room, picked the syringe up, and put it on the bedside table.

"Gentlemen, the patient has a concussion as well as deep hematomas on the back, neck, buttocks, and legs. There are fractures as well. Burns. Because of the concussion, she is on light pain medication. If she didn't have a concussion, she would be on heavy pain meds." He eyed them waiting for the implication to sink in. "Don't upset her. Don't let her sleep." He was very serious.

"Not my first rodeo," Grayson said without inflection. He stepped past the nurse and into the room. The nurse followed him in.

"Stephanie, these policemen want to ask you some questions. If you get fatigued or you just want them to stop, you let me know. Push your call button." He fussed with it and moved it so she would know where it was located. "I will be right back. Remember, you need to stay awake for another seven hours." The nurse gave them a knowing look and hurried out of the room.

Stephanie had half her face covered with a cold compress. The rest of it was puffy and turning colors. Her right hand was heavily bandaged, the other bruised and splinted. She smiled weakly, "Hey Joe, wtho'ss your friend?" She blinked her eye and studied them for just a moment. "Oh, he'ssth your bossth? I ssthaw 'im earlier at t' classth. Am I a ssthusthpect or ssthometh'n?"

"Stephanie, this is Detective Sergeant Grayson. He's going to ask you some questions," Joe told her softly.

"Sthure. Thesthe guysth beat t' sthit out'a me. I'm not goin' anywhere." She giggled, "Stho hittin' on me when I'm trapped again?" She stiffened immediately. "No laughing."

"I don't think you should be laughing, Ms. Blackraven," Detective Grayson suggested. "Can you remember what happened to you? Take it as slow as you need to." Joe pulled out a notebook. Grayson clicked on a recorder.

"Sthure. Ya know I'm dwugged?" They both nodded. "Stho if I drift off topic, you gon'a cut me sthome sthlack?"

"This is not a legal deposition, Ms. Blackraven. I just want to know what happened to you."

"Okay. I got busthwhacked. They were waith'n for me in the clump ah treesths right outsthide ah the Cramer build'n. I cut through there to sthave a couple of stheconds. Two of 'em in sthki masthksth. They must'a col' cocked me as I sthepped int'a cover. Cause I hit t' ground and had a flash back to, ah, early life difficulty."

"When was this?"

"Well, I wasth sthixteen and disth cute guy a' sthchool, who wanted t' date me. M' Uncle Raymond, he'sth t' guy that raisthed me after my momma died. Anyway, Uncle Raymond an' I had harsth wordsth, and he told me if I thought I was sthuch a big girl then I had to prove it by beat'n him. Stho we went out t' the barn and stharted a real sthlap down. He didn't pull t' punchesth, either. He knocked m' around good, even if I wasth a second-degree black belt."

Joe had a sinking feeling. It could be either the medication or her brain got damaged. Punch drunk wasn't just an expression.

"No, Ms. Blackraven, I mean tonight, as you were leaving the Cramer building. What time were you leaving?"

"Wha'?"

"Tonight, the guys who attacked you, what time was that?"

"I don't know, it was dark. T' dean kept me a' ta' clasthsroom show'n 'em how t' set a circle and drop it." Her one eye started to sparkle, "Joe, t'ey gave me my doctorate. Isn't tat cool. I'm Doctor Blackraven now. I t'ink you owe me two coffeesth."

Joe smiled, he couldn't help it.

"Ms. Blackraven, if we could go back to the attack?"

"It wasth Calvin," she licked her lips, "'e wasth cute and sthweet and could talk up a sthtorm. Well, ta firssht date wasth fine, but ta sthecond . . . damn 't, I 'ate it 'en Uncle Raymond isth right."

"No," Grayson cut her off, "not your past, tonight. What about the ski mask guys?"

"Wha," she got a puzzled look.

"Let me try, sergeant?" Joe asked quietly. He got a hand gesture toward her. Joe pulled a chair over and moved the stand holding her bags of IV fluid. "Stephanie, we have a problem. Can you help us solve it?"

Her exposed eye seemed to sparkle. "Sthtate t' problem."

"The problem is we don't know about what happened tonight. You were leaving the classroom tonight, and you got attacked. What can you tell me about the attacker?" Joe tried to make it sound like Bruce had sounded earlier.

"T'ere were two men. Bot' over six feet tall. Bot' wore ski masks. Dark clothesth, blue jeansth, bootsth. No, one 'ad sthneakersth. One of t'em, t'e one with t'e broken nosthe, sthpoke well. Ta one wit' ta disthlocated knee and bruisthed throat didn't stheem as educated. He wasth more sthtreet."

"How did they get the broken nose and the knee, Stephanie?"

"I did it." She smiled, "I got ta one who picked me up with a palm sthtrike. He wasn't ta one that hit me." Stephanie stopped and moved her jaw around for a moment. "Interesting, no pain. Anyway, the one that hit me got a knee to the inside of his knee and an elbow strike to the throat. I got his knee, probably broken. Then I ran, well, tried to. Uncle Raymond was right about that too, the bad guys just kick you when you're down." Her eye seemed to wander off, like she was looking somewhere else. "I'm not pretty anymore; do you think that will matter, Joe? Will you still like me?"

Joe froze. *Focus,* he thought, *Stay focused. Then you can . . . what can I do?*

"Bremer," Grayson's tone was neutral.

"I still have this problem, Stephanie." Joe's voice was a little rough.

"Call me Steph." Her eye had tracked back to him, and she tried to smile. "State the problem."

"Okay, Steph. The problem: you got attacked outside the Cramer building. How did you get to the physics building?"

"I went to the lighted sidewalks. Then I went to the rape alert post. The red lights on top make them visible. I could see the physics building from there. When they spotted me, I hit the button and ran to my lab building." Her eye got wild as she looked randomly around the room. "I can't remember anything else until I woke up here." She reached out and grabbed Joe's hand with her bruised one. "How did I hurt my back? How did I burn my hand? Am I brain damaged?" Her eye was tearing up.

Joe patted her hand. "I think your brain is fine. I don't know about the rest, Steph. We'll be trying to puzzle that out."

"I think that's all we need from her tonight," Detective Grayson announced softly. "Ms. Blackraven, you heal up. We will need your help when you're better. Joe, walk with me."

Joe patted her hand again. "I'll be back." She didn't let go for a moment, then, like she made some decision, she released him. Joe went into the hall.

"Not as much as I hoped for, but better than nothing," Grayson commented as they strolled down the hallway. "I' will talk to the nurse and make sure she gets a private room. Stay with her until you get relieved by a uniform. It seems like your hunch about the gangbangers using magic is on target. They probably had someone in her class. You probably saw them today, yesterday. Sleep late, and be in my office at noon. Bring whatever you have on her class and suspects." He turned and walked off, then stopped, looking back. "Good job." He turned and walked off.

Joe smiled. Detective Sergeant Grayson didn't say that very often to anyone. Joe started to walk down to the nurses' station to ask about coffee, but something made him turn. A dark figure was just stepping into Stephanie's room. Joe pulled his gun and ran.

For a big man, he moved pretty quietly when he needed to, all that hunting. He slowed at the corner of the room and bent low to peer around the corner; careful to expose as little as possible. The dark figure was fuzzy, which didn't make sense, since Joe was looking right at him. He was sitting in the chair Joe had pulled over and speaking quietly to Stephanie. Joe eased around the corner, aiming his gun as he moved. "Don't move, or I will shoot you."

The guy made a very girl-sounding yelp, started to get up, then stopped. Like it took a second or two for Joe's words to sink in. "Don't shoot!" a woman's voice hissed. "I'm not hurting her. I'm here to help."

"Joe." Stephanie's voice was kind of singsong. "It's Rosemary, my faculty advisor. Ease up on the gun. You know your finger's on the trigger. You're not supposed to do that unless ... Oh, Rosemary, don't move."

Joe stood up and pointed his gun at the floor. He could still aim quickly, but it wasn't pointed at anyone. "Why are you blurry? Why are you here?" he demanded.

"I enacted a don't-see-me spell, which obviously doesn't work well. I am here to help her. I have a healing, ah, symbol for her to use." Rosemary didn't seem happy about explaining, but Joe was holding a gun. She looked like she had sucked on something really sour.

"You have a symbol that will heal her?" Joe asked. He couldn't quite keep the doubt out of his tone.

"Can I move, officer?"

"You have a symbol for curing?" Stephanie was fascinated, Joe could tell by her tone. "Have you tried it before? Were there tests?"

"Steph, hold up." Joe moved a little closer, but didn't holster his gun. "How did you know she was here? This is not the closest hospital to the university."

"Can I move? Or are you going to gun me down, like some lawless cretin in the streets?" Her tone said it all, when it came to what she thought about police.

"You can sit back down in the chair and remove that spell. It's giving me a headache." Joe's tone also conveyed a message. He would shoot her in a heartbeat, if she gave him cause. She sat down slowly and made a motion in the air with her hands. The fuzziness stopped, and a handsome woman appeared. Darkish hair with grey streaking through it, trim figure in dark clothes. "Don't move closer to Stephanie. Now, how did you know she was here?"

"I am on her list to contact in case of emergencies. It is on file, here at the hospital," Rosemary stated with a haughty tone, like she was talking down to a stupid student.

"Why would they have your name?"

"Stephanie was injured a year ago, and she made the entry into her record at that time. Apparently, they kept her waiting then and she didn't like that, so she had a note created. This is her hospital of choice."

"I have a protector," Stephanie sang softly in a little girl voice, with a cute smile on half her face. "He's my boyfriend."

Rosemary glanced over at her with an amused smile. "Shhhh, honey. Yes, you do, and he's annoying."

Stephanie giggled a little and then stiffened up with pain.

"So, they call you in case she gets admitted?"

Rosemary gave a small nod.

"Then why are you sneaking in here in the middle of the night?" Joe asked.

Rosemary's lips puckered in disapproval like she was sucking a lemon. "I am not family, so not allowed in until visiting hours. Her injuries suggested that she needed aid quicker than that. Letting wounds like hers go for hours can cause scaring, thus incurring complications when healing, especially brain injuries."

Joe holstered his gun. "How reliable is this sp … ah symbol?" He glanced at Stephanie.

Rosemary gave him a little smile. "You do seem to have her best interests in mind."

"He's sweet on me," Stephanie announced in a cute girl voice, making Joe blush. "He probably brought those gangers down on me, too." Joe scowled on that one and felt like someone had just hit him in the stomach.

Rosemary reached over and patted her arm in a motherly fashion. "He probably just sped it up a little. Once you had heard about the robberies on the news, you would've put the pieces together and then decided to do something. Thus, they would've reacted. They were probably already watching you."

Stephanie nodded slightly.

"The symbol is very reliable. There is a coven of Wicca I have been working with for some time now. They introduced me to it. I can use it, but I don't have much of a gift, as it were. Stephanie, however, is very gifted. While I could only provide a very limited type of cure, she will probably be able to affect a complete recovery in a very short period of time."

"Joe," Stephanie whined in a little girl voice. "I want to see it."

"What kind of meds have they been giving her?" Rosemary asked in an alarming tone. She moved over and looked in Stephanie's eye. "Her pupil is grossly enlarged; her pulse rapid, the swelling is getting worse."

Joe reached over and hit the call button. There was no chime in the room, and it didn't light up. He remembered the clumsy orderly with the dropped syringe. Joe reached up and pulled the IV bag down and crimped the hose with a knot to stop the flow. "Give her the symbol," he ordered. "I'm going to get a nurse."

Rosemary hesitated for just a moment, then shook herself. "Wait, let's try this first." Pulling a sheet of paper out of a pocket, she moved to the edge of the bed. "Stephanie, listen closely. This is a new type of invocation of a symbol. When I show it to you, I want you to visualize it in your mind's eye as stretching over your body. Can you do that?"

"Yes, Rosemary." Her voice sounded very childlike, very trusting.

"Here is the symbol." She held up the paper. "Let me know when your visualization is complete, and I will tell you the next step."

"Oh, this is a good one. Complicated. There's five symbols interlinked," Stephanie said with delight. Her tongue stuck out between her teeth just a little bit as she concentrated. "I have it all over my body like a big blanket."

"Oh, what a bright child." Rosemary's tone was soothing and motherly. "Now, you have to want it to work. Want it very bad, very, very badly. It will make the pain go away." Rosemary pulled a No.2 pencil out and put it in Stephanie's splinted hand. Stephanie screwed up her face like a child concentrating. "Do you have the will?" Stephanie nodded slightly. "Say 'goddess hear my prayer.'"

"Gods hear my prayer," Stephanie's little girl voice echoed with sincerity.

Rosemary frowned. "It will have to do. Say the word 'heal' like you do and give it the way."

"Eal-Hay," she mumbled and poked herself with the pencil eraser.

There was a soundless compression of air that pushed Rosemary off the bed and rocked Joe back a step. The smell of burnt rubber spread throughout the room. The heart monitor froze and then started buzzing madly.

Joe stepped over, hauled Rosemary to her feet as he checked Stephanie's pulse, steady and regular. She was glowing very faintly. "Is there anything else you can do for her?"

Rosemary looked confused then shook her head no.

"All hell is about to break lose. You being here will be hard to explain. So, you should leave." Joe had been walking her to the door.

Joe could see comprehension bloom on her face. She looked into the hall. "Call me. Tell me how well it worked." With that she scurried off, away from the nurse's station, waving her hand and speaking softly.

Almost on cue, a female nurse appeared from that direction. Joe waved at her, "Come here! Something has happened." Joe didn't yell, but he whispered damn loud. "Where's the male nurse that was in here earlier?"

"There's no male nurse on duty for this shift," she stated abruptly.

Stephanie lay on the bed with her eye closed. The nurse quickly checked her vital signs, examined the monitor, and reset it so it would stop buzzing. She picked up a syringe on the bedside table, studied it, looked at the twisted tubing for the IV, disconnected the sack and all the tubing, and then hurried out of room. "I have to check her chart. Don't leave her alone."

"Don't lose those things, they are evidence," Joe shouted.

Stephanie opened her eye to look around the room. She had stopped glowing. "Hey, Joe. Where am I?" She looked around a little more. "What am I doing in a hospital? What are you doing here?"

Chapter 6

Joe was running on a quad espresso with a coffee chaser. He had been at the hospital all night, mainly chatting with Stephanie. They had been swapping growing up stories. Her life as an orphan raised by a mysterious great uncle was as strange to him as his growing up in a large family was to her. He hadn't wanted to leave. He only ran home to change into his suit so he could look somewhat presentable to Detective Sergeant Grayson.

The detective's office wasn't really an office. They had been the victim of the soft-sided office cube fad that had swept through the business world. Accountants loved them because they didn't cost much, everyone else thought they sucked for lack of privacy in a crowded spacc.

Joe knocked on the top of the wall, "Sergeant, are you in?" His voice came out more as a rumble.

Sergeant Grayson looked up and rose. "Let's go into the boardroom." He grabbed a folio off his desk and led the way. They had a room with white boards in it for case images. It was easier to visualize if they put them on the wall, built a timeline, and wrote notes near the pictures. Joe noticed there was a picture of Stephanie on two different boards in the room, meaning two different cases. Joe involuntarily moved over to scan the boards. One was labeled Margret Vanderhousen with a picture of a pretty, blond, mid-thirties, single professor at Bosh-Gates and dead. The other was Sylvia Bloomerton, late fifties, handsome, single professor at Bosh-Gates and dead. These were murder cases.

"That's why I was in her classroom yesterday. Ms. Stephanie Blackraven has popped up in two different murder cases as possible sources of information," Grayson explained. "And if what you tell me is true about last night, she may be another potential victim." Grayson didn't seem too happy about it.

"Yes, someone tried to kill her last night. We were there and saw the perp. It was that male nurse. He administered an excessive dose of morphine and another drug, yet to be identified into her IV fluid. We must've stepped in just as he was administering it. It was meant to look like an accident." Joe rubbed his eyes before he could catch himself.

"Did you get any sleep?"

"No sir. I stayed and tried to keep them, the hospital personnel, from screwing up the evidence. I mostly succeeded. We have several partial prints and one really good one. They problem is, it doesn't match anyone on record." Joe spied the coffee pot in the corner and moved toward it.

"Why didn't she?"

Joe gave his sergeant a puzzled look over the cup. "Why didn't she what?"

"Die."

"Oh, that." Joe sipped. He was just too tired to come up with a good lie. "Her faculty advisor, Rosemary Stein, snuck into the hospital and gave her a symbol to use for healing herself. It was pretty amazing." Joe took another sip of coffee like nothing had happened.

"What?" He had the sergeant's attention.

"She used magic; no, she'd call it science, to heal herself." Joe smiled around his cup. "The hospital staff was tearing their hair out trying to figure it out. She has made a full recover. No breaks, no bruises, no drug overdose, nothing. Hell, it regrew her fingers. She thinks it even healed a knee injury she took a year ago."

"Are you kidding? She was beat to a pulp. Don't get me wrong, she struck me as one tough lady, but come on." For the first time since Joe had known him, Sergeant Grayson was startled.

"Everything healed. Only problem is she can't remember much, especially the symbol she used."

"Damn, that would be some medical breakthrough. Rosemary Stein should still have it?"

"She might, but Steph is the only one who can make it work. Professor Stein admitted that much to me. Apparently, it's been bouncing around the Wicca community for a while." Joe sipped more coffee before going on. "It would make a real difference in medicine, which is why they're hounding Stephanie about it. I left just when she got fed up and threatened to sue them for malpractice, because of the drug overdose, thus forcing her to use experimental methods on herself. That backed them down." Joe chuckled at that one and the visual image of her getting up in that pompous doctor's face.

"Why were you in the classroom yesterday to see the young lady?"

Joe was too tired to really think before he answered. "I was acting on a hunch. The three breaking and enterings you gave me were too weird. The facts, as they stood, didn't make sense, unless the bad guys could walk through doors. I had checked out the households, and there weren't any discrepancies, so they had to use magic to get in and out." He poured more coffee, blew on it to sip. "I had heard about Steph on campus and decided to ask her if it was possible. I hit pay dirt. Not only possible, but she and her assistant, Bruce Richardson, identified the partial symbol and told me how it could've been done." Anger at the attempt on her swept through him, causing his hand to tremble and coffee to spill.

"Joe?" Grayson asked.

Joe ignored the implied question, "I'll bet dollars to doughnuts, the guy who worked the symbol was in that class." He set down his coffee and opened his notebook to extract a page with a picture on it. "Andrew Stone, student, petty thief, and deeply in debt. He is a student in the class and there when I approached Steph. My gut tells me he sic'd those assholes on her." Joe put the picture on one of the boards and turned to Grayson.

"Campus police picked up two men last night due to a rape alert, one with a broken nose and another with a dislocated knee and bruised throat." Grayson held up his hand before Joe could even move. "Not your job. They will be processed and charged with assault and attempted rape. They both have records and gang affiliations. I gave your information about the symbols to Seattle Metro, well, to all the neighboring police departments, and they would like to speak with you and Ms. Blackraven. There have been other robberies with weird shit. If," he paused to get Joe's attention, "you can convince her to help."

Joe frowned, "Me, her, what?"

Grayson smiled. "Well, since she is your NAG, I thought you should escort her."

"NAG, sir?"

"You know, not-a-girlfriend, NAG."

"Oh funny, not ... ah ... sir." Joe really was not amused. This was one of those things that was going to make the rounds and quickly.

"Well, be that as it may, since someone has already tried to kill her, we're assuming it's because she is either providing info on the gangs or because she is somehow related to the murders. Whichever, she warrants protection while aiding the department." Grayson had gone back to the stone-faced look. "Also, we got some funny hits on her record. So, that warrants looking into as well."

Joe cocked his head and squinted. "Funny hits, what does that mean?"

Grayson moved over to the computer and punched in a search routine. "It wasn't on her, exactly, it was on the guy who raised her, one Raymond Blackraven. The Montana residence checked out, nothing of note in his Montana record, but when it went into the joint data store, which pushes into the FBI and other Homeland Security sources," he pushed away and let Joe see the screen. It was flashing the secure profile warning, indicating that the data was locked. "And then," Grayson pointed at the phone in the room, which started ringing. "Go ahead."

Joe picked up the phone. "Bellevue police department, Officer Bremer speaking."

"Officer Bremer, this is Agent Holstrom, FBI. Did you just try to access information on Raymond Blackraven?"

Joe raised an eyebrow at his sergeant. "Yes, I did."

"What is the purpose of your search?"

"I was seeking background information on an emerging data source we have, a Stephanie Blackraven, who was supposedly raised by him, her uncle."

"Yes, he did raise her in Cascade, Montana, located in Cascade County. Did you need any other confirmation?"

"I was hoping to get some background. She provided some antidotal information that seemed to indicate a rough upbringing."

"I'm sorry officer, all other information is classified." The FBI agent sounded sorry, but Joe didn't think he was.

"So, if I need that information, then who do I have to apply to so I get cleared?"

"You won't get cleared, good day." He hung up.

Joe pulled the receiver away and stared at it and then slowly set it down. "I wonder what that means?"

"Well," Grayson started, "At a minimum, it means we aren't going to get any information from them. It also may mean there is more to Ms. Blackraven than we see right now. It also means we would have to get the information from her directly."

"I don't like the sounds of that," Joe blurted out. "I mean, we're going to ask her for her help. It seems kind of crappy to spy on her at the same time." Joe scratched his head. "If she's not a suspect ..."

"Not spying, just nosing around. I've run into this before, and it normally indicates the person was some kind of government spook. The kind they don't want people messing with for various reasons. These are also the kinds of people that the government made deadly and are afraid they are working on US soil." Grayson stepped over to one of the boards with his back to Joe. "Both of these victims were associated with the same university as Ms. Blackraven is currently attending. Both of these victims were women. Ms. Blackraven also knew them or worked with them. This is starting to look like there was some kind of ritual involved with the killings, I would like her opinion." He turned back to Joe. "Can you do that? Get her involved with this case without compromising the department."

Joe frowned, "Isn't that what detectives are for, I'm just in training."

Grayson picked up his folio and slipped a shield out. The badge was bright and shiny. "That's right, detective, that is what they're for." He held the badge out to Joe. "You are also officially assigned to these murder cases."

Chapter 7

"Bigfoot has been sighted again around Skykomish. Scientists from the University of Washington are proposing an in-depth investigation about the legendary creature." The immaculate talking head smiled from the flat screen, "Story at ten on King 5 news."

Stephanie hit the off button and tossed the wired controller back on to the rumpled hospital bed. She rose from the "comfortable" chair, as opposed to the uncomfortable chair, to go look out the window. She also carefully held the back of her gown closed lest she flash her naked bottom at the room.

Symbols and images were flashing through her mind's eye. It was like the working of the healing on herself had broken something lose within her head. It was seeking a way out. Carefully, lest she power one, she started calling them to her mind's eye by name or category, since she still didn't know what most of them did, reviewing them, and then putting them away. She knew she could call them from that memory slot later. It seemed as if she was remembering every symbol she had ever seen.

"You'd think they would let that creature alone after all these years. He obviously doesn't want attention." The seismic voice rumbled from the door. She whirled around, almost losing her strategic hold on the gown.

"Joe, you scared the crap out of me."

His glower quickly became a big toothy grin. His face wasn't anything great, with all the bony ridges, deep-set eyes, and squareness of it, but, as Uncle Raymond would say, it had character. She kind of liked it.

"What are you doing here?" she asked. "Again."

"I heard they were going to let you out today, so I thought I would stop by and provide security." He got serious. "We caught the two who beat you up, broken nose and smashed knee guy. But we still don't know anything about the guy that was here in your room."

"You mean the one that tried to kill me?" A smile spread across her face at Joe's tone. He was really worked up about this. "That's okay, Joe. I know you're working on it."

"There's another thing. The department has asked me, to ask you, if you would help us with a couple of investigations?" He was giving her a pretty intense look. She didn't know how to interpret it. "In exchange, we will provide protection for you."

She smiled impishly. "Do I get a cool badge?"

"Ah, … no. We'll issue you a little cheesy plastic card with your picture on it." He pulled it out of his pocket and let it dangle by its lanyard. "Mainly, it's to let us know that you are an approved person at crime scenes. I'll hold on to it for now, since you don't have pockets." He stuffed it all back in his pocket. "So, will you help out?"

"You should get Bruce's help, too." Joe gave her a questioning look. "He's smarter than me, and we're partners in symbology. I have the gift, but he does all the database work."

"Okay, I'll get him added to the list. He's not being targeted by bad guys, so he won't be included in the protection."

"Are you going to be my protector?" She gave him a playful, but shy, little-girl look, batting her eyes like the women do on TV, flirting with him. He fell for it. His face looked like she had hit him with a bat.

Joe blushed and did a kind of "aw shucks" look away while smiling slowly. "Ah … ah … Yes, I will be your liaison. We're going to try and keep your exposure to a minimum."

Looking down at her flimsy gown and then around like she was trying to see her back, "You can't see through this, right? I'm not exposing anything now? Did you peek at my butt?"

"Not yet, no … I mean, … ah, … no."

He's just too easy. She smiled at him. He made her feel warm inside. "Sure I'll help, since it's you asking." Pointing at the paper bag, she asked, "So, what's in the bag?"

Joe seemed to just notice the bag in his hand. “Oh, they cut up your clothes when they brought you in, so I borrowed some of my sister’s things to see if you could use them. Unfortunately, they’re a little bigger then you are, my sisters, that is.” He handed her the bag.

“Did you ask them first?” She looked into the bag. “This is a lot of stuff. How many sisters do you have?”

“Three. Mom said it was okay. They’ve outgrown those.”

“You drove forty minutes up to Index to get me hand-me-down clothes? Hey, did you see Bigfoot? Index is only about 15 miles short of Skykomish.”

He shook his head mumbling.

She couldn’t help but tease him. It was too much fun. Right on cue, he blushed and lost the ability to speak. He only did that when it was something about her. “You know there’s a Target just over the hill in Woodinville, not five minutes away. Or,” she walked over to the closet, opened it, and carefully with a strategic hold in place, bent down, rummaged around, and pulled her keys out of the plastic bag for her effects. The police had kept her backpack. She jingled them, “Gone to my apartment.” Joe mumbled something. “What was that?”

“I had to go up by my folks place, anyway, and . . . ah, I didn’t, ah . . . well, ah.”

She was just being mean, teasing him, but he was cute. Here was this huge mountain of a man who had trouble talking to her. She liked him, and she was pretty sure he felt the same way about her.

“He said he didn’t know what size you are or how to get you bras and panties.” Bruce stepped in the room, holding up a Target bag and two others from the scary mall boutiques. “I, on the other hand, am a shameless hedonist and had no problem embarrassing the sales lady. Hi Joe, you shouldn’t let her do that to you.”

“Do what?” Joe bristled at him.

“Never mind,” Stephanie butted in. “You two he-men get out of my room. I want real clothes.”

“You goin’ to tuck that shapely rear end away, instead of flashing it to everyone?” Bruce asked, teasingly. “Joe, here, won’t have anything NOT to look at.”

"Bruce!" She let out a little laugh. "Leave him alone, and yes, clothes. I want out of here. Maybe you could go intimidate the nurses, so they could expedite my discharge?" She shooed them to the door and closed it firmly.

Joe's bag had the right size underwear. *How did he figure that out? Hmmm* . . . she thought, *more material for teasing him.* Blue jeans from Bruce's, even though they were designer and cost more than jeans ever should, she put them on. Ahh, one of Joe's sisters was a real mountain girl, flannel, a little big, but fit just fine over the really tight shirt Bruce had bought her. What the hell was he thinking? There wasn't enough material to keep the girls from getting frisky, not that breasts her size weren't prone to leading the way in any shirt. Sneakers, neither pair fit, but they would work good enough to get her home. Joe's bag had a hairbrush, toothbrush, and some generic travel makeup, not that she used any. "Must've been his mom." She smiled as she mumbled out loud, "I'd like to meet her." Then she paused. That might send the wrong signal to both Joe and his family. Or was it the wrong signal? "Shit," she said, "this is where having a mom would've been handy. I'll have to ask Rosemary."

She snorted, thinking about what Uncle Raymond's advice would be. If she were a guy he'd say, *Just screw her and get it out of your system.* Instead, she would hear, *Ladies need to be ladies, don't encourage the boys.* Being raised by some kind of cross between a mountain man, cowboy, and merchant soldier from the turn of the last century had its drawbacks.

Finishing up in the bathroom, she stepped out and right into the nurse, who had a habit of not knocking. "You're dressed," Nurse Barge-right-in blurted out. "The doctor wanted …"

"I don't care what he wanted. I am out of here," Stephanie abruptly stated. "I said I would give you guys a day. You've had it. Now, clear my paperwork so I can leave."

The nurse started to sputter again.

"Look, I'm leaving within the hour with or without the paperwork completed. There is nothing wrong with me." She gave the nurse a firm look. "The cops won't help you. They're on my side."

"Very well, Ms. Blackraven." She presented papers with a flourish and a smile. "If you ever figure out exactly what kind of magic you did, I would really like to know."

"Science, not magic. It's you along with about every other doctor in this place, that wants to know." Stephanie was reading the paperwork. "I'll be working on it. I want to know, too."

"That is Doctor Blackraven, by the way," Bruce announced with a haughty tone. He was standing in the doorway holding a diploma up so she could see it.

"Bruce!" Stephanie exclaimed. "How did you get that? Is it real?"

"Rosemary. She started working it the moment you walked out of the classroom. I knew you weren't interested in walking, so she gave it to me to give to you. They do want to have some type of ceremony." He handed her the cardboard-backed paper.

She was moved, tears formed; for some reason, holding this piece of paper just made it all real. "Three years, despite what Rhinebolt could do," she whispered.

"Congratulations, doctor," Joe said, smiling and holding out some roses to her.

"Doctor Blackraven, you earned it," Bruce solemnly stated. She hugged him and then Joe.

"Joe, how did you know? Where did you get the flowers? They're beautiful." She was touched by his gesture. He gently brushed a tear off her cheek with a strange expression on his face.

"I took them off a cart down the hall." He moved his eyes side to side while squinting like a shifty thief. "We should go before they call a cop." Laughing, they all fled the hospital.

Stephanie's apartment wasn't anything great. It was in a slightly more reputable neighborhood than the U's student housing, and it had two bedrooms. Her building set in a little cul-de-sac that gave the illusion that it was all alone in the trees. That was the secret of Puget Sound, all the trees made it seem like it wasn't a city of millions crammed up against the ocean.

Bruce pulled his stylish late model BMW into the cul-de-sac. It was full for the middle of the day; three dark Suburbans, one truck, and people sitting in all of them. "Shit," Stephanie blurted out, "That's Uncle Raymond's truck." She pointed at a beat-up Ford F250 4x4 with two large utility boxes in the bed. Almost on cue, a six foot, lean, weathered cowboy got out wearing blue jeans, a dark blue shirt, a jean jacket, and a tan sweat-stained cowboy hat. Scarred, very capable hands were hitched by his thumbs to his pockets, and a weathered leathery face that had huge amounts of character. They got out of Bruce's car and waited as the cowboy slowly walked over to them.

"Uncle Raymond, this is a surprise." Stephanie was trying for a nice neutral tone, instead of screaming frantically and running into her apartment. It wasn't that she didn't love him, but more like, she had done and said some really not nice things to him, then ran away to college. Things she wished she could take back now. He also seemed to know just the right thing to say to really piss her off. She loved him, just didn't like him most of the time.

"Princess," his whisky voice was a whisper as he nodded to her. He shifted his eyes to Bruce. She had forgotten about Bruce. "Queer."

"Straight," Bruce shot back.

"Homo."

"Hetero."

A faint smile played on Raymond's lips. He seemed to like pushing, ... well, ... everybody. "How ya doin', Bruce?"

"I'm okay, Ray. You seem to be a little off. You all right?" Stephanie could tell Bruce was ready to either throw down or shake hands. As he said to her often, he was gay, but still a guy.

Uncle Raymond offered his hand to Bruce. "I'm sick, but, hey, life's short." Bruce shook his hand. Guys shook hands, not girls. It was like stepping back into the 1950s, and she didn't know all the rules.

"Your eyes are a little yellow, Ray, and skin tone is off." Bruce was acting concerned. He had only met Uncle Raymond a couple of times and those times hadn't been all that pleasant. But he was smart and observant. "You lost weight?"

Bruce was right, Stephanie thought, *he does look thin.* "Uncle Raymond, are you WORKING?" Stephanie was getting concerned. Her uncle didn't look healthy. She couldn't really place it, but he seemed deflated a little. Then again, she hadn't seen him in four years, and that time had ended with her throwing him out of her apartment. Even looking ill, he was still dangerous, and he had a look in his eyes that was all serious.

"My princess gets bashed around; I come to check it out." He gave her one of his cold smiles.

"He with you, Ray?" Bruce interrupted, nodding toward a guy getting out of a truck.

A bigger man, full of life, with his sandy blonde hair cut short in a military haircut, normal looking, somewhere in his mid to late thirties, was gliding toward them. His face had character, too and a couple of scars. Stephanie could tell a master class fighter when she saw one. She had been raised by one. This guy was in his prime and dangerous.

"Yeah, that's Nelson. I wanted him to meet Stephanie."

"How about the guys in the Suburbans and the two over by the corner?" Bruce nodded toward them.

Uncle Raymond smiled his approval. Bruce had done something else he liked. "Yeah, they're all with me. I'll call a couple of them over in a minute. Don't be reachin' for your heat."

Stephanie was shocked, that was what Uncle Raymond called a gun. "What?" she squeaked, looking at Bruce.

"Bruce, here, is carrying. I don't what him to confuse Nelson … or the others. This is all friendly." Raymond explained it like it was a chance meeting between old friends.

"What the hell is going on?" Stephanie demanded of both of them. It felt like she was in high school again with Raymond coming in to talk to the boys, but not her.

"You get beat up, the lab has been broken into on three different occasions; … I'm being careful." Bruce stated.

"Don't go gettin' all riled up, Princess." Uncle Raymond was being all calm and nice. Something was up, and it made her nervous. He was hardly ever nice. "I just brought you some stuff you might need, and I have some papers for you to sign. That's all."

"Uncle Raymond, I don't need any stuff." Her mind was jumping around wildly as she tried to imagine what "stuff" meant this time. It could be anything from a camping tent to a sniper rifle to a .50 caliber machine gun, maybe even a rocket launcher. She had gotten beat up, so it was probably weapons.

"Girl, you just got the crap beat out of you." He studied her for a moment. "And you look great, like one of them pin-up girls out of Soldier of Fortune. What's goin' on? I was told concussion, broken ribs, maybe fractured arm, hand blown off." He was studying her hard now.

It was making her nervous self-consciously, she pulled the flannel shirt closed. *He must be sick, if he missed all that until now,* she thought. "I used a symbol to heal myself. It was kind of a panic, since someone tried to kill me with a lethal overdose of meds the other night."

"Lethal." Uncle Raymond froze for a moment as he got his anger under control. Then she saw a wave of pain pass over his eyes. His voice was colder than normal as he spoke, "Nelson, would you kindly mosey over to Mr. Riedel and ask him if he knows anything about this."

"Yes sir," Nelson replied.

Stephanie though he was going to salute before turning. He marched over to the closest Suburban to chat with a guy in the backseat.

"Uncle Raymond, what's wrong with you?" Stephanie was getting worried and pissed off. "Who is Mr. Riedel, and why would a Mr. Riedel know anything about me being overdosed?"

"I'm sick, Princess." He paused and glanced over to the Suburbans. "Let's get all this other stuff out of the way, then we'll talk."

"What other stuff?" She bit the statement off.

He didn't respond while waving at the guys talking. "Come on over and bring the papers," he ordered.

Joe's sneaky police SUV pulled into the cul-de-sac. She just didn't think it was fair that the police got to drive around in unmarked SUVs. How was a law-abiding, but nervous, citizen going to avoid them? He pulled up, but as he got out, two other guys in suits, muscle wearing suits poorly, got out of a Suburban, and moved over to intercept him.

Uncle Raymond didn't miss that. "The cop with you?"

Bruce glanced over. "That's Joe, her boyfriend."

"He's not my boyfriend."

Uncle Raymond got "that smile" on his face. She had never really learned what it meant, but things got interesting when he smiled that way. "Joe Bremer, Bellevue cop, new detective. So," he glanced back at Stephanie, "you're his NAG."

"What!" Stephanie exclaimed.

"NAG, not-a-girlfriend. It's what his co-workers are calling this girl he's fallen for, but can't really pursue cause she's a suspect or whatever they call it nowadays."

"NAG," Bruce was laughing. "I can't wait to see Joe's reaction to that."

"He won't like it," Stephanie said. She pondered on it and then flashed a quick sly grin. *More material for teasing Joe*, she thought.

Something wasn't right about the situation, so she pulled her mind back to the recent conversation. *I'm not playing Uncle Raymond's game!*

She took a deep breath and mentally stepped back, putting all the emotion away. It was time to go 'engineer' all over this problem. She looked around. *Four in that Suburban, four more in that one, eight, two by the side of the building, ten, two more over by that Suburban, twelve, two more harassing Joe, fourteen people total. Uncle Raymond didn't want Bruce to pull his gun, so they are all armed; personal security? He is working.* More people got out of a Suburban, one in a really expensive suit, the other in an almost as expensive suit. L*awyers,* she thought, *with two nervous, dangerous-looking types.* She looked back at Uncle Raymond. *Face shallow, eyes sunken with dark rings, eyes yellowish, little crow's feet at the edge of his eyes, indicating pain. Uncle Raymond always had a reason for what he does. He didn't say he wasn't working, either. He's trying to keep me off balance. Why?* She never could figure out exactly what it was he did, but while growing up, she had accidently answered the phone on a number of occasions to find someone from the government on the other end.

Another suit, a very expensive suit, walked up with a briefcase and an air of importance about him. "Princess, this here is Mr. Riedel, he's got some papers for you to sign, fingerprints and a DNA sample."

Stephanie's mind went into overdrive. What was up with Uncle Raymond just showing up, being sick, him picking on Bruce again, the "stuff," Nelson, bringing up the police harassment of Joe, and his backward way of pegging Joe as her boyfriend. It all seemed to be directed at keeping her off balance. She looked at him hard and then blinked. “You’re dying! You have cancer.” She blurted out. “You’re here to pass ownership to me. I’m your only heir.”

“Too damn smart,” Uncle Raymond mumbled and pursed his lips like he did before saying something abrupt to her. “Everybody dies. Just sign the papers, and I’ll leave.”

“No,” She shook her head while stepping back. “No! I want to talk to you. Really talk, none of this last century, condescending, let’s keep the women folk in the dark for their own protection, shit!”

He shook his head and half-turned away from her, but she wasn’t giving up this time.

“I want your word, sworn by the knives you make, that you will talk to me, or I’m not signing shit.”

“Princess …”

“No! No! Not this time. I have things to say to you. Things to clear up. I’ve said some mean …” She fought hard for control. “And I need to …” Her throat just closed up.

He nodded his head without really saying anything. Then after a moment, “Okay, I’ll give you another chance to tear my heart out.”

“Swear.”

“I swear by the Bone Knife that I will give you a chance to talk to me.”

“Today, now, right after I sign this stuff.”

He was defeated. “Okay, today, right after you sign the papers.”

Mr. Riedel chuckled a little and muttered something under his breath.

“What, what did he say?” Stephanie wanted a target. She rounded on him. “You aren’t a part of this. Why are you here?” She stepped closer to him, getting in his face. “What did you say!?! Who are you?”

Uncle Raymond obviously heard his comment. “Mr. Riedel, just put the papers out and shut the fuck up. Someone has already taken a shot at her. You know what would happen …” Uncle Raymond pulled a small cell phone from his pocket, just far enough so Mr. Riedel could see it and his finger on the one. Mr. Riedel paled and started getting things spread out on the hood of Bruce’s BMW.

Everyone else froze in place. “Princess, please sign the papers where indicated. I will explain all that I can after that, but not in the middle of the street.”

“I work for the government.” Mr. Riedel sounded smooth and cultured. “And that’s all I can tell you.”

“Steph,” Bruce said in a worried tone, “I think you should just go along with what the nice government man wants you to do. Just sign what he wants you to sign.” He patted her on the back.

Bruce was spooked, too.

There was a scuffle from up the cul-de-sac, and Stephanie turned to see Joe all but picking up one of the suits by the lapels. The other one was pulling an expandable metal club called an ASP out. “Joe,” Stephanie called out in alarm. “You two leave him alone. Are they with you?” She started toward them only to have Uncle Raymond grab her arm. She almost pulled him over, which is what stopped her. She turned and looked at him in surprise. She had never in her wildest dreams ever thought of him as frail.

The two suits weren’t having much luck intimidating Joe, and now he was holding the ASP. It looked like two hound dogs worrying at a bear. “Nelson, would you go save the guards from the princess’s, … ah.”

“NAB, sir.” They all glanced at him as he gave them a smartass smile. “You know, not-a-boyfriend.”

Uncle Raymond smiled, “Yeah, something like that.”

“Bureau of Indian …” Bruce looked Uncle Raymond in the eyes. “Department of … Princess isn’t a pet name, is it?” Bruce said in a low tone. He had been glancing at the papers being spread out.

Stephanie decided that if looks could kill, Bruce would’ve died right then. Uncle Raymond’s left arm twitched like he was going to do something, but he didn’t. “Not here, not now,” he coldly whispered.

Stephanie, honest to God, didn’t know what was going on. She had never seen Uncle Raymond like this or Bruce. Joe, she was just getting to know, but she didn’t think he was acting like he normally would. It was like they all had some secret guy language, and she didn’t have a translator. She had spent her adult life taking control and managing her affairs. Now, she felt adrift. She was not giving up. She was going to control her life.

“Fine.” She stepped up, started speed-reading, and then froze. She looked at Mr. Riedel and then at Uncle Raymond. “These don’t even have my name right.”

“It’s right,” Uncle Raymond said in a whisper. “I just never told you your whole name. Sign, then we’ll go talk.”

Stephanie studied him and then reluctantly turned and signed.

“You don’t have to read them,” Mr. Riedel offered. “I have copies for you.” He pointed to a legal-size manila envelope.

She just glanced at him and went on reading before signing.

“Hey, Steph,” Joe’s seismic voice rumbled out. “You okay?”

She glanced up to see him red faced and quivering, ready to throw down. “No, but it’s family shit. Ya know?”

“With the government?” Joe rumbled out.

“Yeah, go figure,” Stephanie sarcastically replied.

“Hi,” Uncle Raymond threatened, “you must be Joe Bremer, her not-a-boyfriend.”

Joe’s voice dropped even lower in pitch. “Yeah, and you must the uncle that liked hitting her when she was little.”

“Shut up!” Stephanie bellowed. “We are not doing this here. All of you, just shut up. Let me finish this, and then we’ll go inside.” No one said anything; they just glared at each other. She went on reading, scowling, signing, glaring at Uncle Raymond, signing, and then literally signed the last page with a bloody thumbprint.

Chapter 8

Mr. Riedel collected the papers. One un-named lawyer opened his laptop while the second one plugged in a scan wand. Mr. Riedel handed them the papers, they scanned her signature on every document, closed everything up, handed an envelope to Stephanie, and they all nodded to Uncle Raymond and left. No one spoke.

"Let's go inside." Stephanie started digging out her keys.

Her apartment was spacious for a college student. The living room connected to the dining room with a kitchen attached, and sliding door led to a small deck on the outside. Pretty standard arrangement, two bedroom, they filled it up.

Nelson went around pulling drapes and checking the other rooms.

"What about the other guys outside? Will they be joining us?" Bruce asked.

"They'll stay outside."

"Security? Perimeter?" Bruce asked with a raised eyebrow.

"You're pretty observant for a queer."

"You're pretty sexy for a dying old guy," Bruce countered with a smile.

"Guys, shut up and sit down," Stephanie interrupted before they could really get going. "And you," she rounded on Joe with a finger pointed, "keep what I told you about my childhood memories to yourself or in context." Joe frowned. "He didn't just beat me, most of that I earned."

Stephanie turned back to the settling men and put a totally insincere smile on her face like a good hostess. "Does anyone want anything, a beer, or maybe a pint of whisky?"

"Water," Uncle Raymond stated. He was having trouble sitting down. Finally, he moved over to take one of the straight-backed kitchen chairs.

"Why don't you let me get those drinks, while you talk to your uncle?" Bruce offered. Stephanie just nodded and pulled another kitchen chair into the living room. She realized after she sat down that it was closer to Joe.

Uncle Raymond cleared his throat, after taking a sip of water. "Joe, you goin' ta be able to leave your badge outside for this discussion, or do I have to ask you to leave?"

"Just how many laws are we talking about here?" Joe rumbled out.

Uncle Raymond smiled a cold smile. "It really depends on what she asks. I'm not going to hold back much. I've killed people with government sanction. Not much is in your jurisdiction."

"Hmmm … Well, I should probably go then. What I don't know, I can deny." Joe stood up.

"I, … um, …" Stephanie stuttered to a stop.

Joe looked at her, cocked his head, waiting for her to speak.

"It … ah … It would probably be best," she finally got out. She was pretty conflicted about Joe. She wasn't very good with the whole boyfriend thing. She had chosen poorly in the past.

Joe gave her a funny, soft smile and then turned back to her uncle. "So, you are her only living relative?"

"I raised her. She's got others kickin' around in England. I'm the oldest one I know of."

"So," Joe paused as he made a decision. "Beings as how you are her senior male relative present, I would like your permission to court your niece."

"What?" Stephanie blurted out. She was working up to being really pissed at him, but couldn't, since she was thinking about what a great guy he was. She was also scared all of a sudden by what Uncle Raymond might say.

"Steph," Joe looked her in the eyes as he hurried to explain. "It's really old school, but I thought what the hell, he's old school. Anyway, it's better than having him show up to kick my ass sometime."

"Joe, he's an old man and dying. Kick your ass?" She frowned at him.

"You're kidding, right? He's like a punch line to a joke." Joe was serious.

"Which joke?" Nelson asked.

Uncle Raymond raised his eyebrow in question as Joe turned to look at him. "Why don't you pick a fight with an old man? Answer, cause he knows he can't take a beating, so he'll just kill you."

Uncle Raymond smiled at that, and Nelson gave a wry smile while nodding.

"Got that right," Bruce added while setting light beer out for everyone. When he sat down on the other side of Stephanie, he quietly whispered, "Congratulations. He's a keeper. Don't screw it up."

"You should've asked me first," Stephanie blurted out.

Bruce winced and shook his head.

"I did," Joe answered softly. "Remember the coffee?"

"Oh, yeah. But that's not courting."

"Split'n hairs, Princess," Uncle Raymond rasped out. "Detective Bremer, you goin' to treat her like a lady? You goin' to be a gentleman?" He was dead serious.

"I'm sitting right here."

Joe looked down to meet Uncle Raymond's steely-eyed look with one of his own. "Yes, sir, she is a lady. And I will be a gentleman."

"As long as she wants you to be one," Nelson leered.

Joe hmmmed, smiled, and nodded.

Stephanie didn't know what to say to that, so she scowled, said nothing, and tried to glare at both Uncle Raymond and Joe.

"It would put my mind at ease knowing there was someone else who cared for her." Uncle Raymond's smile had turned inward for a moment. "Okay, Detective Joe Bremer, you have my permission and blessing, for what's it worth."

"Thank you, sir." Joe was very serious. He turned to Stephanie. "I will be outside, right outside." He got up and left, closing the door softly behind him.

This was all just too surreal for Stephanie. "Uncle Raymond, you can't ..."

Uncle Raymond cut her off. "You know, it's your fault I'm dying of old age."

"What?" Stephanie laughed weakly. "Is not."

"If I hadn't taken those years off from my old profession, I would've died earlier in a back alley of some Third World piss-hole or in a ditch in a banana republic." He sat back from making his point. "By the time you were done with me, I wasn't young enough to take on those jobs and knew it."

"Done with you!" she exclaimed. "You were already a dinosaur when you collected me. Anyway, you were the one running my little butt up and down all the hills, buttes, and gullies. Taekwondo in Great Falls, junior rifleman," she was counting things off on her fingers. "Extreme camping, hunting, trapping, gunsmithing, knife making, workouts with all your old buddies on 'real fighting.'" She made quotation marks in the air. "My God," she said as she threw her hands up in the air, "I could shoot better and fight harder than any guy in my high school. You taught me to shoot just about every different kind of rifle and pistol made." She turned to Bruce, "You know I could field strip, inspect, and reassemble a militarized AR-10 in under twenty seconds. That was in the dark. I can build one in about thirty minutes with all the parts." She turned back to Uncle Raymond, who was smiling faintly at her. "I was your little soldier of fortune pin-up girl. If I hadn't grown breasts, you would've never known I was a girl."

Uncle Raymond harrumphed at that. "Want t' bet. You were a pain in the ass." Before Stephanie could explode at him, he went on without raising his voice, "You were also my only experiment in raising a child. I tried to show you what I knew. Teach you stuff I knew and liked to do. It was only later I realized I should've asked you more what you wanted. Then you went and turned into a girl."

"AR10, twenty seconds?" Nelson asked.

"Is that all you got out of that?" Stephanie shot back.

"It's a pink camo, modified AR-10, .308 auto, more punch, longer range. I almost shot a guy over that camo job. He thought it was mine," Uncle Raymond chuckled. "It was the only way I could get her to carry the damn thing. She wasn't having any of those yucky green or black ones." He tried and failed to make his voice sound like a girls.

"Pink?" Bruce asked. "Camo?"

"Yeah, it's in the closet. You want to see it?" Stephanie asked.

"You don't even like pink!"

She confessed quietly, "I did it just to piss off Uncle Raymond."

"An automatic weapon, it's illegal to own one," Bruce stated.

Stephanie patted his knee, "That's okay. One of those papers I signed gave me unlimited weapon ownership in the US. I could go buy a tank if I wanted to, I think." Bruce stared at her.

"Oh yeah," Uncle Raymond said while digging out his wallet. He pulled out three different plastic credit card sized cards, a couple sets of keys with little controllers on them, a couple of other keys on a ring, and handed the lot over to her. "Here are ID cards and keys to stuff: the Suburban outside and the storage lockers we talked about before you threw me out last time. You'll also be getting your real birth certificate by registered mail in a day or so."

"Real birth …"

"Don't ask, just read it. You'll understand right away."

She got up, shaking her head, to collect the assorted items from Uncle Raymond and handed them to Bruce before she sat back down.

He was staring at the cards wide-eyed as she stated, "I don't need your stuff."

"The bruises you should have on your face say otherwise."

She took a deep breath to settle herself and then focused on Uncle Raymond. "So, what was all that about outside? Most of the papers I signed were for things that couldn't have been legal, like all the land from the Bureau of Indian Affairs. How can I own an Indian reservation?"

"I was tying up loose ends."

"Uncle Raymond, you said the truth."

He took a big breath and let it out. "It's a legal fiction. I have land all over the country, several countries, and I didn't want them to take it away from you. I made a deal. You are of Indian heritage; in fact, you are a princess, as Bruce guessed."

Bruce waved.

"The North American Indians didn't have princesses," she stated with some assurance.

"Who said it was NORTH American?"

"Hmmm … How could you've made that kind of deal? It's the government." Stephanie was a little in awe of that.

"Are you sure you want Bruce to hear all this?" Uncle Raymond asked in exasperation.

"Yes, yes I do. Bruce has had my back for a couple of years now. If he liked girls, we might've been a couple."Bruce waved again, this time with a limp wrist.

Uncle Raymond frowned and took a sip of water, then shook his head. "Could I get a couple fingers of Scotch?"

"Ray, the doctor ..." Nelson started to say.

"Yeah, I know, but damn, I'm dying anyway."

"Glenlivet, top shelf, over the fridge," Stephanie told Bruce as he got up.

"Damn! That's my girl." Bruce rummaged quickly and brought in a water glass with a couple inches of brown liquid.

Uncle Raymond took a sip. "Now that cuts the crap in your throat." He gazed off, obviously collecting his thoughts.

"I think I'll just start near the beginning, Korea in the fifties, Vietnam in the sixties. It was a dump, way worse than what you guys get to read about. I was a kid, Indian half-breed, back when we were still discriminated against by both sides. I was raised in England during WWII. Dad died, that would be your great-great-grandpa. He was a Brit, kind of an ass, but he did teach me a few things: stiff upper lip and all that rot, no whining, what." Uncle Raymond did a great British accent. "Mom brought us back to the States, to a reservation in Montana, and married a Cheyenne shaman, had a daughter by him that would be your grandmother. I joined the army to piss Mom off. Sis had married a Brit, too. That would be your grandpa. I actually liked him. Damn, your mom married a Brit, too, but he died when you were real little, living in England."

"Anyway, I kind of broke with the family, lost track, just didn't care about family. Didn't fit on the reservation, too much white in me, too much drive. Stepdad tried to bring out my Indian side. He was the one that showed me how to craft the knives. It didn't work to connect me to the tribe. It just set me further apart. I didn't much like the Indian way, and they didn't like me much, either. Today, you would call me rebellious."

"I joined the army and went to Korea. That worked okay, got some training, specialized in being sneaky and knife work. I just worked the stereotype; all Indians are good with knives. Nam was a whole new education."

"The brass just couldn't get through their heads it was a dirty kind of war. I got in trouble." He took a sip of Scotch. "We had captured some Cong, and we needed information from them. I got it, but the officer in charge didn't like my methods; maybe it was the screaming." Uncle Raymond chuckled like it was an old joke. "He had me arrested, sort of, we were in a war zone, but that wasn't going to work, people were going to die. So me and four others hurt a couple of people, sneaked out of camp, and conducted an unauthorized mission. Freed some captured POWs, killed a whole mess of Cong, and generally cleaned up a mess caused by some Washington army asshole. I was a hero, so they couldn't court-martial me, instead they gave me a medal and suggested I leave the army. That was when I got recruited by a different army, a black ops army." He took another sip and leaned forward, pointing with his glass in his hand.

"Ya see, there was a group in Washington that had been watching. They learned the Nam lessons; there were some types of fighting that wasn't for regular soldiers. This kind of fighting took killers, sneaky killers, Studies and Observations Group, SOG. Today, you would call it Special Operations Group, or black ops." He smiled a cold smile as he sat back. "I got recruited even before I left the country. Me and some others were sent back out into the jungle to do other stuff." He paused briefly as something passed over his face and took his breath away. "Well, that was the beginning. All through the sixties and seventies I got training, did jobs, all kinds of unpleasant jobs, government-backed jobs. I specialized in accidents. I ended up working for organizations with letters instead of names."

"Now, they all thought I was just some dumb Injun, so no one noticed that I kept records of every event, every adjustment, every deal for the good of the country, and the locations of all the bodies. Some of them were in the US, others in allied countries, others in bad guy territory."

"You were a spy?" Stephanie couldn't keep the doubt out of her voice.

"Oh yeah, 007, license to kill." The Brit showed up again in his voice. "That was me. Only I didn't travel in the high-life lanes, I was more the low-life type. Keep to the dark, no trail, no MO, nothing to track me by. I snuck in and out, only an accident left behind. Hell, I was behind the Iron Curtain so many times I had my own road." He rattled off some sentence, it sounded Russian.

"Iron Curtain?" Stephanie had heard about it, but couldn't remember. "You speak Russian?"

"You kids!" Uncle Raymond just shook his head and got the nasty tone he used with her. "The Cold War, Soviet Union, any of that ringing a bell?"

"Oh, yeah, ancient history." Stephanie narrowed her eyes at him. He knew just what to do to piss her off. *Hmmm, if he was a spy then he would be good at manipulating others,* she thought. *Like his grandniece.*

Uncle Raymond smiled and sipped. "Anyway, by the end of the eighties, I was training and planning more than I was in the field, which turned out to be a good thing. I had established my own network, worldwide." He frowned and harrumphed, "Not to be confused with the World-Wide-Web. It was connections, people, HUMINT it was called. Then the wall fell in '91." He took another sip. "Ya know, the Berlin Wall, signaling the end of the Cold War. Peace broke out." He laughed outright at that, until he was reduced to coughing, and turned red.

"What's so funny," Stephanie asked.

Nelson looked concerned, but answered, "There was no peace. Nothing had really changed, just been destabilized. Instead of one big bad guy, now there were lots of different types of bad guys looking for US ass. Congress, controlled by the intelligencia liberals, used it as an excuse to start cutting the military, Foreign Service, CIA, betraying our allies around the world. There was a big RIF, reduction in force. There was a time when the navy didn't have enough officers to captain all the ships Reagan had built. Under the Clinton administration, almost all the HUMINT resources were released from service, which got many of them killed. It set the stage for 9/11 and most of the other …"

Uncle Raymond made a gesture, and Nelson stopped talking; like throwing a switch. "No politics." Uncle Raymond cleared his throat. "Not a good time.

They tried to cancel my contract, permanently. I went private. This is when they found out about all those records I kept. Governments around the world that I had been contracted out to got interested in me staying alive. Our government got the message. I was like Hoover with little dirty secrets."

He cleared his throat again, "You got any questions? This was all pretty much pre-you."

"I don't even know where to begin." Stephanie looked away. "How many people did you kill?"

"Thousands. I stopped counting after a while. Why does everyone ask that?"

"No, I mean how many did you kill personally?"

"Hundreds." He pulled out his bone knife from nowhere, with the cross-hatched grip, and twelve-inch, rune-inscribed blade. "The grip was smooth when I started; every nick on it is a kill." The thing was covered with marks.

"They were all bad people, right?" Stephanie couldn't help but be impressed.

"No. I would do anyone to get the mission done: women, children, old people, innocent, guilty, whatever it took to get the job done. I'm a murderer." He smiled a cold smile. "I am not a nice person. I have done terrible, terrible things, and I don't care. Some of it, at the time, I enjoyed doing."

"You aren't all terrible; you gave up your whole life to raise me." Stephanie quietly added. She was troubled by the fact that it didn't really bother her that her great uncle was a murdering assassin. She thought it was pretty cool, and it explained soooo much.

Uncle Raymond froze for just an instant and then smiled. "Lapse in judgment?"

That made everyone laugh, except Stephanie. "Not to me. I'd lost everything, everyone in the fire. If Mom hadn't pushed me out the window … I still remember standing in the foster home when you came in the door with that social worker in tow." She gazed off, seeing the red and angry face of that terrible woman from Child Services. Stephanie was just another American Indian half-breed, just one more mouth to feed. No one wanted her. A tear broke loose and trailed down her face. "You fought for me, from the very first." She laughed weakly in memory. "I don't know what you said to that woman, but she ran away. She stopped telling me how much trouble I was to her."

Uncle Raymond got serious as well. “Damn, you always did know just what to say,” he muttered. “I told her you were my grandniece, and I would kill her and everyone else in her office, if she didn’t get the fuck out of my way.”

That made Stephanie laugh, “I think she believed you.”

“I meant it.” He took a sip of Scotch with a dark look on his face. “I was contacted for a contract on an American Indian woman and her daughter. I didn’t really investigate cause the money wasn’t good enough.” He gazed off in space. “I look back now and see that it wasn’t some kind of cosmic message. It was a warning. It was someone with a purpose. They wanted my niece, your mom, and you dead. Hell, I didn’t even know you were back in the country. Last time I’d bothered to check, you were in the UK. Anyway, when I got the call that my niece had died in a fire, I put the pieces together. It rocked my little narrow world,” he added with some heat.

“I had a great hate built up by the time I showed up to get you. I had to track you down through several agencies, two states. It smelled. I caught up with the hitter, but he didn’t know anything useful. But he was connected through the black ops arena. Didn’t you ever wonder why or how you ended up in North Dakota, when you guys lived in Browning, Montana?”

“No, I was a kid and in shock.” Stephanie shook her head. “You did tell me you gave up everything for me.”

“I didn’t give up everything.” Uncle Raymond looked uncomfortable. “I just told you that because you were being a little bitch. You used to piss me off …”

“The feeling was mutual.”

“I could’ve lived without the pedophile, pimp charges.”

Uncle Raymond stopped her cold with that. Stephanie just closed her eyes as the nausea hit her, “I am so very sorry for that. It was not true. You never touched me. You may have hit me while we were sparing, but … I can’t tell you how sorry. That was the meanest …”

“You didn’t?” Bruce blurted out. “There’s a national list, the FBI keeps it. You pressed charges that …”

“I did.” She opened her eyes and just let them all see the tears. “I was fourteen and wanted something; I can’t even remember what now. I came up with this great idea.” She closed her eyes and let the tears run. “I am so sorry, can you forgive me? Please forgive me?" This ghost had followed her for years. It still made her sick to the stomach whenever she thought about it.

"Yes, you're forgiven. Stop worrying about it, you were set up. Officially, it never happened." That snapped her eyes open, "Yeah, THEY set you up."

"What? How?"

"That school counselor you liked so much, they were paying her to get you away from me." Uncle Raymond took a sip of Scotch. "She confessed everything. The charges were never filed. No record was ever made of the event."

"How," Stephanie eyed her uncle. "What did you do?"

"I broke into her house at night when you were at a sleepover. Drugged her whole family to sleep, then I put dotted lines on all three kid's necks, the dog's, and her husband's. He was cheating on her, and I had pictures of that as well. I left the pictures on her stomach while she was naked, spread eagle, tied down in the living room. I had set her family on the couch so she could see them and the line. Then I woke her up and told her I would kill everything she loved or knew if she didn't come clean." He chuckled, "She told me everything. I let her keep the money. I back trailed the source through a chain of people to someone in New York. At which point, the trail went cold, as in a dead body, as a cut out."

"How, … what, … why didn't you tell me!"

He looked away for a moment, then down. "That one really hurt. I wanted to teach you a lesson." He paused again, "Then, when I realized just how bad you really felt, I felt stupid and petty and didn't want to talk about it."

Stephanie blinked a few times, thinking about what it would've been like from his side. She had cleaned up her act after that, at last realized there was more to it all than her wants.

"Say something," Uncle Raymond prompted quietly.

"I'm processing. This is a lot to recalculate on the fly. That little incident has haunted me for years, once I realized how stupid it had been." She collected her thoughts. "You were the only person that cared anything about me, I stabbed you in the back, and twisted the knife. I guess you could say it caused me to redefine myself." The room fell into an awkward silence.

"Just exactly what was your business in Cascade?" Stephanie asked after a moment. She just couldn't get her head around it all.

Uncle Raymond chuckled again and sipped more Scotch. "Didn't I just tell you, I was a spy and assassin?" He chuckled at her look. "I had a welding business, ran a few cows, fixed cars. I just didn't do too much welding or car fixing or anything else there. Oh, we did eat the cows. I was running a private contacting business of … ah … specialists at the same time. Cell phones and the Internet where starting to pick up speed after 2000. After 9/11, things started booming in my security business. All the HUMINT resources thrown away in the nineties, let's just say the gov'ment needed me again."

"Why didn't I know any of this?"

"You were a kid, and I tried very hard to keep you out of it. It was the kind of stuff that could've gotten you killed." He took another sip of Scotch and got thoughtful. "Almost did, as a matter-of-fact. Anyway, boys seemed to be attracting your attention about then."

"That would've been the barn, slap-down time frame," Bruce mentioned.

Uncle Raymond smiled broadly, "She told you about that, huh? I was never so proud as the day she called me out to the barn. The words she had learned." He shook his head in wonder. "Anyway, she almost kicked my ass that day."

"No way," Nelson blurted out. "You, General?"

"I. … Shit. … You. … Not." Uncle Raymond emphasized every word. "I was pissing blood for days after that fight. If I hadn't started fighting dirty, she would've had me. Of course, I let her get too close at first. I didn't think she had it in her; she suckered me with the cryin' and blubberin'."

"You staged that!" She blurted out and then fumed quietly to herself. She thought she was going to die in that fight. She hit him with everything she had, held nothing back. She had been trying to kill him, well, at least hurt him real bad.

"Hell no! You were hot after that asshole Calvin, and all he wanted was pussy. I told you that." He winced, with a surprised look on his face, and paused for a moment.

"True, you did tell me. It was the second date when he tried to force himself on me." Stephanie was reliving the whole date rape scene again, picturing it all in her mind's eye. She was still mad at Uncle Raymond.

Uncle Raymond shocked her out of it by laughing. "Then you broke his arm, his nose, and just about punched his balls up into his chest. The look on his dad's face when he came by to have it out with me for beatin' up his kid, and I explained it was you that done it and why. That was one of those priceless moments." Uncle Raymond was laughing again and banging his knee. "I had to hold you back when you came off the porch to do it again." He was wheezing as he choked out, "They ran for their pickup with you scapin' at me to get at them. I've never loved you more than at that moment." He got a funny look on his face, and then started choking for real, with blood running out of the corner of his mouth.

Stephanie froze.

Nelson moved quickly for a big man. He popped a pill in Uncle Raymond's mouth and injected him with something. "He needs to lie down for a moment." Bruce helped lift Uncle Raymond and take him back to her bedroom. "He'll be fine in a moment. Just don't get him to laughing anymore, okay?"

"How sick is he?" Bruce asked as he laid him back.

"Sick, the doctors only gave him a couple of months. Cancer, bunch of kinds." Nelson actually sounded worried.

"What are you to him?" Stephanie asked.

"I am his adjutant, his aid, if you will."

"So, what's this about? Am I going to inherit his … ah … whatever kind of business? You called him general." Stephanie was sitting on the bed holding her uncle's hand.

"Yeah, he's a retired Army General. The, ah, business, that will pass to others. You get his favors."

"His what?"

"Favors." Nelson got a nod from Uncle Raymond. "People in our business don't really work on money, oh, we get paid a lot, but we do owe others in our business things, favors. You scratch my back, I scratch yours, kinds of things. Favors. A lot of people owe him. He's transferring all that to you. I'm your point of contact for the favors."

"I don't want …" She shifted her attention to Uncle Raymond lying pathetically on her bed, petted his hand, and fought not to cry; she hated crying. "You can't die. I'm just starting to know you."

"Shhh," Uncle Raymond whispered, "Of course I can; everybody does."

"Uncle Raymond, there's a symbol, it worked on me. I can heal you." Stephanie was excited now. "I can find out what it is and use it on you. It replaced my fingers and even healed my torn-up knee."

"Why don't we give them a few minutes alone?" Stephanie heard Bruce say. Nelson, at a look from Uncle Raymond, left the room. Bruce shut the door behind him.

"Princess, listen to me," he reached up and brushed her face with the back of his hand. "I've done bad things. There are a lot of things I just don't want to live with anymore. Let me go. Visit the ranch when I've passed. Go to the knife forge, look around. I've left stuff for you there. Trust no one." He passed a thick envelope to her. "Here, lock it up, keep it secret, read it later. Trust no one. They're after you more than me. There are several government agencies that are looking for handles on you. I couldn't figure it all out. Started looking too late."

He paused again to take a deep breath. "The conspiracy is out of Europe. They had all our relatives killed: great-grand, grand, mother, sister, everyone. It passes through the females. I don't know what IT is, but they are trying to kill you all off."

"Uncle Raymond, not everyone is out to get you." Stephanie couldn't keep the bitter tone out of her voice. He had been paranoid her whole life.

"Just 'cause I'm paranoid doesn't mean there isn't someone trying to get you. Remember the hospital." He grabbed her hand and shook it gently. "I am not important. This is about you staying alive. I've done all I can to make you safe. Now it's your turn. I'm done." He slumped back against the bed. "Trust no one."

"I've got Bruce and Joe, I think."

Uncle Raymond's eyes snapped open, "Bruce is ex-army, airborne, ranger, he was being groomed to come into the dark. Joe, I don't know about Joe. He has brothers in the military: marine recon, army ranger, I don't know about him." He closed his eyes for a moment. "Damn, this is a pain. You aren't ready."

"Uncle Raymond, you can't go. I love you." The tears were leaking out now. "I can heal you."

"Nelson," he called out, "We need to leave." Quieter, he added to her, "Make your own choices. I've given you all the tools I can. Trust your instincts."

"Yes, sir," Nelson called out as he knocked on the door.

"Steph," Joe called from the living room, "My boss called, he wants us at a crime scene."

Uncle Raymond brushed the tears off her face. "I've known all along that you loved me. If you love me, you've got to let me go. Just let me die."

"Did you say you could heal him?" Nelson was intense as he helped Uncle Raymond up.

"Yes," Stephanie whispered softly, she hated crying. "I healed myself, but I can't remember the exact symbol. I'll contact my mentor and get it from her."

"Who's her mentor?" Nelson asked of Bruce.

"Rosemary Stein, Professor Stein at the U," Bruce volunteered as they helped Uncle Raymond out.

She tried not to, but cried for a few minutes on her pillow when they were all out of the room. It was all too much, too fast. Joe came back in as she was wiping her face. She looked at him, "Can I trust you?" She felt very vulnerable.

Joe got a funny look on his face and pushed the door to. "I won't hurt you on purpose, but I've never had a girlfriend before. No experience." His voice just rumbled out of his chest. "You can trust me." He looked concerned, serious, "but maybe we should take it slow."

Bruce's voice came in from the other room, "Put cold water on your face, it will help with the blotchy look."

Stephanie patted Joe's chest as she moved toward the bathroom, "Okay, fair enough, we'll take it slow," she quietly said. "Let me un-blotchy my face, and then let's go look at a crime scene."

Chapter 9

"So, what can we expect at the crime scene?" Stephanie asked as she came into the living room. She had changed her mismatched sneakers for a pair of her own and swapped the flannel shirt. It was late fall and raining. Go figure, raining in Seattle. Her light Gore-Tex jacket would work for the rain. Grabbing her backpack, a new one since the police had kept the old one, she slipped her pistol into the front pocket while shielding it with her body, as she tried to not let Joe see.

"What do you mean?" Joe asked cautiously.

"Well, I've never been to one. I don't have any idea what to expect, and if you want me to do something, I may need tools." She looked at Bruce, "You ever been to a crime scene?"

He did the shifty eye thing. "Like, as a criminal, no. As an investigator, no. I do watch TV, unlike you. Cop shows are all about controlling access and evidence."

Joe went detective. "We are looking for your professional opinion about what might have happened. So, bring whatever you think you might need to render that opinion. Whatever you would need to find or identify symbols. We shouldn't have to worry about scene contamination. They've had hours to investigate. There is a dead person. So, it may be smelly, messy, upsetting, and nauseating."

"Great, I've never seen a dead human. You didn't say it was a killing?" Stephanie turned and grabbed a pair of old boots to swap for her sneakers. "Let's swing by the lab and pick up the spectral range cameras, magnetometer, spare laptop, and the portable symbol library."

"I loaded the symbol library onto your Wearable as an app."

"That's right," she nodded, "I remember now." She thought for a moment, then turned back to Joe. "We should probably take two cars. Bruce keeps some analysis materials and tools in his trunk. Murphy says that we won't have what we really need."

Joe looked confused, "Murphy?"

"Yeah, you know, Murphy's laws." Stephanie didn't see the spark of understanding in Joe's eyes so she added, "Murphy's law: anything that can go wrong will go wrong and at the most in-opportune time. And the engineering corollary, well one of them: whatever you really need to fix the problem, you will have forgotten to bring."

Joe snorted and rubbed his chin. "I'll follow you in my SUV. Hold it; wasn't your lab blown up?"

"Nope," Bruce supplied. "Her lab is at the other end of the hall. She blew up somebody else's."

"Now hold on. I didn't blow, … well, … I guess I did, with a symbol." She was thinking hard and something was swimming to the surface. She needed to be somewhere quiet for a time. Shaking her head, she refocused, now was not the time to empower a symbol. "Anyway, mine was broken into again."

"Yep, they didn't seem to get anything, except to slag the printers and your new desktop. I locked it up with padlocks yesterday. I have the only keys." Bruce took them out and jingled them.

Stephanie smiled. "Okay, we'll swing by and pick up the cameras and my extra laptop. Then we'll go to the crime scene. I think we have a plan."

"Do you need the gun?" Joe asked.

"Yes, I think I do. I have a license. Someone beat the snot out of me, and someone else tried to kill me. I think I do. It's in my backpack just in case."

"May I see your concealed carry permit, please," Joe asked. "I want to insure it's current."

Stephanie fished around in her backpack to find her wallet and then presented it. Joe looked at the issue date and handed it back. "Looks good."

Bruce handed him a different one, while smiling. "Here, try this one."

"You're carrying, too?"

Bruce smiled and nodded. Joe looked it over and handed it back. "Try this one." Bruce handed him yet another CCP. "It's hers."

Bruce handed him the other cards she had gotten from Uncle Raymond.

Joe scowled at it for a moment, "What the ... I've never seen a CCP like this before. It looks official, federal. Wow, you could carry just about anything with that license, class three and up."

"She's got a pink camo, fully auto, AR-10 in the closet, maybe she should bring it."

"That's a little over the top." Joe had disbelief on his face. "I think we police can protect her at a crime scene. There will be a lot of police there." Joe pondered for a moment. "However, if you keep your gun in your backpack, you can't set the pack down. That would be leaving it unattended or uncontrolled. I would recommend you wear it holstered, out of sight."

Stephanie gave him a wide-eyed look as she processed what he told her. For a second, she thought he was channeling Uncle Raymond. "Okay." She opened a closet and picked up a slim leather holster, found a belt, threaded them both around her waist, and let the jacket hang. "How's that?" Joe nodded. Stephanie grabbed her backpack. "Let's go."

She stepped outside and stopped. "Poop! I can't leave that Suburban sitting there. It'll get ticketed or towed." She went back in, got the keys, and moved it to her parking spot. Her truck was still at the U. The Suburban was brand new, powerful, with lots of space, and little doors and hatches to look behind. She didn't have time now, but later. It would be fun. New car and she did like guns. They weren't practical living in an apartment, going to college, but she did like them.

The drive was uneventful. She had too much to think about to talk. Her mind was rolling over the past several days' events. There were pieces missing. She kept probing them like a toothache.

Joe waited outside, talking on the phone, since they were going to run in a grab the tools.

The physics building looked the same except when she got to the stairs down to the lower labs. The rail was freshly painted as were the doors at the bottom. The doors looked new, and there were security cameras that hadn't been there before. It had only been two days since she had been beat up, but repairs were already made. "Bruce, were the doors damaged that night?"

"Must've been. They were working on them yesterday when I came by to assess and lock up. The hallway is still scorched."

Stephanie had stopped at the bottom of the stairs and was running her hand over the railing. Memories started trickling back. "I slid down the center hand rail because I couldn't walk. Nylon lab coat, I was going way too fast." Her voice was a whisper. "I must've flown off and hit the doors; no, the floor, then slid into the doors." She took a step over and bent down to a spot near the center doors. "I woke up here and scrambled to get inside." She opened the door and moved slowly down the hallway. "I was having trouble walking so I stayed near the wall. When I got to the door to the lab, it was open." Bruce rushed before her to open the door. She looked into his eyes. "Does this make sense?"

He nodded. "Yeah, they found blood on the floor outside and on the base of the doors. Scalp wounds bleed a lot. The hospital said you had torn open your scalp on a tree branch. This wall had a trail of blood smeared from the doors to the lab door. What did you see in the lab?" He was talking quietly like he was trying not to break her train of thought.

She scanned her eyes around searching for something. Then it came back to her. "There was a guy with a ski mask in the lab. He was standing over by the printer. When I turned away, broken nose was coming through the doors." She pointed back to the doors by the stairway. "Broken knee probably couldn't make the stairs. I pissed broken nose off, insulted his lack of intellect. The only word he knew was bitch." Bruce smiled knowingly, but didn't say anything. "Then I turned to run, … well, hobble away." She turned toward the other end of the hallway. "When I got to the center of the hallway." The hallway was blocked by a barrier of hanging plastic and yellow police tape. She waved beyond the barrier. "There was another ski mask coming through those doors. That one had a gun, a dart gun, a tranquilizer dart gun."

"He, he shot at me. The dart stuck in my backpack. I went," she paused looking around, then just pointed in the right direction. "Through the door to the Directed Energy lab. I called 911 from there. He followed me. I could hear him stumbling around chairs. I broke for the lightning lab in the back, and he threw a chair at me. I was on the floor and crawling." She turned to Bruce. "I must've turned on the lightning generator."

Bruce shook his head no. "The breaker was off."

"That's what he told me. Snotty like, I got mad. Really mad." She stopped, and her mind raced for a moment as she searched again for a memory. "He said something else to me, and I got really pissed, killing pissed." Her voice caught as the memory flooded into her, and a symbol locked into her mind's eye. "I invoked a Norse storm symbol from the ninth century. It was the one found in that Lord crypt in Norway." She turned to Bruce. "Holy shit! It worked. I called up a lightning storm. I'm lucky it didn't kill me."

"It killed the lab," Bruce said with a little smile. He motioned her over to the plastic barrier. There was a slit in it, and he invited her to look through.

Stephanie glanced around first to see if there was anyone watching. She felt guilty for peeking. Through the opening, she could see the scorched and burnt walls in the hallway. The room beyond was even worst. She couldn't see it all, but she did see melted chairs and benches. All the windows between the adjoining spaces had been blown out, and they had been the heavy-duty jobs with the wire mesh inside.

"Wow, did they find anyone dead in there? That asshole had been standing in the doorway."

"No, Steph, you didn't kill anyone. There was no reported body, or at least the police didn't say anything about that."

"I need to sit down," Stephanie announced and started walking back to her lab. "I need to tell Joe. There were four of them, not two."

"Four?"

"Broken nose, broken knee, printer destroyer, and dart gun boy, that makes four. The police only got two. There are two more out there. Oh shit."

She pulled out one of the stools in the lab and perched on it. "These symbols are even more dangerous than we thought. My God, a freestanding natural lightning strike has millions of volts of electricity in it. That can convert to thousands of amperes with the right resistance. Did it ignite combustibles in the room? Why wasn't the fire more intense?"

"I don't know. We should ask the police. They're the ones who took all the data." Bruce walked over to pull out two camera cases and then a bulky meter.

He turned back to her, "You know what really has been bothering me?" She gave him a raised eyebrow look as if to say the other events weren't enough. He snorted. "Why didn't they steal the equipment in here? If these guys were breaking in for money, these cameras alone are worth thousands, not to mention the computers, o-scopes, screens, there are a couple of hundred thousand dollars' worth of equipment in here."

"One point one million. I got a big grant. Department of Energy," Stephanie corrected while wiping her hair back out of her face. "All of it would be valuable, but hard to sell. Some of it you and I designed specifically to look for residual symbol energy." She looked around for a moment and then sucked in a breath as it came to her.

"They were after information." He gave her a puzzling look. "Think about it. They burnt up the desktops by shorting out, right?" Her eyes got huge as a thought smacked into her. "The symbols … they were after my research. The symbols …" Her voice trailed off as she followed her scattered reasoning.

"Hey," Bruce broke her train of thought. He was holding up a backpack. "This is Andy's." He sat it on the bench and rummaged in it. "Laptop, textbooks, whoa, what have we here?" He pulled a book out with papers stuffed in it. "And these are your research notes on identified symbols."

She hopped off her stool and hurried over. "That isn't a textbook. That's a gaming book."

"Dungeons and Dragons, Players handbook, as a matter-of-fact. Why would Andy … Oh … oh, wait a minute." Bruce set the book down and flipped to a specific section. Once there, he started flipping through more pages.

"Bruce," Stephanie said in a singsong voice.

He slammed the book shut. "Damn, Andy is the thief." He turned to look at her. "He's the guy working for the gangbangers. I should've known."

"Bruce," she made waving hand gestures. "Data."

"Right!" Bruce took a moment looking like he was to collecting his thoughts, just like he always did before delivering a conclusion. Then he reeled away again, slapping himself in the forehead. "Of course, it's so obvious."

"Bruce, I may have to hit you. I've had a couple of stressful days."

"Sorry, Doctor Blackraven." He said it in a mocking tone. "Okay, okay," he quickly added as she stepped toward him. "Look, last winter, right at the beginning of the semester, Andy came to me looking for work. He told me he was having trouble scraping together the tuition, and he was pretty good at information organization. I put him to organizing data, the initial steps in the symbol library. Then in about March, he came up with this idea that the symbols could be like the spells in D&D. He games in my world. We had some sessions together with some others. Anyway, I helped him do some initial matching of symbols by relationship to names of spells listed. Harmless stuff, I thought he was starting a world." Bruce flipped open the book to a spell page. Written all over the margins were symbols, incomplete symbols using her standard, symbols she quickly recognized as correlating by theorized name or subjective meaning. "He compiled them and cross-referenced them to the game spells. I'm assuming some of these actually work since ..." Bruce flipped to another page with the symbol near a spell defined as opening all doors. "This is the symbol Joe had."

"He was stealing my work!"

"Our work, but yes." Bruce flipped through some more pages. The number of symbols got fewer and fewer. "My hypothesis is that he is the one breaking into our lab, trying to steal more information, more symbols for higher powered stuff."

Stephanie looked up to meet Bruce's eyes. "His grades dropped at mid-term last semester, and I dropped him as a lab assistant. I wouldn't put him on during the summer. He no longer had access to the database. He didn't talk about needing money then. We did a lot of work between April and now. The break-ins started at the end of last semester." She turned and walked away. "So, why burn up our computers? Spite? To get even?"

Bruce pulled out the printed material. "He was trying to dump the library, the whole library to the printers." Bruce paused, looking at her expectantly.

She was puzzled for just a moment, and then it hit her, "Ah, he didn't know about symbol interference. Whoa, we never tried stacking all of them. The interaction between the symbols was causing an even greater effect then we calculated. The stacked group ..."

"He never got them all out. That's why he kept coming back. They would start printing and then reach a certain point and combust or short out or something. Whatever it was, it destroyed not only the printer, but also the computer it was connected to."

"And a table once," Stephanie corrected him, "Don't forget the table. I wonder what order they would print in if we just dumped the library." Stephanie was reaching for her Wearable. "Grab that spare set of materials." She set down her Wearable and grabbed a wire basket.

Bruce came over with a collection of separate pages, not stacked. "These are the first twenty."

"What does he have printed out?" Stephanie thought for a moment. "And are they printed back-to-back? I think that's the standard setting for our printers."

Bruce gave her an 'ah' look. "Yes, back-to-back. Looks like he has the first thirty here."

"Okay," Stephanie scratched her nose as she spoke. "So, the hypothesis is that he was printing them out in a back-to-back format and just letting them pile up in the printer. So, if we drop them into this tray in the same order and alignment like they were printing, we should be able to manage the interference and measure the possible interaction."

"I concur. What about a safety margin?" Bruce asked. "After all, it did destroy several sets of equipment."

"What'ch ya doin'?" Stephanie and Bruce tried to jump the bench as they both went for their guns. Joe smiled from the doorway. "Drawing a gun on a police detective is not a good idea. You guys need to pay more attention to your surroundings."

"Joe," Stephanie hissed, "You scared the daylights out of me."

"For a big guy, you move very quietly," Bruce said, sounding relieved.

"So, you get back to your lab and decide to run an experiment?" Joe asked.

They both looked sheepish and wouldn't meet his eyes. "What did you two find?"

"I remembered some more about the night I was attacked," Stephanie explained excitedly. "And I think we've figured out who the thief is and why."

Joe nodded, "Well, this wasn't the crime scene I was supposed to bring you to, but it is a crime scene. Dazzle me," he added while sweeping his arms expansively.

Stephanie walked him back out into the hallway and then through all the events as she had remembered them. Then she took him back into the lab and explained what they had found there.

Joe was rubbing his chin and studying his notepad. "So, there were four assailants. We only caught two of them. You think Andy is the gangbanger using symbols because of what you found in his backpack, the D&D stuff? I kind of lose it there."

"We've already explained it twice," Stephanie said.

"One more time," Joe smiled.

"Okay, he was my lab assistant last spring. It gave him access to the lab, and that was when Bruce got the idea for the symbol database as a reference. Andy didn't do well that semester, and his grades dropped. He got fired as a lab assistant, thus losing access to the symbols and their effects translations. Under the pretense of using them for D&D, Bruce helped him correlate some of them to the spells in the game. There were a few that worked." She pulled over the book again to show him. "Here is the symbol you showed us from the robbery."

"Wow, good work," Joe said while jotting another note. "We should put everything back into his backpack and take it with us." At their puzzled look, he added, "Evidence." They both did the "ah" thing and nodded their heads. "How did he know they would have those effects?"

"My guess is experimentation. He had to have tried it out. Andy did have the knack. Not a real strong capability, but he could power a symbol," Stephanie admitted.

Joe's phone rang, and he had it out and up to his ear in seconds. "Bremer." A pause. "Yes, sir, I have Doctor Blackraven and Mr. Richardson with me. We stopped by their lab so they could pick up some analysis tools. A visit here triggered a memory return for the doctor. I have the full story. What you need to know right now is that there were four assailants, not two. When she got down to the lab, there was one in her lab and another with a tranquilizer gun down the hall. They were trying to kidnap her." Joe listened for a moment.

He covered the phone with his hand, "Steph, did they shoot the tranq at you?"

"Yes, I think they did. The dart stuck in my backpack as I turned."

"Do you have the dart?"

She thought for a moment. "I don't think so."

Joe lifted the phone. "They did fire at her, but she says she doesn't have the dart. It struck her backpack. Yes, sir. Yes, sir. On our way." Joe hung up the phone. "Well, good job. Let's load up and head to the other scene. They're waiting for us." Joe looked around. "What are we taking?"

Stephanie and Bruce started pointing at things.

Chapter 10

Bruce and Stephanie followed Joe in Bruce's car. He was the one with the address. They continued their discussion about which symbols might do what and started making plans on how they would test which ones. They were making a list by priority; low power first, based on possible effect, purely on the basis of the name of the symbol. Not exactly a qualitative method, but the only one they had. Stephanie had copied the relevant pages out of Andy's book so she could study them as they drove and because Joe had taken the originals as evidence.

"You know," she finally decided, "complexity seems to be relative to assumed power level. The more complex the symbol, the more power Andy has assumed it has, which doesn't necessarily follow."

"Joe's slowing down. It looks like we have arrived." Joe's SUV turned into a rundown business park in the northeastern part of Bellevue. Bruce was waved off by two policemen in uniform standing near a barricade. "If we assume that each symbol represents a packet of energy," he reasoned as he turned, "then the more parts to the symbol the greater the energy concentration." Bruce was forced to drive down to the adjacent parking area almost four buildings over. "Or," he continued as he parked and got out of the car, "the work to be accomplished is more complex."

"That is another assumption." Stephanie pulled her backpack out of the backseat along with two equipment cases. "The fact is, we don't know. We need to conduct some tests about general symbol types, measure the energy output and effect. We need to continue with our research while confirming Andy's assumptions. Maybe, when they catch him, they'll let us talk to him before they lock him up."

"You're right," Bruce conceded as he pulled an equipment dolly out of the trunk and started loading it with more equipment cases. "Talking to him would be good. Where are we going?" He looked around through the rain, well, mist really. The office park was overgrown with untrimmed trees of all types. It was pretty obvious that no one had been keeping up the grounds.

"It's over that way." Stephanie pointed. Just between the buildings, through the overgrown trees, they could see a police car blinking. "You need help with anything?" she asked.

"I got it. But next time, we load everything in Joe's car. He gets to park closer." In trying to dodge one puddle, he stepped into a disguised, deeper one. "This is going to ruin my shoes." He shook the mud and gunk off his shoe as he walked.

"Should've worn boots. Stay on the sidewalk." She danced around another puddle. "Ah, there it is."

Joe waved from across another parking lot. He hurried over. "Let me take that?" He reached for one of her equipment cases.

Stephanie pulled it out of his reach. "No, you don't. I carry my own equipment."

"You can help me," Bruce said while giving him a pouting look. "I don't have any feminist hang-ups." Joe glared at him as he grabbed a couple of cases and then pointed the way with one of them.

Joe started juggling the cases, trying to get their plastic badges out. Stephanie sat hers down with practiced ease and helped him with the badges. The policeman at the barrier smirked as he identified Joe, "Detective Bremer." The officer was in his rain gear, and Stephanie couldn't see him well. He did have smiling blue eyes as he enjoyed Joe's efforts.

"Officer Paulli," Joe nodded back, "I have two consultants."

Officer Paulli didn't say anything, just kept smiling, and head nodded them through. She figured Joe would hear about it later. Names recorded, gloves handed out and donned, and they were allowed to enter the crime scene. It smelled like sewage and burnt meat, but she still couldn't see anything.

Detective Sergeant Grayson stepped around a plastic sheet hung from a rafter to keep the misty rain out. "Good evening and thank you for assisting the police. Anything you find here cannot be discussed in public without being cleared by my office. Any interesting, ah, mag, ah, symbols discovered are also not to be discussed and will be considered evidence in this investigation. You can't use the information until it is approved by the DA's office. If you agree to these conditions, please sign this form." He held out a clipboard to them with forms on it. They signed. He looked it over and handed it to Joe. "This way, please. You may want to leave your equipment here until you get more comfortable with the scene." After stacking the cases and parking the dolly, they stepped through the plastic curtain.

It was a big open area. A warehouse, raised ceiling, exposed metal rafters, big garage door on the other side of the room and right in the middle of it, under glaring, hastily rigged spotlights was a deflated body, hands contorted, body ridged. He was on the floor with arms and legs spread wide. There were burns, deep burns, third degree, into the muscle and bone, on his wrists, chest, and both sides of his neck. It appeared like the moisture had been sucked out of his body, and the skin was pulled tight on his face. It had hurt because his face was frozen into a contorted, horrific, now soundless scream. His shirt was burnt. Blue jeans soiled. There were fluids congealed near the body.

Stephanie's hand flew to her mouth, "It's Andy! That's his belt buckle, his jeans. He still has that special pencil in his shirt pocket. Oh my God. Who did this to him?"

"You knew this man?" Sergeant Grayson glanced at Joe.

Stephanie nodded. "Yeah, he was a student in one of the classes …" she glared at the sergeant, "The same class you showed up at. Is that why you wanted me here? You think I'm somehow responsible for this?" She was getting pissed.

"No. I don't think you had anything to do with this." He glanced back at the body. "According to the coroner, this happened about the same time you were getting overdosed in the hospital." He gestured at the scene. "This is not the first one of these we've found. I was hoping you could tell me what, why, and how it was done."

Stephanie looked at Grayson then Joe. "I have no idea." She turned back to the horrific scene. "What can't we touch?" Her ire was cooling toward the sergeant, but she wanted a piece of whoever had done this to Andy. He was one of her grad students, damn it, even if he had been stealing from her.

Detective Grayson made a sweeping gesture of the area. "It's all yours. Don't touch or move the body. The coroner's meat, ah, ambulance is late."

She turned her attention to the area surrounding the body, studying the floor. She crouched down and scraped her fingernail on it. "Sealed concrete, non-porous surface, looks almost like it was varnished or epoxied; this would take a symbol." She stood up and walked to the area in front of the garage doors and examined the floor and then walked back over. "The floor is different over there. Someone prepped the floor here for symbol work. Bruce, let's get to work?"

Stephanie pulled off her backpack and knelt on the floor outside of the body leak zone at the edge of the sealed area. She pulled out some rubbing paper and a soft leaded pencil. Bruce went back to the equipment cases and brought them out.

"Is there a table or bench anywhere around here I could use?" Bruce asked while popping open one of the foam-lined cases. Joe shrugged and went to look. Bruce pulled out a black cased magnetometer, hung it around his neck, and let a microphone-looking magnetic sensor down by its cord to hang just above the floor. He started looking at the device and walking around the room, not anywhere near the body.

Stephanie was intent on her tracing, so was startled when wing-tipped dress shoes showed up in her area of vision. "You're blocking my light. We're going to be at this for a couple of hours, if we get any traces. So, you staying out of the way would help us the most." She glanced at Sergeant Grayson scowling at her as she pulled a can of spray graphite and graph paper out of her backpack.

"It would be helpful if you would give me some hint of what you and Mr. Richardson are doing or looking for," Sergeant Grayson stated patiently as he hadn't moved. "This is a police investigation."

She didn't like people looking over her shoulder or thinking they were in charge of her, but it was an investigation. "Okay," Stephanie conceded. "Standard analysis, I'm trying to determine where the edge of the symbol area would be, assuming there is one. Bruce is using the magnetometer to determine if there is a magnetic field induced into the floor." She started creating a rough sketch of the area with the body as a reference in the middle. She then pulled out a compass and noted where north was on both the graph and on the floor. She moved to the north pole of her drawing.

"Then why is he walking around over there?" Sergeant Grayson continued to hover over her.

"He's getting a random sample of normal floor or assumed normal at this point."

"Another question." Grayson tapped his trousers with a notebook. "Why magnetic?"

"We have found through our research that the activation of a symbol causes a molecular level change that leaves an energy signature, normally that equates to a magnetic change from the surrounding area. We're assuming that if anything was done, it was done near the body." She waved her hand around in a circle surrounding the dead guy. "On this sealed portion of the floor. I'm about to test for sympathetic resonance with a symbol intonement." She slowly traced a symbol in the air above the paper with the eraser end of a pencil. As the faint glowing symbol wavered in the air above the trace paper, she sprayed the graphite above it. "Etect-Day!" she said while poking at the symbol. The graphite flew to the paper in a random pattern. "Hmm," was all she said as she moved to another compass position.

"Another question." Grayson seemed slightly more interested. "Are you wearing a gun?"

That stopped her. "Yes." Stephanie looked up to meet his eyes. Grayson just looked back without commenting further. Stephanie slowly removed her jacket so everyone could see it on her belt. Grayson gave her a very slight smile and reached down. She gave him her coat. That made him give a real smile, and he motioned for her to go back to work.

Joe came back in with two uniform policemen carrying a folding table. "Perfect," Bruce said. He came over and set down the magnetometer and started setting up a laptop. He started plugging in the cameras, imagers, and the grid projector. Using the IR camera plugged into the laptop, he then took several pictures. There was no flash with the first camera. Then he used a flashing camera and took pictures from all the points of the compass.

Stephanie continued with her efforts to identify an edge, and when the last flash pictures were taken, she grabbed her backpack, papers, spray can and moved over to the table. Bruce had extracted the memory card from the flashing camera and inserted it in the laptop. As Stephanie came over, he picked up the magnetometer and continued to walk around taking measurements. They didn't speak, just kept working. Finally, after she had measured the distance across the sealed area, both north-south and east-west, entered some data in the laptop, erected the grid projector on a tall tripod, and the computer beeped, she spoke. "Grid is up." Four red dots appeared on the floor at the cardinal points of the compass outside the sealed portion.

Bruce walked over and plugged the meter into the laptop and then walked to the north red dot. "We ready?" he asked.

"Hold it," she announced while holding down a key on the laptop. Turning to Sergeant Grayson, she asked, "Can we shine red laser light on the body?"

He thought for a moment, "Yes, I don't see a problem with that."

She lifted her finger off the key, nothing happened. "Bruce, it's not ready yet. Why does it do that? Indicate it's ready while it's still calibrating?"

Bruce smiled at her and shrugged, "I don't know."

She frowned at him, "You should fix this."

He didn't say anything, just snorted.

A moment later, a red grid appeared on the floor with a highlighted compass rose on it. "Do the cardinal points line up?" Bruce nodded. "With the body in the way, you're going to have to do it by hand," Stephanie told him.

"That's okay." Bruce frowned at her. "Any other obvious items you would like to tell me to do?" Stephanie frowned at him while twitching her head toward the detective sergeant.

Bruce smiled. "Nervous much?" He smiled at her look. "Stop worrying, I already have needle swing. Something powerful was done here with symbols," Bruce commented.

"It's up. Any time you want to start. Mark the edges first, so I can initiate the overlay computation. I think we have a positive IR indication as well." She was starting to get excited. This was a big symbol.

Bruce went to each point of the compass, marked the floor, and took a measurement. Just as he was finished with all four points, two men with a wheeled gurney came through the plastic. Officer Paulli had also found a couple of folding chairs. He and Joe chatted as Joe took them from him. Joe opened one and offered it to Stephanie with a little bow. She smiled and gave him a little curtsy before sitting down.

Sergeant Grayson came over. "They're going to remove the body and the lab people want to examine the area under the body. Why don't you explain what you two have done to this point?" Stephanie shut off the grid projector.

"We have established a grid reference for the magnetometer measurements. We will use the grid as a point to fix all future measurements. The first camera was a scanning IR imager. The second was visible spectrum. The computer is linking them with the references points on the grid, which will allow us to overlay the magnetic signature on top. Then we will use the ultraviolet imager. These four overlays should allow us to discern what was traced on the floor. I will try the symbol of sympathetic resonance again to see if it will pick anything up once we have it localized. I can already deduce that it will be complex, more than likely a series of concentric circles of symbols. Someone went to a great deal of trouble to try and hide this."

"Hey," Bruce called out to get their attention. The body had been lifted away and was being wheeled out of the room. The area that it had been lying on was being investigated by two guys and a woman with LAB on their coats. "We have holes drilled and rings installed under his arms and legs. We also have blood at several points under the body and on the outer portion of the sealed area." Bruce watched for a moment. "Can we get the mollies removed, they will interfere with the magnetic, ... ah, ... never mind they're taking them." He went over and replaced his microphone device with a push-broom-looking device on wheels.

"When the lab people are done," Stephanie continued, "Bruce will take the magnetic sensing bar and slowly roll it over the area in both orientations. It will cover a two-foot swath at a fixed distance from the surface. Then we take the ultraviolet scan and let the computer work." They continued to watch as the lab people swabbed, sampled, bagged, and finally cleaned up and carried off everything. They gave the sergeant a form and nodded as they left. Stephanie turned on the grid, and everyone froze. The grid was glittering in places, mainly where the body had laid. She switched off the grid, but black lines were crosshatched where the body had been. She and Bruce looked at each other and then at Joe. "We don't have a clue." She announced to Sergeant Grayson's unasked question. "The glittering stuff reacted to the laser. It must have been photo sensitive," Stephanie theorized.

The sergeant pulled out his phone and called the lab people back. They asked and were told the frequency of the laser. Then they swabbed, stored it away, gave another form to Grayson, and left. None of them spoke after the initial questions. A uniformed policeman, big, but not as big as Joe, he was handsome in a solid kind of way, older than Joe, it was Officer Paulli again, without rain gear on, showed up with coffee for everyone.

"You're a life saver," Stephanie said to Officer Paulli. He just smiled and tipped his hat.

"Do we keep going?" Stephanie asked Sergeant Grayson while sipping.

Grayson nodded yes. Stephanie motioned to Bruce. He started slowly sweeping the sensor across the area. It was slow going since he could only sweep in one direction at a fixed pace, and then after the entire area was done one way, he rotated ninety degrees and did it all again. When he was finally done and putting away the sensor, Stephanie turned off and removed the box that produced the laser grid only to replace it with another lensed device. She spent several minutes trying to get it aligned with the grid until Bruce saved her by doing it.

"This takes a few minutes," She stated to the room. She motioned for Joe and the sergeant to come over to the laptop. "Here is what we have so far." The screen showed six windows. In each were different types of images. She waved at them generally, "Each of these is one of the images we compiled, and you can see the pictures." She pointed at two of the windows. "This is the grid," she pointed at another. "The computer is currently building the image from the magnetic scan. It will take some time because it has to be accurate to a couple of hundredths of a millimeter. Location and orientation of a symbol or collection of them, is very precise. This is aligned with the IR images and the UV ones. Those also have to be compiled by computation." She stepped away and motioned to Bruce. "Would you show them the demo of what it's doing?"

"Not on that, it's busy. We should've brought a desk top with a quad core and thirty-two gigs of RAM." He reached down and pulled up another laptop. "Let's use this one." He brought it to life and started fiddling with it.

"I have an idea," Stephanie announced. "Bruce, can I have your car keys?"

He nodded toward where their coats were lying, "Coat pocket."

"I'll be right back," she said as she grabbed her coat and headed out of the building. She saw Joe look up from across the room, point at Paulli, and then point at her. Paulli nodded and followed after her.

Stephanie was hurrying along. Her mind was buzzing with a possible symbol application. She would use the detection symbol, but over a much larger area. She could take the cover sheet Bruce kept in the car and then use the can of graphite spray over the whole area. It should give them a faster glimpse of the symbols. She had never tried it on an area that large, but if she used the technique Rosemary had walked her through for healing herself, visualizing the symbol over a large area. Stephanie came to a complete stop.

"Oh my God," she said to herself while walking in a small circle. The memory of the complete process from the hospital flooded into her mind. The symbol, the application of it to her whole body, the invocation, she had it all. She could heal Uncle Raymond.

She started off like a shot for the car. She would get the drop cloth, the light one, then go back, and tell Bruce.

"So, bitch, we want our witch's book." The harsh accented voice cut through the night. A bare-chested man stepped out of the darkness near the trees. He was followed by another from the other side of the sidewalk. The second had his coat thrown open and was festooned in silver jewelry she could see glittering in the poor light. Both men were average height, which made them six inches taller than her, and heavy bodied. The bare-chested man was heavily muscled like a body builder, and of obvious Mexican descent, with dark hair all over his body. He had tattoos on his chest, neck, both wrists, and upper arms. She couldn't quite see them clearly. They were symbols, complex symbols, and for a fleeting instant, she wondered if she could get him to take his pants off to see if he had symbols on his legs.

"Aren't you cold?" blurted out of her. She could see the rain beading on his chest hair.

He smiled an unpleasant smile, "Why, chica, you want to warm me up?" He rubbed his groin for a moment suggestively.

"Ah, no." Her mind was slowly catching up to the conditions and implications. "What witch? What book?"

"Andy's book," Silver boy purred out. "He was our witch." She saw several other figures in the darkness. "Give it to us now, and we won't kill you."

"Go'n ta fuck you up, bitch. Nobody with a gun to save you now." She knew that voice. Broken nose stepped out. His face looked like it still hurt.

"You really should increase your vocabulary," just seemed to leap out of her mouth.

A bright light flashed on. "Police! Nobody move." Officer Paulli stepped up with a gun in one hand, a flashlight in the other, his wrists supporting each other.

"Wolf," Silver boy growled while touching his silver items. Stephanie saw a faint luminescence dance on his silver. But the bare-chested guy's howling immediately attracted her full attention. The symbols had lit up on his chest and neck with racing greenish-silver light. He had his head thrown back and was howling into the rain. At the same time, he ripped his pants off. Yep, symbols on his legs. She watched, spellbound, as his face started to elongate, and his chest rippled.

"Shit," erupted from her side as Broken Nose stepped into a deep mud puddle and temporarily lost his balance. That was all she needed to break the spell of fascination from the howling guy. She immediately dropped into a low front stance and punched Broken Nose in the groin, followed by a jumping front kick to his solar plexus. He slammed backward into the mud.

Isn't training great, she thought as she scurried behind Officer Paulli. The problem was Paulli had too many targets, and a guy changing into a wolf in front of him.

"Werewolf," she heard Paulli say to himself. "Run, doctor!" he said to her. Then his gun started thundering, shattering the hissing quiet of the rainy night. Wolf guy was jumping with the impact of every bullet, but it was just pissing it off.

"I'm goin' ta ram this in you, bitch." Broken Nose was up, kind of hunched over, but he had a big knife held out in front of him.

"So not going to happen," she screamed as she drew her Millennium. It briefly got hooked on her coat. But before he could shuffle forward more than a few feet, she had it free, and shot him twice in the chest and once in the head. He went to the ground. She moved from the spot, looking for other targets.

Paulli shoulder checked her out of the way as something heavy smacked into him, where she would've been. A big dog was savaging the downed officer. Stephanie emptied her gun into its side. All that did was attract its attention. She butt-scooted back from it as she fumbled for a spare magazine. She didn't have one.

The wolf was huge, with red eyes glowing, as it snarled and growled at her. It was taking its own sweet time closing on her. She realized it was toying with her. It knew she didn't have anything to hurt it with.

"Wolf, back off." The voice of Silver Guy cut through the growling. "We need her. Kill the cop."

Wolf glanced behind it, barked a kind of parody of a laugh, and turned away. Stephanie did the only thing she could think of, what women had been doing since the dawn of time. She screamed, as high a pitch as possible, as loud as she could. The wolf froze and then looked back at her in seeming disgust. She pulled out a pencil.

"You goin' a poke him in the eye?" Silver boy scoffed with a laugh.

It was the one symbol she used more than any other, always in demonstration of the power in symbols. It was so familiar that it just leaped into her mind's eye already formed. She poked at the wolf with the pencil. "Ash-Flay." A brilliant photoflash exploded into the face of the wolf and its glowing, red, sensitive eyes.

The wolf yelped in alarm.

She poked at it again, "Ash-Flay." And again, and again, and again. She couldn't really see it herself. She was blinded by the continued explosions of light. She visualized its eyes and how the symbol would overlay them, poke, "Ash-Flay." A howl of pain erupted into the night.

"What the hell," she heard from a different voice further away.

"Officer down," she screamed as she butt-scooted further away.

"This isn't over, chica," she heard Silver Boy say. "Wolf to me. Wolf here, wolf, wolf." He kept calling to lead the wolf away.

A bunch of flashlights appeared between the buildings. She crawled back out to where Paulli lay. She found him by touch. Her hand came away wet, and it wasn't water, but it was warm. "Hang in there, officer, help is coming." He was making whizzing, slurping, bubbling noises that no human body is supposed to make. She tried, but just couldn't make her eyes come clear. All she saw were dazzling bright spots.

Visualizing the symbol she had used in the hospital, she expanded it to cover the officer. She detailed his form by the touch. Concentrating hard, she poked at him with the remains of the pencil, "Eal-Hay." A symbol flashed bright and settled into his body. It was different this time. It was like her strength was getting sucked away. She quickly found herself lying over the top of him without the strength to move. "Oh God," she prayed, "let him live."

Just before fading off to blackness, she thought she heard a voice, "He will."

Chapter 11

Joe was standing out on Stephanie's little deck, looking off through the trees, but what he was seeing was her blood-soaked body lying on the ground, white as death. He growled again at just the thought and the coffee cup cracked in his hand. The scene just seven hours ago was still fresh; paramedics, ambulances, Officer Paulli, who should've died but hadn't, the general pandemonium of an officer and consultant attacked at the scene of a crime. She had to kill someone, someone they had arrested, and then released, to protect her own life. His relief when they found her unhurt, but exhausted from her symbol work to save Paulli's life.

"That's two, man," Bruce said from the little kitchen. "You keep bustin' her cups, and she's going to kick your ass."

Joe took a deep breath and went inside. "I thought you were going to the lab?"

"I did and now I'm back and you didn't hear me either leave or come back. Good thing there are other cops outside." Bruce was leaning casually against the cabinet. "You need to get some sleep."

"Now that you're back, I think I'll go do that. Wait, doesn't she have a guest room?"

Bruce chuckled, "Yeah, but it doesn't have a bed." He smiled at Joe's look. Bruce motioned and then led him back to the guest room. Bruce opened the door and stepped aside so Joe could look in. The room was filled with equipment, electronic equipment, meters, o-scopes, little plastic boxes filled with parts, a bench with little metal arms with clamps on them, racks of tools neatly stowed.

"Whoa," Joe breathed out, "That has got to be the biggest desktop I have ever seen. Four monitors, huge ones. What gives?"

Bruce smiled some more as he motioned Joe out of the room. "Lest we disturb her sanctum sanctorum or wake her up," he whispered as he led Joe back to the kitchen.

"Her undergraduate degree is in electrical engineering, master in systems engineering, as well as archeology for the symbols. That room was where her initial research was done, as well as the creation of most of the initial tools and test equipment we use now," Bruce explained.

"I thought you made all the tools?"

"Lately, she did all the initial work. I only joined her team about two years ago. My undergrad is in physics, with a masters in same and soon," he knocked on wood, "a PhD. I do applied energy, thus my interest in the symbols." Bruce topped off their coffee cups. "She's been working on these symbols for years, ever since her first masters." Bruce put the coffee pot back and studied Joe over his cup for a moment before adding, "Personally, I think it's in her blood, magic," he added quietly.

"Don't let her hear you say that," Joe smiled chidingly.

"Don't I know it!" Bruce laughed.

"You know her pretty well?" Joe asked.

"No, no, don't get me in the middle of this."

"In the middle of what?" Joe asked.

"You trying to figure out how to get in her pants." Bruce was smiling faintly and shaking his head.

Joe was instantly furious at Bruce for even the suggestion that he had base intentions toward Stephanie.

"Whoa, big fella." Bruce set down his cup and stepped back. "Christ, you've got it bad."

Joe took a deep breath and let it out slowly, then did it again. "I don't know what to do. All I want to do is keep her safe, that's how I was raised. Honor, protect, cherish women, and then I think of her last night lying there ... the blood ... I thought it was hers; she was so white. I, ah, got her into this." There was another crack.

"That's three," Bruce said. "How much do you bench press?"

Joe looked down like he had forgotten the cup was in his hand. "Shit." Coffee was dripping on the floor. Joe rushed the cup to the sink to dump it and then threw it in the garbage.

"You need to take a chill pill, big guy. First, you've got to understand she's not exactly your classic, raven-haired beauty. You see this little, cute, petite, stacked, sexy woman that could stop traffic if she just tried a little." Joe just nodded. "Yeah," Bruce confirmed with his own nod, "She's a beauty. She also has this hellcat inside her. And a temper." Bruce shook his head like he didn't believe it himself. "Holy shit! She can go bat shit sometimes."

"She isn't going to let you just cherish and protect. And if you even try it, she will dump you like yesterday's bad coffee. You're going to have to let her be her, which means she always says the wrong thing, she will always jump and then wonder how high it should've been, she will always blow something up first before actually doing the precise calculation, and she will never ever back down. She was raised to kick ass and take names. You should get her to talk about her Uncle Raymond sometime."

"You love her, too?" Joe quietly asked. He finally understood the heart ache saying. He had never allowed himself to go this far before. He was pretty sure it was the big L with her. He got this strange feeling in his stomach just thinking about her.

"She's like the little sister I never wanted but got. So, yeah. But you have got to get a handle on this or it will drive her away." Bruce sipped his coffee some more. "Don't you have sisters?" Joe nodded. "Then it's time for you to get some counseling."

Joe started shaking his head, "No, no, no, if they even got a hint of this, they would make my life a living hell."

"Joe, if your feelings are as strong as I think they are, then they're going to find out. And I think they may surprise you."

Joe stood looking at his latest broken cup in the trashcan. "I'm going to go get some sleep. And buy her some more cups. I'll be back later in the day. Don't let her go anywhere without me."

"Hah, like I could stop her." Joe shot him a dirty look. "I got it," Bruce added seriously. "Go."

Joe left. His drive back to his apartment was a blur of restless contemplation without conclusion. He wandered his apartment, unable to settle down, until finally he called his younger sister, Abigail. He had been the closest to her when they were growing up. She was the one who talked to him the most. When he realized he was pouring his guts out to her about Stephanie and the messed-up situation, he abruptly hung up and went to bed. She had just listened without comment through most of it. Amazingly, it had made him feel better, and he fell right to sleep.

The phone brought him up from sleep. "Bremer."

"Joe, Rosemary's missing," he heard a female voice say.

"What? Who is this?" Even as she said it, his mind told him.

"It's Steph, you know, the woman you keep almost getting killed." She laughed lightly, but he felt like a knife had been rammed into the hilt.

"Hey, Steph," he tried to sound casual as he heard Bruce say something harsh to her in the background. He also checked his watch for the time. Two p.m., he had gotten about five hours of sleep. "I'll be right over. Don't go anywhere until I get there." He waited to hear something from her.

"Okay," was the subdued response.

He hung up and started dressing. He had to actually stop a few times to calm down. He did armor up, though. He put his tactical gear on under his dress shirt as well as the extra weapons and new cool Kevlar woven pants. Be prepared was his new motto. He carried his full tactical pack out to the car.

Checking in with his office, he found that they had been made aware of Professor Stein's disappearance. Sergeant Grayson wanted him to bring Steph and Bruce to the professor's office on the chance they would understand something the police had missed. Professor Stein was Dr. Blackraven's mentor and apparent best friend. Joe remembered to stop and buy her coffee cups, heavy ones that wouldn't break easy.

She and Bruce were standing in front of her apartment building near the back of the Suburban checking something out as he drove up. Neither one was caught unaware, both turned at the sound of his car. He grabbed the cups as he got out, nodding to the two uniform policemen in their car.

Stephanie was standing outside with pajama pants and fuzzy slippers on with some kind of canvas raincoat, very cowboy, pulled around her. Hair kind of frizzled out and an air of disregard for it all. Just the sight of her took his breath away. "Hi," was Joe's witty opening.

"Hi back at ya," Stephanie commented. "Why are you smiling?"

"Ah," Joe froze up again. He decided the truth was the only way to go. He couldn't seem to keep track of anything else around her. "You look great. Ah, … I'm glad to see you up and walking around. I was scared for you last night."

"That wasn't your fault." Stephanie blurted out. "Those lowlife, greasy, belly-crawling piss ants were lying in wait for me at Bruce's car. And a werewolf, did you know about werewolves?"

"Steph!" Bruce exclaimed. "God, didn't we just talk about this?"

"What?" She looked between the two of them in confusion.

Joe decided to disregard the comments. "You shouldn't be standing out in the open. They might decide they don't need you alive anymore." Joe stepped over to physically impose himself between her and the condos across the cul-de-sac. He also got a look into the back of the Suburban. The cargo floor was up, and he could see at least six tactical-looking rifles: two subcompact machine guns, three tactical rifles and one long gun. All of them looked very modern and tricked out. Bruce dropped the lid and moved Stephanie back to close the cargo doors. Stephanie hit the button to lock it.

"Good idea, let's go inside." Bruce hastily said with a smile. "Stephanie, you need to get your clothes changed."

"Why? I'm supposed to hide here all day." She did not sound thrilled.

"Well," Joe began slowly. "We need to go by your lab to see if the stuff is done calculating or whatever it's doing. And Sergeant Grayson would like you to take a look at Professor Stein's office to see if you can spot anything out of place."

"Really! He wants me to try and help find Rosemary?"

"Yes, that was what he told me."

She squealed, hugged him quickly, and then ran into her apartment, doing some kind of goofy chicken run that was cute and endearing for a girl, but would get any guy shot. Joe looked at Bruce in confusion.

Bruce shrugged and started walking toward the apartment, "Don't ask me. Must be the fuzzy slippers. I think she's happy to help with Rosemary. She's been bitching about not being allowed to do anything since she got up."

"You know," Joe started as they turned. "For someone who has been almost killed a couple of times in as many days, you'd think she'd be a little less excited about the police dragging her to another crime scene."

Bruce just shrugged. "She wants to help. She wants to be doing."

Not long after they got inside, Stephanie came out into the living room wearing blue jeans, a close-fitting canvas shirt with special pockets in the front, specifically designed to work around her breasts, a wide belt, and cowboy boots. Then she walked around arming herself; a gun in a holster on the right side, two magazines in a holder on the left next to her Wearable, extra magazines in two of the front pockets on the shirt, a lock-blade knife in a back pocket, a long-bladed hunting knife in a sheath in the left boot, and six pencils in pockets on each sleeve. The hunting knife had swirls and waves on the blade. She was not a big woman so everything was kind of compact and packed just so.

"Is that a different gun?" Joe asked.

"Yeah, you police confiscated my Taurus cause of the shooting. This is a Springfield Armory XD subcompact. It's a little bigger than the Taurus. I have small hands." She held them out to show him. Then with a smile and a hair flip, she dove in to the closet to drag out a bag and a gun case. The bag held body armor cut to her size and shape. The gun case held a pink camo AR-10 with tactical sights. The case had five side pockets for thirty round magazines, four were full. She held up the armor, "This has Dragon Scale and should be able to stop a grenade. I can wear it under my rain slicker. I also have tactical pants with Kevlar and more Dragon Scales at strategic places." She gestured at the rifle, "That is self-evident." She met his eyes, "Do you think I need them?" She was very serious.

"Damn," Bruce exclaimed. "I feel safer just being near you."

Joe was conflicted. He was affronted that a civilian should feel like they needed to be armed. But on the other hand, she had almost died being escorted by a policeman. She did look hot in her Rambo-ina outfit. "If the bad guys see you have a vest on, they aim higher. Put the vest on under your shirt. It looks like it's designed for it, closer to the skin the better. We'll put your rifle and gear bag in the back of my SUV. If it goes south again, we retreat to the SUV and arm up." He thumped his own chest to show the plates he had on. "I have my tactical gear in the SUV as well. Where did you get Dragon Scales? You're talking about the ballistic plates, right, not really scales of a dragon?"

She smiled sweetly, "I don't think dragons have surfaced as a species yet. These are the plates."

"Those are really expensive and limited in distribution," Joe probed.

"Uncle Raymond did the deal. They were in his last load of 'stuff.'" She made quotation motions with her fingers.

"You're going to have to tell me more about your great uncle." Joe was frowning.

Stephanie stopped smiling and turned to Bruce. "Don't you pack a Smith & Wesson .40?"

"Yes," Bruce said slowly. "And thanks for reminding the detective."

She grabbed a box of shells from her workroom and handed them to him. "Here, load up a magazine with these. I found out that lead bullets do not stop werewolves; it just pisses them off. According to the Internet, silver does affect them, and that isn't just the fantasy sites. Dr. Bloomerton has an extensive white paper on the B-G site on lycanthropes. I put silver nitrate into these hollow points and sealed them with hot glue. I haven't shot any yet, but they seem to load okay." She eyed Joe.

"I'm a .45 guy," he stated.

She smiled at him and handed him a box. "I thought so. I had Bruce pick up some .45 ammo as well. Here, gift to my boyfriend, potential werewolf killers."

Joe didn't know what to say to that. But it did light up his day. *Boyfriend*, he thought. *Oh yeah.*

Chapter 12

Joe pulled into the main campus of the U. "Turn here," Stephanie blurted.

Joe gave her a look.

"We're going to Rosemary's office, right?" Stephanie asked.

Joe nodded.

"Then turn here." She was leaning across the front seat, pointing. "I'll show you the closest place to park." Joe smiled and nodded. She frowned. "Stop looking at my chest and just follow directions." She was smiling on the inside.

"But," Joe blushed and started following directions. Bruce snickered from the backseat.

They ended up turning through several narrow lanes and then pulled behind a building in a lot surrounded by trees. It wasn't a very big lot. It was well hidden and labeled as faculty parking. Joe parked as she directed. They got out, and Stephanie nervously pulled her jacket down to make sure it covered her gun. She met the guys at the back of the SUV. Pointing at the closest building, "That's Rosemary's building." She pointed across the lot. "That red Ranger is my truck." She turned and pointed to the building closest to it. "That is the back of the Applied Physics building, where my lab is."

"I'm going to run over and check on the data," Bruce announced while starting to trot across the lot. "I'll meet you at Rosemary's office."

"Bruce!" Stephanie exclaimed and then froze. She had this terrible feeling and didn't know how to express what she was thinking.

Bruce turned around with a puzzled look, then came walking back over. He studied her for a moment and gave a quick one-arm hug. "Wow, you don't have to worry, I'll be careful, and right back. You've got the big guy with you." She saw them exchange a look, ending with a nod from Joe. "You'll be fine. I'll be right back." Bruce repeated and trotted off.

"Sorry," she apologized to Joe. "I guess I'm a little nervous after last night." She felt really embarrassed. She hardly ever had "girl" moments.

"They'll have to go through me to get to you," Joe rumbled out with absolute seriousness. "Which way?" he gestured.

She smiled, shook her head, and pointed the way while walking. "So, how do we know Rosemary is missing?" There was a small sidewalk from the parking lot through trees to an entryway.

"Sergeant Grayson said that someone called in a disturbance last night when we were at the other scene." Joe led the way, slightly ahead of her, opened the door for her, and motioned her through. "Uniformed police officers were dispatched; they found the door to her house ajar, forced entry, and signs of a search." Stephanie motioned for a right turn at the corner. Joe nodded and continued explaining, "Another unit was dispatched to the U, here, and they found signs of forced entry and hasty search."

"Why did you guys react so fast? No offense, but lightning speed for police response is not what we expect from a phone call. Oh …" She got wide eyes for a moment as she tracked the problem through. "She's a person of interest as well, and you thought …" Her voice trailed off.

"Yeah, that's pretty much it." Joe nodded toward the uniformed police officer down the hall. "Is that where her office is?"

Stephanie nodded, "Yeah, that's it." Apprehension flooded into her. Rosemary's office had always been a secure place, a bastion of comfort and serenity in a world of chaos. Now it too had been assaulted by the real world. She dreaded what they would find.

"Stephanie!" A woman's voice called out from an office up the hall. Marsha Portman appeared from the office. She was a no-nonsense, grey-haired, mature lady in her sixties, large, and hard as steel at times, but always there for you. Stephanie thought of her as a battleship; big and imposing stops for no one, crushes all in her righteous path, but a giving heart of gold for those Marsha decided deserved it. She was the office manager for the soft sciences. She called herself their secretary and was damn proud of it.

She came charging down the hall. She didn't even come to Joe's chest, but he hurried to get out of her way. "Stephanie," Marsha said again as she surrounded her in a protective bear hug. Marsha towered over Stephanie. "We heard you'd been raped and beaten, in the hospital with life-threatening injuries." She pulled Stephanie away to arm's length to look at her. There were tears standing in Marsha's eyes. "Then, on the news this morning, those pictures of the shooting, attack at a police scene, and there you were again, in the middle of it. But here you stand, cute as a button, and pretty as ever." Marsha hugged her again, with more restraint the second time, as tears leaked down her face. "What's going on? How did you get out of the hospital so soon? Doctor Moorcastle, MD, has been calling, trying to get ahold of you for a medical procedure or some kind of incant ... ah, symbol for medical application? He's pushy, I don't like him."

Stephanie's heart warmed as it always did around Marsha. She always made Stephanie feel wanted. It had taken almost a year for Marsha to decide that Stephanie was a "good girl," but from then on, it was all cookies at holidays, little gifts for every occasion, and invitations to holiday meals with Marsha's family. This outpouring of heartfelt feelings made Stephanie a little teary as well, but she brutally suppressed it. "I'm fine, Marsha. I didn't get raped. As a matter-of-fact, I broke one guy's nose and the other's knee, then ran off."

Marsha gave a little sharp intake of breath and then a short, rough laugh. "You go, girl." She gave Stephanie a little shake to emphasize her approval. "You show those walking penises where they get off."

Stephanie smiled at her abrupt change, "I did get beat up."

"Steph," Joe interrupted her. "No case facts."

Marsha rounded on him like a mother bear protecting her cub. "Who are you to interrupt Doctor Blackraven? Young man, I would have you know that this is an institution of higher learning, and it is expected that respect be shown to those ..."

Stephanie had heard this lecture before and needed to intervene before Marsha got into full protection mode. She had never had Marsha apply this to her before, only to Rosemary. "Marsha," the older lady stopped talking immediately just like she did for any tenured professor. "Marsha, this is Detective Joe Bremer. He's my police liaison. I am helping the police with several investigations. He's okay. He's got a handle on the police stuff. I don't want to mess it up."

Marsha turned back briefly to glance at Stephanie and then seemed to study her a little more. She turned back to Joe. "Well, I see," she stated in a different tone. "Hmm, Detective Bremer, I expect you are here with the other police, and you have accompanied Doctor Blackraven to inspect Doctor Stein's office?" Her tone implied that Joe should be answerable to Stephanie, not the other way around.

"Yes, ma'am," was all Joe said. His eyes were saying something else, but Stephanie didn't know how to read him yet.

Marsha nodded as if everything was as it should be. "I will leave you to it." She turned back to Stephanie. "Doctor, when you have a moment, please come speak with me." She gave Stephanie's hand a little shake.

Stephanie smiled at Marsha's abrupt change and nodded to her, as she had observed Rosemary to do. "Of course, Marsha. Right after the police are done with me."

Marsha turned and charted her course back down the hall away from them.

"Wow," Joe breathed. "She is formidable."

"That's kind of a big word for a cop, isn't it?" Stephanie teased.

"Word-a-day calendar," Joe said without pausing.

Stephanie laughed at the quick retort. Her laugh made Marsha stop and glance back.

"We should get at it," Joe encouraged, motioning down the hall with a sweep of his arm.

"You just want to get away from Marsha, before she comes back and kicks your ass."

Joe nodded in all seriousness. "Damn straight. She reminds me of my mom." He moved her down the hall.

Rosemary's office was actually two rooms, an outer meeting room with bookcases and filing cabinets lining the walls, but no real character, an inner room which was her office. Her office was a pleasant room with a cozy nook containing two chairs and a small table set just so in front of the window. It was a place to sit and have tea during an intimate discussion. Her desk was a roller-top model pushed up against the shared wall. The walls had pictures of country scenes, flowery meadows, and a glade with a stream running through it. There were little curios and knickknacks sitting around on the bookcase shelves. There were plants everywhere.

There wasn't much sign of searching in the meeting room; a couple of filing cabinets were opened, and a few books had been pulled off shelves and lay on the table. The inner room was where chaos had struck. All the drawers had been pulled out of the desk and up ended over the floor. All the little cubbies in the roll top had been disturbed. Piles of papers had been pushed off the desk. An entire bookcase of books had been pulled out. Even some of the plants had been smashed to the floor.

Stephanie took it all in with a sharp breath. "What am I supposed to be doing here?"

"Look around," Joe said, stepping out of the office into the meeting room. He was supposed to give her room, and he kind of filled the space. She had thought of it as spacious until he stepped into it. "See if there is anything you can see out of place, like not supposed to be here, or anything missing, that should be here."

Stephanie looked around at the chaos. "Can I touch anything?"

"No. Try not to," he answered from the outer room.

"Hmmm." She sat down in one of the nook chairs and started scanning the room, one section at a time, recording everything in her mind's eye. It took all her willpower to keep herself from getting up and setting things to right. After scanning the room, she tried again by just looking around. Then it jumped out at her right away, some of her favorite things in Rosemary's office were gone.

"Joe," she called.

"Right here," he said as he stepped into the doorway.

"There are little things missing, a carved piece of wood that used to set there on the shelf." She pointed at the place across from her. "And a crystal figurine, there. Her journal. Little things."

"Keep looking around and name them off. Don't worry about value, just let me know." Joe was writing in his notepad.

She named off a couple dozen items after studying the chaos. Most of them were precious things to Rosemary. Little things, things she wouldn't want to lose or get broken. A thought struck, and just as fast, she decided to keep it to herself. These were the things Rosemary would take if she was leaving, running away from something.

"We should go look at her house!" Stephanie said as she jumped up and moved to the door.

"Why? What did you see?" Joe asked while searching her face intently.

Stephanie froze for a moment. "Why do you think I saw anything?"

Joe slowly smiled. It really did change his face. He had a nice smile. "'Cause you jumped up and rushed the door after making a little startled noise. The noise was cute."

"Did not."

"Did too." Joe was still smiling.

She sucked at lying. It was just easier to tell the truth. "I'll tell you if you don't write it down."

Joe laughed a little and then lowered his pencil. "Okay."

"All the stuff that is missing is the stuff Rosemary truly valued. It's the stuff she would take if she was leaving, not wanting anyone to break or handle."

Joe frowned. "So, you're saying she took them, knowing her office would be searched?"

Stephanie looked up into his dark eyes. "I don't know about the search part, but it's the stuff she would take if she were leaving permanently. The most valuable personal items, things she has collected, one piece at a time over the years, mementoes of her life. All of them were very special to her."

"We should go look at her house to see if her normal traveling stuff is gone," Joe noted while putting away his notepad and pencil. The pencil had a burnt eraser on it.

Stephanie smiled as she noticed the pencil. "That was what I said before, pencil thief."

"I didn't steal it. You dropped it. I was just recycling it. Can't let a perfectly good pencil go to waste."

"Right," Stephanie agreed with a heavy dose of sarcasm as they walked out of the building.

Just as they stepped into the parking lot, her cell phone rang. "Hello."

"Stephanie Blackraven?" a serious male voice she almost recognized asked.

"Yes, this is she."

"Nelson." He stated his name like he was reporting an important fact. "Your great uncle was just killed in Portland. Car bomb. Sorry."

Stephanie stumbled into Joe and grabbed on to him to keep from falling over. "What? What did you say?"

"This is Nelson, your great uncle's aide. He was just blown up by a car bomb in Portland, Oregon." His voice was flat and unemotional.

"Oh my God! What, ... what?"

"Get a grip. I need you to get in your truck and drive to Portland right now."

"Steph, what is it?" Joe sounded concerned.

She pulled the phone away from her ear. "My uncle has been killed in Portland. I need to drive there."

"What? Killed? Who is that on the phone?"

Stephanie put the phone to her ear. Nothing. "He's hung up. It was Nelson, my uncle's aide, deputy, helper, whatever. He said he needed me in Portland. I've got to go." She pushed away from Joe and started toward her truck.

Bruce and Tom came running from the Applied Physics building. Bruce was yelling something at her, but she couldn't make it out. Her mind was fuzzed over after hearing of Uncle Raymond's death.

Joe stepped in front of her. "Steph, wait. Let me call the police in Portland."

"What?" She was stepping around him. Joe grabbed her shoulder. She automatically blocked it and went for a wrist grab. He reversed and grabbed her other shoulder. She blocked that. He grabbed at her forearm. She moved to block that. They were circling and trying to get a hold on the other.

"What the hell are you two doing?" Bruce yelled at them. "We've got trouble." Stephanie and Joe stopped trying to grab each other and turned to look at Bruce. "T R O U B L E! Listen."

She took her attention away from Joe and Bruce and heard sirens. "What now?" she exclaimed.

"They've barred us from the lab. They're calling it a crime scene and won't let us at the data we have cooking," Bruce announced in exasperation.

"I don't care! Uncle Raymond is dead. I have to go to Portland." Tears choked her voice.

"Whose they?" Joe asked.

"The police is they." Bruce turned his attention to Stephanie. "Uncle Raymond's dead? Aw shit, I'm sorry." Bruce took her into a loose hug. "Steph, I am so sorry." Tears were clouding his voice now. That broke something in her, and tears started flowing.

"Steph," Joe begged. "Please, let me call before you go rushing off. It might be a trick."

Hot anger ripped through her as she cut him off. "Yeah, so he was a murderer. I know you don't care, but he's my uncle." She shrugged her way out of Bruce's embrace.

"That's not fair, Steph. I don't know anything about your uncle." Joe sounded hurt, but she was too angry for it to register.

"Yeah, well, now you never will." She turned away and started digging her keys out of her backpack.

"Steph, please," Joe begged. There was real pain in his voice. "This may be another ploy." He moved around to stand in front of her again.

"What?" It was the pain in his voice and eyes that got to her.

"Three attempts on your life in four days. Someone wants you out of the way. Now, suddenly, your uncle is killed in Portland. I don't know much about your uncle, but I do know he is tough, durable, and smart. If he has survived this long, then this strikes me as a little too convenient."

"What are you saying to me?" She stuttered out as she hit the unlock button to her truck. It beeped not too far away, saying it was unlocked.

"I'm saying don't go rushing off on one phone call from some guy you just met." Joe stepped closer. The sirens were also closing on them.

Stephanie took a deep, steadying breath and let it out, regaining her center. "That makes sense. It would take me about five hours to drive to Portland, anyway. What's another hour to check it out?" She nodded slowly as the hot anger receded and reason returned. She was suddenly embarrassed by her hot words to him. "Joe, I'm sorry about what I said. Why don't you follow me to my apartment, and we can call from there." She pushed the remote start button for her truck.

There was a *whump* noise from under her truck, and smoke suddenly appeared. Joe reacted instantly by grabbing her, spinning her around, and shielding her with his body, her back to his front. His back was to the truck. She saw Bruce and Tom diving to the pavement ten feet away. Then Joe dove sideways for the pavement, carrying her with him. They were in the air when her truck finished blowing up. She heard Joe grunt as the shock wave hit him. His huge body cushioned her from the explosion. She landed in his arms, on her side, on the pavement. The force of the blast tumbled them a little. She was stunned for just a moment and then scrambled to look at her truck. It was a burning hulk.

Joe was unconscious, limp, and on fire. "Bruce!" she shrieked. "Help me with Joe." She jerked her jacket off and used it to started beating at the flames while pulling him away from her burning truck. They were twenty feet away, but apparently that was too close. She could feel the heat. Joe was huge and heavy, but she still managed to drag him another ten feet. Bruce and Tom helped her pull him further from the fire. They stopped dragging him when they were across the parking lot. They had also gotten the fires on him out.

Stephanie checked to see if he had a pulse, and he did. She did notice the trail of blood they had left from dragging him.

"Hey," he rumbled out quietly. "You okay?"

"Yeah," she breathed out. "I'm fine. You took the hit. How are you feeling?"

"I told you they would have to go through me." He sighed and closed his eyes. "It hurts a little."

"Joe," she said as she touched his face. Blood had started leaking out of his mouth. She grabbed a pencil.

"Don't move! Slowly lie down on the ground. She's armed." Peripheral vision showed her two uniformed policemen with weapons drawn and aimed.

"This is Detective Joe Bremer. He saved my life just now when my truck blew up. Now I am going to try and save his." She said it all slowly and calmly. She brought the symbol for healing to her mind's eye. Another detail came to her, she remembered Rosemary telling her to ask the goddess for help in healing herself.

"Lady, I said hands in the air."

She ignored them. The symbol filled her vision, and she spread it over Joe. She built her will. She really wanted this to work. He had saved her life by spooning her to him, and he wanted to date her. She didn't want to lose him now.

"Lady, I'm not going to tell you again. Hands up and drop the pencil." The policeman had moved in front of her.

"I'm going to help him!" Stephanie stated calmly, closing her eyes and focusing on Joe's bleeding form. "He's a detective for the Bellevue police." She nodded toward Joe. She looked up to the sky, "Goddess, hear my prayer for this man, my protector. Aid me in his healing."

"Are you Stephanie Blackraven?" one of the officers asked at the same time. "I know we have a warrant, but she's the one that helped Paulli."

Stephanie ignored them and gave her will the way. "Eal …"

Bang!

Something heavy struck her chest and smashed her into the asphalt.

She heard a voice, "P rr oo tt ee cc tt oo rr." Or was it a siren.

She couldn't breathe.

The lights and sounds seemed to be swirling into a dark spot.

"Down!" she heard someone scream. "All of you on the ground now!"

"You shot her," Bruce screamed. There were sounds of scuffling and smacking, then a *ttzzit.*

"Down, or your next."

"What the fuck are you doing? You shot her," someone else yelled.

"She was kneeling, holding a pencil," a woman called out.

"She was glowing. Didn't you see that? She was going to do something. That glow ..." Then with more conviction, "She was going for her gun."

"You asshole! She had a pencil in her right hand. That's the side the gun's on."

"Two are armed, one of them is down. Shots fired. Blackraven is in custody. Officer down. We need an ambulance and aid car," a voice stated.

There was a huge weight on her chest.

Chapter 13

Stephanie came to lying on her side as someone tried to rip her shirt off. Her chest hurt, bad. Her head hurt a little, and her shoulders were wrenched behind her. Then it came rushing back. "Joe," she said. She tried to reach her chest, but her hands were restricted. "Shot, I've been shot." She weakly flailed around on her side.

"Miss, hold still, I'm trying to see where you're hurt. Who would handcuff someone they just shot?" It was a graying paramedic who was trying to get her shirt off. "Get these damn cuffs off her!" he demanded in exasperation.

Stephanie's mind snapped back with crystal clarity. "The releases to my vest are on the sides. How's Detective Bremer?" she asked calmly or at least tried to. It came out kind of mumbled.

He fiddled with her hands and then rolled her onto a stretcher with wheels. "Who is Detective Bremer?" he asked while rolling her over a little bit, and she felt his hands pawing under her shirt. "Ah," he burst out in relief, "you got a vest on. That's why there's no blood."

Stephanie cleared her throat. "Catches are on the sides." It came out better. "I feel like I've been hit by a truck. Ah, my truck." She tried to get up. He pushed her back down. "They blew up my truck."

"Lady, are you going to be a problem?" He looked her in the eye as he said it. "You're lucky he didn't aim higher. Now lie still while I check you out." She smiled at his tone as she shook her head. "You can sit up, but only to let me get your vest and shirt off you." He was old enough to be her father and seemed to be getting some type of ironic humor out of the situation. "Okay, then. Don't make me have to cuff you again." She gave an involuntary squeak of pain as she tried to move. He helped her to sit, and then he stripped her to her bra. He lifted it off briefly, to poke underneath it. "Sorry, I need to check."

"No worries. I think it may have cracked a rib or two." She groaned as he poked. "Damn, the vest worked. It seems to have distributed the impact over a large area, only I'm not that large. That must be why my whole chest hurts."

He smiled at that. "You seem pretty large to me." There was a twinkle in his eyes and crinkles in the wrinkles at the corners. "It did work, but he uses a cannon."

"That could be construed as sexual harassment . . ." she started to say, then he pressed something, and the pain stopped her comment.

"Yep, cracked something." He continued to play with her chest. "You're what, twenty-five, twenty-six years old?" She nodded, trying to breath.

It hurt.

"If you're done feeling up my suspect," an office was standing over them, "put her in my car." He laughed roughly. "Maybe I want a turn."

All the humor faded from the paramedic's eyes, "Officer Crunkle, it is unprofessional for you to stand there and eye my female patient while I am examining her. Please step away. I will let you know when she is ready for transport." The officer harrumphed, but moved away.

She looked around as a way to distract herself from what the paramedic was doing. Joe was on a stretcher not far from her. There were six or seven police cars. She couldn't see Bruce. Lots of people were yelling. Phones lifted for a better look.

"Stephanie," she heard Joe weakly call out. "You shot?"

"Yeah, I'm here, Joe. I'm okay," she yelled back.

"Hmm," the paramedic said as slipped her bra painfully back down and then helped her put her shirt back on. "You probably have cracked ribs, but then again, maybe not. Your vest was well made and fit perfect. It did its job. Your left breast is going to swell and be painful. You might want to get some ice on it." She started to smile and say something only to have him cut her off. "No, I am not trying to be funny or sexist. It is going to hurt. You also got a bump on the head from when it smacked into the asphalt." He glanced around and then asked softly, "Was it Crunkle that shot you?"

She glanced up to locate the officer just ten feet away. She nodded yes.

"I'm going to ask you real loud if you want to go get checked out at the hospital," he spoke softly, pausing to catch her eye, "You say yes, as loud as you can. You do not want to be in his car."

"Why?" she whispered.

"He's not the sharpest tool in the shed and if the scuttlebutt around here's true, then he's dirty. Goin' have nothing to lose by doing something else stupid." He wiggled his eyebrows at her. "He shot a cute co-ed holding a pencil, while she was saving a police detective from getting burnt up. His career is toast."

She glanced down, trying to see his nametag, only to find his name covered by tape.

The paramedic commented. "The police have your gun and other stuff. I'm going to have to handcuff you again. Sorry." He seemed to really see her face. "Hey, you're that Doctor Blackraven, the wizard that saved Officer Paulli last night. I was on that call, too."

She nodded as she tried to pull her shirt closed, but the buttons were gone. "Engineer, not wizard. No magic, just science. Yeah, that would be me."

"Right," he said with a smile that reached his eyes. "No magic. Sure." He thought for a moment, "So," he started, somewhat confused, still talking softly. "You save a policeman's life last night, your truck blows up, you pull another cop out of a fire, and the police shoot you today?"

She snorted, "Yeah, go figure. I guess no good deed goes unpunished."

He snorted, "That's the way it seems to work. I think somebody's out to get you. How's the pain?"

She thought about it. "Not bad, all things considered. I've gotten hurt worse in a sparring match."

"Martial arts?"

She nodded. "What's your name?"

He smiled, glancing at his nametag. "I cover it up because of all the weirdoes and nuts we come in contact with. Just call me Roger."

She smiled. "Thanks, Roger, for helping me."

"You're welcome. From what I can see, you're one of the good people." He smiled at her, "I think that big guy over there saved your life. Looks like he took the blast, lucky thing he was standing where he was and had full tactical gear."

"It wasn't luck," Stephanie locked eyes with the paramedic. "It wasn't luck. He grabbed me from behind and hugged me to completely cover my body. He's a hero." She licked her lips and quietly asked, "How is he?"

The paramedic glanced over toward Joe. "He got a good knock on the head, some deep cuts on the backs of his legs and butt, scrapped up leg, bled a little. That's all we can see. He needs to go to the hospital." He glanced back and patted her arm. "And so do you. They'll check you both out."

"Aren't you done yet?" Officer Crunkle barked.

"You just lie there and try to rest." He patted her arm as he stood up. "Young lady, do you want to go to the hospital?"

"Yes, I do," she yelled as loud as she could and jerked at her handcuffs to make a show of it. "Take me to the hospital. Don't let that police officer have me. He already shot me for no reason. Now he wants to rape me." She heard some kind of yelling commotion start out of sight.

The paramedic fought not to smile as he winked at her. "All right then, I've got to talk to my partner." He moved away, talking loudly to the other policemen about her condition. Officer Crunkle was drawn away with him.

Tom appeared, kneeling at her side. He looked rumpled, but not burnt or bleeding.

"Tom, what are you doing here?" she asked.

"I was helping Bruce out in the lab and then this." Tom looked worried.

"I'm okay," she hurried to assure him.

Tom glanced away and then back. "We don't have much time. The police are not going to let you go to the hospital; they're going to take you downtown. There is other stuff going on. What you need to do is stay calm. These charges are bogus. I'll call to get you legal help."

The adrenaline of the situation was helping her process information even faster than she normally could. "You're not just a grad student. What is going on?"

He glanced around again. "Your great uncle hired me to keep an eye on you. We have protocols in place for a situation like this. I'm a grad student, but I'm also in his organization. I'm sorry to have to tell you. He was killed earlier today, which has set in motion a different set of protocols, all designed to keep you safe."

She teared up again at remembering the loss of her uncle. "I remember. Nelson called. He said I was needed in Portland."

Tom blinked, and his head ticked to the side, "What? He called?" Something was running around behind his eyes. "We don't have time to discuss this here. Go with the police; be calm, smart, and professional. I'll arrange for legal help and extraction." He started to get up, and Stephanie tried to grab his hand.

Damn handcuffs, she thought as her hand pulled up short. "Wait," she whispered. She saw a group of people heading towards her and noticed a large crowd of noisy campus folk had gathered. "Bruce, what happened to Bruce?"

Tom smiled. "He jumped the cop who shot you and got a few good licks in before they Tasered him to the ground. He's going to the police station, too. I gotta go." And he faded into the collection of cars.

She noticed there were several students taking pictures or videos with their cell phones. Marsh was raving at a policeman while being restrained by another.

Where had the fire trucks come from?

Someone called out her name, but she couldn't see who it was, so she weakly pulled at the handcuffs and tried to look innocent and hurt. Surely somebody was getting her performance on camera. Getting some kind of story out would help, she hoped.

There was a bunch of yelling between the police and the paramedics, she was having trouble tracking.

Officer Crunkle came over to uncuff her, and she kicked him in the balls to get him off her. She almost blacked out from the chest pain. They cuffed her hand and foot and dumped her into the back of a patrol car; she hoped it wasn't Officer Crunkle's squad car.

Joe had actually struggled up off his stretcher to take part in the yelling when Crunkle came over to her. He was yelling loudly when they start to move her. He had pushed someone in a suit, then fell to the ground again, which had pretty much ended all the yelling and got him handcuffed to a stretcher and quickly rushed out of there. She couldn't see much after that. Her chest was starting to hurt more, and her shirt fell open again.

She was hurt, terrified, and alone in the world; nothing had prepared her for the brutal reality of the last four days. The only person she could rely on was herself. Tears were leaking. "No, damn it!" she admonished herself. "Uncle Raymond would kick my ass. I will not go out crying like some pathetic princess waiting to be rescued." Pulling back from the brink of despair, she started reviewing her assets and information. She had a lot of time to think and plan.

Stephanie didn't watch much TV, but what she had seen had her expecting to go through some kind of process procedure at the police station. Strip search, documentation, mug shot taken, crappy orange suit put on her, statements documented, and being dumped into a smelly cell with other female detainees.

That wasn't what happened.

Instead, Crunkle and another officer carried her into the police station through a non-busy door, to a very sound-absorbing little room, handcuffed her to the chair with her shirt gaping open, exposing her bruising chest to Officer Crunkle, with his split lip and bruised face, and another officer who didn't look happy.

She asked them a great number of questions that they didn't answer. It was only when she started verbally harassing them that she got a reaction. Junior high school training apparently did have a use. Pretending she couldn't read their nametags, she named Crunkle Dickhead One and the other Dickhead Two. She didn't think they liked her. She had no idea how much time had passed when they finally stepped out of the room.

As soon as they left, she worked a pencil out of the left sleeve pocket with her mouth and dropped it into her right hand. She had a plan and was tired of being cuffed and gaping. She decided early on to try the symbol to unlock her hands. It was the symbol Joe had brought to her in class. She drew it from memory, powered it with her will, “Lock-Unhay,” she quietly intoned. There was a pulse of air pressure.

The handcuffs fell away, her bra unclasped, her pants zipped opened; basically every lock, clasp, fastener, and connector in the room she could see, came undone. A few ceiling panels fell loose. For a moment, she thought the recessed lights were going to fall on her. Unfortunately, the door to the room also clicked open.

Damn, she thought. *That one works really good. I should probably experiment somewhere else.* She didn’t move.

Detective Sergeant Grayson stepped through the door flanked by the Dickheads. “What in hell did you two do?” He took in the condition of the room, her clothes, and froze for an instant and then rounded on them.

They had a very quiet, yet intense conversation she couldn’t hear, which left both Dickheads white and angry and Grayson red and shaking. It ended with Grayson shouting very quietly, “I don’t care what your orders were. She has rights, and you have violated them.” He turned his attention to her. “Dr. Blackraven, if I uncuff you, are you going to act civilized?”

She smiled her prettiest. “You mean, am I going to pound the crap out of the Dickheads here?”

She could see Grayson struggle not to smile. “Yes, are you going to refrain from that?”

“If you let me put my clothes on, I will even thank you. But I want their names and service numbers.” Stephanie didn’t know any lawyers, she didn’t like lawyers, but for this, she would find a good one.

“All in good time.” He moved over with a key.

She stood up and let the cuffs clang to the floor.

Both officers froze in shock. Dickhead One pulled his gun, almost aimed it, and finally struggled out, “Hey, how did you . . .” before catching himself.

“Shit,” was all the other said while stepping back.

Stephanie smiled faintly and nodded to Dickhead One to make Grayson glance over. “I just didn’t want to get shot again for fixing my clothes.” She went about setting her wardrobe to right, or a right as she could make it, as she asked, “Detective Grayson, would you hook my bra for me? I can’t reach it with my shoulders and chest all bruised up. How's Joe?" she asked as she turned her back to him. She also noted out of the corner of her eye, a scowl and a head nod from Grayson got Dickhead One's gun back in its holster.

"He's at the hospital being checked out. No permanent damage, just banged up a bit. He'll be fine." He didn't say anything else, but his body language screamed that there was more.

"Joe's a hero. He saved my life at the risk of his own. Did Dickhead One there tell you that? And why wasn't I allowed to go to the hospital as well? After all, Dickhead One there did shoot me in the chest after I pulled Joe away from the fire when my truck was blown up." She sounded the picture of innocence. The buttons were gone from her shirt, so she cross-tucked it in front to close it as best she could.

"Lieutenant Drakeson ordered your arrest." He said it very slowly and quietly, so that only she would hear. He had his back to the officers. "He had reason to believe you were responsible for the murder of Andrew Stone. They were afraid of your ma, ah, symbol stuff. Your search and restraint was against the law." He added that very quietly. "It violated laws and police procedure."

Stephanie started to say something smart-mouthed, but something in his eyes stopped her. He was very tense. "Thank you," she said as she finished setting her clothes as right as she could. "Where are my other possessions?" She was processing the data.

"Procedure would be to impound them until the investigation runs its course," Grayson added deadpan.

She kept studying his eyes. He was trying to tell her something more.

"Grayson, what the hell are you doing with this prisoner?" A tall, not as tall as Joe, clean shaven, distinguished black man yelled as he moved from the outer room to her cell.

"That would be Lieutenant Drakeson," he quietly stated to her before turning. Louder, he said, "Trying to preserve the foundation of evidence and arrest and limit the sexual harassment charges."

"Is it normal police policy to strip female prisoners naked and then let the guards examine them minutely?" she asked the room with icy clarity. "Do you do the same for the male prisoners?" She met the newcomer's eyes with cold calculation.

"We didn't . . ." Crunkle started, but was cut off.

"It is for terrorists," Drakeson stated.

"Then you must have me mistaken for someone else. I was arrested for murdering a dead man." She turned back to Grayson. "I want a lawyer." She paused for dramatic effect. "Now, before I get raped." She locked eyes with Dickhead One then glanced at Dickhead Two. "Or shot again."

"We can hold you for forty-eight hours before filing." The lieutenant was pretty smug.

"Even terrorists get due process of the law," she stated with absolute surety; even if she didn't really feel sure. "And that means I get legal representation. I am a US citizen with no previous arrests, no outstanding anything; I don't even have a parking ticket. I have been unduly assaulted, seized, and searched. Subjected to sexual harassment and demeaning confinement. I also am protected by the Bureau of Indian affairs as a religious figure and the State Department of the US of A as a protected individual due to my religious standing. I want my lawyer now. You all will be lucky if you keep your badges, especially the Dickhead twins." She delivered it all with icy cold clarity while gesturing at the two officers.

Grayson was looking at her with new respect, the lieutenant with contempt and the Dickhead officers with beginning fear.

"We should add she is delusional to the profile," the Lieutenant stated. "You Miss, are a grad student at a little backwater university in Bellevue. Don't threaten me with your pretend status."

Stephanie had never been so scared or felt so alone, but there was no way she was going to let this guy know that. She pulled herself up to her full five foot nothing height, in blue jeans, torn open shirt, and cowboy boots.

"That is Doctor Blackraven to you, civil servant."

Drakeson clinched his jaw.

"Unlike you, I had to study hard and earn my position. Brown nosing wouldn't get me anywhere." She turned and stepped away with her nose held high. Good thing she had Rhinebolt as a study model, or she never would've known how a pompous asshole should act. "You seem to be behind in the knowledge department, but I guess it is to be expected from a simple servant, oh," she waived her hand airily. "Sorry, that is civil servant, poor education and all, for your type. Now, be a good simple servant and summon my lawyer." She waved him off in Rhinebolt's most irritating fashion, totally dismissing him as she moved to stand in the corner with her back to a wall. She was also flexing her shoulders, trying to get them to work properly again.

Grayson stepped in to grab the lieutenant as he lunged for her. "Sir," he stated calmly, "there is a great deal about Doctor Blackraven you don't know." Drakeson glanced at the sergeant and then back to her.

Shouting voices came in from some outer space. Legal words were floating in the air. The Dickhead twins exchanged a look, and One went out. Two just stood there and looked uncomfortable. The lieutenant and sergeant were talking quietly but intensely. Dickhead One came back in, white as a sheet, to whisper to Drakeson. He also turned pale and shot Stephanie a piercing look just before rushing out of the room. There was more shouting outside.

Grayson stepped over close to her. "Whatever happens, get clear of here. Somebody got to Drakeson, politics or bribe, don't know. Stay clear," he whispered to her. "Sorry, we don't work like this. I don't understand what's happening."

She nodded. Dickhead One and three suits came into the cell. Two of the men had very expensive suits on, she didn't know how much they cost, but she bet it was a lot. Both men were tanned, lean, sharp looking, with piercing eyes and briefcases. The taller had a delicate diamond stud in one ear. The third suit was Tom. His suit wasn't as expensive, but he did clean up well, and he didn't look out of place with them. He had too much muscle for the suit. She had never noticed that about him before. He stepped forward slightly. "Doctor Blackraven, are you okay?"

"No." She was pissed and wanted the world to know. "They left my clothes open, pants unzipped, displaying me to the room, and chained me to this chair for hours. Those," she pointed at the Dickheads, "two were left in here with me. He's the one that shot me because I had a threatening pencil." She pointed at Crunkle. "No one would give me a phone call or anything. They wouldn't even let me go to the bathroom. Finally, Detective Grayson, the only decent man here, came in to help me. I want out of here, and I want justice."

Tom smiled and nodded. The other two turned predatory. Ear Stud turned to the lieutenant. "We would like to consult with our client. Please leave the room and turn off your recording devices." His tone was cultured, rich, and very condescending.

Drakeson's cell rang just as he was going to say something. He answered it "Drakeson. Yes, captain," and froze. Nodding a few times, he finally said, "Yes, sir," and motioned everyone out of the room. The police grumbled, but all of them left the room, closing the door. Ear Stud held up one hand to forestall Stephanie from speaking.

Tom removed a cell phone-size device from his pocket, watched it for a moment, and then nodded. Ear Stud smiled and motioned for her to sit down. "We are under retainer from your great uncle. I'm Walter Pleasance and this is my partner, Otto Stubens. We are lawyers. Do you agree to let us represent your interests?"

She studied them for a moment while still leaning against the wall. "Why should I trust you?" She was alone, but Uncle Raymond was smart, and even after his death, he was looking out for her. She closed her eyes with a brief pang of loss. She thought she had known him only to find she didn't have a clue and wouldn't be able to learn.

That brought them all up short. "What other choice do you have at the moment?" Otto asked with a slight sneer.

She continued to study them calmly. *Now is not the time to show emotion*, she thought. *They could be just another ploy.* "I can have a public defender summoned. I can use my phone call to bring in other council. Why should I trust you? You could be a part of the plot or plots to kill me. After all, there have been four attempts on my life in five days."

Her bold statement seemed to set them back. It made Tom smile. Walter pulled a packet of documents out of his briefcase. "We have copies of all the documents you signed for your uncle, as well as others signed by your great uncle." He studied her for a moment. "Really, we have no concrete proof. Your great uncle called in a favor from us on this. We have a note from him for you, but it could be forged."

"You know my uncle was killed today in some kind of a car bomb."

They looked slightly troubled, but Walter continued. "Yes, we know. That sets into motion several other events. The least of which, it causes his fortune to pass to you along with all his other possessions and holdings. But let's focus on this …"

"How many favors?"

"What, well, four at least from me." Walter glanced at Otto.

"Is that really important?" Otto asked. She just stared at him. "I owe him my life. So, let's call it one big one."

Stephanie nodded once. "Okay. So, you two are his legal representatives here in the Puget Sound area?"

"Yes, well, our firm is." Otto relaxed slightly.

"He's had you on retainer here? For how long?"

Walter smiled. "When did you move here?"

Stephanie frowned; it was a good answer. "Let me see the note he left me."

Walter pulled out the sealed envelope with her name on it and handed it to her. It looked like his handwriting, but she was not an expert. She tapped the contents to one side and tore off the end. One page was inside.

"Princess," she read, "if you are reading this, then shit has happened. Yep, they are mine. Read the other letter." The bottom was signed Unc. He always signed his notes to her Unc, short for uncle. Yep, it was all Uncle Raymond. She closed her eyes to hold back the tears. She would not cry in front of these people.

"We're sorry for your loss."

"Sure you are." It came out much colder then she intended. "So, this means you work for me. I pay the bills now."

Neither of them liked that statement. Otto looked like he had swallowed something bad. Tom was grinning at her.

"Yes," Otto finally choked out.

"Here's what happened." She recounted everything from when she set the symbol in the lecture hall until now. She left out all the personal items about her and Joe, as well as the healing symbol and police specific information. Other than that, she told them everything and in as much detail as she could remember. They all looked impressed and took notes.

"It was a werewolf?" Tom just didn't seem to be able to get a grip.

"It was a man that turned into something bigger than a timber wolf. That spells werewolf in my book."

"You stopped it with a symbol that made a flash of light?" Walt asked.

"Yes," she said as she reached for a pencil. She only had four left. "You want a demonstration?"

"Yes," Tom said at the same time as Walter.

"Later," Otto interjected with some emphatic hand motions. "Later, after we get her extracted and legal action in motion. Time is not our friend on this." Walter nodded agreement.

The two lawyers sat quietly for a moment. They looked at each other, exchanged a few cryptic words, and then Otto pulled out his cell phone while standing and moving away.

Walter stood up to pace a moment, obviously in thought. He visibly made a decision and turned to her. "Just stay here with Tom. Sit down and remain seated, looking young, cute, innocent, and vulnerable. Don't kick anyone else in the balls. We'll take care of getting you out of here." He started to step away and then turned back. "Did I say don't talk? Well, don't talk."

"Bruce," Stephanie said as she poked her finger on the arm of the chair. "Bruce Richardson, my lab assistant and friend, get him out as well."

Walter looked at her, smiled like the shark he was, nodded, "Okay, no extra charge."

"The senator please," she heard Otto say into his phone before he stepped out of the room.

Walter followed him, pulling his own phone. "Hi, I am Walter Pleasance. I represent Doctor Stephanie Blackraven. I would like to speak with the district attorney, please. Yes, I can hold." Then he was out of the room.

Stephanie started thinking. The problem was that she didn't have enough information about what was going on. Assumptions would have to be made then evaluated later for accuracy. "Why would someone want to kill me? Why would they want to kill me now?" she asked herself.

"Doctor, don't talk," Tom chided her gently. "They may have turned back on the recorders." He showed her the device that now had blinking lights on it.

"May I have a piece of paper, please? Call me Steph. Every time someone says doctor, I look around to see who it is."

He nodded, smiled while he pulled a notebook out of his inner coat pocket and tossed it to her. Catching it, she pulled a pencil out of her sleeve pocket. She started writing down all the questions she could that centered on her and the past day's events. She filled three pages. She numbered the items and then started sorting them into columns on another page. On yet another page, she started annotating items she would need to get to help in her problem solving.

Sitting back, she started looking at all the items she had noted and slowly started annotating them and occasionally making additions to the lists. After studying them for a while, she listed them all out in a different pattern and order. Circling some and drawing lines between others. She studied that for a while and then listed them again in yet a different order. She tore all the pages out of the notebook, then laid them all out on the table to study.

Greyson stepped into the room. "What are you doing?" he asked. "Everything you create in here is evidence."

She looked up. It took her a moment to reorient. "Okay. I'm just trying to figure out your murder and the attempts on me. You're welcome to the notes."

"Steph," Tom chided. "You're not supposed to talk to the nice officer."

She frowned and sat back in her chair. She collected all the notes and handed them to Greyson. He took them with a wry smile. "How are you feeling? Is it starting to hurt?" He was trying to tell her something with his eyes.

"Yes," she said slowly as he nodded faintly. "Yes, it's starting to hurt real bad." Greyson glanced at the door and then back at her, making hurry-up motions. "My chest is swelling. I may pass out." She gave him a raised eyebrow look, trying to ask him if that was what he was after.

He gave her a brief smile and stepped over to the door. "Doctor Blackraven is starting to go into shock. Get an aide car here with a paramedic," he shouted out into the room.

Tom stepped over, removing his coat to drape over her shoulders. Quietly, he whispered, "Unfocused eyes, vacant look, hell, just lean over and rest your head on the table."

She glared at him for a moment. Like she didn't know what shock symptoms were. Slowly, she leaned over the table to pillow her head on her arms. Tom tucked his huge coat in around her.

Other people charged back into the room. She ignored all of them and their questions.

She must've dozed off because she woke up when a loud argument with her name in it moved back into the room. It just wasn't that large a room. Otto was squared off against Lieutenant Drakeson talking legalese at him. Drakeson was shouting back about obstructing justice. She ignored it all and put her head back down on her arms.

"Hi," the familiar calm voice of Roger the paramedic said.

She glanced up. "Didn't we just meet earlier today? What are you doing here?"

"There just aren't that many paramedics in Bellevue. It's night now, and you aren't doing very good." He set his medical toolbox on the table. "You seemed to have passed out during interrogation, must have something to do with being shot."

She smiled weakly at him, "Ya think?"

"Can I get you to set back?" He had pulled out a stethoscope and flashlight.

She started to sit up and froze as her upper body cramped. "Ahhhh," was all she could really say.

"You," Roger pointed at Tom. "Help me get her onto the floor. Everybody out of the room," Roger bellowed over her cramping body. Everything from then on was pretty straightforward. She was stretched out on the floor, painfully.

"Roger," she whispered to him as he bent over her, "I'm not dying. I just cramped up."

"Get an oxygen bottle in here and the gurney," He yelled over his shoulder and then leaned closer to her, flashing a light in her eyes. "They don't know that. You look like shit, young lady." She tried hard not to laugh. He fussed with her until his partner and the gurney arrived. Then she was moved to a gurney with ice applied to her chest and painkillers ingested and wheeled out to a waiting ambulance through a gauntlet of yelling suits.

"You're all over the news," Roger whispered to her after they got her past the suits. "They're playing it like the police dragged you out and shot you like a dog while you were saving some poor policeman's life." Roger winked at her. "Your university friends seem to be doing a good job of casting you as the heroine and the police as the villains. They got some good cell phone pictures from the scene, too." He leaned over close to show her an image from his phone. It was of Crunkle in the act of shooting her while she was on her knees over Joe. "Like I said, his career is toast." Roger chuckled and patted her hand.

Tom and Walter rode along on the short distance to Overlake Hospital, which was the closest.

She was whisked right into the emergency room, through to X-ray without getting any, and out to a limousine with the explanation she was going to a private facility.

It was a very nice facility, very complete. They did all the normal doctor stuff, administered pain meds, and she went to sleep. She never even got a chance to tell them no.

When she woke up late in the night, she was in her own apartment. She got up long enough to find and load her shotgun and put it close to the bed.

Chapter 14

Loud pounding on her door brought Stephanie out of her spare room. She wasn't exactly dressed for company, with sweat pants and a built-in bra tank top she was using to hold the ice on her chest, all covered by a big purple sweatshirt. She was heavily into frump mode even by her standards. Stopping short of opening the door, but not directly in front of it, lamenting the lack of a peephole, she finally asked, "Who is it?"

"I have some stuff here for Stephanie Blackraven." The woman didn't sound too happy about it. "It's from Joe Bremer."

Stephanie shifted the 12 gauge Home Defender to a right, one-handed grip and opened the door with her left, using the door as shield. "Come in."

A tall, broad-shouldered woman with a single golden-brown braid hanging down her back, wearing boot-cut blue jeans, black biker boots, good figure, leather biker coat, made Stephanie think of a Viking war maiden, as she came in like she was ready to sack and burn something. She was carrying Stephanie's gun case for her AR and gear bag. Tom was following the young woman with a puzzled look on his face, until he glanced behind the door to see her standing there with a shotgun ready for use. He nodded his approval of her readiness.

"I'll be right outside." He pulled the door shut as he backed out.

"I have a bone to pick …" her voice trailed off as she turned to see Stephanie with a shotgun.

"Who are you and why do I care?" Stephanie had had a couple of hard days and a bad night. Her chest was aching, as anticipated, and she was having to rotate ice on and off to control the swelling. Her left breast felt like it should be three times the size of the right, but wasn't. She had also started stretching just to keep everything from seizing up again, which made her chest and shoulders hurt like hell. She had a symbol for healing, but was afraid to use it. And she had private security guards, hired by her lawyers, that wouldn't leave her alone. They wanted her to pack up her stuff faster so they could move her to a "safe house" for her own protection. She had called to see how Joe was doing, but the calls were being blocked by the hospital and police. And to top it all off, she was a celebrity to the press. They were hounding her for a statement. She had been firmly instructed by her lawyers not to say anything.

The young woman went wide-eyed and took an involuntary step back. "Ah, could I get you to set the shotgun down?" the young woman asked politely. Stephanie figured she couldn't be out of high school. She was a little pale, with tear tracks on her face. Then it hit her, this had to be one of Joe's sisters. Who else would've gotten her stuff out of his SUV?

Stephanie's mind slipped into overdrive; they wouldn't let her calls through, Joe wasn't out of the hospital, he had pretty bad visible injuries and unknown internal ones. He was under observation for something in an observation ward. They were keeping him isolated, just like they did for intensive care patients. He was a detective who had been in the news, so anything negative was newsworthy. A family member, who had recently been crying, had shown up unannounced at her door. Her conclusion was that he could've had fatal injuries, and no one wanted to talk about it.

"Shit!" Stephanie exclaimed and leaned her head against the wall. "Did Joe, … ah … They said he only had superficial wounds." She was tearing up again. "Is he, … ah …" She choked up with a little sob. It was becoming too much.

There was a short silence. "Oh no, God no, he's not dead or anything. Joe's fine. He's really angry at the police. Joe's going to be okay. Could you put the shotgun down?" She seemed a lot nicer now. "Please."

"Sure," Stephanie whispered, wiping at her face. "I've had a couple bad days. Lost my uncle to a car bomb." She propped the gun so it couldn't be seen from her deck if someone were outside, but within easy reach while moving to the door. "Sorry, it's just, I tried to call him, and they wouldn't let me …" Stephanie wiped the almost tears out of her eyes and took a deep, calming breath that almost doubled her over from the chest pain.

"Are you okay? Is there anything I can get for you?" The young woman was worried now and definitely at a loss.

"No, I'm not okay. Some asshole policeman shot me in the chest yesterday and Joe got blown up and nobody will tell me anything." Stephanie was holding her chest and leaning against the wall again. "Who are you? Which sister? God, this was not how I wanted to meet his family. I'm dressed like frump girl and … and … I'm just pissed at the world. Hell, we haven't even had a real date yet!!!" Stephanie decided not talking anymore was best.

Stephanie didn't want to look her in the eyes, but Uncle Raymond hadn't raised a coward. Steph pulled herself together and straightened up. The young lady was looking around her apartment while Stephanie had herself a mini meltdown. "Hi, I'm Stephanie Blackraven."

"I'm Abigail, Joe's youngest sister," she announced with a smile and a slightly impressed look on her face. "You have every right to be upset, if even half the stuff happened like the news said it did."

"Those assholes didn't get anything right," Stephanie blurted out. The shocked look on Abigail's face brought her up short. Stephanie closed her eyes and took a not-so-deep breath. "Allow me to start again. Hi, I'm Stephanie Blackraven, your brother's not-quite-a girlfriend. He and I have had six very interesting days together. I'm glad to meet you."

Abigail giggled. Stephanie tried not to wince.

"It's nice to meet you, Stephanie," she shyly said. "Ah, Joe sent me over with your stuff. He was worried that you might need it. He, ah, said you shouldn't worry about him." She blushed and looked at the floor for a moment. "He really likes you. He asked about you the first thing when he woke up." She paused, glancing at Stephanie.

Stephanie frowned and then smiled as she thought about Joe. "So, how's he doing?"

"His butt's all torn up, fifteen stitches. Legs got about twenty each. He's healing up good and should be out of the hospital later today or tomorrow. They, ah, the police won't tell him anything either." She giggled again. "So, ah, what really happened? I've heard it on the news and everything, but, like, they never tell the truth."

"I stopped watching TV about ten years ago for just that reason. I have no idea what they've been making up." She glanced back to the door. "You want something to drink? Coke or water or something?"

"No, thank you." Abigail looked around again. "Can I sit down?"

"Sure, sorry. Let me get the gun out of your way." Stephanie stepped over, grabbed the gun case, and moved back over to the table.

"Well, the news has been showing your burning truck and the clip of that policeman shooting you. They're blaming it all on gang violence. The Internet is showing all sorts of stuff that was taken by college students. There's one site that's claiming it's all a police cover-up for something about murders. They've got some interesting stuff: yelling between police officers, you being, ah, examined by a paramedic while chained to a stretcher, Joe pushing around somebody and then falling down and being chained to his own stretcher." She sat down and leaned forward. "So, what really happened?"

Stephanie glanced back at her eager face and then turned back to her rifle. Her hands took on a life of their own as she decided what to tell. "Well, your brother took me to the U to look at one of my professors' offices that had been broken into. It was a mess, and I saw some stuff that gave us another clue to chase. When we came out, I got the call about my uncle having been blown up, … in a car in Portland." She paused as the pain of Uncle Raymond's death washed over her again. She also realized she had field stripped the rifle and the upper assembly was laid out on the table for inspection. With a little laugh and a swipe at tears, she inspected the firing pin to make sure it was still seated properly. Uncle Raymond had told her about a trick the bad guys would pull on rifles by taking out the firing pins, so the soldiers wouldn't know it until they tried to use them. He had made her check every time after her rifle was out of her control.

"Anyway, Joe wouldn't let me just hop in my truck and race off to Portland. He got in my way and made me see reason, which saved my life the first time. He was standing between me and my truck when I hit the remote start. The bomb didn't go off right. There was like this pre-explosion, which allowed him time to spin me around and hug me to him, ya know my back to his front, before it really blew. That saved my life a second time." The rifle was all back together.

She set it down and faced Abigail. "Your brother saved my life, twice. He's a hero. He took the whole blast on his back." She wiped at her running nose. "When I was on the ground and everything started tracking again, I started pulling him away from the fire and beating on him with my coat to put him out. He was on fire as well." She had to stop and look away for a moment. It was like it was happening again.

"I had pulled him across the lot by then and saw the bloody trail he left. It scared me. I thought he was dying." Stephanie took a not-too-deep breath. "I decided to use a healing symbol I had discovered last week. I was right in the middle of the Will and Word when Dickhead One shot me in the chest. Everything went kind of scratchy after that."

"OH MY GOD!" Abigail exclaimed, "You pulled him across the parking lot. You're just a tiny thing. How did you do that? You only weigh, what, about a hundred pounds. He must weigh four times what you do." Abigail's eyes were wide with wonder.

Stephanie smiled. "Thanks, but I weigh a little more than that. I'm pretty strong, too. Anyway, I had to. He had just saved my life. I had to pull him away."

Abigail was beaming and excited as she jumped up from the chair. "Wow, Joe said you were beautiful and tough, but, you are really pretty. But wow, pulled him across the parking lot and put out a fire on him. You're like five foot nothing. Wow, pretty and tough. Then that policeman shot you. Ah," Abigail got a confused look on her face. "Why aren't you, ... ah, ... like, in the hospital in intensive care or something. Bullets, like, hurt."

"I had a Dragon Scale bulletproof vest on. It spread the impact across my chest." Stephanie stepped over to the closet and pulled it out. She had already replaced the section of plates that had been damaged and the liner. It wasn't like she was sleeping very well.

"OH MY GOD! You've got a vest. That looks better than Joe's. Where did the bullet hit?"

Stephanie sighed and went into her workroom and returned with the impacted section of plates. One of the central ones and the surrounding interlocking six were visibly deformed. "This is the section that was over my left breast. As you can see, it did its job."

"That's amazing. You're amazing. You, like, take guns apart and fix bulletproof vests. Joe said you're a genius. He says you're a doctor in engineering and symbols and stuff, which makes you a wizard with magic and everything."

Stephanie didn't think she had ever been that young. "I am not a wizard. It is not MAGIC, its science. But I am a doctor of applied symbology. Do you want to see how a symbol works?"

"OH MY GOD! Yes, yes, please." Abigail all but clapped her hands and hopped up and down.

It made Stephanie smile. She reached over and picked up one of the many pencils she had strategically placed around her apartment just in case. Old Faithful all but leaped into her mind's eye and then appeared hovering in the air in front of her. *That's never happened before*, she thought. The last time she had used it, it was as a weapon. Hmmmm, it made her think. "Abigail, …"

"Call me Abby, everyone does. And, well, since you're Joe's girlfriend and all … ?" Abby let it trail off as a type of question.

"Okay Abby, look at the wall, not at the symbol. The last time I did this it was to stop a werewolf and something may have changed."

"SHUT UP, you've seen a werewolf! OH MY GOD! You used a spell to stop it?"

"It is a symbol and it's not M A G I C, it's applied science. Okay?"

"Yes, ma'am," Abby said somewhat deflated.

Stephanie realized she had said that last part a little stronger than she had intended. The symbol was still hovering there. That had never happened before, either. Normally, when she took her attention off the symbols, they faded very quickly. *Hmmm,* she thought again. "Abby, look at the wall, not the symbol, so look at the wall now." As soon as Abby turned away, she said, "Ash-Flay." And poked with the pencil. The flash lit up the room, blinding her briefly.

"Oh my God!" Abby whispered in obvious wonder. "You did that with that symbol?"

"There's energy stored in the symbols. With the Will, the Word, and the Way, it can be released in a controlled manner." Stephanie realized she was lecturing.

A knock at the door was followed by, "Doctor Blackraven, are you okay?" It was Tom.

"Yes, Tom. Sorry; I was giving my guest a demonstration."

The door opened, and Tom's head poked in. "Was that the same flash symbol you showed us in class?"

"Yeah."

"Well, it's about a hundred times brighter now. It's gotten the news vultures all excited. You may want to hold off for a while from any more experiments." He thought for a moment. "Let me know when your guest is leaving. I think we had better escort her through the press. They seem to be circling, sensing news in the water or something."

"Okay, Tom." She didn't say anything else, so he pulled his head out and closed the door.

"Wow, you have bodyguards?"

"Who did you think those guys were that stopped you outside?"

"I didn't think about it. I was pretty pissed off."

Stephanie got a hint at the real reason for Abby's visit. "So, why were you all pissed off at me?"

Abby got real quiet and stared at her hands.

"Abby, we're friends now, right?" Stephanie prompted. "Why were you mad at me?"

"I saw your picture on the TV and heard all the stuff they were saying about you." She was barely speaking and wouldn't meet Stephanie's eyes. She just stared at her hands.

She's really distressed, what can I do? I'm terrible at this stuff. What would Rosemary do? Stephanie hesitated and then went over and put her hand over Abby's. "Abby, what is it?"

There was a short pause, then, "And, … well, … you're really, really pretty and smart and a wizard and a doctor, and I thought you would be like those girls in college that were so mean to Joey. He's never had a real girlfriend; they just took advantage of him. I thought that you were just using him 'cause he was a cop and … well … you couldn't really like him. They used to be so mean to him." Very quietly she added, "They used to call him Joe-Joe, the dog-faced boy in grade school and, … ah, … ah, … and he did save your life. I'm bigger than you. I was going to kick your ass if you hurt him. Now, I feel really stupid because you are really nice and you cried when you thought, ah, … well, … I was scared."

Well, that seemed to work. I have to remember this, Stephanie added and then went on to ask Abby in a soft tone, "Why were you scared?"

Abby had tears leaking down her face. "I saw the TV stuff, showing your burning truck and Joe lying on the ground with you kneeling over him. At that time, they said you had done it, blown it all up, and were in the act of finishing him off. I hadn't heard anything from the hospital or my folks. I thought Joe was dying. Then the only thing I heard from him was to go pick up your stuff and bring it to you. Joe's still in the hospital, … and, … and they're running all sorts of tests, … and nobody will tell us anything. I'm worried about Joe."

Stephanie shook her hand a little. "I would never hurt Joe, never on purpose, anyway. I like your brother. I haven't had many boyfriends, so I'm not sure where this will lead. We're taking it slow until we figure it out. But I like him a lot. Do you understand?"

Abby turned away to wipe at her face. "I told you I felt stupid. I could see right away you and he had something, and now I may have screwed it up for him. He's a really good guy. He may not be all that handsome, but he's a really good guy."

"Abby, you haven't screwed anything up. I like Joe. I even like the way he looks. His face has character, and it really lights up when he smiles. Hell, we may even get to go on a date one of these days." Stephanie was surprised when she realized she did like Joe a lot. She liked him so much she was worried about what his sister thought of her.

Abby giggled just as the front door creaked and started to swing open.

Stephanie took two steps and snatched up the 12 gauge to aim it at the door. Bruce froze in the half-opened doorway.

"Told you, you should knock." Stephanie heard Tom's mocking voice from the hallway.

"Wow, you're fast," Abby breathed out, staring wide-eyed at Stephanie's shotgun.

"Hey, Steph," Bruce said a little breathlessly. "Please don't shoot me. This is a new jacket. Who's your friend, who's … been crying?" He sounded puzzled.

"Bruce, you asshole, knock next time. I could've shot you." Stephanie clicked on the safety and put the shotgun back into its position. "This is Joe's little sister, Abigail."

Bruce looked between the two of them, "Steph, should I come back later?"

"Why?" Now it was Stephanie's turn to be puzzled.

Bruce looked heaven word as if for guidance. "So the two of you can finish your girl talk … about Joe."

"Does Joe know about him?" Abby interjected.

"Girl talk? What are you …" Stephanie turned back to Abby, "Yes, Joe's met Bruce. Bruce is my lab assistant-slash partner in crime." Steph was suddenly having trouble keeping up with the conversation. It was like she was missing some hidden queuing.

"Crime?" Abby's eyes were wide again.

"It's an expression. Bruce is a PhD candidate in applied energy. He and I have been working the symbols together for a couple of years now."

Bruce was doing his squinty eye thing, like when he studied something, then, worst of all, he smiled. "Abby, did Joe tell you that he asked permission to court Steph?"

"What! Really?" Abby was excited again. She grabbed Stephanie's hand in both of hers.

"It's no big deal." Stephanie tried to down play it. "He asked my Uncle Raymond if he could court me, before my uncle died."

Abby was shocked. "He did? Was your uncle your oldest male relative?"

Stephanie was puzzled, since that was almost the same wording Joe had used. "Yeesss."

"OH MY GOD! You two are practically engaged! He never told any of us that! Gran is going to be so proud of him." Abby was really excited now.

"Engaged! Whoa, wait a minute," Stephanie was feeling a little panicked. She pulled her hand away from Abby's clutches. "I didn't agree to that." She got a puzzled feeling. "At … least, … not … yet."

"Wow! Joe really lo …" Abby went wide-eyed and abruptly stopped talking. She looked around, like she was checking if she had everything. "I should go now. Joe warned me not to stay too long." She very abruptly leaned in and gave Stephanie a careful-not-to-hurt-her hug and then was out the door.

"I think I've stepped into the Twilight Zone," Stephanie exclaimed, resting her head in her hands.

"Nope, the family zone, almost as weird, but nebulous." Bruce was smiling at her like she had done something good.

"What the hell does that mean?"

"Oh, you'll find out. Anyway, I told you Joe was a keeper," Bruce replied cryptically as he slipped into the kitchen. "You want something to drink since I'm in here?"

"Yes, a glass of water would be nice. I need to take some more painkillers." Stephanie sat down, rubbing her chest.

Bruce came back in with a Coke and a glass of water. "Here you go. Hey, thanks for sending the legal help my way. Those guys are real sharks. I even got an apology from the police for them Tazering me."

"No problem. The police really screwed the pooch on this. I still can't believe that asshole shot me."

"He's dead," Bruce stated as he sat her water down.

"What? Who's dead?" She forgot about the water.

"Crunkle, the guy who shot you. They found his body this morning in an alley not far from his apartment. Gang-style killing; him kneeling and one to the back of the head."

"Holy shit!"

"Yep," Bruce took a sip and waited until she had taken a sip of water before adding, "The news are speculating that you did it."

Stephanie sprayed water all over. "What?"

Bruce laughed quietly and moved further away from her. "Yep. You're in cahoots with the gangs."

"That's bullshit, and you know it!"

"Yep, but I thought you should know before you get near the media." Bruce sipped his Coke. "That lieutenant, the one Joe works for, he got suspended, …

without pay. Apparently, he was the one who put out the warrant for you, and he didn't have just cause."

"What the hell?" Stephanie's mind was really racing as she got up to get the ibuprofen. She downed the pills and motioned for Bruce to follow her, "Come here, I want to show you something." She led him back to the spare bedroom.

She had pulled down all three 4 x 8 whiteboards from their ceiling racks. "I started trying to figure out what was happening. I've recorded all the assumptions and facts. There are more of the first than the second." She pointed at the respective lists on one of the boards. "Then I started trying to analyze them for potential points of congruity." She gestured at the second board that contained lots of interlinking circles.

"It's the symbology," Bruce blurted out while looking at her work.

"Yeah. That's the conclusion I've reached as well." She pointed at one column. "Symbology linked to Andy to the gangs. It breaks there. I can't figure out who or why they would be trying to kill me. That truck bomb was definitely an attempt to kill me. Everything to that point links back to the symbology. Why kill me? How does it relate to Andy's death? The gangs didn't kill him."

"Your uncle." He turned to look at her. "Them trying to kill you has to be a linked to him passing." Bruce turned to face her. "He was notorious and connected. Maybe they figured he gave you or left you something."

His face clouded up as he stepped over to gently take her in his arms.

"I'm sorry he died." Tears were openly running down his face. Bruce could get emotional, and he didn't try to hide it from her. "When that policeman shot you, I thought you were dead." He was crying now. "I thought something truly special had been removed from this world. I'm so glad you aren't dead."

Stephanie patted his back as they slowly rocked from side to side. "I'm not dead yet," she said in a really poor imitation of the scene from Monty Python and the Holy Grail. Bruce chuckled. "Stop crying." Stephanie chided him gently, "You're going to get me crying again."

Bruce pulled away, wiping his face. "You're like my second little sister, only I didn't like the first one this well."

Stephanie got quiet as she contemplated the events listed on the boards, giving Bruce some time, and distancing herself from his emotional outpouring.

Her chain of thought took her through the gang attack and then to the symbols listed in Andy's book. The symbols popped up one after another as she tried to link the implications of them.

Bruce touched her arm. "Steph, stop thinking about whatever you're thinking about."

"What?" she mumbled.

"Steph, look around you."

Steph changed her focus to the room. Glowing symbols were floating in the air, lots of them. One by one, she thought of the symbols and visualized them returning to her mental file, and they winked out or faded away, depending on how well she knew them. The ones winking out she knew really well, the others she had to concentrate on.

"What were you doing right then?" Bruce was using his quiet study voice.

"I was thinking about the chain of events and how it linked to the symbols in Andy's book. I started reviewing the symbols to see if there was a relevance to the sequence of events."

"And they started appearing in the air." Bruce thought about it for a moment. "It was really cool, too. Ah, when did this start, this sudden appearance?"

She thought for a moment. "I think it was after the werewolf, when I used the flash one as a weapon."

Bruce started nodding to himself in obvious thought. "Has anything else changed in your visualization or manipulation?"

"Yes, the flash symbol just appears now like this. It appears fully formed. I don't have to draw it, and it's more powerful. I did it earlier for Abby, and Tom said it was a hundred times more powerful."

"Was he in the room?"

"No, he was guarding in the hall."

"I think you need to be careful, more careful than normal. All it would've taken is the Will and the Word, and you would've launched them all."

Stephanie thought about it for a moment and then nodded her agreement.

"Hey, Doctor Blackraven," a voice called out from the living room.

She glanced out to see one of the larger guards in his military type, tactical black outfit, standing there. He was ruggedly handsome, with scars on his face, and looking like he was trying not to be angry.

"Yes."

"How's the packing coming?"

Stephanie felt that little fire of anger start in the pit of her stomach. "I told Tom I would let you guys know when I was ready."

"I don't work for Tom," he snapped.

That did it. She was fully pissed now. Stephanie pulled herself up to her full five-foot height and stalked into the living room. "So, just who do you work for?"

He was slow in answering. "I work for the agency." Tom had moved into the room behind him.

"And do they pay you?"

He was getting more wary now. "Yes," he slowly responded.

"And who does the agency work for?"

"Look, doctor, I'm just trying to do my job here."

"I see. Well, the agency was hired by my lawyers. And I pay my lawyers. So, who do you think pays your salary?"

He was angrier now, his dark eyes were snapping. "You do, doc. I work for you."

"Then why in the hell are you bugging me about my goddamn packing?" she yelled.

He was a little red in the face now, but spoke in an even tone. "Doc, you're paying me to keep you safe. I can't do that here. We need to move you to someplace else. Now, we can do that with or without your stuff. Once moved, you can fire my ass, get a new team leader, and I'll move on. Until then, would you kindly pack your shit, so I can make you safe?" There was a purposeful pause. "Please."

"Stoneman," Tom emphasized his name.

"Tom, you're too close on this one. You know her and like her. That has compromised your judgment. Back off," Stoneman continued in the even tone.

Stephanie was drawing in a breath when Bruce grabbed her arm. "Steph, ease down. The man is only trying to do his job." She whirled to face him. He held up a mirror to her.

Her eyes were literally sparkling with light motes. She forgot all about the guard.

"When did, … How long, …" her voice trailed off as she watched the effect fade with her anger.

"Got me," Bruce shrugged. "How about I help out with the details here?"

"What?" she asked. She was still puzzling about the light in her eyes.

"Stoneman, there, is right. You need to move somewhere else." He glanced over at Stoneman and nodded toward the door. "I can help with your packing, shit, I can get you packed. Why don't you grab your essentials and go with them? I will see the rest of your stuff comes to you. Okay?"

"Bruce, I don't want to impose on you."

"You won't be. It would make me feel better knowing you are somewhere safe. Make sure the place has a lot of room. We are going to need to have you practice some symbols. I've been making plans, too."

"You sure?"

"Yes. Get your stuff and go." He pulled out a cell phone. "Here take this. It's a pre-pay, and I have my new number in it already. Call me when they have you settled. Just push the one."

Stephanie was going to argue, but realized she was just being contrary. "Okay. Don't bother with the quad cores or the monitors. I'm buying new ones. I do want all the drives and the backups." Her mind was pinging from subject to subject, like the metal ball in a pinball machine, smacking from subject to subject, waiting for the flippers to add a new vector.

She shuffled into her room to stuff flannel shirts in a bag; she packed other items, basically all her clothes since she couldn't decide, but she wanted to make sure Bruce saw the flannel. He hated flannel. She dropped the bags in the living room and started packing her gun stuff; shotgun, rifle, and her one remaining pistol. The police still had her others.

As Bruce was helping her squeeze back into her dragon scales, since she couldn't do it on her own, she asked, "Do you still have all the raw data from the crime scene in your car?"

"Yes."

"Bring it, too. I want to finish the analysis on it."

"Tom," she called out a moment later. "I'm packed. Let's take the Suburban."

She hugged Bruce as the guards hauled away her bags. "I'll call later and let you know where to come. I'll have a room for you as well."

"Good idea. By now they have figured I'm a target as well, they being the gangs. I'll pack some of my stuff and follow as well. Now go." Bruce shooed her toward the door.

She went and just let the guards do what they wanted without her adding her two cents.

Chapter 15

"Is this a good idea?" asked medically suspended, former Officer Paulli.

"Probably not." Joe had gotten fed up with the hospital, so he and Paulli had left. No release paperwork, they just walked out during the early morning shift change when everyone was distracted.

Joe's wounds had healed completely in twelve hours, another medical miracle for Dr. Blackraven. Then his blood work came back and that was when the long confused faces came to repeat tests, no answers, just more tests. He had been moved to the same quarantine care area as Paulli. The same things had happened to Paulli, and then Paulli was suspended while the police force struggled with the implications of his test results.

"Do you even know where you're going?"

"Yes," Joe rumbled, while Paulli gave him a look. "Sort of. I got directions from Bruce, Steph's research partner. Her hiding place is out here on Welch road, on acreage."

"I don't think we're even in a town anymore." He looked around through the misty almost rain. "I think this is unincorporated Snohomish County. We left King County about ten minutes ago."

Joe couldn't tell him the direction felt right. No one feels direction, but he knew Stephanie was this way. "Look, Lost Lake Road goes this way. Then it turns into Welch Road. We follow that for two miles, and it's on the right."

"There's a river out here someplace."

Joe glanced at him. "When we hit the river, I'll turn around."

"Don't you have a GPS?"

"Just sit there and shut up."

"Rookie," Paulli muttered under his breath. Paulli had been Joe's partner when Joe was a fresh caught policeman. Anthony Paulli had shown him the ropes for four years and never let him forget it. Paulli had recognized Joe was smart and capable, because he started pushing Joe to the detective path right away and telling him about it. That was when he wasn't calling Joe an idiot for doing rookie things. Joe owed him.

They continued on in silence, watching the forest go by. The vine maples and alder trees grew in and around the cedar and pine trees. Blackberry bushes were growing up through the lower branches of the leafy trees. They formed a wall of greenery some twelve feet tall in places. It was almost impossible to get rid of the blackberries once they had gotten a firm hold on an area. The blackberry walls were broken by driveways and five-acre lots along Welch Road. Most of the houses were set back into the forest out of sight behind the blackberry walls.

"Why are you slowing down?"

"We're getting close."

"How and the hell can you tell?" Paulli was looking back and forth along the road.

"There," Joe pointed at a break in the blackberry walls that had a strip of flannel cloth stuck into the blackberries on one side. "Bruce said he would mark the driveway for me." Joe glanced over at Paulli's disbelieving look. "He hates flannel shirts, and Steph wears them all the time. So, any excuse to do away with flannel ..."

Paulli just shook his head as they turned into the driveway. It turned abruptly right and then, after two truck lengths, turned left, effectively hiding the gates from the road. Joe pulled to a stop in front of the fancy closed wrought iron gates. "A gate was not mentioned."

"Don't move too fast. I think there's a guy off to the right with a rifle pointed in our general direction." Paulli kept his hands low as he got his pistol out.

Joe rolled down his window and stuck his head out slowly. "Party of two to see Doctor Blackraven." He rumbled it loud enough to be heard at the gate, but not too loud in case they had unwanted and unseen observers. Steph was hiding after all.

There was a long pause and then a digi-cam-covered guy stepped out of the blackberries on the driver's side. "Who are you?"

"Joe Bremer and Tony Paulli, ah, she would know him as Officer Paulli," Joe supplied.

"Wait one," The guard said before he started speaking low to himself.

"She's got some pretty good security here," Paulli observed.

"Yeah, go figure." Joe was a little confused by this. He was wondering what she had gotten herself into. What he had pushed her into.

The gate started to open. "Go up to the house, and you'll be met. Don't leave the driveway," the gate guard ordered.

Joe waited until the gate was open and drove through. His 4 x 4 barely fit. It was a black, three-quarter ton, diesel Ram 2500, jacked up with skid plates on the bottom from the days when he worked his way through college as a lumberjack. Given his escape from the hospital, he didn't want to drive the police SUV. It was rigged with a locator GPS, as part of the digital policeman program, and he wasn't sure he wanted the department to know the location of Stephanie's new place

"Electric gate, at least three cameras. Those were automatic weapons, not exactly legal," Paulli observed. He glanced at Joe. "I gather you didn't know about any of this?"

"No. Last time I saw her, she was living in a two-bedroom apartment in Redmond. And that was just two days ago." Joe drove on.

"Well," Paulli's southern background worked its way into his drawn-out start, "There have been five attempts to kill her in six days. Can't fault the woman for being careful, but where'd the money come from?"

"The uncle that raised her was blown up about four seconds before they blew her truck." Joe was trying hard not to growl in anger. It just tore him up to think of her alone in the world. "She must've inherited money or land or, … I have no idea." Joe could feel Paulli's eyes on him.

"She's alive, Joe, just focus on that."

There was about half a mile of driveway winding through the trees and dense underbrush.

"Get a load of that house," Paulli quietly exclaimed. It looked like it was some kind of old English mansion, grey stone, multi-paned windows, pond in front of the covered entryway. The four-car garage gave it away as not being from the Middle Ages. It even had a tower on one corner with parapets. There was someone on the top of it. The entrance, most would call it the front door, was like a medieval castle gate, dark heavy wood with black iron bands on it.

The house and grounds were looking shaggy around the edges, like no one had cared for it in years. The pond was green and had stuff growing in it and it wasn't decorative stuff. The blackberries were moving into all the green spaces around the front. All of the, what once were, decorative trees had been canopied by blackberries. What the blackberries didn't want was covered in knee-high weeds and grass. The exposed wood on the house looked very weathered.

As Joe pulled his truck up, the doors opened, and an over six-foot tall, heavily muscled, dark clad, professional stepped out. Paulli would've called him a "hard man" had they run into him on the streets. Meaning he was a killer or a street fighter or both; it changed based on how Paulli was feeling at the moment. The hard-man's face was square-ish, weathered, and scarred. Joe and Tony both got out of the truck and strolled over to the newcomer.

"I'm Stoneman, the lead of Doctor Blackraven's security detachment." He didn't sound too happy to see them. "Damn, you're big, you must be Detective Bremer?" He did not offer his hand.

Joe nodded to his statement.

"Who are you?" Stoneman asked of Paulli.

"Why do I care if you know me?" Paulli snapped back.

Stoneman's eyes turned flinty, deadly. "I'm the guy who's trying to keep Doctor Blackraven alive. Are you two going to make that harder or easier?"

Joe watched them square off like two big dogs looking each other up and down. "Well," Paulli's voice developed a southern draw, "The way I see it, Bremer and I already took a bullet for her. So, we've passed the first test, that being keeping her alive. What have you done?"

Stoneman squinted at them for a moment. "Explain?"

"Bremer, here, took the blast of her truck blowing up, using his body to shield hers." Joe started to say something, but Paulli wasn't having any of it. "I took her out of the path of a werewolf and let it have me."

Stoneman's stance changed slightly. "You had your throat ripped out three nights ago, and she healed you with magic? You must be Bellevue Police Officer Paulli."

"Yep. Ex-policeman, they medically retired me yesterday, well almost. The bureaucrats haven't figured a PC way to spin it, but they will." Paulli didn't sound happy.

"Are you a werewolf now?"

"I'll tell you after the next full moon."

Stoneman looked them both over and then shook his head. "You two are going to make my job harder." He adopted a stoic resolve and turned toward the house. "This way. Don't reach for your guns, bad things would happen. She's in the workshop out back blowing shit up. Maybe you could convince her that not blowing shit up would make it easier to hide her location?" He didn't really have his heart in the request.

Joe rumbled with a laugh. "She must be working on her symbols. No way in hell she's going to stop doing that. It also explains the acreage."

The inside of the house was a reflection of the outside. Very English; dark woods, old seeming lighting fixtures, a grand entryway with stairs sweeping to the left and right and in need of some tender loving care. He expected to see a butler step out to ask for his coat.

The house was huge, but he didn't really pay attention. He wanted to see Steph.

They swept out of a big living room with a fireplace the size of his truck, onto a stone paved terraced patio that lead down to what once had been a rolling lawn. Now it was just an overgrown field with weeds. There was a barn off to the right, complete with fences and sheds. To the left was a collection of other buildings, and since Stoneman was leading them that way, Joe figured it was the workshop. The sudden sound of pops, like firecrackers going off, seemed to support his guess.

Stoneman frowned as he opened the door and stepped through. They walked into an open bay with a high ceiling. The equipment doors on the other side were wide open, leading out into a kind of covered work area, like a giant carport for semi-trucks, tables were set up to one side and in the middle, which then lead out into a field. Out in the field, behind the building, was a smoking drum of some kind. All Joe really saw was Stephanie.

She was wearing blue jeans and a flannel shirt hanging loose, black hair in a ponytail down her back, holding a broomstick blackened on both ends, like it was a sword. From behind her, Joe could just see the hint of the graceful curve of her neck and cheek.

"There's your NAG," Stoneman announced.

Joe caught himself before he actually grabbed Stoneman, but it was close. The look on Stoneman's face was pure surprise. Joe amazed himself, he didn't use to have a temper, but he was so pissed he was seeing red and wanted to break the man in half. "I don't like that expression," Joe rumbled out when he stopped growling.

"Noted," Stoneman said while holstering his sidearm.

"He has that effect on me as well, Joe." Stephanie was walking toward them. "And for future reference, Mister Stoneman, you may call me his girlfriend. Now go away." Joe felt his anger evaporate and a new warmth in his middle.

"Before you go away, would you tell your man up there to stop pointing a rifle at Detective Bremer. Are they here to guard you too?" Paulli quipped.

Stoneman's jaw tightened as he gave Paulli a dirty look, but answered Stephanie, "Yes, ma'am. Have you found a replacement for me yet?" His hands also made a few abrupt gestures, apparently calling off the guards, since they all turned away.

"No, your organization hasn't seen fit to get back to me." She smiled prettily at him. "Good thing I'm not asking for anything important."

"Hey Steph," Joe rumbled out. "You're looking good."

She smiled for Joe as she walked toward him, setting down the stick as she went by one of the tables.

"Where's Tom?" Stoneman asked.

"I sent him off for more equipment," Stephanie said without taking her attention off Joe. "You said he wasn't a very good bodyguard, so I've found another use for him." Stoneman turned and left, muttering to himself.

"Yo, big man," Bruce called out. He was by one of the tables typing on a computer. "They get your shapely ass sewn back on?"

"Yeah," was all Joe could manage as an answer.

"Bruce, behave," Stephanie admonished. "Who's this you've brought, oh, ... Officer Paulli, good to see you." Stephanie offered her hand to him to shake. "Thanks for knocking me out of the way." She was peering at his neck.

Paulli smiled and tilted his head up and pulled his shirt and coat down to expose his neck. "Tony, to people who save my life. It healed up with only a little scarring." He bent at the waist as he brought her hand up to kiss it. "Thank you for saving my worthless hide."

Joe watched Stephanie blush as he throttled the urge to punch Paulli in the face. "He may be a werewolf," Joe muttered as a way to get even.

Stephanie froze for just a moment and then seemed to lean in to study Paulli's face. "Are you sure? What kinds of symptoms are you having? Do you feel any different?"

Paulli gave her hand a little pat as he released it. "No and none and no. Them damn doctors, they seem to think that's the case. Stupid blood work."

"I know someone that has been studying the phenomena for a year or so. Do you want me to connect you to her?" Stephanie seemed to be fascinated. "Do you see better? Can you smell more things?"

Joe noticed how pretty she got when she studied something. She squinted her eyes just a little bit.

Paulli snorted, "I don't know." He stepped back from her intense scrutiny, rubbing the back of his neck. "I haven't really thought about it."

Joe noticed Stephanie's eyes shifting from side to side for a moment as she looked down. "Ah, shit," she exclaimed suddenly. "They're going to fire you. The police don't know what to do with infected personnel, so they get rid of them in case you pose a threat to the public. Did they already tell you?" She looked back up at him.

Paulli looked shocked for a moment, then rubbed at his eyes, "Damn Joe, you're right; she is smart." He pulled his hand down so he could meet her eyes. "Yes, ma'am, they told me yesterday that I would be medically suspended. But you're right; they're just tryin' to find the PC way to get rid of me."

"You can work for me!" Stephanie announced.

Paulli was shocked again. "What! No, no, I just came by to thank you for saving my life. I'm not looking for charity."

Stephanie snorted in a very unladylike way. "Charity my ass, I'll work you like a dog." Bruce burst out laughing. She rounded on him. "What the hell is so funny? This man just lost his job."

Bruce was walking over to the group. "Don't you get it? You said 'work him like a dog' and he's going to be a werewolf." Bruce chuckled again.

"But I didn't mean, … ah," …" Paulli started hee-hawing right along with Bruce. They all started laughing.

"I need a beer," Bruce announced to the group. "Who else?" He pointed at each in turn, getting nods from them all. Then he looked up, "Frank?"

The guard up on the catwalk frowned down on him. "Bruce, damn it, you know I'm working. Stop pointing at me up here, I'm supposed to be invisible."

"Right, sorry." Bruce didn't sound sorry.

"You, Detective Bremer," Stephanie commanded. "Come over here and bend down so I can get at your face."

Joe froze for a moment and then did as she asked.

Stephanie gently cupped her hands around his face. She gave him a kiss on the left cheek, "That's for saving my life by not letting me get in my truck right before it blew up." She kissed him on the right cheek, "That's for taking the blast and saving my life a second time." She got an evil glint in her eye just before she slapped him lightly. "That," her voice became harder, "is for not calling me and telling me you were alive. Instead, sending your sister around to spy on me."

Joe reared up. "That's not …"

Stephanie cut him off with a sly look. "I'm not done. Bring your face back down here."

He hesitated, not understanding what was going on. The kissing was nice, though.

"Don't make me climb you!" Stephanie warned. Joe bent back down. She gently cupped his face, "This is for not dying." Tears were in her eyes as she kissed him full on the mouth.

Joe was in heaven. He was afraid to do anything to startle her. It might make her stop. Finally, she pulled away a little bit. "Yes, by the way, you may court me," she added with a little peck on his nose.

Joe couldn't help himself; he swept her up in a hug. He surprised her because she gasped.

"Joe," Bruce yelled. "What the hell are you doing?"

"She gave me permission to court her."

"Crunkle shot her in the chest. It's all bruised up."

Joe was shocked. That hadn't been a gasp of surprise; he was crushing her. He had hurt her. He almost dropped her.

Paulli was laughing so hard beer was coming out his nose.

"It's okay, Joe," Stephanie finally breathed out. "I'm okay. But could you set me down?"

Joe very gently set her back on her feet. Her face was white, and she clutched at her chest.

"If you want," Bruce said as he handed Joe his beer, "you could ask to see her bruise. It's mostly around her breasts."

That started Paulli laughing again.

"I'm sorry, Steph, I forgot about you being shot." Joe felt really bad.

"It's okay, Joe. Mister Paulli, would you cut it out? Joe didn't know about my chest."

Paulli was laughing harder. Bruce was trying hard not to laugh, "I don't know about that, Steph. He can't seem to take his eyes off them most of the time." That started both of them laughing even harder. Joe noticed Stephanie's mouth twisted as she tried not to laugh with them.

Joe lifted his beer to Stephanie, "Girlfriend."

She momentarily glanced down shyly and then smiled an impish smile while hoisting her beer right back at him, "Boyfriend." They clinked their bottles and sipped.

They drank some more, and then Stephanie nodded toward one of the rooms off to the side. "Let me show you something."

That started Bruce and Paulli laughing again and asking if they could see, too.

Stephanie rounded on them. "When you two boys are done laughing about body parts, join us in the boardroom." She turned and took Joe's arm.

Joe rather liked her on his arm. He didn't care where they were going.

Stephanie led him into a room where the walls were lined with flat-white painted plywood. There were note cards on it, lots of cards put on with thumbtacks.

"I've been trying to figure out why someone would want to kill me," Stephanie stated without preamble. "I've captured all the facts, primary assumptions, secondary assumptions, as well as preliminary conclusions based on the assumptions. It's not perfect, but it's the best I've come up with. Some of the conclusions are pretty interesting." She had been walking around the room pointing at things as she talked. "This is more your kind of problem solving than mine." She rounded on him and looked him in the eyes. "I don't want to share this with the police because some of it is very personal. But I would like your opinion, if you can keep it to yourself."

Joe cleared his throat. "That won't be a problem. I've been medically suspended like Tony." Stephanie's eyes widened then narrowed. "They think I'm a were as well." He made little quotation gestures as he said 'were.'

"What kind? When would've you been infected?" She was getting pissed. "That's stupid!"

Joe was trying to figure out how to tell her it might run in his family, when Bruce brought Paulli into the room. "It's our boardroom. We're trying to figure out why they're trying to kill Steph."

"There are three crime trails here," Joe blurted out. They all turned to stare at him. He carefully moved around Stephanie to the stack of blank note cards. He grabbed some and a pen. "We have attempts on Stephanie's life." He jotted it down and put in on a blank space. "We have the gangs and their robberies." He jotted another note and posted it. "We have the serial murders, of which Andy Stone was only the most recent."

"The what?" Stephanie exclaimed.

"Serial …" Bruce's voice trailed off in shock.

"Joe," Paulli warned, "That could …"

"What?" Joe cut him off. "Get me fired? They've already asked for her help. That's what put her in the way of the gangs." He jotted another note, but Bruce posted it. "There have been three of these ritualistic murders, like Andy's, in Bellevue. That was why Sergeant Grayson wanted your help. We didn't have any clues." He jotted names and handed the notes to Bruce.

Bruce read them as he posted them, "Oh no! These are all professors, Steph. You know these women. Knew these women," he corrected himself sadly.

Stephanie stepped over to read the cards and then started shuffling around the room, duplicating note cards, using a different color, and posting the new ones in different orders. The three men had been driven into corners to stay out of her way. Bruce would dart in to add something and then step back. After a while of muttering, making circles on papers, adjusting more cards, Stephanie stepped back, twirling her hair and biting at the ends of it.

Joe thought she was extra cute when she did that. He hadn't seen it before.

"Joe," she finally said. "You should stay here. Move in with me."

Joe was shocked. "Move in with you?" he repeated. "Steph, we just ..." He didn't know how to go on.

Paulli smiled and started to say something smart, but Bruce made a very serious gesture that stopped him. "Why is that Steph?" Bruce asked, trying to sound casual.

"I think there are three points of congruity and three, maybe four points of weakness." She nodded to herself and then stepped up to the board. "The first point of congruity, as we both identified, is symbology." She pointed at the column of cards to emphasize her point. "The second congruity is my Uncle Raymond and everything associated with him." She motioned up and down another column. "Final congruity is Bosh-Gates University." She studied the cards. "Weakness, we have those close to me: Bruce, Rosemary, and now, my boyfriend." She smiled as she said it. "Joe. Then Abby, his sister, as being a possible. They could've seen her enter my apartment and leave somewhat happier." She stepped back to look at the men. "Joe can be safe here, just like you are, Bruce," she finished, answering Bruce's question.

Joe couldn't help it; he was smiling at her. She had asked him to move in with her. His mother was going to have a cow. He had a girlfriend, and he was going to live with her.

"What?" she said to him, with a smile playing on her lips.

Joe couldn't answer; he just looked at his shoes. She just had that effect on him.

"Tony," Stephanie stated after a moment of confusion over Joe. "We may have more serial murders."

It brought Joe's head up. He had only been told about the three. "What others?" slipped out.

Paulli looked shocked. "Well, I didn't do it."

That seemed to stymie Stephanie for a moment. "Nooo," she finally said slowly. "You asked about why I would offer you a job earlier. It's because of your police experience. My lawyers have received several requests for my services from other police departments in the area. I didn't understand before now. I thought it was gang stuff, but serial murders with a symbolic signature; that would definitely be me. I can't afford to go wandering about, so I would need an agent. That would be you. You could go gather facts and data and bring them here to us for analysis." Joe could tell she was thinking hard.

Paulli smiled and shook his head. "I don't need a job. I got money, at least enough for now. How about I just help you? You're trying to solve crimes here, and I'm all over that." He crossed his arms over his chest. "Anyway, it just fun watching Joe and you not talk to each other." Joe gave him a dirty look, which just made Paulli chuckle.

Stephanie obviously didn't get the joke. "Of course we talk. When we're near each other, … Anyway." She waved her hands as if to clear the air. "I'm sure there are indications at the other crime scenes of the use of symbols. We would need to provide you with …" Her voice trailed off. Once again, she seemed to be deep in thought.

Joe leaned over closer to Bruce. "Are there little lights dancing in her eyes?"

Bruce nodded without taking her eyes off her.

"When did that start?" Joe was a little concerned.

"Recently," Bruce whispered.

"How long was she doing symbols today?"

Bruce turned to look at Joe, "How do you know we were …"

Joe gave him a wry smile. "Stoneman was bitching about her blowing stuff up. I figured you guys were running through Andy's spell book seeing what correlated."

"You two done?" Stephanie asked with hands on hips.

"No," Bruce said imitating her stance. "What were you thinking about right then when you were talking to Tony?"

"Why?"

"Joe noticed your eyes lighting up again."

"I was thinking about the symbols we found at Andy's death site and how Tony would collect the same kind of data without the complicated tools. Perhaps, there are symbols he could use by proxy." Stephanie was thinking again.

"What symbols?" Joe asked.

She smiled for him. "Come see." She led them out of the boardroom and down to the larger of the two remaining rooms. There was computer equipment lining one wall, impressive computer equipment, and a box hanging from the middle of the ceiling at the other end with cables running to it. "We don't have it all yet, but we will." She pressed a few keys on one of the keyboards, and the box projected a red image on to the floor.

The image was of a circle with three rings of symbols arrayed around a center. In the center of the circle was a likeness of a man spread-eagle with his head pointed to the south, according to the compass rose. There were several symbols specifically placed around the man.

"This is a likeness. It won't work like this. The floor is too porous, and the total layout isn't finished yet." Stephanie had picked up a broom handle to point with and proceeded to lecture. "I expect this to be more complicated than the Solomon Circle you saw earlier this week, Joe. But it comes from the same era. The outer ring of symbols is for containment, almost exactly like the Solomon Circle. The next two I am unsure of, but I will understand in time. The computer has to finish the data integration." She handed the broom handle to Bruce, like passing the talking stick at a town meeting.

"We have deduced how it was drawn," he picked up the tale. "As a matter-of-fact, this is how it was laid down for poor Andy. They used a laser projector just like this one and painted the floor with photosensitive paint with a fast curing time. They probably prepped the floor, set up the laser projector, and then waited for the victim." Bruce pointed at the head and each of the tips of the extremities. "As you can see, the distance is very precise from the innermost circle, so they had to have had the victim's height before inscribing the image. Then adding the height, they could instantly lay the device." He tapped the stick on the floor twice. "Conjecture at this point, but with another sample, we could compare." He handed the stick back to Stephanie.

"I've sent Tom out to get a higher quality video projector and a twelve by twelve screen to shine the image on. Since we don't intend to bolt someone down in the middle of it, we'll project it perpendicular to the floor; it will be easier to study that way." She set the stick near the door. "Our serial killer is very proficient with symbols, a master symbologist. So, based on that, we can make some assumptions about the power of the final construction." She swept her eyes around her audience as she would in any lecture to keep the student's attention. "It's really powerful, and it used the life force of the person in the middle of it to power it." Picking the stick up, she circled a collection of symbols. "These, I think. I will know for certain when the computer gets done, and I can study it all." She turned back to look Joe in the eye as she added, "He has also studied near Bruce and me. What he did is an almost exact duplicate of our methods. We didn't do it, but somebody from Bosh-Gates did; someone who has seen our research."

"So, who would have had access?" Joe wondered out loud.

Stephanie started playing with her hair, obviously in thought.

"The only place I know it was recorded in detail was in a white paper Steph published about ten months ago," Bruce supplied. "She might have mentioned it in her thesis."

"No, it wasn't in my thesis. There were two papers: one on symbol site surveys and the other was a detailed description of the setup and method. That was the one ten months ago."

A phone rang, and everyone started digging them out. It was Stephanie's. "Hello." She listened for a moment and then looked up at the group. "This will take a minute. I'll be back." With that, she walked out of the room.

Chapter 16

Stepping into the impromptu electronics lab next door, she closed the door behind her. "Hi, Mr. Stubens." She greeted her lawyer cheerfully, not really liking him, but determined to get along. She didn't even know him that well. It hadn't even been a full day yet.

"Good morning, Dr. Blackraven." He didn't sound like he was having a good morning.

"Mr. Stubens, how about you call me Steph or Stephanie, and I'll call you Otto. If nothing else, it will speed up our greetings."

He laughed on the other end of the phone, a real laugh, too. She liked him a little better for that. "Very well, Steph. I have several items for you. Are you somewhere you can speak freely?"

Glancing around, she said, "About as good as it gets here, shoot."

"We have staff coming out to the house. A butler named Lawrence Peabody, cook, Maggie Turns, and maid, Agnes McDoogle. They are all trained, experienced in the primary jobs as well as being security specialists. The women can go with you where the men can't or shouldn't."

"I don't need more bodyguards. What the hell am I going to do with them when I move back to my apartment?" Steph threw her free hand up, even though Otto couldn't see it.

"Hmmm, two things, one; your apartment was firebombed last night. You aren't going back there. Two, this isn't going to be over quick. It may be a year or more before we can get this figured out. And yes, all of your possessions were moved out before they struck. No one was hurt, but your landlord evicted you."

"Well, shit!"

"Precisely!" He was back to being curt and sounding pissed. "That brings up another item. Stoneman has asked me to ask you to, quote, stop blowing shit up, unquote. It makes noise and will attract attention."

"He can piss off. I have work to do, and it's going to require I practice loud, noisy stuff. I will explain it to him again. By the way, where are we on getting me another security group?"

"We are no further then yesterday when you brought it up. It's not easy to find reliable, professional security personnel, especially the caliber needed in this situation. I could probably contact some of your uncle's old associates."

"No, that won't work. I . . ." Uncle Raymond's letter had been very specific about some things and people. "Keep working on it the other way."

"Very well, next topic. The phone company is going to install DSL for you right now, should be this afternoon. We . . ."

"Is that dual line DSL?"

"Yes. As I was saying, we are paying an expedite fee, so it should happen quickly. It'll be followed up with the gigabyte trunk you wanted, but they'll have to run the fiber just for you."

"Ouch. Ah … isn't this just a temporary location?"

"No, you bought it, well, the corporation bought it, because we all expect you to blow it up or burn it down." He sounded serious.

"Pish posh," she said just to get his goat. For some reason guys, especially intense professional guys, didn't like the expression. "Can I afford it?"

"Easily."

"Then I want it in my name. If I'm going to blow it up, then I want to bear the cost." She glanced at her phone again. "We get real good cell service here. Can I get 4G wireless or a higher speed signal that way?"

"There is a cell tower very close to the property, which has other advantages. So, you should be able to support all the wireless you want. But in this case, they can bring the fiber over from there instead of the road, which will defray some of the costs. I have already given them the go-ahead. On a similar front, we have more paperwork for your signature. One of us will be by this afternoon to talk you through it."

"Oh, hey speaking of money, I loaned that black credit card you gave me to Tom so he could get some more equipment."

There was a long pause. "Perhaps, I should get you a couple of lesser cards you can loan out. That one is a titanium card."

"Yeah, I know, but I needed a lot of stuff. Titanium is like over a 100K limit right?"

"Yes, the limit is very high."

"How high? Maybe I want to buy my own island."

"You do remember that this law firm is the executer of your inheritance." His statement had a little threat in it.

Stephanie took a deep breath and let it out. She didn't like threats or anyone controlling her money. "Yeah, I do remember you TELLING me, but I haven't seen the paper yet. So, maybe you should bring that today as well. Assuming no one kills me."

"It was not my intention to threaten you, your freedom, your inheritance, or to make you angry. If I did, then I apologize. Your uncle appointed us as executors and provided you with a healthy trust fund. I just want to make sure you get to enjoy it."

Stephanie counted to ten. "Look, I don't like someone controlling my money or even pretending to. I have had my life turned upside down …" She had to stop and take deep breaths. It hit her again, Uncle Raymond's death, people trying to kill her, and how alone she was in the world. Tears started leaking.

There was a gentle knock at the door. "Steph, are you okay?" Joe asked quietly. "Can I come in?"

Maybe she wasn't so alone. She gave a short prayer out loud, but not loud enough for Joe to hear or the phone. "Oh God, please let Joe be for real and give me the patience to not drive him away." Serenity and security seemed to settle over her. And off in the distance, she heard a bird call that almost sounded like a word.

"Doctor Blackraven?" Otto was still on the phone.

"I'm here. Hold on a moment." She covered the phone again, wiped her face. "Joe, I'm fine. Give me a couple more minutes."

"You don't seem fine to me," she heard him rumble.

How did he know? “Later,” she said with a hand motion no one could see, pulling the phone back up. “Hi. I’m back with you, what’s next?”

“The Snohomish County and King County sheriff’s departments, Lynnwood police, and Bothell police have again requested your assistance.”

“I have an ex-policeman I’m going to send to them to collect data, so I can analyze it here. Should I call them?”

“That won’t work.” He paused again and she could hear him harrumphing to himself. “As much as I hate to say it, you would be required to go in person. It will put you at personal risk, so I advise against going.” He finished like he was expecting something.

“Of course I’ll help them.”

“As I thought. Perhaps later this afternoon?” Otto really didn’t sound happy.

“You knew I would go.”

“Like a bee to honey. I will tell the various departments that you will help. Texting the respective numbers to your phone now. Well, if there is anything else you need, let me know.”

“Law suit against the Bellevue police department, first for shooting me and then for firing, well, medically retiring, Officer Anthony Paulli and Detective Joe Bremer for possibly being were . . . creatures. The department is trying to figure out a PC way of making it right. Hurt them. Make them squeal like pigs.”

“Are the two policemen at your current location?”

“Yes, they’re staying here and helping with my investigation.”

There was another pause on the phone then, “Investigation? What investigation?”

“My investigation into why someone or ones are trying to kill me. I’m not leaving it up to the police.” She ended the last on a raising note.

“Ah … very well … is there anything this firm can do to help?”

“You’re doing it.”

“Very well, we will take statements from the gentlemen this afternoon as well as gaining their agreement to have us represent them. Is there anything else?” He paused, giving her a chance to speak. When she didn’t, he said, “Good day. We’ll be in touch.” He hung up.

"Shit," Stephanie exclaimed. "I have to tell Stoneman we're taking a drive." After a moment, she smiled to herself. For some reason she liked needling him.

She opened the door to find Joe leaning against the doorjamb like a giant James Dean. "Hi," he rumbled out.

"Did you want to talk to me?" she asked.

He reached out really slowly and gently brushed a tear streak on her face. "You're not alone, you've got me."

She stifled a gasp, "How did …"

"I don't know. I just felt like you needed me." He gently pulled her into a hug. He was big, but soft and smelled like Old Spice. She liked it.

"Hey," she heard Bruce start in his teasing tone. "You two should …" She felt more than saw Joe's head turn. Apparently Bruce saw something as well, as he finished in a different tone, "Take a few minutes to talk."

She wiggled to pull away from Joe and then took his hand to tug him into the room. Joe closed the door. "There's only one chair." She gestured at it and then was shy all of a sudden.

"That's okay, I can stand."

"No, I want you to sit down." She smiled at him. "Then I can sit in your lap."

Joe froze for a moment. With a funny smile playing on his lips, he pulled the wooden office chair out and slowly sat down.

Steph promptly walked over and crawled into his lap, her right, unhurt side towards him. He wrapped one arm around her. Resting her head on his shoulder, she asked, "What did you mean by me not feeling fine to you?"

"I knew you were sad all of sudden, and I wanted to help you."

"Really, how did you know that?"

"I don't know." He nuzzled the top of her head. "You smell good."

Steph giggled, she hated when she did that. "I was just thinking the same thing about you." She pulled away so she could look at his face. "I don't know how this is supposed to work. Every relationship I've ever been in ended badly."

Joe smiled and leaned in to kiss her, but paused a few inches away. He had brown eyes rimed with gold. She hadn't noticed that before.

She smiled. "Are you doing the 90 percent thing from the movie Hitch?" The movie had been about a dating consultant for guys, teaching them how to get out of their own way with women.

He shyly smiled back at her, "Yeah."

"Do it again." He leaned in again and paused. This time she kissed him. It was nice.

When they separated, he cleared his throat, "I'm not good at this dating thing, either. You're my first real girlfriend. According to my sisters, we're supposed to do nice things and help each other."

"That seems like a good start. You're not going to try and keep me from doing my job, are you? I'm not a Barbie kind of girl; you can't put me on a pedestal. I have things to uncover and discover." She leaned in 90 percent of the way and paused. He kissed her.

"Well," he started after they separated again. "I'll try not to, but I get these funny feeling around you. I get really angry when I think of you being hurt, sad counts, too. I didn't used to be like that. I didn't have a temper at all. I just can't help myself when it comes to you. So, I must like you."

"You're not going to hurt me, are you?" She batted her eyes at him and leaned in again.

"Never!" She found out he rumbled really loudly when she had her ear on his chest.

She'd never felt this way before. "You make me feel safe. Secure, warm inside." She wiggled into his arms a little more.

"Hey, Steph," Bruce called out from the other room. "Tom's back with all the stuff. He got us lunch, too."

"We should go out," she whispered to Joe. "They may wonder what we're doing." She didn't want to get up.

"They probably think you're wiring me up to something," Joe commented while looking around.

Steph laughed out loud. "I don't think so. Let's go." She started to slide off, but Joe hugged her again and then gently set her on her feet.

"Before we rush out there, I should tell you I got a message from Rosemary," Joe commented.

Steph turned back to him. "Why didn't you tell me?"

Joe's eyes shifted like he was trying to decide something. "Are you mad at me?"

That set Stephanie back as she realized she was mad at him. But how did he know? "Ah ... yeah ... but not really. How did you know?"

"I just ... knew." He settled back into the chair. "I don't think this is normal in a new relationship. I mean, you hear how a couple starts anticipating their partner, but I think it takes a little longer than a week."

Stephanie smiled, "It's been a very stressful week. I know it's aged me."

"You didn't cast a spell on me or anything, did you?"

Stephanie started to give him a hot answer about it being science not magic, but then paused as a thought struck her. "I might have." She remembered her attempt at the healing symbol and the strange siren at the end when she got shot. "Or something might have." She turned away and buried her face in her hands. She felt terrible, lost, the serenity and warmth shattered. "This isn't real. You have a symbol on you, making you like me."

His hands gently settled on her, pulling her back against him. "It's real. I liked you before your symbol stuff. I fell for you in the classroom, when you trapped yourself in the circle." He gently turned her around and tugged her hands down until she looked at him. "I liked you from the very first. I would use the other L word, but you might run away screaming." She could tell he was studying her face. "I was referring to how I can feel your emotions, not how much I like you."

She smiled at that and the feeling of hopelessness eased away. She noticed the gold in his eyes was more pronounced. "I like you, too."

"Are you okay?"

"No, not really. I'm grieving, which I'm finding out is a lot like PMS. I get wild mood swings, random intense emotions, and every once in while, it just floors me that he's dead, and I have a mini-melt down crying."

Joe's face was frozen in an amazed state. "Ahhh ..." was all he really got out.

"Is that too much information?" She was feeling kind of stupid for just dumping what she was really thinking. "Now you know why guys don't hang around me much. I just blurt out the truth."

Joe's face slipped into a sloppy smile. "It's fine. I've just never had a woman say that stuff to me. My sister used to, but, well, not since I moved out."

"Well, I hope you get used to it." She patted him on the chest. "I tend to say what I'm thinking all the time. By the way, what's Rosemary's message?"

"She wants to meet with you. She says she has information on some activity around Bosh-Gates and the serial killer." Joe was all detective again.

"Where and when?"

"Her instructions are to text her phone that you're on your way, but don't say the time or where. She'll meet us at the place you two liked on Vashon Island."

"Vashon Island." Stephanie was puzzled. She and Rosemary hadn't gone to Vashon . . . Then it hit her. She knew where. "It'll have to be tomorrow. We have too much going on today."

"What've we got today?" His brows furrowed together.

"Well," she smiled, "you have to go get your stuff and bring it back here. Then we have to go visit a couple of police stations in a random order. Then my lawyers are coming by to explain and have me sign things. They also want to talk to you and Tony."

"Oh," he said while standing. "We are busy." He gestured for her to precede him out the door.

When she walked out, the central area was all a bustle of activity. Tom had backed a panel truck up to the smaller bay doors. Bruce was picking through boxes that Tony was unloading. The truck was loaded with all sorts of boxes. Tom was standing over at a table looking at Stephanie's notes on the symbols.

She shooed him away. "We'll do symbols later. Help with the unpacking."

"You're going to let me try some of those, right?" He grinned while walking back over to the truck.

"Maybe. If you can show me you can remember and form without looking at notes."

"God, what is it with you and tests!" he exclaimed while climbing into the back of the truck.

"Safety first, I don't want you to blow your hand off like I did." She wiggled her fingers at him. "Hey," she called out to Tony. "Careful with the electronics. Just bring it all over here."

"I'll get it," Joe stepped in. "Just point at the ones you want first."

They all pitched in. Stephanie took the electronics. Bruce was moving the machines and machine tools into the other end of the building. Tom helped Bruce. Joe and Tony played crane. They both were really strong. Stephanie quickly lost track of what everyone else was doing as she unpacked, setup, and then initialized a hard drive server stack. The graphics and associated symbols took up lots of hard drive space. The phone people showed up and connected the DSL lines. It worked right the first time. Now they could connect to the university, even if it was slow communications. Slow was better than nothing. The monster desktops were initializing and downloading updates from the Internet. It would take them a few more hours before they were fully up and running. Then they could run all the machines as a distributed computational network and really start crunching numbers.

She finally caught up to Bruce and Tom at the lunch table. She was missing someone. "Where did Joe go?"

Bruce swallowed. "He and Tony went to get their stuff." Glancing at his watch around the chicken thigh he held, he added, "They should be back any time now. You want Joe's stuff in your room?"

Stephanie blushed and looked away for a moment. "No, I think we need some more time to get used to each other. Let's put him across the hall from me."

Bruce just nodded while taking another bite. "This place is pretty cool, Steph. I have to ask, are you really, really rich now?"

The loss of her uncle hit her again, and she looked away. "Yeah," her voice was thick as she answered. "He left me everything. I didn't realize how rich he was. He never showed it."

She felt Bruce's hand on her shoulder. "It's okay, Steph. You aren't alone." He shook her a little. "Now we can buy cool shit we don't need."

She chuckled and snagged a chicken breast. "Where did you put the projector and the big screen?"

"The barn," Tom chimed in. "It was the only space big enough. We ran a fiber line to it and installed two more of the big desktops. They're initializing now."

They caught up on all the equipment placements and capabilities around bites. Stephanie finished first and walked back over to her symbol notes while nursing a Mountain Dew. Joe was confusing her and her uncle's loss kept unsettling her; she needed a distraction.

"Time for work," she decided and after a moment, she picked up her notebook and wandered out to the back of the workshop. It was where they had the range for symbols. Glancing up, she noticed an array of cheap video cameras. She looked closer; maybe they weren't so cheap.

"Hey Bruce," she called. "What's with the video?" She was pointing at the cameras.

"Well," he started from right behind her. "We talked about how the symbols were almost too fast for us to discern the effect, so I thought we would use high-speed video and analyze the results from it after the fact. You know, slow it down so we could see it."

"Good idea. Fire it up! I want to try a few more before people show up." She picked up the broomstick and stepped into the box they had marked on the floor. It was like a shooting range and that was the way they ran it.

Bruce pushed some buttons on the laptop and then stepped out of the covered area looking around. "The line is set," he told her as he came back inside. "The line is clear. Fire at will."

She started up with a couple of dart symbols that make fiery lights fly at the barrel. She made some notes about how it seemed to function. Then progressed to a mystery symbol, but there was no effect she could see. It felt like she was triggering something, but nothing seemed to happen after the glowing symbol disappeared. She did that one three times, made notes about what she could tell, and then moved to a different one. It was frustrating and exciting. She kept working them. The area light symbol was impressive.

A little later she heard, *Push it away from you,* as she gave it the Will, said the Word, and was just giving it the Way. The resulting explosion blew her back on her butt. Luckily, it had been twenty feet away before it detonated. Her skin was burning, and she was having trouble seeing.

Something told her to do the healing symbol. Without thinking about it, she called the healing symbol, laid it over herself, and mumbled the words. She started feeling better right away.

"Steph? Steph?" she heard Joe from a long way away. Then she was lifted from the ground and put on a hard surface. Hands were touching her body: head, neck, shoulders, arms, legs. They were trying to figure if anything was broken.

Stephanie glanced off to the side and saw the shimmering blue image of a woman. Dark hair, strong face, buckskin thigh-length dress, no it was a gown, no, it was ... shifting. The woman looked like she was frustrated and was making a gesture with one hand from Stephanie to herself and back. The other hand was making a duck-quaking movement.

Stephanie's head was pulled over, and Joe bent to look in her eyes. "Steph, can you hear me?" He was gently wiping her face with a wet cloth.

"Of course I can." She looked back over, but the blue lady was gone.

"There is no 'of course,' I've been talking to you for five minutes."

He seemed frustrated, worried, and had golden-yellow eyes. He also had a beard. How had he grown a beard?

"Your eyes have lights dancing in them. We should get you up to the house."

"I'm okay, Joe. Really, I'm fine. I just got knocked on my ass."

"Look at your clothes."

Stephanie looked at her arms. The sleeves were burnt brown, as was her shirt and legs. "Wow, I almost blew myself up ... again."

"Ya think," Bruce said as he walked up. "No almost about it. We got the fires out. Your face is ..."

"If you hadn't suggested I push it away, I could've been seriously hurt."

Bruce and Joe looked at each other. "I didn't say anything, Steph. Did you do that healing symbol on yourself? I thought you were afraid of it."

"You told me to, so I did."

"It ... it wasn't me. Steph, I didn't say anything. I had looked away to talk to Joe as he came in." He looked worried. "Your hair is growing back." He took the cloth away from Joe and brushed it on her brow. "And you have eyebrows again. I agree with Joe, I think we should go up to the house. Maybe talk about this away from the ... ah ... here."

"She okay?" Stoneman asked from the range.

"We got the grass fire out," Tony added.

Stephanie sat up. She was on the table with her notes. The end of the car-port they were using as the range was blackened with char or soot. "Ah ... just how big was the explosion?"

"It rocked this shop building and blew off some shingles. I would say a small satchel charge," Tom told her.

"What in the hell were you doing? You could've killed yourself!" Stoneman yelled at her as he stormed into the building. "They probable heard that explosion in Bothell and Monroe."

"Well ...," Stephanie started.

"Crap, do we need an ambulance?" Stoneman asked as he got a good look at her. "Holy shit! You scorched your clothes, why aren't you burnt? The heat it would've taken to burn your clothes should've seared your skin."

"She did a symbol," Bruce supplied.

Stoneman paused, a little unsure. "We should take you up to the house and get you checked out. I have an ex-navy corpsman on the team."

"I'm fine, now," she added, "Did you guys see a ..." She trailed off as she thought about what it would sound like should she bring up a ghost-like figure after getting blown onto her butt.

"See a what?" Joe asked.

Bruce was looking at her now. "See what, Steph? This is uncharted territory. If you are seeing or hearing things, we need to record it for analysis."

"If we go up to the house, you can meet the new additions to your group as well as get checked out." Stoneman seemed to actually be concerned.

"There was a blue wavery thing over by the wall," Frank called out from above. "Is that what you saw, doc?"

"Well, yeah," Stephanie reluctantly acknowledged.

"You heard voices, too?" Bruce asked.

"You know," Stephanie said. She was starting to feel put upon. "Let's go up to the house and let the medical type check me out and tell you all I'm fine. Then we'll talk about what I saw and heard." She hopped off the table.

"What was the last symbol, Steph?" Bruce asked.

"Well, explosive or explosion or fire gush, I guess is how it would translate into English." They were all trouping toward the house in a loose gaggle. "I think it was actually a collection of three symbols, not one complicated one. It seemed to go together differently than the rest." She thought about it for a moment. "Yes, definitely three. You know, I think I can break down the individual components to determine …"

The air to her left turned into blue-violet ring pattern, and she felt a gentle push. Then there was a loud crack. There was another swirling pattern. Since she was looking right at it, she noticed there was a center point of white with higher frequency colors swirling off from that. A meaty thunck, followed by a howl of pain, followed by a crack.

"What's that?"

Stonemen drove her to the ground, yelling into his radio.

Joe let out a howling growl; he was facing the back part of the property. Through a gap in Stoneman's covering her, she saw another swirl of colors with a white center right in front of her face. Then a scarlet fountain pulsed out from Joe's leg. Someone else jumped on the dog pile. She could still see a slice of Joe's leg and foot. His pants leg was pulled bulging tight, and his foot was splitting out of his boot.

A group of five guards pulled Stephanie up off the ground and hustled her into the house. She caught a glimpse of Joe, standing out on the lawn, slightly hunched over and roaring at the sky. He had ripped part of the way through his shirt and pants. He was growing hair over his exposed body at a visible rate while it thickened, and his hands had expanded to the size of dinner plates with long claws.

"Please God, not Joe! Help Joe, please!"

Just before they forced her into the house, she saw Joe pause, shaking his head side to side.

Chapter 17

Stephanie woke up in a pleasant, windowless small room of dark rich paneling and deep pile carpeting. She could've slept on the floor, as the carpeting was so deep, instead of on an air mattress. She had had the strangest dream. A woman had tried to talk to her about something, but she didn't speak any language Stephanie knew, a lot of hand gestures and pantomime. It had turned into flashes of friendly wolves and bears, symbols, weather effects, green plant growth, night skies, and zombies. It was very confusing, frustrating, and tiring and she was glad she woke up.

It took her a moment to remember where she was and why. She didn't know where, but she remembered why and shot up off the floor. "Joe," she blurted out.

A strange feeling of warmth suffused her, as she felt him nearby. It had something to do with the dream.

"I can feel him, too. He's that way," she realized out loud while pointing. "He's right, not normal in a relationship." The door to the outside was obvious, and it opened with a little out rush of air. "Positive air pressure, no gas is going to be leaking in. This is a panic room." She giggled to herself, "My new house has a panic room." The door was thicker than her forearm was long and had steel plates on both sides. Just outside the door was a storage room with partially filled shelves. They looked to be loaded with groceries and other staples. There were also two of her security personnel standing looking surprised at her.

"Hi," she chirped.

"Ma'am, you're supposed to be sleeping." He didn't look particularly happy to see her.

"Well, I'm not." For some reason she didn't trust them, and it pissed her off that they were here. She walked out of the room into a hallway that had a stairway to the left and many doors to the right. Right was toward Frank, who was sitting in a lawn chair in front of a door ending the hallway. He stood as she came toward him.

"I'm glad to see you mobile, ma'am, but aren't you supposed to be in the panic room?" The last part was directed more toward the guys trailing her.

"I was, now I'm not. Open the door."

"Doctor Blackraven, you can't go in there. It may not be safe …" The guard ran out of steam as she rounded on him.

"My boyfriend and Tony, a guy that has already saved my life once, are in there. Are you telling me it isn't safe to be near them?" She didn't know how she knew they were in there, but would figure it out later.

"It might not be. They almost turned into … ah … something dangerous …" he trailed off again.

"Well, we'll just see." She turned around and tried the door. It was locked. Now she was really pissed. "Frank, please unlock this door and tell Stoneman I would like to speak with him, right now." She was trying to be calm, but was thinking of the symbol of unlocking things.

"Doc, I'm not supposed to …" She glared at him. "Ah, … Doc … your eyes are glowing."

Stephanie heard a sidearm clear a holster. She slowly turned toward the terrified guard holding his pistol at his side. "You're fired. Reholster your gun and get off my property." She noted that the other guard had his gun trained on the scared guy. He was also talking into a throat mic.

"Steve," Frank smoothly interposed himself between Stephanie and the scared guard, "Ease down and do as the Principle has stated. Right now."

Steve slowly holstered his gun and then backed away from the group.

"Frank, please unlock the door."

"Yes, ma'am, as soon as Steve rounds the corner." Frank wasn't taking his attention off the guard. "Kiel, would you see that Steve makes it upstairs?"

"That leaves only you down here. We were told two-man rule applies."

"Kiel, I'll be fine." Frank was still very calm.

"Steph," she heard Joe's voice through the door. "Are you okay? What are you mad about?"

"They have this door locked, and I want to ... ah ... see if you're hurt." She was going to say touch you, but decided that was too much information. Stephanie could see the light from her illuminating the wall.

"Kiel, right the fuck now," Frank was still being calm.

Steve had his hand back on his pistol, but was hurrying. Kiel shrugged, "Your ass," and turned to follow Steve.

"Doc, just give me a moment." Frank was still calm.

"I've asked you repeatedly to call me Steph."

"Yes, ma'am, and I've told you I don't call the Principle by her given name." He turned to the door and used his keys to unlock it.

"You call me 'doc' with is a familiarized version of doctor. It's like using a shortened version of my name. I don't understand."

"No, ma'am. Just consider it mystic guard shit and let it go."

"If I asked you why they are locked in, would I like the answer?"

"Ah ... ah ... No ma'am."

"Good thing I didn't ask then."

"Yes, ma'am. Here you go. Enter slowly so as not to excite the other guards. Ah, okay."

"Sure Frank, but only cause you asked nice." She patted his cheek as she stepped into the room. She liked Frank because she *knew* he liked her. *How do I know that?* she thought for an instant.

It seemed they were having their own drama with guns and guards.

The room was another dark paneled one with no windows. Dark cherry wood shelves covered three of the walls with lights shining on the walls above the shelves, giving it a museum kind of effect. The last wall was a floor-to-ceiling slate fireplace, a spiral stairway rose to another doorway, and rich deep pile carpeting completed the picture. The cheap metal and web lawn chairs did detract a little from the expensive feel of the room.

Joe was standing a few feet away, barefoot, basically wearing a blanket with blue jean cutoffs. He had a very hairy chest; she suddenly wanted to run her fingers through it. Tony was across the way in a lawn chair, nursing a beer, wearing a sleeveless shirt and cut-up jeans, barefoot.

Three guards with submachine guns on friction slings across their chest at-the-ready were standing strategically around the room, clear fields of fire with no chance of hitting each other. They didn't look nervous, only attentive. Bruce was perched at the top of the spiral stairway, legs dangling down, with Tom holding a scoped carbine at the edge of the landing. She could tell he wasn't sure whether to aim at Joe or Tony or the guards.

Stephanie counted to ten then did it again. "Okay, everybody with a gun drawn, out!" No one moved. "Guys, I have had a really interesting day. Actually, I don't know what day it is. Now, if you can't figure out who the bad guys are from the good guys, then I just don't need you around."

"Steph, they're here to protect you, and I don't have a problem with that," Joe quietly commented.

"I do."

"Why? You do realize Tony and I almost went lycanthrope when you were shot at." Joe was still being calmingly quiet. "I was so angry …" His voice trailed off as he gazed off in the distance. "All I could see was red until you spoke to me."

Stephanie started to snap a hasty answer, but her mind went into overdrive analyzing what she had seen. "I was shot at. There was an assassin just off the back fence line." She looked at Joe. "I didn't speak to you. I got hustled off into the house. You were …" She didn't know how to finish.

Joe nodded. "Yeah … changing."

Bruce spoke up from the top of the stairs. "Those equations that you triggered earlier, the ones we couldn't see the effect from, were some type of shield or force field. It appears like they stopped the bullets, well, kept them from hitting you. They did ricochet around. That's why you are … ah …"

"Alive," Tom finished for him. "Your symbols saved your life again, doc."

"Interesting hypothesis, any data? Was anyone hit?"

Tom nodded slightly, "Well, yeah, both Joe and Tony caught a stray."

Stephanie was shocked. "Are you all right?" She rushed up to bury her hand in the hair on his chest. It made all the security types tense up. She felt the calm flood through her the instant she touched Joe.

He smiled at her and covered her hand with his. "I'm fine. So's Tony. Our … change … ah … seems to have caused fast healing, even faster than in the hospital."

"Did you catch the sniper or …ah … stop him?" She swallowed, thinking about Joe and Tony in uncontrollable animal form running someone down.

Tom shrugged. "Someone did. We found him with his throat cut, still in firing position. They must've done him just as he finished the third shot."

The door opened and Stoneman, followed by a man and two women in house staff uniforms, followed him into the room. Stoneman picked up the discussion. "Then someone called 911 to report the shots and kill. How are you doing, doctor?"

"I'm confused and happy to find your scared-shitless, tough-guard types didn't shoot my boyfriend."

"Yeah, I head you fired Steve. They aren't really trained for this."

"Yep, is he off my property yet? What do you mean, not trained for this, what this?"

"Sort of. We need to talk but not yet." Stoneman wasn't happy. "You've been sleeping for three hours and some change. A few things have happened since we got you into the house. But before we get into that, I thought you would like to meet your household staff and approve them staying." He motioned for the uniformed people to step forward.

They lined up like it was an inspection. The guy was over six feet tall, neatly cut black hair with a touch of silver at the temples, square face with piercing brown eyes. He was wearing a black suit, high-polished shoes, white shirt, the perfect stereotypic butler. He seemed to be just quivering with readiness for anything as he stepped forward and bowed from the waist. "Lawrence Peabody, mum." His British accent very pronounced, "I am your gentleman, or as you say here in the States, properties manager. If you'll have me." He bowed again and stepped back into line.

A thin woman with an impish face and deep blue eyes stepped forward and curtsied. She was wearing a blue and white dress topped off with some kind of dust cap to hold her hair. "Agnes McDoogle," she said with very pronounced not British accent, but definitely from the UK somewhere. "Housekeeper, mum.

I'll keep this lout from turning the house into a man cave, mum." There was a twinkle in her eye and a little smile on her lips.

The last woman was large, with strong forearms and hands, and slate grey hair pulled back into a bun. She had on the whites of a chef without the hat. Her face was that of a kindly grandmother; rosy cheeks, happy smile and generous eyes brimming with unshed tears. She stepped forward as well.

Before she curtsied, a memory slammed into Stephanie. "I know you." She stepped forward to take the woman's arm. "You used to give me cookies, only you didn't call them that. We used to have tea in a special ... ah ... place" Stephanie looked them over again as memories tickled. "I know all of you!"

The woman beamed. "Yes, mum, crackers we call 'em. I didn't know if you would remember. You were just a tiny thing." She was very British as well.

"I don't … I don't …"

She patted Stephanie's hand. "I was your nursemaid, mum, from your father's side. We all are from your father's side." She bobbed a very slight curtsy. "Maggie Turns, mum."

"But how?" Stephanie took an involuntary step back. "My mother was running from England."

"Yes, mum," Maggie agreed and started to reach into a pocket. Guns were cocked all around the room. "Easy there, laddies." She didn't seem concerned. "I just be a reach'n for a note." She slowly pulled out an envelope and held it out to Stephanie. "We got a call a few weeks ago from your great uncle which started us this way. Then we heard about his pass'n and contacted your solicitors. I'm very sorry for your loss." Stephanie thought she meant it. "I've been holding that for some time."

Stephanie glanced down at the letter. It said "Princess" on the outside in her uncle's hand. She tapped it to one side and tore off the end. She pulled out the papers.

"Princess," it started. "Damn'd if you didn't run off. I don't know your frame of mind, how long it's been, or what's happened so, if I'm alive, get the hell out of England. Your dad was killed, and no one seems to know why. Or they won't talk to me. I left this note with them in case you started tracking down your roots. This old biddy was your nanny. Yes, you have family in England. Now get out! It isn't safe.

"If I'm dead, get the hell out of England. I guess you're on your own now. Be smart and be tough. Don't let the bastards see you bleed.

"Maggie Turns is good people; you can trust her. You can trust what she tells you. She was very close to your mother. Ask her for proof." It was signed Unc with the image of a knife under it. There was also a picture of a younger Maggie.

Stephanie was fighting for control. No tears in front of these people. She looked back up at Maggie, wiggling the letter at her. "Prove it."

Maggie smiled, but it wasn't grandmotherly. "Okay, laddies, I'll be pulling a knife out to hand to the missus now. So, don't go getting twitchy." She slowly pulled out a ten-inch bladed knife from the middle of her back. It had a very distinctive damask-type blade and an elk antler handle. There were scriptish symbols etched into the blade. "The Bone Knife," she offered it hilt first.

Stephanie took it and looked it over. It had her uncle's sign on it. She pulled a symbol from memory and tapped the blade with her finger as she intoned, "One-Bay." The symbols on the blade lit with an eerie green fire. She offered the blade back to Maggie, who took it without hesitation.

Maggie pricked her finger and used the drop of blood rubbed along the blade to extinguish the eerie green glow. She smiled at Stephanie when she was done, wiped the blade, and made it disappear. Stephanie hadn't seen the completed ceremony for years. If it hadn't been Maggie's knife, it would've shocked her. It didn't have a lot of power, but it would've been enough to make her drop the blade. She and Uncle Raymond were the only two people who could make a knife like that for someone. *Only me now*, she thought.

Stephanie nodded at her. "You'll do." She gestured at the others, "You vouch for them?"

"Yes, mum. They're like family, they are." Her demeanor changed back to the grandmotherly cook. "Would you be want'n some tea, mum?"

"Tea, no. Coffee, yes, black and food of some type?" Stephanie smiled.

Maggie just shook her head. "You Yanks and your coffee," and went off without even a backward glance at the astonished guards.

"If you won't be needin' us, mum, we have work to be about." Lawrence gave her a slight bow from the waist.

"Sure, Lawrence, please go do whatever it is you do. You too, Agnes. I will want to talk to you all about my father … ah … later."

"Yes, mum. It's been a wee bit of shock," Agnes added with a crooked smile. "We are here for you whenever you'll be need'n us. You should be think'n about change'n your clothes before the bobbies are arriven. They may get the wrong idea if'n your look'n all blown up. Your men as well." She got a wicked smile, "Though I do like a bit of skin and muscle." She winked at Tony as she bobbed a curtsey and left with Lawrence.

Stephanie looked at her clothes and then at Joe. "Bobbies, she means the police?"

"Probably. Someone called 911 about the death, the sheriff's department has already responded. They'll want to speak with all of us, especially you, since you were the target." Joe cracked a little smile. "You do look kind of blown-up."

She smiled back at him, "You are showing skin and muscle."

"It was Kiel or Crimper who called. They have an RF signature for a cell signal. Kiel's is a continuous cycle like for a GPS locator," Bruce announced matter-of-fact. "Don't give me that stunned look, Mr. Stoneman. It didn't take much to deduce what happened and then rig up a cell signal transceiver to use for triangulation. I don't think this place is unknown anymore."

"I already knew the security detail was blown," Stephanie announced, moving to a lawn chair. "It was never secure. The detail was compromised from the beginning." She looked around at the guards, then back at Stoneman.

"How can you …" Stoneman started to say.

"My uncle left me a letter. In it he told me, among other things, that there were persons within his organization that wanted him dead and all loose ends tied up. I'm a loose end, apparently." She noticed both Joe and Tony moving to stand near her. "You, Lieutenant Colonel Stoneman, were mentioned as someone I can trust. He also mentioned something called the Bone Patrol. I guess it is in reference to the Bone Knives he made."

"Sort of," Stoneman gazed off into the distance for a moment. "He was a planner." He muttered cryptically. "Gentlemen," he commanded. He and the other guards in the room all slowly pulled out Bone Knives. Even Tom had one. "We," he motioned around the room, "and Frank, are all that remain of the Bone Patrol. Your uncle formed our little group to deal with the weird shit of the world, things that bullets just wouldn't kill by themselves. These knives would at least let us cut them."

She nodded as she stepped over to Stoneman. He handed her his knife, and she lit up the symbols. His blood put them out, and he wasn't shocked. She went through them one by one without a problem. Her uncle had linked each man to the knife he carried.

Tom didn't hand his over. "I haven't been keyed to mine. The general was going to do it when he got back from Portland." He looked embarrassed by it all.

"That's all right, Tom. Let me see it." He handed it to her. She looked for Uncle Raymond's symbol, found it, and handed it back. "I'll make some time tonight to do it."

"What?" Tom and Stoneman said at the same time. "You can make these knives?"

"Yeah." She looked away to hide the unshed tears. "One of the many things he made me learn to do without explaining why."

The upper door opened, and Laurence stepped through. "Excuse me, mum, the sheriff would like a moment of your time. He is waiting in the library."

Stephanie wiped her face and smiled up at Lawrence. "I have a library?"

"Yes, mum," he announced in a stiff dry English tone. "If you'll follow me, I will show you where it is. Agnes, here, has some clothes for you to slip into as well. Come along, mum. We'll have you spiffied up in no time."

"No new clothes. Let them see me like this. It might make an impression." She shrugged, "After all, people have been trying to kill me. Anyway, I pick out my own clothes."

Bruce groaned. "Not flannel, please."

She patted him on the shoulder as she stepped by. "I may get flannel pants."

"Noooooo," he moaned as if in agony.

Chapter 18

She had a library. She liked books.

She followed Lawrence through the front entryway, up the left sweeping stairway. She hadn't been up this way. The library doors opened out onto the landing, first double doors on the right, before the hallway leading to the west set of bedrooms.

She was stunned as she stepped in. Her apartment bookshelves were built from cinder blocks and one by twelve planks. She looked around the room. Dark walnut bookshelves polished to within an inch of their lives lined the walls and were free standing in some areas. Leather wing chairs, dark wood tables, brass lamps, and books, not many, but hers, it made the room look like it was out of some old castle. Her books didn't even fill one of the shelves. There was a big dark wood desk and other tables deeper into to the room. "Where did the furniture come from?" Stephanie was impressed. It was a big room.

"I contacted an estate furniture warehouse and had them expedite a delivery of furniture, mum."

"How'd you get my books?"

"Your books were delivered earlier with your apartment effects. I stored the rest of your effects below." Lawrence informed her as if it was commonplace.

"Why'd you store them?"

"They really aren't suitable for this house, mum. We have a statement to make."

"I don't have a statement to make." Stephanie was confused by his assumptions.

"Of course you do, mum." He swept her further into the room with his expectation and gave a little bow, "May I present Lieutenant Carpenter of the

Snohomish County sheriff's department," Lawrence pointed at a larger then average beefy man with an honest-looking face. He did have some interesting scars around the eyes and a nose that had been broken sometime in the past. Lawrence bowed slightly, and with a wave of his arm, offered up a normal-sized guy with a pinched face and intense eyes wearing a men-in-black suit, complete with the thin tie and wingtip shoes. "And Special Agent Farmer of the Federal Bureau of Investigation. Coffee will be along shortly, mum," he stated as he started to back out of the room.

"How do I know they are who they say they are? I do have people trying to kill me."

Lawrence gave a single raised eyebrow as a reaction. She took it to mean, You doubt me? Lawrence continued stoically, "Upon receiving their request for admittance, I called the Snohomish County Sheriff's department and had them text me the lieutenant's image. They matched, and they confirmed his intention to visit. I did the same thing to the Seattle FBI office. They had more questions, but in the end, they too sent me an image. These gentlemen are who they say they are." Lawrence smiled faintly and tipped his head. "Is that all, mum?"

She smiled at him, "Yes, I think so. Black coffee for me."

"Of course, mum." Lawrence gave a slight bow and finished his exit.

Stephanie was going to like having a butler, especially an efficient one. "Hi," she said to the two men. "What do you want?"

"Well, that's blunt enough," Sheriff Carpenter stated good naturedly, stepping forward and offering his hand. "You have a dead man out back." She took his offered hand. His could make two of hers. "And I would like to ask you some questions," the sheriff finished.

A noise made her glance over her shoulder. Stoneman nodded at her as he came into the room. She looked back at the sheriff. "The assumption is that he was trying to shoot me. I understand why you would want to talk to me, but," she looked at Agent Farmer, "why is the FBI here?"

Agent Farmer nodded at her, but didn't offer to shake. "There are oddities. I came to ask questions." His diction was precise and formal.

The sheriff cleared his throat, looking a little sheepish. "To state it bluntly, we don't get many murders in this part of Snohomish County. These are really odd. I thought the county could use some forensic help. So, I called and they came. The Bellevue police also had problems with you, odd problems. Assassins are just as odd, so I asked if Special Agent Farmer wouldn't like to tag along."

"Problems with me?" She wasn't really pleased with his phrasing.

"Well," Sheriff Carpenter's face shifted expression, "perhaps I should've said, around you. It seems one of their police officers shot you after your truck was blown up. That would've been after they invited you to help with an investigation. I wouldn't call that normal ... anywhere."

"And that police officer, one Crunkle, is now dead," Agent Farmer added.

"Aaaaand," Stephanie waited. Agent Farmer was interrupted by the efficient Lawrence.

Lawrence pushed a wheeled cart loaded with all sorts of drinks and interesting bite-size food into the room. "I'm sorry about your solicitors, mum. I informed them that you were in a meeting with these officials, but they insisted and followed the food." Walter and Otto were looking professional, but a little harried. They both nodded to her and set down their briefcases. Lawrence just kept going. "Here are your refreshments." He wheeled the cart over to the center of the area formed by the chairs, side tables, and desk. He bowed slightly to her. "Chef Turns also wished me to inform you that dinner is ready whenever you wish to sit, mum. Just let me know, and I will show you to the dining room. Also, a count on how many will be joining you."

"Ah ... I don't know. Ah, where did you get a cart, and how did you get it up the stairs?"

"You have your magic, and I have mine, mum." Lawrence replied deadpan.

"I have SCIENCE, not magic. It is completely definable. God! Why does everyone think it's magic?" She realized after she had spoken that he might have been joking with her.

Lawrence raised one eyebrow. "I used a lift, mum. It runs on electricity." He held up a coffee cup on a saucer to her and a plate filled with crackers and meat rolls. "Black, no sweetener."

She felt a little sheepish about her strong statement, so smiled at his offering. "Thanks." She took the offered saucer and plate. "What, no cookies?" She could tweak him, too.

Lawrence didn't miss a beat; he reached down and produced a plate of cookies with colored sprinkles on them. "Mrs. Turns did say that a woman of your height and figure should refrain from too many of these, mum. Something about hips and tummy." He offered up the plate and then set it within easy reach of her. "Anything else, mum?" Stephanie laughed.

"No, thank you. You may retire. We can serve ourselves." Somehow she acquired a British accent for just a moment. It made her smile. She also had a strong memory flash of a man who smelled of peppermint and tobacco. Everyone was staring at her; apparently, her accent was authentic.

"Ah, we were wondering when you would be showing up, mum. We knew there was still a little Brit in you somewhere." There was a twinkle in his eye as he bowed slightly and glided out of the room.

Stephanie turned to see the sheriff and the agent looking at her. "My life is chaos right now. I don't have a clue what's going to happen next." She waved vaguely after Lawrence. "I have English relatives. The butler, cook, and housekeeper are from them. They came in response to my uncle's death. You want some?" She gestured at the cart and took a bite of a meat roll. "Wow, is this good!"

The sheriff moved in like he hadn't eaten for a week. Agent Farmer took a cup of coffee. Stephanie turned away to sip coffee, so he wouldn't see her smiling at him. He had a prissy, fastidious way. She was stunned. The coffee was rich and, well, great. She took a larger drink. *Damn,* she thought, *if the food is half as good, this cook is a winner.*

"Your cook should open her own espresso stand. This is the best coffee I've ever had," Sheriff Carpenter exclaimed.

"European, very rich." Agent Farmer raised his cup in a salute. "Excellent."

Stephanie motioned them all to chairs. "So, ask away."

"Dr. Blackraven, as your legal counsel, I advise against answering any questions," Walter interrupted. "We should really speak first."

Stephanie realized that lawyers just pissed her off. "Look guys, I keep asking you to call me Steph. Or is this some kind of mystic lawyer crap, like the bodyguards have about using first names?"

They both smiled despite themselves. "It's something like that," Otto supplied.

"Anyway, I'm going to answer their questions about today's shooting, cause I don't have anything to hide, and it might help. Unfortunately, I don't know that much." She sipped her coffee. "I tell you what, we have like a shit ton of paperwork to go through, so why don't you go find the cook and tell her you're staying for dinner and we make it a working meal. I'll spend a few minutes with these guys then come down for dinner. Okay?"

"What's for dinner?" Walter asked, grinning.

"I don't have a clue, but if it's as good as the meat rolls, then it will be great."

The lawyers exchanged a look. Walter got up, collected his briefcase, and left. Otto broke down, loosened his tie, and got a cup of coffee. He made a pleased face after his first sip.

Stephanie smiled prettily at the officers of the law. "So, ask away."

Agent Farmer pulled out a notebook. "You were assaulted and blown up in a physics lab last Tuesday night. Admitted to Evergreen hospital early Wednesday morning and, through a medical miracle of your own devising, you walked out of the hospital a day later, on Thursday morning. Your doctorate was also posted that day.

"Thursday night, you were assaulted by a werewolf and saved an officer's life at the crime scene of a murdered man, a grad student of yours, one Andrew Stone." Agent Farmer looked up expectantly.

"That wasn't a question." Stephanie took another sip of coffee.

Agent Farmer went back to his notebook. "Friday morning, you were invited to another crime scene, the break-in of a Professor Rosemary Stein, your mentor and sponsor. At which point, someone, as yet unidentified, tried to kill you by blowing up your truck. You saved another police officer, one Joe Bremer, recently promoted detective, promoted on Wednesday morning, by pulling him out of the fire." Agent Farmer paused to glance at her again.

"Still not a question." Stephanie took another bite of meat roll. She motioned for Sheriff Carpenter to try them.

Agent Farmer went on. "At the same place as your truck explosion, apparently just after you had pulled Detective Bremer from the fire, you pulled a pencil from your sleeve. I don't understand the significance of the pencil? Bellevue Police Office Crunkle shot you for resisting arrest while holding a deadly weapon, said pencil, and had you hauled, against the advice of the paramedics, to the police station. You were released from the police station under bazaar circumstances on Saturday morning."

Stephanie nodded and tried a cookie. "Mmmmm," she nodded toward the sheriff, "you should try one of these, too."

Otto hastily swallowed. "You should explain to him about the pencil."

Stephanie smirked and turned to Agent Farmer. "I use a No. 2 pencil as a non-conducting implement for creating symbols. I was intending to invoke the healing symbol on Joe, since he was all blown up and bleeding. I never got it finished cause that asshole shot me."

Agent Farmer made a note. "Your uncle, the person who raised you, was killed in a car explosion in Portland, Oregon, at almost the same instant your own truck was blown up. His death also made you an instant multimillionaire, since you are his only heir. Those papers were filed on Thursday as well. Your uncle was also an interesting person with security locks on all his information." He looked up.

"Still no question," Stephanie smiled and toasted him with her coffee cup before taking a sip. Just the mention of her uncle's death gave her a pang, but she wasn't going to let these guys see it.

His mouth twitched, and then he continued, "You disappeared from your apartment on Saturday, and late Saturday night or early Sunday morning, your apartment was hit by a rocket, setting it on fire, arson?"

Stephanie shrugged and went on sipping.

"Monday morning, ex-Detective Joe Bremer, on medical suspension for having contracted some type of lycanthropy through unexplained contact, and ex-Police Officer Anthony Paulli, also medically suspended for the same reason, and the officer you saved on Thursday night from a werewolf, disappeared from the infectious disease ward of the hospital and apparently came here to your hideout, very nice hideout, by the way. Also on Monday, which is today by the way, an assassin tried to blow you up and that failing, took three shots at you. Who is now dead." Agent Farmer flipped his notebook shut. He looked up to meet her eyes. "It has been a very busy week for you."

"Now that dead guy, supposed assassin, is out on your newly acquired fence row with his throat cut," the sheriff finished with almost a laugh. Stephanie wouldn't let her face change expression. "It's kind of odd. Don't you agree?"

"That was a question." Stephanie leaned over and grabbed the coffee pot to refill her cup. "It seems longer than a week." She set down the pot and rubbed her face while talking to herself. "He didn't try to blow me up before shooting at me. I did this," she motioned at her burned clothes. "With an experiment. He shot at me when they were taking me to the house to get checked out." She covered her face for a moment to rub her eyes. It was all catching up to her again. "Why?" She looked up at them. "Why?"

"I'd already called in the FBI because of the other murders. They weren't exactly meth lab busts. I don't have a forensics team. It's just me and six deputies for this section of the county." His tone had softened, and he seemed confused. Did she detect a hint of embarrassment for his lack of capabilities? Or maybe guilt?

"I think she was referring to why her?" Agent Farmer corrected.

"Oh."

Stephanie agreed with a nod. "That's exactly it. Why me? Why now?" She looked over to see Joe, dressed in black shirt and pants, but still barefooted, quietly slide into the room. "I was a grad student at Bosh-Gates for three years, quietly working on an obscure symbol theory. I hadn't seen my uncle for years. Now, in the space of a week, I've been beaten up, blown up twice, burned out, and threatened by gangs, police, Feds, the State Department, and my uncle was killed. Why now?"

"Wow," Sheriff Carpenter blurted out. "I just came to ask you to look over the data from our strange murders. Acting Lieutenant Grayson of the Bellevue police said you were the best at the mag … ah … symbol stuff. He was quite taken with your professionalism." He glanced at Agent Farmer, "I don't consider her a suspect for the killing on her property."

"The evidence, while in its infancy, would support your position," Agent Farmer agreed with the sheriff. "I am still struggling with the lethal-pencil concept."

"Well, I and my … ah … friends? Team … any way, will look it over, but frankly I don't know who to trust with what." She was looking at Agent Farmer.

Agent Farmer's cell phone rang. He answered and turned to listen and almost walked into Joe. The agent's head barely came up to Joe's chest. Stephanie could tell by his short jerk, he didn't know Joe was there. It made her smile.

"Very well," Agent Farmer said and hung up while turning back to them. "Who are you?" He was looking up at Joe.

"I'm Joe Bremer," Joe rumbled out. "You've upset my … ah … Stephanie."

"Can you always tell when she is upset, even when you are not in the room?" The agent's little beady eyes got piercing.

"Not that it's any of your business, but yeah."

"Interesting," The agent turned to Stephanie and the sheriff. "The man on the back fence has no identity. Nothing is registered in any of the databases. But most of his specialized equipment is registered as DHS assets from the Seattle office."

"DHS?" Stephanie asked.

"Department of Homeland Security," everyone said in unison.

Stephanie laughed. "You guys should practice. Can you sing?" Everyone smiled.

Stoneman turned away and started talking quietly into his mic.

Stephanie had a gut feeling about both the sheriff and the agent. She liked them. She got up and walked over to Joe. He smiled as she got closer to him. "Why do you always smile when I walk up to you?"

"I don't know." Joe smiled more.

Stephanie smiled back. "Bend down here. I want to whisper into your ear." Joe shifted his eyes from side to side for a moment and then bent down. "Would you take Bruce with you down to the boardroom and remove all my personal stuff from the boards? I want to take these guys down there." She didn't catch herself in time and kissed him on the nose. He blushed.

"We already did. Bruce thought you might want to share." He grabbed her hand and gave it a little squeeze. "You shouldn't kiss me in front of the other boys, they might get jealous."

"You worried about them teasing you later?" She gave him a wicked grin.

"Yeah, something like that."

Stephanie smiled at him and turned back to the lawmen. "Okay, what are your real questions?"

"What can you tell me about the dead guy?" Sheriff Carpenter shot out.

"Not a thing." Stephanie walked over to sample another meat roll, pulling Joe along with her. "Like I said before, I was working symbols this morning from … let's say, 11:30 to 2:30. Then I did this special one and almost blew myself up. It rattled the shop pretty well."

The sheriff was nodding. "We got calls from all over. Even as far away as Monroe. I'm surprised someone wasn't killed."

Stephanie looked at her clothes. "Well, I did a symbol to heal myself. Apparently, I was quite burnt. Anyway, they were taking me up to the house when the shots were fired. The theory is that one of the symbols I had worked during the session that had no apparent effect, actually created a force field that deflected the bullets. It's a theory. What I know is that two of the bullets hit something directly in front of my face that caused a cascading decreasing frequency of visible light effect. White, at the assumed point of impact, degenerating to red at the outer edges."

Agent Farmer was leaning forward. "The bullets were aimed at your face?"

Stephanie shuddered a little as the implications sank in. "Yes, I think he was shooting at my face. He would've been a good shot because it was a long distance. There was a discernible time lag between impact and sound. And he was picking me out of a moving crowd of men much taller than myself. He even got off the last shot when they had dog piled on me, but left my face exposed. You said fencerow, which means it had to have been at least six hundred yards or so. That's pretty good shooting."

"And between the buildings, with a slight wind and misting rain," Stoneman added. "Somebody got away."

"Why do you say that, Mr. Stoneman?" Agent Farmer was intense.

"He should've had a spotter. All of his equipment was military. They train snipers as two-man teams."

Agent Famer blinked, then set down his coffee, and reached for his cell. "Excuse me for a moment."

The sheriff watched him leave and then turned back. "Did you ever see the shooter?"

Stephanie shook her head. "Nope. I didn't even realize there were bullets until blood sprayed out of Joe's leg."

"Detective Bremer was hit?" The sheriff looked at Joe.

"Yeah. I was rushed off about then, so I can't really comment on anything firsthand. All I have now is hearsay." Stephanie shrugged.

Joe shrugged, "I don't remember."

"You don't remember if you got shot or not? Why not?" Sheriff Carpenter was fairly focused as well.

"I was emotionally distraught over their attack on Dr. Blackraven. So distraught that I was starting into a metamorphosis."

"Metamorphosis, what does that mean?"

"The guards think I was starting to go 'were', unknown type." Joe didn't smile.

Stephanie could feel Joe's emotional turmoil, even if he wasn't showing it.

"We are days away from a full moon, and it was day light. Why or how would you be able to change?"

"Unknown."

Stephanie wanted to reach and touch him. She resisted.

"Ok," the sheriff said as he shifted his focus back to Stephanie. "What did you do when they got you into the house?"

"I went to sleep. Actually, I think I was asleep before they got me inside." Stoneman was nodding in agreement. "I woke up hours later. Like this." She motioned at herself. "My theory is that I was healing from the blast. That's why I just nodded off."

Agent Farmer came back in. "I have to go make some longer calls and arrange some things. Would it be convenient for us to talk again later?"

"Of course, I'll be here all night and probably working."

"Very good, until later then." Agent Farmer offered a little head nod, turned, and hurried off. She heard his steps pattering quickly down the stairs.

Bruce appeared in the doorway. "Hey, ah, Mrs. Turns says dinner is ready, and you all should come eat before it gets cold."

"No, she didn't." Stephanie smiled.

Bruce smiled a little. "Okay, she didn't say that 'cause she's too nice, but she would like to. So, why don't you go get cleaned up and get out of your I-blew-myself-up clothes. Agnes has your wardrobe all laid out for you." Bruce said it like he was expecting some kind of reaction from her.

Sheriff Carpenter rose. "I think I'll get out of your way. I don't have any more questions about the shooting, but I do still have information about the other murders. Would it be all right if I brought that by later as well?"

"Yes. If you and Agent Farmer would return at about the same time, it would probably make this go quicker, you know, not having to repeat things." Stephanie rose with him.

"Great, I'll coordinate with him, and we'll shoot for 9, 9:30 tonight then." He nodded at her and everyone else and made his way out.

Chapter 19

Joe woke up instantly and fully, none of the groggy intermediate stage, asleep to wide-awake. He never woke up that way.

He was lying on carpeting in a dark room, bed to his right. His pillow was Stephanie's clothes. *What am I doing with Stephanie's clothes?* He was even more awake. Rising, he looked over the edge of the bed, and sure enough, he could see the outline of her heart-shaped angelic face. Her little upturned nose, slightly tilted eyes, long lashes, and full lips slightly parted; he really liked kissing those. All the face lines from constant calculation and intense inspection just smoothed out to innocent perfection. She was lying on her side, with the covers bunched up to her chin, and drooling on her pillow. He figured he probably shouldn't share that observation with her.

The door opened, letting bright light slice into the room. It was a big room. "Detective." He could tell Agnes's accent immediately. It was worse when she whispered. "I'm think'n you wouldn't be want'n her ladyship to be a findin' you a peek'n at her as she's a ly'in a bed. You dirty boy, come out of there." The last part had an amused lilt to it.

How did he get here? He remembered a long dinner with lawyers constantly picking at her to sign this or read faster; he wasn't going to let her invite them back. Then Sheriff Carpenter and Agent Farmer showed up with crime data. They had been up really late, first in the boardroom sorting and analyzing the data, and then in the barn, looking at the completed ritual symbol. It was Steph doing that, he was just keeping her company, okay, she didn't know he was there, he just ogled her the whole time. She had fallen asleep in the lawn recliner, so he had picked her up, and carried her to her room. She was so tired she didn't make a fuss.

That's when he got confused because he had put her in bed. Agnes had arrived to shoo him out, so she could undress her and get her settled. How did he end up back in here on her floor? That dream, something about his family's bear totem and ... he couldn't remember.

Agnes was shining a light around carefully so as not to wake Stephanie. She had a chiding, amused tone. "You naughty boy, come out of there, right . . ." her voice froze as she shined the light on him. "Eyes" she breathed out as a knife appeared in her other hand. "Say something right quick, laddie." There was no amusement in her voice now. It was more like cold, killing certainty.

"Sshh, you'll wake her. Shut that light off." He heard Agnes let out her breath as he quietly rose and left the room.

She pulled the door shut behind him. "Shame on you for a sneak'n in there." The amusement was back along with some teasing. "Especially, with her ladyship be'in a sleep'n. She has to be invite'n ya in to play." She smiled wickedly while eyeing his crotch.

"Right." Joe retreated, blushing and embarrassed, to his room across the hall.

His room was huge, but not as huge as her's. He had two rooms, well, three if you counted the bathroom. It was all furnished. The butler, Lawrence, had magically gotten the house furnished the evening before, well, at least the parts Joe had visited. It was like some kind of English oasis: heavy dark woods, embroidered cushions, and thick draperies. Joe's bed even had a tent over it, complete with side panels, and four solid posts holding it up.

He shook his head. His life had become unreal since he had seen Steph in her classroom. Everything was in chaos. All he could think about was her and that wasn't right. Was love at first sight real? Even now, he felt himself drawn to her. He got angry. "No goddamn it." He tore his pants off and grabbed running shorts and a T-shirt. He had to think.

Down the stairs at the end of the hall, out through the kitchen, he found himself running, jogging around the field they all called the practice range. It was raining, but he didn't care. It was the physical motion, the act of moving he craved. Just letting his mind drift, he started going over all the things that had happened in the last week and all the information they had collected. "God, all this has happened in a week," he said to the rain.

After a few times around, he was joined by Tony, who easily kept pace with him, "You runnin'?"

Joe just looked at him. "No. I'm enjoying the rain."

"Thought so." They ran a little longer.

"What did you guys puzzle out last night?"

"You were there."

"Nope. I went to pick the brains of the Bone Patrol, at least the ones who were off duty."

"Oh, I didn't notice you leave."

"You're the detective, so between the puzzle and the girl, I didn't think you needed me. I left all that brain work and strategifying to you guys." They ran a little more before Tony prodded him, "So, what did you find out?"

"Serial killer. At least six vics. That FBI guy decided they should get involved."

Tony whistled. "He launching a task force?"

"That's what he said. Apparently, there are more strange cases like these in the Puget Sound. He's going to put them on it. The first vic was just killed; it was a guy. The next two were women, murdered, raped, and slightly dehydrated. The most recent, well, you saw him."

"Any evidence at the scene?"

"Nothing, everything had been wiped clean; even the rape victims had been cleaned up. Very professional. It doesn't make sense."

"Why?"

"He didn't start sloppy; it was like he was a pro from the beginning. Typical serial killers perfect their MO over time. Or there are more, older killings we haven't found yet. Or the guy has a very strange background."

"You said he?"

"Yeah, we think it's a guy. He strips and rapes the women. The men were clothed. Steph thinks it's his symbol work that's sloppy because of the severity of the desiccation, little for the older kills, really severe with the most recent. That's what she was studying last night."

"She figure them out?"

"Not yet."

They ran.

"The FBI guys found the spotter. Dead. He died hard." Joe told him.

"Hard? Like torture hard?"

"Oh, yeah, and by a pro. The spotter was invisible as well; no records, no listings, no data. But he gave something up before his throat was cut."

"How could they tell?"

"All the pieces hadn't been cut off or burnt. Somebody really wanted the information, and this guy was going to talk."

"Shit, who's the new player?"

"They don't know. Kill site was cleaned by a pro. This guy's just evil or really intense."

"The doc hear any of this?"

"No, thank God, she had gone to the barn to study symbols."

"You know," Toney glanced over at Joe, "the Bone squad mentioned how her great uncle had faked his death in the past by being blown up."

"No shit." Joe said. "Do they think he's faking it?"

"No one would speculate. They just left it hanging." Tony ran on, than added, "But, according to them, he was a pro at bad stuff. This sounds like something he could've done is he wasn't like, eighty."

"Yeah, he was old but savvy." Joe respectfully noted. "He could've had a younger accomplice."

Tony nodded with a grunt.

They ran on in silence.

"That was only one of the prongs on the board, what about the other two?" Tony asked

Joe kind of shrugged while running. "Couldn't figure the gangs, and Steph didn't want to talk about her uncle."

They ran some more, just breathing and listening to the rain.

"I can help a little with the gangs. I had Bruce pull up the data online that professor had compiled. Sylvia Bloomerton, she had been building the data since 2000 on enchanted creatures. The turn of the millennia seemed to have more significance than people realized. Anyway, she had done some work on were-creatures of myth and legend, compiled it, and started drawing conclusions. Werewolves were one of the biggest areas. She had some interesting things in her info, like, she thought the 'were' could be controlled through magic symbols. Symbols like the ones that were on the werewolf that got me. Also, that these symbols would let the 'were' ignore the moon cycle that appears in every piece of literature."

"She was vic number two."

"Damn."

They ran some more.

"She had some direct observation stuff about a werewolf in Montana. The shifting is really painful. The wolf told her that if you can keep it together through the pain, then you are in control, not the wolf."

"Really, damn, I remember rage, not pain."

"Yeah, well, me too. But it wasn't a full moon, we shouldn't even been trying to change. The notes were very specific about that. We may be something else." Tony rubbed rain out of his eyes.

They ran more.

"Did she have anything about how the symbols worked with the change?" Joe realized he wasn't cold.

"Yeah, she had some data on a series of experiments she was conducting with a local werewolf. The local could change any time when triggered by the symbols, but it took two sets, one on the wolf, and one on the witch, her word. She had stuff about how it was moderating his change on a non-lunar cycle."

Joe snorted, "That's a quote, isn't it?"

"Why?"

"'Moderating his change on a non-lunar cycle,' you know what it means, right?"

"Asshole, I may not be a college graduate like you, but I can read." Tony swerved over and tripped him.

Joe did a kind of hoppy change step and caught back up. "Hah, I have a master's degree there, bub."

"Nice step back there."

"Thanks. Anything else from the files?"

"Not on the symbols, her writing was incomplete, and not in a graceful way. I think that's when she was killed. That's the gang connection. Her subject was a member of a local gang, the Loco Lobo, Crazy Wolf. I think they got her. The guy that was controlling the wolf the night I got attacked, had symbols on him and so did the wolf in human form. They lit up like the doc's do when she does her magic."

"Science, not magic," Joe automatically said.

Tony just started laughing. "Whatever, she had other notes on how silver hurt 'were's, just like in the movies, but also fire and chemicals. Also, enough trauma, apparently hit them with enough normal stuff, and they go down. She didn't say what enough meant in real terms, like number of bullets or anything."

"Great."

They ran on.

"Hey, one more thing, I think the Bone Patrol is expecting to have to put us down on the next full moon."

"What?" That almost made Joe trip.

"Yeah, the way they were acting, I'm pretty sure. Frank's up in the barn right now with a rifle, keeping an eye on us. They knew some guys that got bit like me, when they changed, they turned wolf. Apparently, those bone knives they have can hurt were-creatures, actually, they said all types of enchanted monsters. They even told me they cut a demon once. They had been drinking a lot by then."

"I don't think I'm a wolf."

"Really, what do you think you are?"

"Bear. I keep dreaming about my family's bear totem and this blue Amerindian woman who's been trying to tell me something."

Tony stopped running with his jaw hanging open. Joe just kept going. Tony caught back up.

"Black hair, pretty, dark eyes, about five six, five seven, expressive hands?"

"Yeah, that would be her, you having dreams, too?"

"Yeah, ever since I woke up in the hospital. They've become more intense since you showed up. When I see her, she has a bear with her and a smaller woman."

"Huh, really, I see her with a wolf and Steph."

They ran in silence for a moment.

"You like runnin'?" Tony asked.

"No, not really. Makes my knees and ankles hurt and swell."

"Yeah, me, too. Do your legs hurt?"

"No, actually, I feel great. Nothing hurts, I'm not even winded, and we've been running for a couple of hours."

"Yeah and you're bare footed too."

They both stopped running and looked at Joe's feet while he wiggled his toes. "They don't hurt."

"Maybe we should … ah … go talk to your girlfriend about our dreams. If she's awake."

"She's awake. She's in the kitchen, bitching at Stoneman."

"Damn, you can feel that."

"No, I can see her in the window." Joe smiled at Tony.

"Asshole, here I thought you had some kind of mind connection."

"I can tell you she's upset again." Joe focused on Stephanie. "Stoneman fired Kiel and Crimper and sent them away without letting her question them."

"Holy shit, you do have some kind of link."

"Yes and no. I can feel when she's upset, like she can me, apparently, but not what she's upset about."

"I thought you said it was about Stoneman?"

"Yeah, but she told me last night she was going to jump his shit this morning." Joe laughed at Tony's look.

"Jerk." Tony pretended like he was going to slap him. Joe dodged away.

"Yeah, I can still feel stuff about her. I'm tryin' real hard to not let it weird me out. I mean, damn, I've only known this girl for a week."

They started walking to the house.

"She's special, Joe, and I'm not just saying that. I feel like she's going to need you. Need you to lean on, to help her. And you're going to need her as well. This weird shit isn't over yet."

Joe just looked at him. "Is the force with you, Obi Wan?"

Tony thought for a moment. "Ah, yeah, I think it is. This blue American Indian chick in our dreams is part of it, too."

"Holy shit, this is weird." Joe was shaking his head. He had a feeling like he should talk to his grandmother. She was a North American Indian shaman of some type.

"Maybe drinking helps."

Joe snorted. "I don't think so, but you check it out and let me know."

"You're on."

They almost walked into Stephanie as she was leaving the kitchen. Joe smiled as soon as he saw her. She did, too.

She crocked her finger at him. "Bend down here." Joe glared at Tony, daring him to make a comment as Tony stepped by to go inside. She gave him a kiss on the cheek. "Did you sleep on my floor last night?" she whispered.

"Yeah," Joe was waiting for something, but he didn't know what. "Why?"

"I don't know. It's the first time I've slept well since this all started. And I had this dream about a … well, a bear and a wolf," she trailed off. He thought she looked embarrassed.

"Tony," Joe said immediately. Tony stopped and looked back. "Come back here and close the door." Joe led Stephanie over to a bench as he waited for Tony to join them.

Stephanie gave him a crocked, amused smile. "You know it's raining, right."

He pulled his soaked shirt away from his body and looked at it. "Yeah."

"You're steaming. How is it you're soaking wet and steaming while getting rained on?"

"I was running."

She glanced down, "Bare footed?" She was smiling now.

He wiggled his toes. "Yeah. I'm a werebear, apparently." He glanced up to see her reaction. "I've been having dreams about this American Indian woman with a wolf and you in them. In that dream, I'm a bear," Joe announced.

Stephanie looked skeptical, and then Tony added, "I've been having dreams about an American Indian woman, a bear, and this little woman." He smiled at her. "She looked a lot like you."

Stephanie looked up at both of them. "It's still raining, and I'm getting wet."

"Steph," Joe prodded.

"Okay, okay." Stephanie shot up off the bench. "It isn't logical. There is no precedence for this, there is no basis. I … It … NO!" She had moved off a ways and was holding herself tight. After a moment, she turned around. "Yes," she rounded on him. "I've been having dreams, okay. Only the woman can't make up her mind if she is wearing buckskins or gowns. I have bears and wolves in my dreams. They're friendly to me, but no one else. So we are having dreams, what of it?"

"Don't you think it's a sign?" Tony asked.

"A sign of what? That we've all had a shitty week?" She looked at them for a moment. "Look guys, I'm a scientist. I like facts and data. I have a sign that says: Facts and Data will set you free, Alan Mulally 777, 1991. What is the purpose behind this? Where is the data?"

"It may be a spiritual sign, an indication that the Great Spirit is reaching out to us," Joe offered.

"The Great Spirit." She stared at him for a moment. "Holy shit! Just because I have American Indian in my background, you bring up the Great Spirit." The anger dripped off her words. "I don't believe in fairy tales."

"No, it wasn't just because of that, I'm part Indian, too, ya know. So's Tony," Joe shot back. "My grandmother is a shaman."

"No, I don't know." She was yelling now. "I don't know a damn thing about you. I just met you a week ago, just before I got the shit beat out of me." Joe felt like he'd been punched.

"Yeah, well, I wasn't a werebear before I met you." Joe was getting really mad. He didn't want any of this, just being near her made him feel better. He didn't understand any of it. Everything seemed to be spiraling away from him. "I couldn't feel when someone else was sad before I met you." He had moved to tower over her. "I couldn't close my eyes and point the direction to her, before I met you."

"Well, I didn't do that."

"No, but something did."

"That's not rational."

"You can't face it that there's mysterious shit happening and your science doesn't explain it." Scorn dripped from his words. "Before I fell in love with you, I was normal."

She was white and trembling, "Well, if that's the way you feel, then just leave. Get out of my life!" she screamed.

"I can't," he yelled back. "You've cast some kind of spell over me."

Her eyes got big then narrowed to slits. "It's a symbol, not a spell! It is science, NOT MAGIC," she shrieked at him.

"How do you know?" he yelled back. "Bruce said a week ago it was just little stuff. Now you blow up buildings with it."

Her eyes flew wide again. "How dare ... How ... Get out!" She pushed at him, and he didn't move.

"You aren't just going to push me away," Joe bent over to yell in her face. "Calculate that!"

"Get out!" She slapped him, and it hit him like a bolt of lightning.

Joe found himself sitting on the ground with his face stinging. Stephanie was standing with light dancing in her eyes, looking at her hand about ten feet away. Guards were standing shocked at the patio door with knives in hand. Tony was standing off to the side, but between them, only it didn't look like Tony exactly.

He was standing tall with his arms crossed high on his chest, looking down on them like he was the chief, and they were bad little Indians. He gestured up, thunder cracked, lightning made spider webs across the sky, and then a wall of rain landed on them. It happened so fast Joe was blinded by water.

When he could see again, Stephanie was holding him. "Joe, Joe, I'm sorry; I didn't mean it. Please Joe. I told you I sucked as a girlfriend. Say something. Please Joe."

"Wow."

"Joe, I'm sorry. I don't know what got into me."

The thought of him losing her just snuffed the anger out. "Steph, it's okay. I'm fine." He rubbed his face. "What did you hit me with?"

"I ... I don't know. I just got mad and this symbol appeared." She made an angry wipe at the water on her face. "It's too much, too much." He realized she was crying, kneeling next to him. "There are people trying to kill me. I don't know why. These emotions are confusing me. They killed my uncle. I don't know why. My symbols are just jumping into my head, and I don't know why. My theory of symbols being powered by field interaction through Fast Fourier Transforms is falling apart. It disproves my theory. I don't know what to believe. It is not magic. It can't be magic." She looked bleak. "I'm sorry, Joe, Then you said I didn't ... I just lost it. If ... if ... if I could just get a little time without people trying to kill me, I would figure these symbols out." She buried her face in his chest and started crying for real. Big sobs that set her whole body to shaking.

Joe was at an absolute loss. She was strong, logical, and so contained that her crying totally took him off guard. He didn't know what to do for her, so he just took her in his arms and started making shushing noises, while gently rocking her from side to side like he used to do for his sister.

Joe heard Bruce talking. "I'm telling you guys, it was just a lover's spat. You can put the knives away. He wasn't going to hurt her." Joe didn't hear the other comment, but Bruce said, "Well, yeah, maybe she was trying to kill him. I didn't see that part before the rain."

Tom stepped out into the rain. "Post traumatic stress, she's been through a lot in just seven days. The grief is catching up to her. Then Joe has to go and pick on her. He's got anger management issues. Man, did she bitch slap him or what." The last part was with admiration and amusement.

"Leave Joe alone, he's had it rough, too, ya know." Tony stepped over in front of Tom, and he wasn't laughing. "Christ, the man was blown up saving her life. Then they tell him in the hospital that he's going to be a 'were' and fire him. All he's ever wanted is to be a detective. Now he has a girlfriend that does magic and who's got people trying for real to kill her. This is all pretty weird for us. Everything has happened fast, no time to adjust or think things through. And making us mad right now doesn't help." He was doing the quiet police yell by the end. Joe could tell Tony was barely holding it together.

Joe blinked as several things fell into place, "Steph." He shook her a little bit. "Steph, that's it. That's why they're after you. You can figure it out, and they don't want to give you the time."

"What?" She pulled away a little bit. "What did you say? Oh damn, I hate crying, and now I did it in front of you." She realized where she was. "On you," she said, covering her face as she tried to turn away.

"Steph, it's okay." He wouldn't let her turn. "You've been under a lot of stress. Hell, we both are. I'm goin' ta be a bear." He gently pulled at her hands so he could look at her eyes.

"Bullshit, you just think it's a stupid girl thing." The fight was coming back into her.

"I don't think that. You've had it hard, and you haven't had time to grieve for your loss. And there are people trying to kill you." She glanced up at him. "They send police to class so we can cope. Especially in traumatic stuff, like shooting someone, getting shot, getting blown up, or having a way hot girlfriend bitch slap you."

Stephanie giggled. "Did you just call me hot?"

"Yeah, cause you are." He smiled at her.

"I'm sorry I hit you. Are you still going to let me be your girlfriend?"

"Yeah, I'd like you to." He gave her a little peak on the cheek. "But there's a problem. I got an anger problem I didn't use to have."

Stephanie was all serious now. He just realized she was soaking wet even with her hooded rain jacket. "Anger management, what problem? I said I was sorry."

"Steph, I'm going to turn into a bear, a really big, pissed off bear. It won't be safe for you."

"You won't hurt me. I know you won't." She gently put her hand on his face.

"How do you know? I'm huge. I could hurt you without even meaning to. Just falling on you would hurt." He huffed and pointed to where she had been standing. "I could've hurt you right then."

"But you didn't." She looked away for a moment. "I know you won't." She looked back. Her eyes were trying to tell him something, but he didn't get it. "You won't."

"How do you know? If I hurt you …" Joe lost his voice as he visualized a scene in his mind's eye. He almost threw up.

"That's how I know."

"Steph, it might not be me. I might not be in control when I'm a bear."

"You won't hurt me." She looked sad. "Apparently, we now have to be concerned with me hurting you." Joe started to say something, and she put her fingers over his lips. "Sshh, just listen. Uncle Raymond didn't put me in those martial arts classes just to teach me to be tough. It was also to give me an outlet for my anger. I was very angry at the world for how it treated me. It has taken me years to get control and keep it. It appears some of my control is slipping as well." She looked down, and Joe couldn't tell if it was tears or rain dripping off her face. "Our little event here has shattered my control." She looked up at him, and lights were dancing in her eyes again. "I didn't mean to power a symbol when I slapped you, but I did. I could've killed you." Her voice caught, I … I …"

Now it was his turn to shush her. "But you didn't." He looked into her eyes and smiled. "You didn't, and you won't. Weirdness is happening. We'll just have to be more careful of each other."

She patted his face gently. "Slow, we'll take it slow and see where it leads us."

Joe nodded his agreement. "Slow, exactly, we'll take it slow."

She glanced down at herself. "I'm really wet now." She pushed herself up off him. "Why do I always end up sitting in your lap?" A sad smile touched her face.

"Cause you like it?"

She huffed. "Time, you said time. What did you mean?"

"The reason they've decided to take you out, it's so you can't figure out the symbols."

Stephanie looked a little sad. "Bruce and I puzzled that out yesterday, or at least proposed it as a theory. You think it has credence?"

"Yeah! Whoever the serial killer is, he is using symbols to do scary shit to people. He's selected at least two victims from your university, and someone tried to dart you. That definitely suggests they want you out of the way. The only rational reason is that you're a threat. How could you threaten them? You do symbols. There's something about the symbols that they don't want you to figure out."

Stephanie looked sad and felt sad as she turned toward the house. "I'm going to go change and go to work on the symbols."

Joe just sat there and gazed off into the rain. "You okay?" he heard Bruce ask Stephanie.

"No, public fight with my boyfriend with crying, just great. I suck as a girlfriend. You guys don't need those knives. You cut him, and I'll be bitch slapping you as well," he heard Stephanie say.

There was a bunch of muttering that Joe couldn't make out.

Tony stepped in front of him, offering his hand. "Come on, big guy, let's go get cleaned up. FBI will be here soon." Joe took his hand. Tony had to throw himself backward to counterbalance Joe getting up.

"What was with the Indian chief thing?" Joe asked.

"What are you talking about?"

"Right after she slapped me and before the water hit. You were standing there like some heap big chief."

"What the fuck are you talking about?" Tony was wild-eyed all of a sudden. "I was over by the bench the whole time."

Joe shook his head and looked back at Tony. The man was serious. "Nothin', she must've slapped me silly."

"No shit! She spun you around and set you on your ass." Tony was back to himself. "You still have the little girl's handprint on your face."

"Let her slap you, and we'll see how you do."

"Sorry, man, she's not my girlfriend. Bitch slappin' like that is just boyfriend-girlfriend stuff."

"Asshole."

"Who?" Bruce asked.

"Tom," Tony said as he pointed to Tom.

"Heh, don't get me in this."

Bruce laughed. Joe just shook his head and went to get breakfast and dry off.

Chapter 20

Stephanie was cold when she got back to her room, well, suite was more accurate. It was like no place she had ever lived in. Her "bedroom" was the size of her last apartment. She had an entry room with a small kitchen area, a small bedroom barely large enough for the Spartan bed and dresser. Then there was the master bedroom, complete with battleship-size, four-poster bed and expensive bedroom set to go with it. There was a bathroom off the bedroom she hadn't really been in yet. She'd spent most of her time in the newly appointed lab building and barn/theater. They both had bathrooms, one complete with shower. It was dark when Joe had brought her up last night.

She was still trying to figure out how she felt about that. He had carried her up like she was a little kid. It gave her a warm feeling that someone cared that much for her, and at the same time, it pissed her off that he had just picked her up. She was a grown woman and could damn well walk on her own feet.

She decided to take a shower to get warm. Agnes stepped out of the bathroom.

Agnes gave her a warm smile and a little curtsey, "Everything's ready for your ladyship."

"Why do you keep calling me your ladyship?"

"Because you're a lady and my employer." Agnes's face had become blank and innocent.

Stephanie frowned at her, "Rrriiiight?" They stared at each other, but Stephanie blinked first. "Okay, fine. So tell me, why do I have a kitchenette off the outer room?"

"For tea and snacks." Agnes smiled again with a twinkle in her eye. "Perhaps even a late night meal, intimate, if'n you catch my meaning. There is a lift from the kitchen."

"What? You're telling me there is a dumbwaiter from the kitchen."

"Yes, mum."

"Who builds houses like this?"

"If Mr. Peabody's information is correct, and it normally is, it was a Middle Eastern prince, here in North America for education."

"Really?"

"Yes, mum."

This was a type of circle Stephanie had never even dreamed of traveling in, let alone understanding. "Whatever, I'm going to take a shower and get warm."

"Yes, mum," again with a little curtsey. "I've laid out towels and provided what amenities are on hand. Shall I help you disrobe?"

"Hell no!" It just leaped out of Stephanie. "I can undress myself, thank you very much."

Agnes didn't miss a beat, with that little bob. "As you wish. Ring if you need anything, anything at all, mum," She whisked out of the room with a mischievous smile.

The bathroom was a religious experience. Huge just didn't say it: walk-in shower, vanity with angle mirrors, a full-length, three-paneled-mirror set with an articulated arm holding another mirror next to it, another vanity with just drawers, a tub she could use for a fishing pond, and everything in white marble shot through with grey highlights with big plush throw rugs in front of the water projects. Three towel racks, only one with towels, and she found they were heated when she tried to use one to lean against. The one with towels was closest to the shower. "How did she know I was going to take a shower?" Stephaney asked. "Better question, how am I supposed to ring for something when there's no bell? Phones, there're three phones in the room."

Stephanie picked one up. "Yes, mum?" Agnes asked.

"Nothing, just … ah … testing." She hung up.

Shaking her head, she stripped her clothes off and hung them on one of the heated towel racks to dry. The shower was about as complicated as some of her lab equipment, with nozzles spraying from both sides and the back and at three different levels, not to mention it was big enough for six. She got it puzzled out and streaming hot water at her, just as the shivers started. The water was luxurious and calming. Agnes had even put out hotel-like complementary shampoo and conditioner, expensive ones.

Once the warmth started seeping in, she pulled out her problems and started worrying at them. "I have a boyfriend," she said out loud, but not like it was a good thing.

"I have a boyfriend that can feel when I'm sad and what direction I'm in." That one didn't sound any better.

"I have a boyfriend that can feel stuff off me and who thinks he is a were-bear guided by the Great Spirit." She snorted a laugh at that one. "Holy shit, he believes it, too. I like having a boyfriend. What am I going to do?" she asked quietly, bowing her head to the water. The hot water didn't answer.

"Okay, leave that one. Loss of control." She started doing her hair. It seemed longer, requiring more shampoo. "That symbol just popped up when I got angry. I really wanted to kick his ass. Eeep," she chirped as the symbol appeared to her again, and her random thought triggered it. She held her hand away from her as it glowed faintly. She thought about it going away, fading, slowly draining, being washed away with the water, and it still glowed. She consciously pulled the symbol to her mind's eye and then willed it away. Her hand still glowed. She washed the soap back off her face and hair, holding her hand off to the side.

"Crap, now what?" She looked around for something conductive. The water pipes were not an answer. If she set up some type of steam explosion, it could water hammer the whole house. She slid open the shower doors with her left hand and looked around. She tried swatting her hand into a towel, nothing. "Crap."

She touched the floor, nothing. She gently touched the pipe of the heated towel racks, nothing. She sat on the rug and dripped for a moment. Inspiration did not strike. She couldn't walk around with a glowing hand. "Hmm, I slapped Joe. Hit him hard." Getting up on her hand and knees, she kept the glowing hand off the floor, moved over to a section of floor on the side of the room and slapped her hand down. It was like a gun shot. Her hand tingled, but the tile shattered. "Wow, there's force in that. Apparently, intent and physical affect to trigger."

There was a knock at the bathroom door. "M'lady, are you all right?" Agnes was apparently right outside her door. The handle started to turn.

"I'm fine. Had a little accident that's all." The handle continued to turn. "Heh, I'm naked in here. Stay out." She looked for the lock and found it didn't have one. The door started to open. "I said, stay out." Her intention was to throw her weight against the door, but instead, a symbol flashed into her mind's eye, then zoomed out to cover the door, and triggered with her intention to stop the door. There was a soundless expansion of air pressure, the door slammed shut, and seemed to disappear into a seamless wall.

Staring at the door, she realized she had studied that symbol, but hadn't figured out its use. Now she had one.

"M'lady, what have you done?" Agnes sounded more amazed than shocked.

"I'll get back to you." She stepped up and examined what had been a doorway. Now it appeared as if someone had just put the molding around a door shape in a normal wall. "Cool, I like that one." She turned and almost ran into a wavering blue, American Indian woman, who was looking at her sternly.

Stephanie backpedaled so fast her feet slipped out from under her, and she ended up sitting on the floor, naked, with her legs spread and this blue spirit woman standing between them, shaking her head. Stephanie's temper finally kicked in. "What?"

The woman looked startled then puzzled.

"I'm taking a shower here. What do you want?"

The woman pointed at her.

"No way. You weren't around to save my mom, why and the hell would I want you now?" Stephanie pulled her legs in and scooted back to a wall to stand up. "I don't believe in you!"

The blue woman crossed her arms and gave Stephanie a look.

"That's right, I don't believe. Where's the data?"

The woman gestured up and down at herself and then made brief "ta-da" gesture to the sides.

"I don't care. You could be a delusion. Maybe I fell and hit my head in the shower, and all this is a dream."

The woman frowned at her and pointed at the shattered tile and the not-a-door.

Stephanie started to say something, then shut her mouth frowning. "Okay, you got a point. What do you want?"

The woman pointed at her again and then made a gesture like she was drawing someone into her chest to hug.

"But I don't need you. Go find someone else. I don't need anyone." Stephanie pulled a towel down and wrapped it around herself. "Just go away!"

"M'lady, who are you yelling at?" There was pounding on the wall.

"Don't mind me. I'm just taking a shower," she yelled at the wall. Back to the blue woman, she hissed, "I don't need you!"

The woman took on the image of another woman briefly while pointing at Stephanie.

"That's not fair! You leave my mother out of it. She's gone. You let her die!"

The woman pantomimed hugging someone to her, then releasing it toward Stephanie. Her face was a picture of deep sorrow and loss.

Sorrow and loss slammed into Stephanie and had her sinking to the floor in tears; first her father, who was a vague memory of warmth, protection, and peppermint; then her mother, soft, caring, smelling of rosemary and love. Her mother's last act had been to push her daughter out of the window of a burning house to save her. Then her Uncle Raymond; hard as granite, difficult to understand, smelling of tobacco, whisky, leather, and gun powder, but always there for her. He was the rock the world smashed against before it could reach her. They were all lost to her. She was alone.

She was brought out of her grief by something really heavy smashing into the wall. "Joe," she said. She felt him on the other side of the wall. Sad, pissed off, and determined to get to her side. Joe, heavy and angry, hit and shook the wall again.

Something fluttered against her face. She jerked around to see the woman gently touching her. The feeling she used to get when her mother hugged her, touched her heart, and she smelled rosemary and heather.

Stephanie was shocked. "What? You're telling me she's still here? She still loves me?"

The woman stood up with the look of tenderness mixed with sorrow on her face as she nodded. "Yes." Stephanie actually heard her.

Stephanie wiped at her tears. "I'll think about it." She made sure the towel was covering her before she summoned the symbol, visualized it covering the doorway, and then pulling back off of it. The door shimmered and reappeared just before Joe smashed it off its hinges. Then she realized she hadn't known how to take the symbol down before now.

Stephanie glanced over to see the woman with some expression on her face that Stephanie didn't recognize as she pointed at Joe. She nodded, then pointed between Joe and Stephanie with a faint, hopeful smile, making the hugging motion. She faded out as Joe knelt in beside Stephanie.

"Steph, are you okay?" Concern was evident in his face.

"Damn it!" she blurted out.

Joe looked really confused and hurt. "Ah … I can fix the door."

"NO, no, it's just … Okay, so this Great Spirit thing may have some validity." She sounded grumpy even to herself.

He blinked a few times before finally being able to speak. "Ah … what happened?" He was all but growling.

Glancing over his shoulder, she saw Agnes and several of the guards. "Agnes, clear out and take all the guards with you. Please. I'm fine."

"Yes m'lady. All right, m'laddies, ya heard her ladyship, out ya go." Agnes sounded amused.

Stephanie waited until she heard the outer door close. "The Great Spirit, she appeared to me again."

"Again?"

"Yeah, I saw her the first time just after I blew myself up yesterday. Then I was having a moment in the shower, ah, … never mind."

"So, now you believe?" He had a tone she didn't like.

"I always believed. It's just … hmmm … I'm going to need some time on this, okay?"

He started to say something and then caught himself. Joe seemed to be riding the edge of angry.

She didn't want to fight again. "Look, I know this is what started our fi … arg … disagreement earlier, but I'm going to need time to process this. Can you give me some time?"

"You bet. I won't bring it up until you do." He leaned in and pecked her on the cheek. "You all right? You need me to help with …" he glanced around like he just noticed the bathroom, with shower running, wet soapy hair, and her towel.

She glanced down to see that it didn't exactly cover all of her. She looked back up, and their eyes met. She got shy and tugged at it like she could make it bigger to cover her at both ends.

"Maybe I … ah … well … I'll just give you some space here." Blushing red, he got up, picked up the door, and sat it in place from the other side.

Stephanie shook her head. "I've got a boyfriend. We need to go on a date."

She picked herself up and finished up in the shower without any further problems. Got dressed in warm clothes, a proper flannel shirt, water repellant coat, and headed for the barn.

She didn't talk to anyone in the house or on the way to the barn, but she knew they were around. Turning on all the equipment, she noticed the doors and windows had been sealed with plastic and duct tape and a big space heater had been added to the equipment. It looked like a jet engine and put out a roaring blast of hot air, faintly scented with kerosene. The barn was a big space, so the heater wasn't all that close to the hanging twelve by twelve screen. Waiting for the computers to come up, she closed her eyes and slowly turned around in a circle. "Yep, Joe is that away." She pointed back toward the house on the second floor. "I've got a boyfriend, and I can point the direction to him. My life is officially complicated."

Chapter 21

The wireless keyboard let her control the projection monitor and the computers while sitting in a lawn chair. She brought up the completed symbol on the big screen. It started with a big picture of her getting blown up with a little yuck icon in the corner before switching to the symbol image.

"Bruce." Shaking her head, she settled into the lawn lounger to study.

The completed symbol was complex and intricate. At first glance, it resembled a large circular set of runes and other complex tracings intersected by a smaller set. As she studied it, the patterns began to emerge. It was a huge set of smaller symbols combined into a larger structure. The large circular space was where Andy Stone was held down. She wasn't sure about the purpose of the smaller circular set. She put down the keyboard and moved closer.

There, she recognized a cluster of symbols, and another, then a whole string of them. They were a mix of Egyptian and several from other different, ancient cultures. She moved back over to the chair and keyboard. A few stokes and she had a virtual mouse tied to her hand movements. She started picking the recognized symbols out of the greater whole and capturing them in smaller windows. Once the known ones were extracted, she started an algorithm to isolate the remaining ones and start matching it to her database. It was fascinating. She was getting excited. Someone had put this all together from bits and pieces of different cultures. She started studying the ones she didn't know, comparing the angles and symmetry to others. Tracing them with her air mouse, tasting them with the, … whatever it was she had, the knack. Fascinating, it was fascinatingly complex.

"Hey."

Stephanie jerked around. "Bruce, I'm going to put bells on you."

He stepped over and set down a thermos. “Brought coffee.” He poured her a cup as she turned back to the symbols. He waved it in front of her face. “I want to talk to you without the others around.”

She disabled the air mouse and grabbed the cup. “Talk to me, about what?”

“Magic.”

She started to say something smartass, but stopped at the serious look on his face. “Okay, it’s science, not magic.”

Bruce picked up his cup. “To us, it is science to us.” She started to say something, but he held up his hand. “Hear me out. I have three topics I would like to cover then you can ignore me if you like.”

“Okay.”

Bruce didn’t normally take this approach with her, but when he did, he usually had valuable data.

“Magic. What did the common man in 500 AD call the bubbling solution created by pouring liquids and solids together?”

“Alchemy, potions?”

Bruce gave a slight nod. “What about the stargazers who predicted the future through the motions of celestial bodies?”

“I don’t know. Soothsayers, seers?

“How about the old people who helped heal the villagers through collected herb lore or the wisdom of age?”

“Wise men, witches, warlocks?” She shrugged. “Are you trying to tell me that these are the roots of our science today? Chemistry for alchemy. Astrophysics for stargazers. Medical doctors for the village witch? We know that.”

He ticked his head to the side, indicating a point to her. “Not exactly. What they did was called magic by the common person because the common person didn’t know what they knew and couldn’t duplicate it.”

“Are you going to lecture at me?”

“For a minute.” He grinned at her. “The commoners wanted to give it a label, so they could feel like they understood what was happening, even if they didn’t really. Even the practitioners called it magic. In time, when the knowledge was written down and studied for a thousand years, it became common knowledge and thus known commonly. It also was transformed by science into known quantities.

"You made an incredible breakthrough last week when you powered the Solomon Circle. It's never been done before. Since then, you have continued to do things we don't really understand. Our FFT theory really isn't valid any-more, but we'll figure it out. As a matter-of-fact, I have a few ideas, but that isn't my point."

"What is your point?" Stephanie was trying hard to not get mad.

"My point is you have done something repeatable, but not fully under-stood. That is scary to people of science or people around science. It is down-right terrifying to the commoner. They want to label it, so they call it magic. Magic, the term, is becoming a common use item again because things are happening that are not understood or readily explainable by science. Let the people around you call it magic until we can fully define it. It doesn't hurt anything; as a matter-of-fact, it will help. People think they know what magic is, so it makes them more comfortable. Keeping them comfortable is a good thing."

"Why?"

"Because terrified people strike out at those things scaring them; they want it to stop. If it is a person, they want that person to stop. Our very advanced and scientific society isn't very sophisticated when it comes to scary, undefined stuff. People revert quickly to pitchforks and torches. I think being burnt at the stake would hurt."

Stephanie snorted. "You think I should lead them astray cause it will make them feel better?"

"Sort of." Bruce made a chopping gesture with his hand. "Let's table that for the moment and move to topic two. Who funded your research?"

"You already know, it was the Department of Energy."

"You sure?"

"Their name was on the checks."

"My grant's from DARPA for applied energy applications."

"I didn't know you got a grant."

"Yep, but I don't think the money was from DARPA or at least not for en-ergy research. I don't think yours was, either."

"What are you talking about? Why?" She was getting interested now.

"Ten years ago, Bosh-Gates didn't even have a physics department, let alone an applied physics department. Before 2000, they didn't have any hard science departments. They had a smattering of biology and chemistry, but that was really in support of the holistic medical areas and acupuncture. The university was also studying all the mystic areas, and frankly, was laughed at because of it, until after 2000."

"History! What's your point?"

"When magic started showing up, research in magic started. Your funding was the first major infusion of government money to the university in three years. It was your research into symbols that brought me to B & G."

"I know, you told me that when you showed up. Your point?"

"Why would the DOE fund your research? Why would the government be interested in your symbols research?"

"They are interested in the potential for sustainable energy."

"When you're the only one who could make a symbol fire, until six months ago, you were the only one who could make them work. Why would the government be interested in your research if you're the only one who can make it work?"

Stephanie was at a loss now. She had never thought of it in those terms. For her, it had always been the pursuit of symbol knowledge.

"They want you." She had never seen Bruce like this. "They want you until they can figure out how you do what you do and then they won't need you. Your research, our research, is about being able to have anyone power a symbol. Have anyone create a powerful effect from drawings in the air. Think of what a person could do with the power of the symbols? Think of what you are just learning to do with the power of these symbols."

Stephanie glanced over at the complex collection of symbols displayed on the screen.

"Exactly, now they have an example of what applied symbol knowledge does. It isn't pretty. Do you know what it does yet?"

"A little."

He walked over to the screen and pointed at four symbols. "These suggest that it does something with the life force or soul of the individual held in this," he circled his hand around the large circle or the symbols contained there, "region. We saw what it did to Andy. I think it sucked his soul out and transferred it to whoever was," he motioned to the smaller circular area, "in this circle."

"Oh crap!" Stephanie snatched up the keyboard and started typing. On the screen, symbols were highlighted on the main diagram and copies of then started streaming vertically in a column. "These are linkage symbols for channeling energy or whatever."

Bruce waved his arms to get her attention. "Back to my point. The government is now interested in you and your research for a different reason. It's no longer academic. It's now application. And you have shown them its destructive application. What does the government do with potentially destructive sciences?"

"Oh Christ, they try to control them."

"Yep. So, you do magic and can destroy things with it and may be able to teach others to do it."

"I'm a weapon, and I can multiply." Stephanie sat down abruptly and stared at the screen. "I am so screwed."

"Not yet."

She glanced back up.

"They don't know exactly how you do it, mainly because we don't know how you're doing it. If they thought it was tied to an external source, they might stay back longer."

"External source?"

"Yeah, like the Great Spirit is lending you earthly power from her spirit domain."

"Oh, that's bullsh ..." Stephanie allowed him to cut her off.

"Ah, ah," he held his hand up. "Don't. Just think before you speak. You have stated that the Great Spirit has appeared to you twice. You, Joe, and Tony have been having the same dream." She started to say something again. "Ah, ah, hold it. You don't have to acknowledge a deep belief, but you do have data now. Ponder that data, consider what it could mean, collect more."

Stephanie frowned. She had to admit he did have a point.

"Good, keep thinking. Now add back into it my earlier discussion about magic and how it makes the un-knowing feel better. Also, how the government doesn't like uncontrolled destructive capabilities lose. So, I propose you connect it this way. The magic power you have isn't understood yet, and it is influenced by the divine, which would give the government pause. They really don't like religion and how it could affect policies. Further, the commoner feels like you have more control over this mystery power if it is constrained by a deity. It calms them."

"What?" She couldn't keep it contained any longer.

"Steph, you have a collection of professional tough guys around you who are all but pissing themselves over what you can do. They have arrived at the conclusion that you are a religious figure from the North American Indian mythos. They are willing to wait and see what happens."

"Bruce, I'm not going to be parading around like a priestess to …"

He cut her off. "I didn't say you had to. Just consider. Think about it. People are arriving at their own conclusions. Let them; don't correct them while we continue our research. Buy us time."

Stephanie started to say something and stopped. Started to say something else and stopped. She took a deep breath and let it out. "Okay, I will consider it. As you pointed out, new data has been introduced." She was amazed at how she actually liked the idea of it being divinely influenced. "What's your last topic? I would like to get back to the murder stuff. I feel like I'm close."

Bruce nodded. "Okay, last topic. You need to take it easy on Joe and Tony."

"What the hell!" Stephanie almost leaped up off the lounge chair.

"God, would you chill! Your recent life adventures have been pretty traumatic, but the nature of the symbols involvement really hasn't been that bad. After all, we have been working toward this for the better part of three years. Joe and Tony's lives have just been radically altered and in a direction they never in their wildest dreams considered. They think they are were-creatures. The Bone Patrol thinks they are were-monsters that will have to be killed in three days. And probably the most amazing thing of all is that Joe and you have fallen in love during all this."

"Hey … You … What … You know …" Stephanie stopped talking. Nothing was coming out the way she wanted it to anyway. She did have this warm feeling in her tummy. She wasn't alone in the world. The thought of Joe did that to her.

"People make light of it, but in my experience the real thing is a miracle. You two have it. Stop trying to screw it up!"

"Not fair!"

"Is fair. You can't help but poke at it just to see what it will do. It's like an experiment in stress analysis. Joe is walking a tight edge. Not to mention that you two have some type of link that is mystic in nature. He has his emotions and yours mixed in with this amazing life-changing event."

"My life's changed, too." It even sounded petty to her as she said it.

"Yes, it has, but let's face it, you were raised by the apocalypse cowboy, so you have had some training."

"Apocalypse cowboy, God, if only Uncle Raymond could hear that, he would ..." Stephanie trailed off as his loss hit her again. She turned away so Bruce wouldn't see the tears leaking. "Why does it hit me like this?"

Bruce put his hands on her shoulders and turned her into his hug. "Grief can be like that. Plus, you really haven't had that much time to deal with it."

"It sucks. I have cried more in the last week than in the previous ten years."

"Yeah, it does suck. A lot of stuff has happened, but consider, you are tied to Joe just as he is tied to you. Your emotional shell may have cracked when you fell for Joe."

She stepped away from him. "How did you get so wise? You're only seven years older than me."

"It's not the years, it's the miles. I have lots of extra miles."

"What miles? You haven't shared shit with me for as long as I've known you."

"Point. I don't like remembering." Bruce stepped away, gazing off. Visibly, she saw him decide something. He turned back, "There are some jobs in the military that just burn you up. Rangers, Special Forces, I thought I had something to prove. I have seen shit that would turn you white!" Stephanie frowned at him. "Ah, you are white. It worked."

"Funny."

"I was in for twelve years and change, the last four were doing things you're not supposed to talk about."

"Your timeline seems a bit skewed. You should be older, or you started very young."

Bruce sighed, "I graduated from high school at fifteen, college at eighteen, with a masters in physics, genius, remember. I was too young to get a job, and I felt I had something to prove. My sexual orientation caused problems for other people. I allowed people to mess with my head. So, I joined the army. I was good at it. Big surprise, there aren't many smart people enlisting, I did well. The explosive release of energy, coupled with a masters in physics, just lead me to special weapons. I also learned the knack of turning off the smarts and just following orders. That's a hard one because sometimes they want you to do stupid shit stuff. Anyway, the last mission was one of those kinds of things, so I got out."

"Uncle Raymond told me they were grooming you to go into the dark."

Bruce laughed and turned away. It wasn't a funny ha-ha laugh, it was more a I-can't-believe-it laugh. "God, he was some kind of operator and plugged in. Yeah, he had it right. I was being groomed. They were a little pissed when I walked." Bruce stopped talking and gazed off at nothing.

"Okay," Stephanie poked him in the arm. "I'll try not to screw things up with Joe." She waited for him to look at her. "Can I get back to work, or do you have any other annoying words of wisdom?"

He smiled weakly. "I'm all out. I've had my say." He purposely turned back to the screen. "So, where are we?"

"Hi guys," a seismic disturbance rumbled. "Bruce, you pissing Steph off again?" Joe was leaning against the doors.

For a big man he moves way too quietly, Stephanie thought. "How long have you been there?"

"I just got here. I got to hear a little about Bruce the Genius' past."

Stephanie stuck her tongue out at Bruce and turned smiling to Joe. "He was being mean to me. Would you thump him?"

Joe shook his head. "Na, he was probably telling you something you didn't want to hear. There seems to be a lot of that going around this morning." The last part seemed to drip with extra meaning. "I felt you get sad and lonely, so I thought I would come hold your hand."

Stephanie was going to say she had work to do, but changed her mind. "Sure, grab another lawn chair, and we can snuggle while I try to figure this out."

Joe huffed. "You would forget I was here in about a second." He pushed off the doorway and stepped over to her. "Just give me a hug, and I'll go away, so you can work. The FBI should be here soon. I'll run interference."

Stephanie grinned at him and stepped up to hug him. He bent down and she hugged then kissed him. "Give me a couple of hours and …" She didn't know how to finish it.

He smiled. "Have lunch, we'll have lunch. Then we need to go meet your mentor."

"Yeah, that's it." She kissed him again. It did make her feel better.

Joe squeezed her a little and kissed her then stood up out of her reach. "Bruce, try not to piss her off. It really disturbs my concentration."

"You got it, big guy. No pissing off the little priestess." Bruce smirked.

"Don't you start on that," Stephanie shook her finger at him. She pointed at Bruce while she turned to Joe. "Sure you won't thump him?"

Joe shook his head as he turned to leave. "Play nice, kids."

They turned back to the huge puzzle and started picking at it. Bruce fired up another work station and started doing something with the database while Stephanie concentrated on the individual runes. She lost track of the time as she pulled symbols out of the connected mess of them.

"Hey," she pointed at the screen with the air mouse. A symbol highlighted. "Bruce, you see this one?"

He turned away from his station. "What one?"

"The one circled in purple."

"Yeah, what about it?"

"It's mine."

"What?"

"That symbol is mine. I created it from pieces of several Egyptian glyphs. I invented it. What is it doing in this mess?"

"I don't know. What does it do?"

"Nothing, it doesn't do anything. It was in a paper I submitted …" Her voice faded off.

"Steph?"

"I used it as an example in a white paper. It was there to illustrate how a symbol … how a symbol could be used to contain life energy." She turned to stare at Bruce. "It doesn't work."

He looked back at the image. "Well, whoever read the paper thought it did. It is in the greater drawing six times." Bruce concentrated for a moment. "Let me try something. It will take me a few minutes. Why don't you take a break?"

"Okay, you want anything?"

"Fresh pot of coffee."

She picked up the carafe and almost ran into Agent Farmer as he opened the person door mounted in the big door. He was in a dark suit, thin tie, black shoes, he even had on dark sunglasses. She started to make a joke about his attire and decided against it. According to rumor, FBI agents didn't have a sense of humor. "What can I do for you Agent Farmer?"

"You can share with me what you had discovered. I will share with you the data we have from the other five crime scenes."

"Five more killed that way?"

"Yes. At least we think it is. I would like your opinion. I have posted the info in the boardroom."

"Okay, Bruce wanted a minute to do something with the big symbol, so I'll go over and take a look at it."

Bruce looked over. "Hey, coffee."

"After I get him some coffee."

Agent Farmer held out his hand. "I'll get him coffee. You go look. I would like your opinion as soon as possible. It may change our response."

The person door opened and Lawrence maneuvered a large, covered tray through. "Ah, there you are, mum. I have some coffee and munchies that Cook sent for you. Also, Detective Bremer is entertaining several FBI analysts in the other outbuilding, and he would like you to join him." He deftly flipped out a tray stand and placed the huge tray on it. There was a feast of goodies set out. "Also, there appears to be anther contingent of FBI, not associated with Agent Farmer, in the entryway. They are requesting that all your research data be turned over to them. I have them cooling their heels, and I have phoned your solicitors. They are on their way. Is there anything else, mum?"

She just stared at him for a moment. "Ah, I don't know." She stared at him a moment longer then turned to Agent Farmer.

He nodded before she could speak. "I'll take my newly arrived colleagues."

"I guess I'll go look at the boardroom and see what Joe wants. He feels upset." That last statement actually made Agent Farmer do a double take.

"You can determine Detective Bremer's emotional state at a distance?"

She hesitated and then slowly answered. "Yes." Lawrence and Bruce, both shook their heads no.

Agent Farmer squinted at her for a moment. "Don't tell anyone else from the FBI that. But I would like to discuss it later with you." He pulled his phone out and initiated a call while walking away.

"Oops," Stephanie announced. "I better get over to the boardroom." Lawrence held the door for her as she went out.

"Mum," he said as she started to step through. "A word of advice, don't admit anything supernatural to the government."

"Right, my bad."

He just nodded.

Chapter 22

Joe turned to look at Stephanie sitting next to him in the backseat of the Suburban. He could tell before he turned that she wasn't happy, but he knew that without his special connection. She had just wanted it to be him and Tony with her to meet Rosemary. Stoneman had stepped in, and it had gotten loud and ugly. He would remember that for later in their relationship.

"How long are you going to be with me?" Stephanie blurted into the uncomfortable silence.

"Who?" Joe was puzzled by that one. He hoped she wasn't asking about him.

"Not you, Joe." She patted his arm. "Them, how long will I have to have protection?"

Joe covered her hand with his and shrugged. "I don't know. Mr. Stoneman?"

Her security detail lead turned in his seat to look at her. "We've been paid for a month, but I think you should consider longer, much longer."

Joe glanced over to see Stephanie frowning. "Longer than a month, huh? Six months?" Joe could tell the wheels were turning behind her eyes. "Don't know who the threat is, or you do know and don't know how to go to the source?"

Stoneman looked between Stephanie and Joe, like he was weighing something. "It's the source, there are too many possibilities. Your uncle amassed quite an organization; it is highly likely that that is the problem. Someone is trying to take it over, or at least, eliminate you and the cutouts you represent."

Joe was expecting Stephanie to ask a bunch of questions about cutouts, but she just nodded. "Steph, what's he talking about?" She turned to weigh him with her eyes.

"The money and … ah … other things, personal things." She was searching his face for something.

He could feel her internal turmoil. He made a decision. "Never mind, I don't need to know. I trust you. I know your uncle had an, ah, … interesting past. Let's just leave it at that. These other people are just breaking the law. That makes them bad in my book. We find them and arrest them."

She was continuing to study him. "What happens if the law can't do that? What do we do if they are untouchable by the law?"

"There aren't many things the law can't touch, but …" Joe had to puzzle his way through it for a moment. "If they're held outside the law, then … or we … we make them stop. I trust you. I won't drag you in front of a judge."

Her look changed, and he felt a warmth in his chest like nothing before. It made him smile. She reached out to grab his arm. "You would do that for me, just trust my judgment?" Her words were nothing close to the language in her eyes.

"I want … It's …" Joe struggled for a moment, trying to find the right words. "Family, we're courting, that makes us like family. You do … stuff for family. I want us to be family." His words sent her emotions tumbling, smashing between extremes. "If everything works out. Slow, we're taking it slow." He rushed out the last part to try and stop her emotional turmoil.

Stoneman gave him a look that Joe couldn't read before turning back to the front. Joe decided he didn't care; sometimes you just had to take care of business.

Uncomfortable silence settled over them.

"Are we there yet?" Stoneman said with a completely dead tone. Everyone cracked up.

"Now, why are we going to Vashon Island, but it isn't?" Joe asked, trying not to think too hard about what she didn't say to him, but expected him to understand. Tony was real quiet on the other side. Joe could tell he was thinking hard as well. Tony hadn't had a good lunch. Something had happened, and it was bothering him.

Stephanie squeezed his arm, telling him something, but he wasn't getting it. "It's a joke. Rosemary and I were shopping one day, and all the fashion shoppers were out. Fashion, vashion, Vashon, it's a word play about the fashion shoppers, they seem to be really trendy …" Joe couldn't help but stare at her. Her and shopping, fashion, girlie girl stuff; it didn't fit. She was like a female super nerd geek. Little miss flannel shopping for girlie stuff. He couldn't get his head around it. She frowned and let go of his arm. "Ya know, it's not important. We're going to a little sitting area at the edge of Redmond Town Square. It has a little pavilion surrounded by trees that gives the illusion of solitude like an island. Rosemary likes it and thinks it's funny to sit there and mock the shoppers. She likes watching the people; okay, she makes fun of them. Ya know, the human herd." Stephanie smiled.

"The human herd? What does that mean?" Tom sounded offended.

"Rosemary is a Wiccan priestess and a professor of anthropology. She studies cultures and the cross-culture implication of certain fads. She's been studying the upsurge in enchanted events in today's world and how it affects the general man or woman on the street. The human herd refers to how people react in groups to certain stimulus. She thinks those focused on having the latest fashions are just silly and actually developed a recognition standard for various types of shoppers."

Joe frowned. "That doesn't sound very nice. She just sits there pointing and laughing at people as they come by excited about their purchases. I mean, there are some self-absorbed, fluff-headed people out there that feel the latest fashion is more important than food, but …" He just left it hanging.

"You meant fluff-headed women, didn't you? Judging the judger, are we?" Joe was trying to formulate a diplomatic comeback when she smiled and bumped him. "I don't get it either, but she likes it. It became our thing to do when she would take me out to buy girl stuff. She would point and mock, and I would tell her how bad she was. She told me it was therapy for me. I didn't get to do too many girl things growing up. So, she felt it would help me put things in perspective. I think." She smiled at him and batted her eyelashes.

"Okay, I get it now, making fun of the shopaholic posh princesses with daddy's credit card," Tom added with a snide twist.

Stephanie laughed. "Yeah, pretty much. Oops, turn here." She pointed over his shoulder from the backseat, which only worked because the center seat had only a lap belt. "Go over there. That's the closest point to the island. See, it's right there," she pointed.

"What's right there?" Joe was really puzzled now.

"Tom, pull in here," Stephanie ordered. Tom complied. She turned to look at Joe and pointed. "It's right there."

"I don't, ah … ah I don't see it," Joe and Tom said at the same time.

Stephanie reached down, pulled Joe's hand up to point with it. "It's right there."

Joe felt a tingle in his hand, and then he could see a blueish-tinged pavilion with shrubbery planted at several points around it. "What did you just do?"

"Nothing, why?"

"Because I can see it now, and I couldn't before."

"Wow, really." She reached over and grabbed Tony's hand. "Does it work for you, too?"

He jerked like she had stabbed him. Throwing the door open, he all but fell out of the Suburban to get away from her. "Yeah, I can see it." Tony was trying to act cool, but Joe could see the whites of his eyes. Stephanie had just freaked him out.

"Tom, can you see it?" Stephanie asked.

"No."

Stephanie touched the back of his neck, skin to skin. "How about now?"

"Wow, it's kind of bluish-tinged. Did you just scribe a detect mag … energy symbol?" He started getting out of the vehicle as well.

"I don't think so. I don't know why I can see it. But you're right; it is kind of outlined in cyan. I can see Rosemary and another person." Stoneman just raised his hand in the front seat, and Stephanie grabbed it.

"Nothing from me, doc. I still can't see it. Doc, wait here until we secure the area. Tom, stay with her and describe the area to the team, since they can't see it, either." Stoneman got out and Tom got back into the Suburban and took Stephanie's hand. He started talking in low tones into his secret radio. Joe couldn't really make out the words.

Joe watched the team from their vehicle and the one behind them, get out, spread out, and move forward, ten men looking casual and natural. He knew all the guards were armed, but he couldn't see any weapons. They all looked like different men, some in suits, some in jeans, one was a construction worker.

Joe played with the sight he gained by touching Stephanie. He touched her hand. *There*, he thought and lifted his finger off her hand. *Gone, there, gone, there, gone.* He felt Stephanie's eyes on him and her humor at his actions. "So, here's the question, why? Why does touching you let me see that?"

"I don't know why." She was laughing a little at his actions. "I'll have to think about it."

Joe looked over at her and then turned back to keep scanning the surroundings. "The night you got beat up, the first time, Rosemary snuck into the hospital by using a spell. That was how she got the healing symbol to you. The no-see-me thing didn't work this well, but it was working."

"Really, she has a symbol that lets her hide?" Stephanie turned back to look at the professor. "I'll have to ask her about that."

"Okay, Doctor Blackraven, the area is clear." Tom slid out of the Suburban and gestured for them to follow.

Joe and Tony took up positions slightly behind her and to each side with Tom leading.

"Okay, Tony," Stephanie said quietly. "What happened when I touched you?"

"What are you talking about?" Tony sounded angry.

"Tony," Joe cut in. "Just tell us. You've been acting wound up since lunch."

"I had a visitation," Tony whispered.

"What?" Joe and Stephanie stopped at the same time to look at him.

"Keep walking," Tony motioned after Tom. "Ya know the person in our dreams, she appeared to me. Spoke to me."

"What did she say?" Joe asked.

"It's personal. It's about her." He pointed at Stephanie.

"I'm right here."

"I know. It wasn't real clear. I didn't really understand everything, but I think I'm, like your protector or something. Like Joe, I'm kind of linked to you." Tony shrugged, and for a big tough guy, he looked unsure and nervous. He gestured forward. "Could you just go to your meeting? We'll talk about this later."

"Sure," Stephanie said and turned to walk on.

Joe could tell Tom couldn't really see the area. Neither could he, until he grabbed Stephanie's hand. Tony just walked into the area of solitude with them.

Joe felt a tingle and got a whiff of something as they passed the line made by two of the trees. There were six trees in total, evenly spaced around three tables and nine chairs. The center of the six trees was twenty feet or so across. Stephanie surged forward to hug the older woman.

Professor Stein was above average height, a trim figure, and a little grey in her golden-brown hair. Her clothes reminded Joe of a gypsy, complete with bangles and feathers in her hair, but reserved and respectable. She had a cloak with a hood for when it started raining. It was an odd combination, nice looking, but odd. The man with her rose as she did. He was like the quintessential urban male; blue jeans, sneakers, jacket, average everything, nothing to call attention to himself. He was remarkable because he wasn't remarkable in any way.

"Rosemary, I was so worried. Why did you run off?" Joe could feel that Stephanie meant every word. He could also tell that this woman meant a great deal more to Stephanie than being just a colleague.

"I had to, honey. They were coming for me next." She was hugging Stephanie back and rocking a little side to side. "I wasn't the one in trouble." Joe could see the tears glistening in Rosemary's eyes as she pushed Stephanie back to arms' length. "You get beat up, then jumped by a gang the next night. I've been watching the news. My goddess, shot by the police after your truck was blown up." She touched Stephanie's face and looked her up and down. "Oh my, by the Earth Mother's blessing." She had gently grabbed Stephanie's chin and was shifting her face from side to side. "I can see the … What has gotten into you?"

"I've had a hard week."

Rosemary's laughter was like silver bells at Christmas. "That's one way to say it. Then they arrest you for murder. Oh, my little rune weaver, you have had a very hard week." Rosemary hugged her tenderly again with tears streaking down her face.

Joe heard Stephanie snuffle back tears as she hugged Rosemary. "I couldn't have made it without Joe and Tony here and, of course, Bruce."

"Where are my manners?" She stepped back from Stephanie's embrace and dabbed at the tears on her face. She stepped forward to Joe, offering her hand. When he took it, she covered his huge hand with both of her tiny one's. "Officer Bremer, I know I was suspicious of you that night in the hospital. I am sorry for that. I can never thank you enough for saving her from the explosion." She bowed her head over his hand. "The Earth Mother's blessing on you." Joe felt a tingle run over his hand and up his arm. He smelled flowers. Something loosened in his chest as warmth spread throughout him. He felt strong, full of energy.

"What did you just do?" Joe asked while tugging gently back on his hand. She didn't let go.

"I gave you a blessing from the Earth Mother for the help you have given my little rune weaver." Rosemary seemed confused.

"Your blessing flared some kind of … well ... ah ... energy into me. We've been getting a lot of the spiritual stuff recently." Joe pulled his hand away.

Rosemary gave Joe a knowing smile and a little nod before she turned to Tony. "Officer Paulli." She held her hand out.

He held both of his hands up, palms toward her, so she couldn't grab them. "Hi, I'm not going to touch you. I've had enough spirit shi … stuff for the day."

Rosemary smiled, Joe thought she was a very handsome woman regardless of age. "I think you have. Your aura's just aglow with the essence. When the Earth Mother chooses one, it can be unsettling."

"Rosemary, we have a lot to talk about, private stuff. The spiritual is just one item. Who's he? He looks familiar."

"That is my good friend, Christopher Brown. He is my beau and protector." She smiled fondly at him.

Stephanie smiled in shock. "He's your boyfriend?"

Rosemary blushed gently. "Exactly, well like a partner."

Stephanie stared openmouthed for a moment. "Since when?"

Rosemary blushed. "Well, recently. He has been courting me for years, but just recently I found …" She reached out to grasp his hand. "Well, never you mind. He is also head of campus security at Bosh-Gates. It was he who advised me to depart."

Chris smiled at them while patting her hand. "Hi, is that your security watching the courtyard?"

Joe jumped in. "Let's sit and compare notes before we start pointing out people, shall we." He gestured at the tables. There were some things others didn't need to know.

"It isn't just a casual question." Chris's eyes took on a hard sheen. "These people are … bad men, they travel in groups, and they look professional like the ones around us now."

Joe motioned Stephanie to the tables. "They're hers. We're all here to keep Steph safe."

Stephanie stepped over to one of the tables while pulling her backpack off and extracting a laptop. "Chris, I remember you now. You were the campus policeman investigating my lab break-ins." She expertly flipped open the laptop and turned it on. She pulled out a little umbrella that mounted on it to keep the rain off.

"That's right. You called me Barney Fife."

"Sorry about that, but you were acting a little thick."

He smiled while holding Rosemary's chair. "You sure I was acting?"

"Yeah, Doctor Stein wouldn't pick an idiot to be her boyfriend," Stephanie added while making Bruce appear on the laptop.

"Stephanie!" Rosemary's tone was that of a scolding mother.

Chris just laughed, "She's got you there. You do not suffer fools lightly." He patted Rosemary's shoulder as he pulled up a seat next to her. "Your break-ins were the final clue, well, and the attack on you. You see, after my interview with you and Mr. Richardson, I placed a few not-quite-legal web cameras in some strategic places." He smiled knowingly. "I got pictures."

"Really," Stephanie leaned forward. "Can we see them?"

Rosemary held her hand up. "Before we move to the pictures, I want to understand the spiritual reference."

Stephanie frowned. "It's not really part of …"

Rosemary cut her off. "Do not underestimate the nature of the divine. It can be startling, persistent, and dangerous if not addressed."

Stephanie frowned, so Tony jumped right it. “The Great Spirit has chosen the doc here,” he pointed at Stephanie, “as a priestess, and Ms. Blackraven isn’t too comfortable with it.”

Stephanie glared at him.

“And your reason or reasons for thinking this?” Rosemary was calm but alert.

“Well,” Tony’s southern draw was back. “She bitch slapped Joe into next week just for pointing it out to her.”

Joe decided to help Tony before Stephanie got up and practiced on him. “Briefly, because we do have pressing business, we all have had dreams with each other and a figure that could be interpreted as the Great Spirit in them. I term it as the Great Spirit because we all have North American Indian ancestors, some more than others.”

“Oh my.” Rosemary’s hand came to her mouth. “What else? By the look on your face, Stephanie, there is more.”

Now Stephanie was glaring at her.

“Steph had a visitation in the shower,” Bruce spoke up from the laptop. “Enough of one that she shattered a floor tile and made the door briefly disappear. Also, her knack has risen magnitudes in power since last week. She is able to manifest symbols with a thought, provide the Will and the Way with little effort.”

“Bruce!” Stephanie was reaching for the laptop.

“Rosemary, look at her eyes,” Bruce calmly supplied.

“Oh my word.” Rosemary reached out to stop Stephanie from shutting off the laptop as she looked at her eyes.

“There could be other reasons for the changes in her ability,” Rosemary supplied smoothly. She was looking deeply into Stephanie’s eyes like she had found something. “But if the Goddess has appeared to you, that is a different matter.”

Tony held his hand up briefly, and with a deep sigh added, “She appeared to me, too. Just an hour and a half ago.”

“You know, guys, I’m really not very comfortable with this discussion.” Stephanie was glaring at them all.

Joe could tell Stephanie was trying very hard not to get mad and failing. Being able to feel her emotions wasn't always a good thing.

"You know folks," Joe wasn't going to let Stephanie explode again. "Steph and I have already had one fight about this today, we just made up, and I don't want to have another. So, let's write it down as interesting and go on. There are people actively trying to kill her and others even as we sit here."

Rosemary's eyes lit up with a different kind of look. "Made up, is he your beau? Have you found someone?"

Stephanie shut her eyes and let her head hang. "Really not the time."

"Ah," Joe started, "I asked if I could court her and was told yes." He couldn't help it, the smile just leaked across his face.

Rosemary gave a quick intake of breath. "Did you ask it of her oldest male relative?"

"What is it with that?" Stephanie slammed her hands down on the table. "It's like from the last century or something. We are going to move on now. Let's see those pictures and hear the story."

Rosemary's eyes were locked on Joe. He nodded his head yes while mouthing it. Rosemary smiled and slid her chair over closer to Stephanie, giving her a one-arm hug.

"Before we move on, as you say, there is something you all need to understand and internalize." Rosemary shook Stephanie a little and gave her a peck on the cheek, like she was so happy she couldn't contain herself. "Especially you, are you listening?"

Stephanie glared at her and then gave her one grudging nod.

"We define the divine." Rosemary backed away a little so she could made eye contact with Stephanie, Tony, and then Joe. "The divine is not human. Think of it as an alien force or power that walks the earth and reaches out to a very few. Our very interaction with it defines how it behaves." She paused to look at them all again. "It is a very personal interaction. It will take from you just as it gives. Think about it. Don't just pass it off as idle chatter. Explore your interactions with it and the nature of the dreams." Stephanie started to say something, and Rosemary covered her mouth. "No, don't belittle it. No denial, don't shrug it off, young lady. Use that superior intellect of yours and really explore it. When you've done that, we will talk." Rosemary took her hand off Stephanie's mouth and gestured at Chris. "If you please, the pictures?"

Joe thought Stephanie was going to blow up. She was tight jawed, steely eyed, but she nodded curtly to Rosemary and slowly put it all away. Joe wasn't ever going to get between these two women. This was deep chemistry.

Chris bravely took point. "Yes, pictures, yes, but this is all very circumstantial." He pulled a folder out and laid it on the table. "Several women have disappeared from the campus over the last few months under suspicious circumstances. Clair Harrison, Doctor Margaret Vanderhousen, and Doctor Sylvia Bloomerton, all disappeared from their offices or workspaces. It was Rosemary who put the final piece of the puzzle in place."

"They all had the knack," Stephanie supplied.

"Why, yes." Rosemary sounded surprised. "How did you know?"

"Bruce," Stephanie redirected to the laptop. "We were right. The symbol was to pull something away from the victims, it was their ability to work ..." Stephanie frowned like she had bitten into a lemon. "Magic."

"What symbol?" Rosemary asked.

"It's a massive symbol we found at a couple of the crime scenes. I'll pass the name of Clair Harrison on to the FBI. She hasn't been listed at any of the scenes ..."

"Let them go on with their explanation," Joe cut in. "We need them to share first." He wanted to tell Stephanie and Bruce to shut up, since it was an ongoing investigation, but couldn't think of a diplomatic way of phrasing it.

Rosemary looked like he had slapped her. "Detective Bremer, it isn't polite to interrupt ..." She sputtered to a stop as Chris covered her hand with his.

"RM, the detective is right," Chris gently chided her. "This is an ongoing investigation, probably a serial killer case since the FBI is involved. Let's just tell them what we have and let them get on with it."

"As you wish, Chris." Rosemary looked a little shocked at Chris. "Why don't you dig out your little video player then?" Joe smiled to himself. He figured Chris was going to get a little education later.

"I think Professor Rhinebolt is behind all this," Rosemary announced with a haughty air. "He is such a pompous, self-aggrandizing, narcissistic, arrogant, womanizing elitist, who thinks a woman's only contribution to society is on her back servicing the sexual needs of men or popping out babies, male ones preferably. For years, he's been womanizing on campus with his tenure and plethora of doctorates. He was circling around all these women, trying to influence their activities. I don't have to tell you, Stephanie, what a pain in the behind he can be. He held up your doctorate for over a year." She waved her hand dismissively. "Anyway, he was observed near all the disappearances before they occurred. He has also been trying to lure me off campus for the last month. Not to mention his attention for you, my dear. He was always interested in your research, to the point of trying, on more than one occasion, to steal it."

Stephanie pulled the folder over to her and took out several pictures. The first was of a ski-masked individual leaning over the door to her lab. "Andrew Stone," Stephanie announced. "I can tell by his clothes and backpack." Bruce nodded agreement.

The next was a shot of her, hunched over in the hallway outside her lab, with blood running down her very angry face. It made Joe clinch up. He realized how badly beaten she'd been, but to see it ...

There was another of an individual's legs, who had creased dress slacks with the bottom fringe of a sport coat showing, and Stephanie with her backpack held in front of her.

There was another of the sport coat pointing a pistol at ski-masked Andy.

The last one was of two men in army-looking uniforms picking up ski-masked Andy with sport coat arguing with another individual wearing a business suit whose face was in profile to the camera. There was smoke in the background.

"Those are stills from the video," Chris explained. "I think the guy in the sport coat is Rhinebolt. I don't know who the others are."

"Bruce," Stephanie sounded a little shaken. "I'm going to download the video to you. Would you please scrub it and enhance the pictures? The FBI should also see these." She held her hand out to Chris. He gave her the memory stick.

"So, let me see if I have this straight?" Joe asked. "You were called in on a robbery at Stephanie's lab or a series of robberies gone wrong?" Chris nodded. "You decided on your own to put up concealed web cameras to try and capture images of the robbers?" Chris nodded again. "These are the images you got from your cameras?"

"Yes. Also, I have several sworn statements of witnesses around the campus pertaining to the disappearances of the before-mentioned individuals." Chris frowned. "None of it is demonstrative of a crime, but it is suspicious." He patted Rosemary's hand. "I also have personally observed several individuals, not of the campus, stalking Rosemary. I think they meant to take her the night before Stephanie's truck was destroyed."

"So, you were the one aiding her in first escaping and then hiding?" Joe clarified.

"Yes."

"Joe," Bruce spoke up from the laptop. "I have more evidence it's Rhinebolt." Joe gave him his full attention. "I've been running an algorithm to isolate the discrete elements of the greater symbol. So far, I have ID'd 1600 discrete symbols. At least eight of them are from papers Stephanie authored. Rhinebolt has copies of all of her work. There is a record of it in the library database." Bruce pushed something and his video disappeared and a fragment of the symbol appeared with another picture next to it. "The fragment on the right is from the symbol at Andy's murder. The one next to it was recovered by the FBI at an earlier crime scene."

"How did they get it?" Stephanie blurted out.

Bruce smiled. "They read our paper on extracting images and duplicated our methods. But look at the lines."

Joe watched Stephanie lean in, her brow creased in concentration. "The extensors."

"Exactly," Bruce said. "He changed it after you succeeded in firing up the Solomon Circle. Prior to that, it was as Rhinebolt originally scribed it. He couldn't make it work. When you did, he changed his."

"It's still circumstantial." Joe held up his hand before Rosemary could say anything. "But it is more than enough to make him a person of interest and bring him in for questioning."

"Joe, we have another problem." Stephanie was studying the pictures.

"What have you seen?"

"Rhinebolt is working with Nelson, the guy that was my uncle's adjutant. Remember, you saw him outside my apartment before it was firebombed." She had her finger held down on the suited guy in the last picture. "Which means he's got some world-class talent to help him, probably government backing."

"We definitely need the FBI on this," Joe said, pulling out his phone. "Doctor Stein, I recommend you come with us to Stephanie's safe house. Her protective detail can cover you at the same time."

"You have a house?"

Stephanie smiled weakly and nodded her head. "I inherited it from my uncle's estate." Joe watched her tear up and could feel the pain in her heart.

"Oh, honey, not your great uncle?" Rosemary hugged her tighter as she started gently crying.

Joe turned away to make his calls, first to Agent Farmer and then Lieutenant Grayson. They had a lead, and it was solid.

Chapter 23

Stephanie looked up from her latest set of symbol notes to see it was dark and drizzling outside. Her cell told her it was after seven. *Rosemary should have been here hours ago,* she thought.

They had gotten back from the meeting to find the FBI arguing with itself about jurisdiction and evidence. Apparently, they wanted to take all the data pertaining to the symbol case, which amounted to all of her research, away from her. Agent Farmer was squared off against a more politically motivated agent or at least better dressed one. Her lawyers were refereeing.

She had immediately headed for her work area. The less she said to them the better. She did not want to get involved, so she'd worked or at least tried to. Thoughts of the divine, the Great Spirit, Andy Stone's demise, the symbol that caused it, Rhinebolt and what he was doing with Nelson, the FBI taking her research away, just kept chasing each other around in her head. The only way to drown them out was to work, focus hard on complicated symbols. She had even gotten a three-stage symbol to work. She could stand and scribe, then fire off a Solomon Circle on the ground around her by using the knack. She burnt the actual symbol into the dirt with an intensified flash. Of course, at that point it didn't qualify as a flash anymore; it was more like a laser.

The nagging memory of a paper she had read comparing God to a quantum source also kept popping up. She understood quantum mechanics of time domain reflections in faster than light environments, but she was an applied math kind of girl and that paper had all been theory. Engineers were all about applied science, not just theory. The paper had kept harping about the fifth order associations and nodal confluence between chaos structures (what an oxymoron that was, chaos having structure), nuclear resonance, and defining the infinite.

She did get the math angle, but she was all about data, facts and data, that was the way. But what happened to her earlier in the bathroom had been data, it sure seemed real. The Great Spirit turning into her mother … that was just … painful.

Her ringing phone brought her back to the now. She stepped over, saw it was Rosemary, and tapped it on. "Rosemary, where are you guys?"

"Chica, I hear you miss me." It was a very not Rosemary voice.

"Who …" She got cut off.

"No, doctor lady, you listen to me. If you want to see your señora friend alive and unbroken, you will do just what I say."

Panic lanced through her, followed by blazing anger. "Prove she's alive." She was suddenly channeling Uncle Raymond at his darkest moments. It was his drunk, spacey lecture about hostages and how they were most likely dead. Stephanie launched two apps on her phone and then concentrated on the speaker.

"Si' chica," the man sounded smug. "Then she gets to entertain me."

There was a rustling and then, "Stephanie, don't you dare come for me. They killed Chris, just gunned him down. Think, Sylvia, the wolf pack, don't you …" There was a slap and Rosemary cried out.

"There, you see, she is just fine, crazy, but fine." The accented Latino voice was back. "So here is the deal, you bring back to me what is mine, and I will give you back your friend." An evil chuckle was followed by, "Mostly unharmed."

"What is it you think I have?"

"You give me the libro *del* brujo, my witch's spell book."

"Andy Stone is dead. You know that, right? He can't do symbols for you."

"Si'. Two of my soldiers saw him taken. I want his book."

Bruce touched her arm and held up a piece of paper. 'Kidnapped Rosemary???' was written in hasty letters.

Stephanie nodded. She saw Joe in the background with Tony. They looked as angry as she felt. "Okay, when and where? But know this; if you hurt her permanently, I swear by the Blessed Goddess herself, I will rain shit down on you until you beg to die," she screamed into the phone.

Through the phone she heard clothes tearing and Rosemary screaming, followed by slapping. The man was talking to her, but she wasn't really hearing him, she was concentrating on the noise in the background and trying to control her breathing.

"Chica, chica, you hearing me?" He was yelling at her through the phone.

"Not really. When and where?"

"You not hearing me. You don't show up, then pretty old lady becomes puta in my stable." He sounded really pissed off. "We start her training now since you think you so tough. You hearing me now?"

"When and where? Just tell me when and where."

He told her the location and time, interspersed with comments about Rosemary's body. From the comments and the sounds in the background, Stephanie was sure they had stripped Rosemary naked. She ended the call before anger could cloud her judgment further. Her slip had already cost Rosemary. One of the apps had given her a location off the GPS in Rosemary's phone.

She handed her phone to Bruce, "I tried to record the call. Would you see if you can extract it? Also, the GPS locator app is running for Rosemary's phone, would you please pin down the location?"

"Steph," Bruce whispered, "I …"

She cut him off. "Yeah … just … we need to move on this. We don't have much time to get everyone there. Please, just try …" She gestured at the phone. She was shaking, having trouble getting by the rage.

Stephanie turned and ran into Joe's arms. "Please don't hate me, please don't."

"What?" Joe looked like a deer in the headlights. "Why?"

She hugged him hard, "For the things I'm feeling. The things I want to do." She stepped away and looked into his eyes. "For the things I'm going to do. Please don't hate me."

Joe looked puzzled as he nodded.

Stephanie felt a little relief. She was talking to them all, even though she was looking at Joe. "We don't have time for the police or the FBI, and I'm not sure they could handle this anyway. Professor Sylvia Bloomerton was doing research on gangs with werewolves. This must be the gang she was working with." She looked up to the roof. "Frank, call Stoneman and tell him I need him and … and … well, you heard all this. I have a GPS location of Rosemary's phone, and by the sounds, they aren't going to move from there. They won't have time if we're to meet."

"On it," came down from the rafters. "He'll be here shortly. I've already clued them all in. We are mounting up even as I speak."

"Werewolves, load for werewolves, these are the same guys that jumped me last week at the crime scene." She turned to look at Tony. "These are the assholes that attacked you."

Tony just nodded. "What's the plan?"

"Steph, the police could …" Joe didn't get to finish.

"These people have taken Rosemary and are violating her right now. They killed Chris." Her hands were tingling, and she realized one was glowing. "I don't want them in jail. I want them in hell. Do you get me? I want them to go screaming in terrible pain." She was reaching for cold, being very cold. Screaming and ranting would not get the job done. By the look on Joe's and Tony's faces, she thought she had achieved dangerous cold.

Joe started to say something then just narrowed his eyes and nodded. "Family. I got your back."

"Damn right!" Tony added.

Joe pointed toward the house. "Let's go suit up. I think we're going to want to be armed."

"We still need a plan," Tony said.

Stephanie hesitated for just a moment. "Bruce will get the location off the phone. Some of Stoneman's people will head that way now to get into position. We'll all suit up, load up, and plan a route in the cars." She looked around at all the men. "Then we show up, rescue Rosemary, and take care of anyone that gets in our way."

There was a stunned silence.

"I'll tell the Colonel and see if he can't … ah … refine that a little bit," Frank called down.

"Frank, you also tell him I'm going, with or without him. No arguments." She took off for the house with Joe and Tony right behind her.

Agnes was waiting in her room. "Mum, I have a few things for you."

"What?" Stephanie saw a bunch of items laid out on the bed. "I don't have time for …"

She didn't get to finish because Agnes frowned, then grabbed a handful of her own skirt and pulled. The skirt came off with a Velcro separating sound. It was such an unlady-like gesture that Stephanie froze. Underneath, Agnes was wearing black knee-length tights or bulky spandex pants with bulges in some places. "Mum, I've been a guarding women for a few years, before that, I was British Secret Service. Knowing who raised you and the attempts on your life, I packed a few accessories for a well-dressed lady. Now start deedling out of those pants and skinny into these armored knickers." She handed Stephanie black spandex pants just like the ones she was wearing. "I'll explain as you dress."

"I am not wearing a dress to this event."

Agnes dimpled as she smiled. "When I explain why, you will. Now, no more talking, strip." Agnes pulled a few more items out of bags and put them on the bed.

Stephanie stripped. The spandex pants weren't really spandex; it was something else tight and heavy. She was almost too hippy for it. It did have a few interesting pockets. The top was just as tight, but had a built-in bra for holding everything in place.

"My, you are a curvy thing," Agnes commented.

"Yeah, my curves would be perfect if I was ten inches taller, now I'm just top heavy," Stephanie emphasized the girls as she got them settled in place.

"I'll bet you've been have'n ta beat the boy'os off with a stick." Agnes handed her a black silk scarf.

"Normally, I just talk at them, and they run. It seems I'm a little too blunt and smart." Stephanie looked at the scarf. "What do I do with this?"

Agnes stepped over and draped it expertly around her neck and shoulders. "It stops the body armor from chaffing. Yours seems well made, but you never know. I brought a set for you. I like yours better." She handed Stephanie her dragon scales.

Stephanie was amazed; it just slid on over the silk and didn't rub. "Nice."

"Thank you, mum." Agnes gave a little bob as she pulled another case over. "The holsters built into the knickers are for slim-line pistols. These are special composite Walther .9 mm slim grip. I di'na think yours ad fit so I brought a set." She spun around to show her shapely bottom to Stephanie while pointing at the waist in back. "One goes here." She handed a neat little semi-auto to Stephanie.

Stephanie dropped the magazine, racked it to safe, looked it over, released the slide, dry fire it a couple of times, slipped it in and out of the holster a few times, reloaded it with one up the barrel, and slipped it into it holster. "Wow, that just slides in."

"Yes'm, that's what they're made for. The ammo is hollow point, silver-splashed exploding, so don't let the bobbies look at it. I'm sure it's na legal." She picked up another one and turned to show her front to Stephanie, thrusting her right hip out. "This slides into the top of the thigh on the right side. Very few men will pat a woman there for fear of touch'n the privates, if'n you know what I mean. And for those that just want to grab a patch, it's too far over to the hip, and they might miss it. Especially if you slap them really hard, ladylike, you know? 'Cause they've na right to be a touch'n a lady there."

That made Stephanie smile. There appeared to be more to Agnes than she realized.

She handed Stephanie four magazines that slid into pockets down the left thigh. Then a T-handled four-inch punch blade, "This'un goes here." She pointed at a spot on her left thigh. There were five knives in all, one of them her own Bone Knife. "Your Bone blade has a full grip so it's gon'a haft'ta fit the bottom sheath," Agnes explained and pointed. Next, she handed her a lightweight ASP, "You know how to use one of these?"

"Yep," Stephanie nodded, "but this is too light to be much good."

Agnes smiled. "Composite, not metal, don'a wanna set off metal detectors, but don't underestimate what eighteen inches of extra length can a be doin' for your swing. You ever worked a single stick?"

"Yes. Is this composite nonconductive?"

"Yes, mum."

"This will work better than a pencil. I think this one is better than all the rest. Where does it go?"

Agnes shifted her hips again and pointed at a place on her right thigh. "Just be slip'n it in right there."

"You've been wearing all this gear under your skirt the whole time, haven't you?"

Agnes dimpled again. "Yes 'm I have. Now you understand the skirt. It flares slightly at the waist and then flows out and down the leg. It hangs below the knee so you can enter all the churches in Europe without question, not that that should come up tonight. The pockets have slits in them so your hands can slide right through. Everything is within reach. It is also built to pull off, as I showed you." She held up a dark blue skirt with pinstripes. It looked very dressy.

"The fabric of your underclothes is Kevlar woven with ballistic nylon, and those stiffening battens are actual thin ballistics plates," Agnes explained. "It's not goin'a stop a bullet, but it will slow 'm down, works for slashing knives as well. Now, these two knives cross your tummy. Your armor already has the sheaths. Blouse, don't tuck it in, it will hide the knives." She held up a coat to go over it all. "Zip the bottom up about six inches. That will be lett'n you reach the holster." Agnes adjusted it and frowned. "It's a little tight on top, but it'll work." She handed Stephanie her own Springfield XD subcompact. "It's not loaded; there's a holster under your left breast, see 'n if this will slip in there."

Stephanie racked the slide to check the gun. Then she slipped it into the hidden holster.

Agnes was shaking her head. "That's not goin' ta work. It patterns on your side."

"We're in a well-lit room. The light won't be that good where we're going." She walked over into the darkened bathroom. "How about now?"

"You're right, ya can'na be see 'n it in the dark."

Stephanie came back over and pulled the gun out, loaded it, put it back. Two magazines went into her left pocket. She paused, "You know, if I need all three guns, something will have gone very wrong."

"Yes, mum, but better to have them and not need them, then need them and not have them." She looked Stephanie up and down and had her turn around. She put up Stephanie's hair in a ponytail to keep it out of her way. "You're as ready as I can make you, mum." She gave Stephanie a hug, "Come back safe."

Stephanie put on her black shooting gloves, mainly to cover her glowing hand. She almost walked into Joe as she came out of her rooms. He was standing in the hallway, looking spooked and slightly confused. He was also only wearing a black T-shirt and black sweat pants, no shoes. "Joe?"

"Hey, you ready?"

"Yeah, but are you?" She motioned at his clothes. "This it?"

"I guess so. I … ah … had a visitor. She was pretty insistent that I travel light. You look very pretty."

Stephanie could actually see light in his eyes. She took his arm like they were going on a date. "Thank you. Let's go. Surely, they're ready for us by now."

Bruce was waiting for them in the entryway. He was wearing black tactical gear, complete with body armor and mag pouches. "Joe … never mind. Tony brought your truck around. Good thing it's a four door. Let's get a move on." He hustled them outside and into the waiting 4 x 4. Stephanie got in the back. Once inside, Bruce told her, "Steph, take off your coat and your blouse."

"What?" she and Joe exclaimed. Tony stepped on the gas and the big diesel moved out.

"I've got a radio for you. I need to thread it up under your clothes." As Stephanie started to take stuff off, he turned to the two guys in front. "Okay, I gotta ask. Why are you guys barefoot and wearing T-shirts and sweats?"

"I'm not sure about Tony, but I think I'm going to change pretty much as soon as we get on site. I can barely contain it now." Joe was looking straight ahead as he spoke.

"Yeah, what he said," Tony rumbled out.

"Should I be driving?" Bruce asked.

"No," was Tony's surly response.

"Bruce, leave them alone. It … ah … well, ah … it feels right." She handed the XD out of the coat to Bruce. "It's loaded, and there's one in the spout." She shifted and then put her blouse down. "Now what?"

"Body armor, too. I have to thread this earpiece and mic up through the armor."

"I wish you had coordinated this with Agnes. She just got me all dressed for the prom. Here, hold these," she handed him the two knives from her tummy. "There, take it."

Bruce took the armor and started fiddling with it. "Damn, this has the little pocket and there's already . . ." his voice faded off. "Did your uncle get this for you?"

"Yeah."

Bruce barked a laugh. "Damn, he was good. It's already rigged and has the earpiece and mic built in; all I had to do is add the radio. Put it back on. What's the scarf for?"

"Black silk, it keeps the armor from chaffing around the neck."

"Really, I'll have to remember that. I must say that skirt is very fashionable on you. I don't think I've ever seen you wear a dress."

"Shut up. It hides all the weapons." Stephanie slipped back into her armor and got it settled.

"Weapons? I didn't see any," Bruce said, but she could tell the guys in front were paying attention as well.

"I'll tell you in a minute; hand me my knives." Bruce handed them to her without a word. "Okay, it's on," Stephanie told him.

"Tony, I'm going to turn a light on."

"Go for it."

A light came on, and Bruce fished around her neck for a moment. "Steph, give me your hand. This is the earpiece. Put it in."

"Done."

"I'm going to hide it in your hair, behind your ear, as best I can." He fiddled with her ear. "Got it, turn toward the door so I can switch it on." She shifted around and accidently brushed her thigh against him. "What the," Bruce started, "what are you wearing under that dress?" He clicked something, and there was brief static. "The mic is voice actuated. This is a frequency hopping, burst transmission, encrypted radio. Don't talk a lot or you will broadcast on top of everyone else and they won't like it. They all will hear you." He grabbed her hand and put it on a hidden switch. "This will turn the mic on when you want it to be active. It's off right now." He turned the light off.

"Can I get dressed now?"

"Yes, you can," Bruce said as he shifted away from her. "So, what exactly do you have under your skirt?"

Stephanie slipped her blouse back on, then the coat. "Gun."

Bruce handed it to her.

She shifted around, getting it all settled again. "I have armored underwear, three guns, seven knives, six magazines, and a nonconductive ASP."

"Shit!" Bruce exclaimed. "All that, and I didn't see a thing."

"That's the idea. Why else would I ever wear a skirt?"

"I think you look pretty," Joe commented. "Too pretty to be going to break the law."

"You said Agnes dressed you?" Tony asked. "All that stuff hers?"

"Yes, she wears something like this all the time." She reached up to pat Joe. "Joe, you going to have a problem with this?"

"I don't think so." He went quiet for a moment. "If they play it fair and we get Rosemary, then it's not going to be a problem. If they try funny stuff with you, I think I'm going to be a bear, and I don't think bears worry about consequences."

"Damn," Stephanie blurted out. "The backpack, Andy's books, the police have them."

"Don't worry." Bruce lifted something off the floor and handed it to her. "That has a complete copy of his books in it. I copied them all before we turned them over." She could hear him shrug in the dark. "I wanted to study it. Hell, you've been doing symbols from it for the last two days."

"Great, we have a backpack. Anybody know what the plan is?"

"I'd say it's time to call Stoneman," Tony rumbled out.

Stephanie reached up and hit the switch. "Doctor Blackraven online."

"This is Nuc, online," she heard Bruce say twice, once in the truck and then through the radio. Bruce had a call sign.

Stoneman started up without preamble. "Nuc has the location. You will proceed to the parking lot and wait until I give you the go-ahead. You will then proceed to the meet." Bruce pulled up a laptop that was showing a satellite map of the Puget Sound. She could see a flag at Soaring Eagle Regional Park. There was another red flag a short ways away. "My team will be slipping in through the trees to take up positions. Be advised, the backpack has a remote detonation incendiary in it. If it goes sideways, we will move in to extract you and Professor Stein, and then destroy the backpack."

"That's it?" Stephanie asked.

"Yes. Doc, you don't need to know what we're doing. You have enough to concentrate on."

"All right." She wasn't all right, but they didn't need to know that. "If it looks like they're going to double-cross me, I'll let off a flash."

"Good enough. Leave your mic open, we'll get a clue that way. Stoneman out."

"I'm going to turn this off until we get there, Blackraven out." She reached up and pushed the switch. She heard Bruce rustle in the dark for a moment. "Bruce, did you turn yours off?"

"Yeah."

"What are you going to be doing?" Stephanie was starting to worry.

"I'm going to have Tony pull up before we hit the lot and get in the bed of the truck. I'll lie low unless something happens. If it goes bad, I'll pop up and provide covering fire."

"You know, we are or were policemen," Tony said.

"Yeah, well," Bruce paused like he was editing what he was going to say. "You both got kicked off the force because of some bureaucratic crap. So, I figure you want her alive more than you want to arrest me for saving her. Anyway, you'll be a wolf and he'll be a bear, so you both will be tearing them apart anyway and won't be worrying about me. Did you bring your collar?"

"Yeah."

"Collar?" Stephanie asked.

"Well," Bruce started. "The bad guys are werewolves, and he's going to turn into a wolf. So, I figured we should mark him somehow. He's got a stretchy collar with a couple of chem-lights strung on it. That way I'll know not to shoot the glowing wolf."

"What about Joe? I don't want him shot."

"He'll be the only bear there." Bruce sounded very sure of himself.

"How do you know that?" Stephanie asked.

"There have been no reported werebear sightings in the greater Puget Sound. The closest one is north of Granite Falls. Ergo, no other bears on the scene."

Joe snorted.

"What?" Stephanie asked.

"I don't think Bruce will have to worry about picking us out of a crowd. Just don't get close to us when we get all furry. If we can't master the rage, I'll just be a bear and Tony will be a wolf. Our minds will not be in charge. At least that's what Sylvia's notes said."

Stephanie had a sudden terrible feeling. She unsnapped her seat belt and scooted forward. She reached up and touched Joe. He flinched away then settled back. "Joe, I want to kiss you." She reached up and over the seat to find his mouth. It was a good kiss. She gave Tony a peck on the cheek, too. "Thank you for doing this."

Tony glanced back, "No problem."

"I love you, Steph," Joe whispered. "Don't take any chances. If it … if it goes bad … just … just do what you have to do."

She could feel his anger and the concern; it matched her own. "You, too."

The truck slowed to a stop, and Tony turned to look back. "Get in the back, Bruce. It's time. Doc, we switch places, you're going to pull to the edge of the parking lot, and then Joe and I will dismount. We'll fan out and walk in. You get to drive up. Remember; don't start anything until you get the word."

Chapter 24

Stephanie shifted to the driver's seat when Tony stopped to let Bruce climb in the back. She couldn't remember ever being this nervous, scared, and just plain pissed off. According to the GPS, she only had about a third of a mile before she reached the beginning of the parking lot. The trees were thick, and it was misting rain, so visibility sucked.

She'd never been to this park before, especially to a driving range. Golfer's were nuts. Little white ball, hit it, swear, walk, hit it again, swear, she couldn't figure it out. Now she knew she was nervous, she had never given golf a thought before. The park was big with a lot of wooded area, perfect for a bunch of wolves to hide in.

"Stop just ahead," Tony rumbled out from the back. "I want to walk in from the tree line in case they've posted someone here."

"Okay." As the nose of the truck started into an opening that looked like a parking lot, Stephanie eased to a stop. Both doors opened, and her heart leaped into her throat. "Just … don't … I …Crap, I'm so scared I can't think or talk," she finally struggled out.

"You'll do fine," Joe rumbled. "Stick to the plan. I've got your back. Give 'em hell." The last part was almost a growl. "Better turn on your mic."

She reached to turn it on, and the doors shut before she could say anything. "Crap," she blurted out. She heard a snicker through the earbud.

The parking lot was unlit and the truck's headlights cut a huge swath through it. There was like hundreds of yards of cleared land with gentle rolling hills and poles sticking up at different distances. It was dark and raining, so she couldn't really make out what they were. On the far side of the parking lot, she saw a campfire with people dancing around it. "This is a driving range, what the hell are they doing with a campfire?" Stephanie couldn't believe her eyes.

"Gang, bad guys like breaking the law," Bruce told her through the radio.

"Silence on the net." It was Stoneman.

"Sorry," Stephanie whispered. She let the idling truck slowly carry her across the parking lot. She stopped it about halfway there. *It's time to get my game face on,* she thought as she pulled out a pencil. *I need to be that bad girl from high school that didn't take shit from anyone.*

That had been a dark time for her until Uncle Raymond had beaten some sense into her. She remembered that attitude, the mindset, the fire burning in her belly, and brought the symbol to her mind's eye and gave it the Will and the Way. "Eald-Shay." It had stopped an assassin's bullet before. She did it three more times. She had to believe the shield would turn bullets. Two more times.

There were multiple squelch breaks, and then she heard, "Go doc" on the radio. The dash clock said she had five minutes before the appointed hour. She continued idling forward with the truck.

There were twenty of them, maybe more, of mixed races hanging out around the fire; they all looked tough, a few tough-looking women, too. Many of the men were shirtless with tattoos. There were two women huddled over near a table with three guys pestering them, touching them. At another table was a lone woman with four guys near her. That had to be Rosemary, except she was on her knees doing … "No! That can't be her," Stephanie mumbled. That fire of rage started burning a little hotter.

She pulled up about twenty yards short of the main group, turned off the truck, but left the lights on. Hoisting the backpack up on her shoulder, she hopped out and slowly started walking toward the werewolf gang. *One of those guy's arms is as big around as my waist*, she noticed. *Thinking like this isn't going to get me through this.* She had her right hand through her pocket.

They all stopped and turned to look at her. The music played on.

She saw one of the gang push himself off a parking bollard and start limping toward her.

"If it ain't the fucking co-ed bitch, come back for a little more?" Wounded Knee was slurring his words and struggling to walk normal. "You ready for round two?"

"Great, it's Wounded Knee, he's the guy that gave me the concussion last week," she whispered. She kept walking. "I brought the books as demanded," she called out. "I've come to make the exchange." She shrugged off the backpack and held it up. "Back off, gimpy. My business is with whoever took Professor Stein."

"What, can't take a little smack to the head, bitch?"

"I'm walking fine. How are you doing?" She put a little attitude in that one.

"He's got to search you, chica." She heard the voice from the phone call out.

He limped up to her and got in her face. "Bitch, you gotta be searched for weapons. You did kill Amos with your little gun."

"Self-defense, he was coming at me with a knife."

"Still gotta search you, bitch."

"If all you're doing is searching me then fine, but no funny business." She put the backpack down. "You try something, and I'll finish it. I'll do the other knee."

"Ooh, real tough, You ain't gonna surprise me this time. Put your hands up and turn around."

"Not likely. I won't give you a shot at my back." She did hold her arms out from her sides.

He ran his hands down her arms and onto her breasts, squeezing when he got there. The armor kind of defeated that plan, but he did feel the XD. He frowned, "Lose the gun." She heard several gun slides cycle.

She reached in slowly and pulled out the XD and tossed it back toward the truck without turning. She zipped her coat up. "Satisfied?"

"No, spread your legs."

"You better be careful what you grab." She really didn't like this. It was like she knew what was coming.

He started down her waist, then to her hips. She couldn't let him go lower, or he would find the other toys. She shifted her hips to pull away a little, unintentionally putting her butt in his hand, which did make him bend down a little.

"Oooh," he commented as he grabbed her butt. "What …" He had felt the grip of one of the guns.

She let out, what she hope sounded like, a startled scream. Her right hand flashed down and connected with his face. It-Hay, she thought, giving it the Word. There was a crack like thunder, and he went spinning away. "That's not how you treat a lady, asshole," she yelled as he spun limp to the ground. Her right hand probably wasn't glowing now. She stepped up and kicked his good knee as hard as she could. It wouldn't break it, like the other, but it would hurt. Catcalls came from the gang, aimed as much at Wounded Knee as her.

"Chica, that's not how it works." She could tell who it came from this time. It was the guy with all the silver on him by the one woman.

She picked up the backpack and held it up. "You said bring the books, and I would get Rosemary. You didn't say let some loser feel me up. We had a deal. I brought the books."

That brought grudging laughs from some of the toughs.

"He's checking you for guns." He made it sound playful. "You still armed?"

"He was checking for anything, other than making sure I was a woman." She took a deep breath and decided to up the ante. "Anyway, you can't disarm a wizard." She pulled a pencil out, thought of a symbol she had just discovered earlier, and focused the Will and projected the Way to a spot away from her. "Ight-Lay!" Light lit up the area the guy wearing all the silver was standing in. It was like a big spotlight had been suspended about twenty feet up, but illuminated a sixty-foot circle.

You could hear a pin drop, even the music went off.

"Doc, don't antagonize them." It was Frank's voice in her ear.

"Yeah, but you can see Rosemary now," she whispered and started walking forward. She got a squelch break in response, didn't know what it meant, but she got one. The big tough gang members, with biceps bigger than her waist, were wide-eyed and moved away from her to clear a path.

The man wearing all the silver gave her a deep laugh, like he approved. She was pretty sure he didn't, but she figured he couldn't show that.

Ten feet away, she stopped, showing him the backpack. She could see him better than last time. Sculpted bare chest festooned with silver chains, medallions, and symbols tattooed over everything visible, all silver.

"Those two with you?" Silver Boy thrust his chin back toward the parking lot.

"Yeah. You said bring books. You didn't say anything about coming alone." She added a little attitude.

"Doc, stop trying to piss him off." Stoneman sounded tense.

Stephanie ignored him. "Rosemary, you okay?"

"Never better, honey." Rosemary sounded chipper, which set off warning bells for Stephanie.

"*What the hell*, Stephanie thought. Rosemary had a shiner, a cut lip, and her hair was plastered to the side of her head with mud. Her clothes were torn in several places, but she had a skirt on with a top. More than Stephanie expected, based on what she had heard on the phone. She did notice that there was a woman under the table who was naked.

"Get rid of the varita *mágica*, the magic wand," Silver Boy told her.

"Oh, it's not a wand, maestro," Rosemary corrected him sweetly. She turned to Stephanie while her fingers were tracing a pattern on the table, "Literal. Maestro means master. Literally, incantatio depellerent eam. She doesn't use stored manna. She's my little rune weaver."

"You don't get to talk to her, puta. Only to me." Silver Boy looked pissed. "Only the truth."

Rosemary lowered her eyes and started tracing something on the table faster. "I can talk to you. Charm, you are a charmer, aren't you, Maestro? You've charmed me."

"Si', my little puta," he growled.

"Puta means whore, why would you call me that if you are letting me go?" Rosemary's voice was innocent. She rose up and pulled her skirt down and shirt up. "Why give me a lovely symbol on my back if you're going to let me go?" Stephanie could see a tramp stamp tattoo on Rosemary's lower back. It couldn't be a tattoo, they would've just done it, and it would be bleeding.

"Stop talking, puta." It was like he threw a switch, Rosemary stopped talking.

"She has a symbol on her back. Why'd you tattoo her?" Stephanie asked in amazement.

Rosemary slapped her hand on the table and traced the symbol there.

"Literaly incantatio depellerent eam is Latin for literally dispel her charm," Bruce supplied over the radio. Trust Bruce to speak Latin, a dead language. "That symbol on her back may be a charm, as in controlling her. Rumors are about that the gangs are using them to control their whores."

Stephanie needed just a moment to think. With her left hand, she tossed the backpack at Silver Boy, "Here, the books." He caught them awkwardly, like he wasn't going to at first, but then remembered what it contained. Stephanie looked at the shape Rosemary had drawn in the water on the table. She almost had it.

Silver Boy stepped over to the table and put the backpack down.

"I wouldn't open that just yet." Stephanie had his attention again. "It's wired to blow up, so that the books get destroyed, if I don't disarm it." His jaw dropped, and he stepped away from the backpack. She smiled as she shifted her hand in her pocket from the gun to the ASP. "I get Rosemary, and you get your books. Can we go now?"

Silver Boy looked like he'd swallowed something bad. "Sí, you two may go. Go with her puta, but no talking." He looked down at the backpack and added. "Remember to take the present."

Stephanie had the symbol floating in her mind's eye. She got it.

Rosemary reached down and picked up a knife that had been under her, hidden by the skirt. She showed it questioningly at Silver Boy.

"Si', Si', you hate her. Kill her for me," he growled.

Rosemary nodded and turned, smiling, to Stephanie.

Stephanie whipped the ASP out and snapped it to its full length. The symbol was galvanized with her Will and the Way. "Espell-Day," gave it the Word. Rosemary arched her back, screaming.

The world dissolved into chaos.

A rainbow of light appeared in front of Stephanie's face, and she got a little push.

Stephanie heard Silver Boy start screaming in Mexican.

Joe yelled, "Stephanie." Then started screaming or roaring incoherently in rage.

Several gang members were yelling or growling or howling.

The sound of meaty smacks.

The words, "Steph, down" in her ear.

There was another circular rainbow in front of her. Someone was shooting at her. Stephanie jumped forward and swept Rosemary to the ground with her.

They rolled over, and then Rosemary started halfheartedly trying to stab her. "Espell-Day," and a poke stopped that. Rosemary screamed. Stephanie could smell burning meat.

She dumped Rosemary to the side, rolled her over, and pulled up her shirt. The symbol on her lower back was burning into her skin, but it didn't look functional anymore. It looked like a brand. "That's what happened to Andy. His symbols overloaded and burned into his skin."

"Steph, not now," Bruce told her. "Watch out!" he screamed.

A wolf growled, darting in to bite her. She smacked it with the ASP on the nose. It stopped growling, moved back, shaking its head from side to side, while sneezing.

The backpack exploded in a flare of light and smoke.

The light went out.

"Focus, Steph, or you're going to die," she said to herself and to the mic at large. She shifted the ASP to her left hand and pulled a pistol just as the wolf was darting in. She shot it point blank in between its glowing eyes twice. Some of its blood splattered back at her. She couldn't see much in the dark.

"Damn straight, doc, good focus. Hold your position. Help is coming." She thought it was Tom speaking.

"Steph, incomi . . ." Something crashed into her side, flipping her over. A really pissed off Silver Boy was going to kick her again.

She had lost the gun. Still has the asp.

"Espell-Day," The Will, Way, and Word came almost immediately aimed at Silver.

He staggered, screaming. She could see all his silver fetishes, medallions, and tattoos sparkling with blue lightning. Wolves howled in the distance. "You don't have the manna, bruja." He was grunting and growling. "I will stomp you before you can burn me." He stepped toward her.

"Espell-Day," she thrust again. He grunted. "It's science, not magic, asshole. I can do this all day. Espell-Day! Espell-Day! Espell-Day! Espell-Day!" The silver on him was glowing red, and tattoos were sparkling with static discharge. There were two rainbows near her chest. She looked around frantically for the gun. "Black is a stupid color for a gun," she snarled and stood up for a better look.

"No, Steph, stay down."

"Bone Patrol circle." She didn't know what that meant, but she still couldn't find the gun.

Another rainbow. She got hit really hard in the shoulder, and it spun her to the ground. "I hate getting shot. Ield-Shay! Ield-Shay! Ield-Shay."

Silver Boy, maybe she should call him brand boy after this, was moving toward her again. "Why can't someone shoot him? Espell-Day! Espell-Day! Espell-Day! Espell-Day!" He fell to the ground with his skin burning around the tattoos. Apparently it hurt too much to scream, or it could've been the hole in his forehead.

Three rainbows appeared. Things were whizzing through the air, smacking loudly into the ground behind her. Flattening herself to the ground, she started crawling over to use the wolf as a barrier. "Apparently, them changing back to human when they die is an urban myth," she mumbled. Someone laughed on the radio.

"Steph, behind you." Bruce was still with her.

Staying low, she turned to see wolves racing toward her. When they were twenty feet away, a dark hill intercepted them. Her eyes were adjusting to the dark.

Joe was huge as a bear. One swipe of his paw took a pony-size wolf right off its feet and ten feet through the air. It yelped when it landed, but quickly got back to its feet. Joe smashed another one flat with both his front feet; it did not get up. Another one darted in to take a bite out of his back leg, typical wolf tactics. Joe kicked in it in the face in a very un-bear way, making sure his claws got it. Then he rose to his back legs roaring. He was easily fifteen feet tall. HE WAS BIG. He had to weigh over a thousand pounds, maybe two thousand. He was bigger than any bear she had ever seen, including the Montana grizzlies and Alaskan Kodiaks. It was too dark to get a good look at his body contours, but she could tell his eyes were golden cause they glowed. He didn't look like a bear in the stance he took. It was more like a really shaggy man with arms too long and claws; can't over look the long claws. They had to be nine or ten inches. He started shredding wolves. Short swipes, never long enough to leave his side exposed or to throw his center of balance off, he was doing kung fu tiger strikes.

From the side, another wolf easily half again as big as the others, with a day-glow chest, came barreling in. It bowled over one wolf and snapped at another. The one that turned to engage Tony got Joe ripping its side open. The one that turned to Joe got Tony ripping at its hind legs.

It was also very obvious that they both had fought off the pain and still had their minds, because they were grunting and gesturing to each other, adjusting the tactics.

More angry bees whipped by and impacted around Stephanie. The bullets were shredding the body of the wolf she was hiding behind. "Ield-Shay! Ield-Shay! Ield-Shay."

Brrrrrrrrrrr, sounded from the tree line. She turned to see the muzzle flash as one of her attackers went full automatic. "They've switch to automatic. I can't keep the shields up. Help." She sent a call to whoever heard her.

There was a modulated growled followed by a yelping bark. A moment later, a day-glow pony threw itself down between her and the bullets. Tony stated bucking as the bullets hit him.

"Tony, what the hell?"

He turned wolf blue eyes to her and in a growly kind of bark, "You save me. I save you. Give 'em hell."

They had reloaded, and the impacts came faster.

Something snapped in her, she got furious like at the university. This wasn't supposed to be happening. People weren't supposed to be treating her this way.

Fury swept through her as it had in the lab. Nobody did this to her friends. They didn't have the right. The rage swept through her, building pressure, like she was swelling with water. When the hail of bullets stopped, she popped up. "I haven't done anything to you. You think you can take me. Try this." A collection of symbols lined up in her mind's eye. She wanted it on the muzzle flashes in the trees. She gave it the words, "ORM-STAY IGHTNING-LAY."

Lightning shot out from her ASP straight toward the tree line then swerved up into the sky. A gale force wind started in front of Stephanie and smacked into the trees, and a river of rain fell from the sky accompanied by lightning strike after lightning strike.

"Holy crap, Steph! Did you do that?" Bruce exclaimed through the radio.

She sat back on the ground blinking. "What?" A storm raged on a couple hundred yards away, and none of it hit them.

"Tony," she remembered. Pulling the healing symbol from memory, she laid it over his body in her mind's eye, Willed it so. "Goddess, hear my prayer for this man, my protector, and make him well," she heard herself say. She gave the symbol the Way with a Word. "Eal-Hay."

Just for an instance, she saw the outline of the blue woman kneeling over Tony with her hand on his head, and then it was gone. Tony's wolf body sploshed away like it was made of jelly, leaving him glistening, naked, and bleeding on the grass. Even as she watched, the bleeding slowed.

Joe's truck slid to a stop, and Bruce hopped out. "Quick, get Rosemary into the truck. I'll put him in the bed." Stephanie shifted Rosemary over and got her into a fireman's carry. Bruce had to help her. They turned back to see the hulking form of a bear amble over and gently lift Tony, shifted over, and leaned down to put him in the bed.

"Grive," the bear growled out, pointing at Bruce.

Stephanie felt an urgent twitch, like someone poked her in the side. She looked away across the field to see several of her guards standing back to back being circled by wolves. The Bone Knives were flickering with light as they slashed at the wolves. In the center of the circle were two men on the ground. "Bruce, get Tony and Rosemary out of here. We'll help my guards."

"Steph, get in the truck. This was all about you."

Stephanie shut the door. “Come on, Joe, let’s go rescue my security detail.” She saw a symbol being drawn in the air. It was wrong. “No Tom!” She screamed and started running toward them. The hulking form of Joe the bear easily kept pace with her.

Bruce yelled dirty words, but drove off in the truck.

They weren’t going to get there in time. She pulled a symbol up, “Espell-Day!” She directed it at Tom’s work. His symbol flickered out. “Joe, distract the wolves.”

He gave her a guy grunt and roared his challenge. Bears can run fast she found out. He easily pulled ahead of her. “We need transport,” she told the world.

“Where?” Stoneman asked.

“At the light.” She paused in her running to focus. She hadn’t been using this one that much. “Ight-Lay.” The spotlight area appeared around the Bone Patrol. She also took the opportunity to pull her last gun. Symbols were good, but this felt more real. She ran on.

Joe smashed into the circle of wolves, and they scattered. He only got to smash one of them.

She ran up to find Joe sitting on his butt slowly rocking from side to side. The Bone Patrol were all facing him with their knives. “Oh, cut it out,” Stephanie yelled. She ran up to throw herself at Joe. He had bullet holes with blood leaking all over. She scratched his head and rubbed herself against his fur. It was rough fur with pointy ends.

He turned to nuzzle her. He growled something at her. She puzzled at it for a moment, “You don’t know how to change back?” He nodded his head.

“We’ll try a healing.” She heard the racing engine of a truck and a Suburban plowed onto the grass, followed by a second. “After we get you in the back.”

Joe nodded again and stood up. Stephanie heard a rifle get cycled. “Don’t you dare shoot my boyfriend.” She stepped in front of Joe to protect him.

Tom started laughing. “Yeah, like you could cover up even a tenth of him. He’s soo huge.” Tom turned to the guard. “Cut it out! He’s on our side. Get out; I’m driving.”

The sound of sirens off in the distance hurried them along. It took a little effort to get Joe into the back of the Suburban. They took two sets of seats out. He filled all the space and spilled over into the backseat, almost into the front.

Tom drove, Stephanie rode in back next to Joe, with another guard she didn't know too well in shotgun.

As soon as they were moving, she repeated the healing symbol she had put on Tony. Joe didn't change the same way, but he did go to sleep. Bears snore loudly. She took a big breath. "It's only been ten minutes." She looked at her watch like it was lying to her.

"Firefights are like that. A lot of shit happens real quick." Tom wiped his own face as if to reset reality.

"Tom, what did you think you were doing with that symbol? You had it all wrong," she chastised him.

"We were getting chewed up by the werewolves. I had to do something."

"It was wrong. You would've blown everyone up. I told you no symbols until you can get them memorized correctly."

"Okay, doc; that was one hell of lightning show you put on. Wow, did you plaster them."

"Yeah, but ask her if she can remember how she did it?" Bruce piped up over the radio.

Tom laughed.

"We'll still maintain radio discipline." Stoneman was not amused.

"Wait, how many of you got bit by the werewolves?" Stephanie saw a problem. "Isn't that …"

"Later, we'll debrief later," Stoneman cut her off.

"Silence," Tom announced in a strange tone. "I'm being boxed. I've got three vehicles, no there's one behind now." He hit the brakes, sliding the Suburban to a stop.

Stephanie heard a pssst, and something bit her in the neck. She saw the guard in front, on the passenger side, shoot Tom with a dart gun, pssst. Then he turned around and shot Joe until the gun was empty.

She couldn't find her gun. "You traitor," she got out before the world went black.

Chapter 25

Joe was floating in a strange pool. It was warm and comfortable. He didn't want to open his eyes.

"Joe Bremer," a voice called to him. He opened one eye. It was the Great Spirit, or at least the blue lady they thought was the Great Spirit.

"Yes, ma'am," he mumbled, opening both eyes.

"Joe Bremer, my priestess is in trouble. You have to wake up. You need to help her."

"Steph is in trouble? What do you mean trouble?" He was struggling awake now.

"She has been taken against her will. You are her only hope. Feel herrrrrr. " The voice trailed off, and Joe jerked awake.

He was still a bear. The world smelled funny, bad, richer, more smells. Outside, he could hear Stoneman, Bruce, and Tom arguing.

He was still stuffed into the Suburban. He didn't feel very awake, but it was getting better by the moment. The fight was a blur to him. He closed his eyes and sought for Stephanie. He brought up memories of her that invoked strong feelings. She was that way.

Opening his eyes again, he looked around. Very carefully, he reached over with one of his really long claws. He paused to look himself over as best he could. He needed a mirror. Cool, he really was a bear and a big one. His ass was against the cargo doors, and his front hung over the seat almost into the front. He flexed his digits; he had stubby fingers and a thumb with claws attached. He didn't think bears had thumbs. Later, he would worry about it later.

With one claw, he carefully hit the window button to lower it. They didn't notice. "Hi," he tried to say, but it came out as, "Grllii," and pretty loud.

That stopped them.

"Joe," Bruce asked.

"RRRillsss," was the noise he made while nodding his head. It reminded him of when his Labrador tried to talk to him.

"Oh, thank God you're in there." Bruce was visibly relieved. "Someone took Steph. We think the …"

Stoneman stepped over and grabbed Bruce's arm, turning him away. "Don't tell him that. We don't know what he'll do," Stoneman whispered.

Bears have good hearing, Joe found. He could also smell blood. Stoneman was bleeding.

There was a short flurry of activity, and Bruce had Stoneman into a joint lock. "Don't manhandle me again. Do you hear me?" Stoneman gave a brief nod, and Bruce pushed him away.

Joe didn't understand the smells, but it excited him, so it was a problem, something emotional, violent. *Plus*, he thought, *Bruce is pretty angry, upset.* Joe stuck his paw, hand, whatever, out the window and drummed his claws on the door. They scratched and pierced the metal.

"Ggruup," he tried. Oops. Not talking was a problem. He pointed at Tom, then Bruce, the front seats, then the direction to Stephanie. "Ggrrive," he growled.

"You know what direction she is?" Bruce was very hopeful.

Joe nodded.

"Hot damn!" Tom yelled. "Mount up."

"I better drive." Bruce elbowed Tom away from the driver's seat and took the wheel. Stoneman jumped in the front. Tom got in the backseat next to the window and Joe.

"Everyone mount up. We have a direction," Stoneman calmly announced into the air.

Joe smelled Stoneman's blood, and it excited him, made him think of food. He pointed at the blood on Tom's leg. "Grrriiiid," he tried to say blood.

Tom looked where he was pointing. "Blood?"

Joe nodded.

"Does it bother you?"

Joe nodded and pointed at Stoneman.

"He's bleeding?"

Joe nodded.

Tom fished around on the floor and came up with a bag with a red cross on it. "Hey, boss. Joe says you're bleeding. Better put a bandage on it before Joe starts liking it too much."

Stoneman looked back at Tom and then at Joe. Joe licked his lips and gave him a grin. Stoneman had a Desert Eagle in his hand and aimed while putting his back up to the dash.

"What the fuck! Cut it out you guys! Damn it, you knew he was going to turn into a bear. We've only been talking about it for two days!" Bruce yelled. "Joe, point the way, without spearing me in the head."

Tom was trying hard not to laugh. "Colonel, Joe was kidding. Weren't you, Joe?"

Joe tried to look sheepish while nodding his head.

"Asshole," Stoneman muttered while turning back to the front to pull his shirt off.

Joe concentrated again on Stephanie and pointed out the right side of the vehicle.

"They turned. Go right as soon as you can." Tom could see Joe's paw without turning so he took on the role of interpreter.

"Tom eyes and ears," Stoneman grunted. "Shit, I'm going to need stitches. This slash is long, and I can't get to it."

"No," Bruce said. "It's already healing shut."

Joe noticed Stoneman freeze for just an instant, and a smell changed. "That's not good," Stoneman breathed out.

"Joe, hey buddy," Tom was pulling at the fur on the side of his head. "Can you shift your head up higher? I need to change sides." Joe made adjustments, and finally Tom was on the right-hand side of the vehicle.

They found out the hard way that Joe had to be careful shifting his weight. It caused the Suburban to sway dangerously. They were on two wheels for a moment.

Tom had belted himself in and unpacked a laptop and a flat monitor mounted in a special frame. He had a headset on. "Joe, which way?"

Joe thought about Stephanie and pointed. He was starting to get upset. She felt hurt or scared. “Ggriiive rrrrasssr.”

“Joe, what is it?” Tom asked.

Joe made a forward wave motion with his hand. “Rrrasssr.”

“Go faster?”

Joe nodded.

“Something change with Stephanie?” Bruce asked from the front.

“Police scan has a lock. Apparently, there are three cars racing a motorcycle ahead of us. The police are vectoring units. Turn left up here. We can cut over to a four lane.” Tom was studying the screens.

Joe spent the next bit trying not to think too hard about Stephanie, but still get a direction. She was scared, and it was making him angry.

“Joe, direction?”

He pointed, but it wasn’t in the direction they were driving.

Tom was doing something clever. He was having them turn in different directions, Joe pointing, while drawing lines on one of the screen. After a moment he said, “Got ’em. I’ve triangulated their current location based on Joe’s pointing. Looks like they are at an industrial park on the other side of highway 520. Turn right here and get on the highway. Then take the first exit and go left at the light.” He repeated the directions and the address to someone on the radio or was it a phone. Joe was losing track. Stephanie wasn’t happy about something.

Bruce swerved and swayed, but got through the turn and onto the highway. He put his foot in it, and the Suburban really picked up speed.

“Joe?”

He pointed.

“Yeah, baby, they stopped moving,” Tom shouted. “We have them now.”

“We are running out of time. If they stopped moving, then they are at the site. The last symbol site was in an industrial park.” Bruce pushed for more speed and took to the right-side carpool lane, using it as a speed lane. It was late at night so the traffic was light.

“Don’t kill us on the turn,” Stoneman commanded. “Joe weighs a ton and that will make us unstable.”

"Right." Bruce started concentrating.

Joe felt a stab of pain. Stephanie had just woken up and realized where she was.

Bruce hit the turn going too fast. Suburbans are heavy to start with and with Joe it was like turning a whale. Luckily, the Jersey barrier kept them from spilling off the intersection, and Bruce righted them. "It's only paint and a dent or two."

Joe roared his approval.

Ahead, they saw flashing police lights and cars piled up. "Those are the cars that boxed me earlier," Tom supplied as they got closer.

Joe pointed toward Stephanie, "Urrrrrn."

Tom was getting good at this. "Yeah, that should be where she is. Second building over, just behind that complex."

Bruce brought them to a sliding stop. "Police."

There was a clicking on the driver side window. Joe didn't move his head, but glanced over to see a police officer with his gun out clicking it on the window. *Bad form*, Joe thought. *You don't pull your sidearm unless you intend to use it.*

Bruce slowly brought his window down.

"What's the big hurry, mister? I clocked you at over a hundred back there on 520."

"My name is Bruce Richardson. I work with Doctor Stephanie Blackraven. She has been kidnapped and is about to be killed. These men are part of her security detail, Expedite Security."

"What?"

"Doctor Blackraven has been working with the Bellevue police and the FBI on a serial murder case. The serial killer has abducted her. We are chasing them." Bruce pointed forward, "Those cars up there are part of the kidnapping."

"Don't move." The officer stepped a little further away from them and keyed his radio. "Dispatch, I have a stopped vehicle with three males and a stuffed bear in the back. They say they're part of an ongoing police investigation involving one Doctor Blackraven and the FBI. Please advise."

"Say again?" the radio voice asked.

He did. Joe huffed. Time, the clock was ticking, and he was getting anxious.

"Be advised we have an AP out for one, Stephanie Blackraven, doctor regarding gang violence and killings. There is also a of interest notice for Bruce Richardson, … ah wait one." The radio voice seemed to get excited.

"Didn't you say you were Bruce Richardson?"

"Yes, officer, but we are running out of time." Bruce pointed. "They are right over there and could be killing her even as we speak."

Joe didn't like the sounds of that. He was getting really anxious.

"Guys," Tom was staring at him. "Guys, we should do something. Joe seems to be getting excited back here."

The officer stepped closer. He was still pointing the gun at Bruce. "What the … are you talking about." He seemed to be editing his speech. "You," he wiggled his gun at Bruce. "Hands on the wheel." Bruce complied. "You," he pointed the gun at Stoneman. "Hands on the dash." The officer looked spooked.

"Officer, do you mean to shoot us?" Stoneman asked calmly.

"No, not unless you do something that warrants it."

"Then why are you pointing your sidearm at us? We have offered no resistance nor have we threatened you in any way." Stoneman was going for cold, the tone a superior would use.

"Ah."

Joe could see the officer thinking hard. He also lowered his weapon to the ready position.

The radio crackled. "Be advised the FBI has issued a stop and detain order for all members of Expedite Security in conjunction with the Blackraven AP. There is also a were warning in effect." The gun came back up.

"That's it, everyone out of the car, ah truck. Move slowly."

Joe, careful to keep his paw below the window, reached over and pushed the button to lower the window. The officer instantly trained his pistol at the opening. Joe lunged as fast as he could, which turned out to be very fast. His first thought was to smack the gun away, but his claws would shred the guy's arms. Instead, he hit him in the face with the palm of his paw/hand, roaring at the top of his lungs. The officer went off his feet to his butt in record time and, more importantly, didn't have time to shoot.

"Go," Stoneman ordered.

Bruce whipped the wheel to the right and floored it. The big V-8 answered with squealing tires, racing noise, and swerving rear end. The Suburban was up the curb, on the grass, and down into the empty parking lot in a blink. That's when the law caught up to them, the law of physics.

Too much bouncing, too much weight, and too much speed caused the Suburban to swerve, then fishtail, and finally do a slow, graceful roll onto its right side.

"That kind of shit only works in the movies," Stoneman observed calmly while lying on the door.

Bruce was hanging from his seat belt. "It got Joe away from the police for a moment. Go Joe, save Steph!" Bruce yelled.

Joe had braced himself when Bruce started moving, which wasn't all that hard, considering he took up the whole back of the Suburban, so he wouldn't land on Tom.

When the Suburban stopped, Joe bunched his hind legs and kicked as hard as he could. The cargo doors exploded off the back, and Joe started shimming out the back.

He pointed. "Gggrrrrrnnng gggrrrrt ssssssrrrrrrph."

"He's going to get Stephanie," Tom supplied.

"Yeah, baby!" Bruce yelled and then yelped. "Ah, I think I broke something."

Stoneman said something about dealing with the authorities.

Tom was talking quietly to someone on a radio or cell.

Joe's feeling of Stephanie's fear slipped away. It was like she was gone. He reared and roared and bolted toward the buildings.

It was late at night and raining harder, hopefully that would make it harder for people to see him, not.

Startled cries rang out, then shots. He felt little thuds in his side, but he picked up speed.

He rounded the central complex at a full run. He could run fast.

There were three cars, a van, and a big panel truck. The van and the truck were close to a building entrance.

A man with a rifle rose up from behind a car and took aim at him. Joe swerved and shoulder blocked the car. It slid sideways into the man, taking him to the ground. Joe stopped and stomped on him once. Then he took off running; she was close.

Brrrrrrrrrr sounded off to the other side followed by heavy impacts to him. He stumbled and went into a shoulder roll. He saw another man in tactical gear reloading. Joe leaped up and closed with him. Another swipe and the guy just went to pieces.

Joe moved as another automatic rifle opened up. He didn't think he was hit.

He saw three guys ahead, one was shooting at him. The other two were doing something with a tube. That didn't look good for him. He swerved again to get behind the truck. Joe reached down and grabbed the frame under the truck and lifted. Yes, he was strong. He roared for extra strength.

The truck slowly toppled over on the tube guys.

Joe didn't wait; he cut around the front of the truck to run right into a started rifleman. Joe's swipe bent the rifle and the guy's head.

Joe was running on instinct. He realized he didn't really have control anymore. It was like he was riding along in this tank body that really wanted to get to Stephanie. He just gave it ideas and insight.

Joe tucked his head down and ran through the glass entryway. There were two guys there with automatic shotguns. Those hurt. He kept moving his head around so they wouldn't shoot him in the eyes. They did shoot him everywhere else.

One swipe each. Ballistic plates didn't seem to stop claws.

Down was toward Stephanie. Looking around, he spotted a sign to a stairway. Sure enough, stairway down.

Going down stairs was, apparently, a skill on four legs. He jumped to the bottom and let the wall stop him.

Tired.

Bleeding. Energy seemed to flow out with his blood.

Another door got smashed through. He could see her in a big room, naked, spread-eagle on the floor. He rose to his full height, roaring his defiance.

A wall of bars made of light slammed down in from of him. It hurt to touch them. Then it got hard to breathe. Another man stepped out and started shooting him with darts.

He roared again and then toppled over. His last clear sight was of Stephanie looking at him from the floor and crying. He tried to tell her he was sorry for not saving her.

He looked on helplessly as the man in the suit coat knelt down and slapped Steph. Then he started undoing his pants.

Joe couldn't move; he couldn't do anything to help. She was going to get raped, and he couldn't do anything but watch.

He raged inside his head, but he was tired and had trouble breathing.

Another guy in tactical pants dressed above combat boats stepped into view. He was yelling, but Joe couldn't really understand what was being said. It did stop the guy in the suit coat from taking his pants down.

Breathing was getting harder. His vision zoomed down to just a black tunnel ending in his view of naked Stephanie. He didn't want his last look to be like that. He thought of her as she had sat in his lap and kissed him. Her little judgmental laugh he found so cute. Her eyes as she gazed up into his. The way she bit her hair when she concentrated.

The rage just went away. He'd found his happy thought, maybe he could fly like Peter Pan.

He felt a liquid whoosh as his form changed. He was human again, but everything faded to black.

Chapter 26

Stephanie was walking through the forest, heavy with underbrush and cedar trees. Water gently dripped down and pooled in the carpet of needles. Up ahead, she could see a clearing with a little stream bubbling through it and moss on the banks.

Sitting in the clearing on a stump that had arms like a chair, was the Blue Lady, to one side a shot-to-hell bleeding wolf, and on the other side a really big sleeping bear.

"Hi," Stephanie approached tentatively.

The Blue Lady put her hands on the heads of the animals and breathed in deeply. Swirling light flickers streamed up her arms and into her. Letting out her breath, she smiled, "Greetings Stephanie Blackraven. Be welcome to my place."

"You can talk to me?"

"Yes, you have let me in, called on me directly for aid."

"Yeah," Stephanie wasn't happy about that, uncertain about what followed. "I did do that. I believe you exist." She looked around. "So, what now?"

"Now you take your place as my High Priestess. You have already saved one of my hand maidens from enslavement."

Stephanie shook her head, "What?"

The Blue Lady placed her head on the bear and breathed in again. More lights streamed up and into her.

"You aren't like stealing his memories or anything, are you?"

"What if I am?" Her smile was a little more predatory now. "He too has asked for my aid and given himself to me."

Stephanie didn't like the sounds of that and was getting pissed. "He did it for me. I'm responsible for his … ah, condition."

The Lady's smile froze like a freeze frame. When she moved, a ghostly image of Rosemary was standing behind her. The Lady opened her mouth, but it was Rosemary who spoke. "Remember, my little rune weaver, she is an alien, unused to human emotion or thought. You define the nature of the relationship." Rosemary's eyes narrowed. "If you want it rough, it will be rough."

The Lady closed her mouth and waited.

Stephanie started to say something smart-mouthed, but stopped. Just for an instant, she channeled Uncle Raymond and his constant haranguing her about her sharp tongue. She hung her head for a moment then looked back up. "Is Rosemary the handmaiden?"

The Lady nodded.

"What is it you want me to do for you, exactly?" Stephanie was trying to be calm and collected.

"You will be my representative to the human world. They need to be made aware of the reawakening of …" It was like a static interrupt. Sound was made, but the sound didn't make sense.

"I'm sorry. I didn't get that last part."

The Lady tried again, but it had the same effect. The Lady frowned and looked at Rosemary.

Rosemary blinked a few times and looked off into the distance. "Interference and there is no frame of reference for the concept you are trying to explain. She, ah … we need more experience before we can frame the concept for discussion."

The Lady glanced down at the wolf and bear. "They don't have it, either," Rosemary supplied. "I think she needs to learn more before you can really explain. I certainly don't have a reference that would work. That's why you need her."

The Lady turned her attention back to Stephanie. "You are mine, do you agree?"

"I will be your High Priestess and convey a yet-to-be-determined message to the world. I will do it in my way and at my pace, since you can't explain the alien concept to me. That is all I can agree to at this time." Stephanie steeled herself to be smashed.

The Lady considered for a moment. "That was what I said."

"Then I agree."

The Lady seemed content. She stroked the head of the wolf. "This one is more in tune with me, but he is not connected to you like this one." She patted the bear.

Stephanie couldn't help but smile. "That's because I'm falling in love with the bear. He's my big Joe bear, isn't he?"

The Lady looked up sharply and frowned again. Rosemary yelped, "Crap."

Stephanie was abruptly jerked back into a world of pain and light.

She was being held down by two men and another was trying to take her clothes off. The tight pants were giving them problems. In a very uncoordinated and unladylike fashion, she started fighting them. Elbow here, bite there, kicking, she even got one of the knives on her legs out and cut one across the face. That's when she got punched.

When she came to again, they had her bolted to the floor. Her bare butt pressed against smooth cold stone. She was still groggy and fuzzy, but looking everywhere and thinking. Her face hurt. There was no symbol laid down yet, but there was a projector mounted directly over her with the cords running along the ceiling over to a bench. She could hear yelling and the distance sound of guns. There were two guys in the room, no, three. One was standing to the left of the only door with some type of hose connected gun. Another, Nelson, the traitorous bastard who had been Uncle Raymond's deputy, was near the right-hand wall holding a bulky over wide rifle with a huge magazine, and the last, ten feet or so to her left, Rhinebolt. He couldn't tear his eyes away from her. They were moving up and down her body.

"What, asshole, never seen a woman before?" she spit out. "Oh that's right, you have to rape women to get anything." He didn't like that.

"Stop staring at her tits, doc, and get ready." Nelson didn't seem to like him, either.

"I'm not just staring at her tits. I'm also ensuring the spell I placed on her severs the connection to whoever is tracking her magically." The sneering arrogance just oozed out.

"Well, it's too late for that doc, because it's just about here." Nelson motioned to the other guy.

There were lots of shots fired, screaming, roaring, and then silence. She caught a faint scent of Joe's feelings. She tried hard and got a glimmer of Joe's rage. He was just over there and coming down. She levered herself up as best she could, which wasn't very good. They had her down tight.

Something heavy impacted a wall and shook the whole building. Then another thunderous roar, and the door and part of the far wall shattered. A bloody monstrous bear plowed right through it all. It hesitated for an instant as it saw her, then reared onto his hind legs, and shook the building with its roar, stepping forward on its hind legs. Bloody strips of fur hung off its sides, bleeding holes were everywhere. Part of its chest was like hamburger. Its paws were blood up to the elbows, the claws glistened with it.

To her left, Rhinebolt spoke a sentence in Latin, and Stephanie saw ribbons of light stream toward Joe to solidify into a cage. He had never been that good with the knack.

Joe smashed into the light cage and roared again. It stopped him.

Stephanie's vision blurred. He was so beat up. All the blood, it was all for her. She hadn't even told him she loved him. Tears started running down her face, she couldn't help it, as she watched him get gassed by Hose boy and darted by Nelson. She couldn't feel him anymore.

"I told you," she heard Rhinebolt condescending to the others. "The cage will hold him and the gas. How could you have doubted me?"

"Joe," she screamed. Twisting toward Rhinebolt, she shouted, "You bastard, you're going to die for that. You're going to die screaming." Getting angry helped clear her head.

Rhinebolt stepped over and slapped her face. "Shut up, you good-for-nothing doxy." He stepped around where she could see him better, and he started undoing his pants. "I've wanted to do this to you for years. It's all you're good for. You stupid co-ed, thinking your theory's had any merit."

"Professor, you don't have time," Nelson said, walking over. "The bear ripped up our backup and lookouts. Right now, it's just me, Jones, one guy on the roof, and he's pulling out. He reported activity moving this way. If the bear was close enough to get here, her detail can't be far behind." He looked down at Stephanie like a man checked a side of beef. "She's a fine piece of ass, but you need to do the spell so we can get out of here."

Rhinebolt looked up like Nelson had told him Christmas had been canceled. "No, I've waited so long."

"I don't give a shit. We have no time. This little bitch has cost me seventeen good men." Nelson stepped over to Rhinebolt, grabbed him by the neck, and pushed him toward the computer. "Now, do your bit, or I'll just shoot her so we can leave. I was paid to get you subjects, not die, or go to jail."

Rhinebolt put his clothes to right and then went to check the computer, muttering the entire time.

Stephanie looked around frantically. She didn't have a pencil. Then she heard a faint voice, *Project away.* It sounded like Rosemary.

Could she do that, visualize, and then push the symbol eruption far enough off her hand to keep it from hurting her. She snorted, *I'm going to die hideously here soon, anyway, so what have I got to lose?*

She visualized the healing symbol settling over the still form of Joe. He had changed back to a bleeding human. She focused and gave it the Will and the Word. "Eal ..." Rhinebolt stuffed a gag in her mouth.

"Stupid girl, think I'm going to let you intone while I'm working. It's a ball-gag. I use it for my special time." He ran his hand over her body, lingering at sensitive areas, playing with her. He shoved his fingers into her. "Ohh, you are so nice," he crooned at her, leaning closer.

There was nothing she could do to stop it. She was helpless. Her tempered flared, *You are only helpless if you let yourself be,* she thought. She started looking around for opportunities.

"Professor! No time! I'm not going to tell you again. We have no time," Nelson calmly told him. "I've got the symbol, I don't need you anymore. So, what's it going to be?" Stephanie looked over to see him aiming a pistol at Rhinebolt, no, it was at her.

The professor lurched away, pausing just a moment to spit on Stephanie. "She needs some of my bodily fluid. Normally, I use something else, but that will suffice." He went back over to the computer and pressed several keys.

The projector started flashing an intense red beam on to the floor. Stephanie could see the symbol taking form. She screamed her frustration into the gag.

Think, Stephanie told herself. *You do your best work under pressure.* She started reviewing the theory in her head, but her thoughts were jumping everywhere. *Focus*, she told herself.

The foundation of it all was the formulation of the symbol, the Will to make it so, The Way or direction it should go, and the Word to trigger the release. She couldn't speak so … If it was a trigger, then maybe it wasn't a spoken word, but the effort to speak it. She could still do that. She focused on Joe again, laying the symbol, gave it the Will to work, she knew the Way, "Eal-Hay," she garbled around the gag. It triggered.

Yes, I have a way. Thinking hard, she pieced together the master symbol. *What can I do? Wait, the floor is photosensitive. All I need is a few minutes.* She brought out old faithful.

"*No*, the Lady spoke.

What, oh, if it looks like this won't work, Nelson will just shoot me. She would've slapped her forehead, but her hands were tied down. *The frequency, too, it has to be exactly the right light frequency, or the paint won't pick it up.*

"The symbol is down," Rhinebolt announced, like he had an audience. "Now to check it." The projector whirred, and a different lens clicked into place followed by a flash. "I also get a picture of you, all spread out there, my pretty," he laughed manically. "It would be better …" He cut off as he glanced over at Nelson, "Philistine," he muttered.

He's nuts, Stephanie realized. Whatever this was, it had finally cut that final string holding his sanity.

"It's ready." His voice was breathy in anticipation. Apparently, so was another part of his body, everything was just standing at attention.

The sound of a scuffle and two shots brought her attention back to the front of the room. Hose boy was lying on the floor bleeding. Nelson was stumbling back away from another figure, who was slowly sliding down the right-hand wall.

It was Uncle Raymond.

Stephanie screamed. She was in emotional overload.

"Ahh," Nelson cleared his throat while looking at the bloody hand he took off his stomach. "That hurts." He looked back over at Uncle Raymond. "Why couldn't you just die like you're supposed to? Everyone else does."

"Asshole," Raymond breathed out. "Disloyal asshole."

Nelson chuckled. "That's what you taught me, General. Highest bidder."

"You let her go, and I'll show you how it all works." Raymond was struggling to talk. His head rocked over so he could look at Stephanie.

"I already know how …" Nelson started.

Bang!

Professor Rhinebolt screamed and fell to the floor. Uncle Raymond had a small handgun hidden by his left leg out of Nelson's sight.

Bang!

Nelson shot Uncle Raymond in the left arm.

"Professor, you still with me?"

"Yes, I am, no thanks to you. Luckily, my previous treatments have made me somewhat immune to simple bullets."

"The clock is still ticking, or should I just shoot her now?" Nelson aimed at Stephanie.

"No, no, it's all prepared." Rhinebolt limped over and stepped behind Stephanie's head, probably into the smaller circle. He started speaking Latin.

Bang!

Nelson shot Uncle Raymond again. She saw Uncle Raymond grimace and look back at Nelson. "Don't go away yet, old man," Nelson gloated. "I want you so see what happens to your little niece. It's quite the show."

Stephanie snapped, and her temper flared again. The symbol set she had used twice now appeared in her mind's eye. Lightning Storm!

No! the Lady said. *That would kill you all.*

I'm going to die, anyway.

What of Joe, you'd kill him, too.

He's alive? Stephanie barely believed her.

Yes. There is hope if you're smart. You and Joe can both live. The Lady was persuasive.

Stephanie growled in frustration and laid a healing symbol on Uncle Raymond. She started searching for another symbol to use on Nelson. A simple one slid into place. "Art-Day," was garbled into the gag. Little fiery embers of light appeared about two feet above Stephanie and shot off at Nelson. Only two of them hit him.

He didn't even turn all the way around, he just briefly looked. "Goddamn it, professor, I swear I'm going to just shoot her."

Bang.

Nelson shot Uncle Raymond again.

She tried one at Rhinebolt, but it seemed to fizzle out before getting to him. His eyes widened as he noticed. She went back to aiming at Nelson.

The professor's Latin sped up.

Art-Day, Art-Day, Art-Day, Art-Day. The little pieces of light kept flying. Nelson muttered, and apparently tired of the pesky little impacts, he turned to level his pistol.

Bang!

Nelson's brains sprayed out the side of his head. She saw Uncle Raymond let his right arm drop, and the tiny gun fell away. "Never turn away 'til their dead, dumb ass." He flopped his head over so he could see her. "Sorry, Princess, age caught up to me. I love you." He slumped, eyes closed.

"*Goddess*, she yelled in her mind. *Hear my prayer! Please lend your healing hand to my uncle and greatest protector.* The healing symbol flashed into her mind's eye.

And a cool shiver ran over her naked body, quickly followed by a little whoosh as the Solomon Circle closed around the greater symbol, cutting her off from everything outside it.

She was getting really tired of Rhinebolt. *What the hell*, she thought. "Art-Day." She just kept triggering the darts. They sprayed against the inside edge of the circle force field. She triggered them as fast as she thought of them.

Rhinebolt almost stopped incanting. She guessed she had surprised him with that one.

The symbols were coming so frequently that they were forming a string in her mind's eye. Inspiration struck, the string of simple symbols reminded her of an equation, a polynomial. She kept at it, only adjusting the end/edge of one symbol and the beginning/edge of the next. She had it. She stopped triggering them as she formed a different string of symbols with an almost an equal sign and a recursive variable.

"Omatic-Autay Art-Day," she mumbled into the gag.

There was a sputter above her, and then a constant stream of fiery darts started spraying at the inside of the force field. She didn't have to concentrate on the symbol now. *Time to look for some way to screw with Rhinebolt*, she thought.

Rolling her head back, she caught sight of Rhinebolt out of the corner of her eye. He was standing over her, waving his arms like he was conducting an orchestra, only he was wide-eyed, staring at her automatic dart equation.

She remembered blinding the werewolf with her flash symbol. She visualized the light of her flash symbol boring into and through his eyes, when she had it. "Ash-Flay," she garbled into the gag.

He screamed as his eyes exploded.

That stopped his chanting.

She looked back over to see her darts turning the force field red where they were impacting. The big symbol was continuing to be empowered. Frantically, she studied her surroundings for anything else she could screw up. She saw Joe move, shifting his shoulder.

"I don't need to see to absorb you, cunt," Rhinebolt hissed out before he started chanting again.

She tried the unlocking symbol. Apparently, the cuffs holding her arms and legs weren't locked on. All that did was make Rhinebolt's pants fall off and the gag loosen. *Why did the flash and unlock work and the dart not?* If she ever, *No,* she stopped. *When I get out, Bruce and I will study it.* She was back to altering the big symbol.

The big complicated symbol hovered in her mind's eye. She was tracing the power-conducting portions of the symbol when she heard a bell-like sound.

Blinking a few times to refocus her real eyes, she noticed her fiery darts had etched a hole through the force field. *That might be enough to get a symbol through,* she estimated.

Uncle Raymond was still hunched against the wall. She could see blood bubbling out of his mouth. *He's breathing*. Excitement almost overwhelmed her. *Where there's life there's hope.*

"*Goddess*, she yelled in her mind. *Hear my prayer! Please lend your healing hand to my uncle and greatest protector.* The healing symbol flashed into her mind's eye.

"*You don't have to yell. I've been listening since the last time you asked.* The Lady sounded like Professor Stein speaking to an errant student.

Please heal him, please. Stephanie had never begged for anything, but she begged for this. "Eal-Hay."

She saw Joe crawling toward her. Incredible pain lanced through her body. *It's now or never*, she thought.

Rhinebolt was chanting louder, like he was coming to the end.

Ah, my Rune Weaver, heal yourself now. Then let's look at this pesky symbol, the Lady commanded.

Stephanie did as she was told. The healing gave a respite.

She heard voices, familiar voices. She ignored them. She ignored everything outside the symbol.

Focusing everything, she sent herself into a fugue state of absolute concentration. It was like time stopped for her on everything, but the symbol. The pieces of the symbol flashed through her mind's eye as she reviewed it all.

"*Here, here, here, here, and here, make these changes,* the Lady told her.

"Frequency, we have to have the frequency of the light right, red at 647.1 *nanometers.* The entire process of light amplification by the stimulated emissions of radiation creation flashed through her mind's eye.

"*Ah, that's how*, she heard. *Time is short. Visualize. Focus, WILL IT SO.*

Stephanie gave it everything, The Will, The Way, and the garbled Word. "Ange-Chay Ash-Flay."

She didn't see the flash.

All she got was mind-blanking pain. She screamed until she had no air left.

PAIN!

Blackout.

Chapter 27

Joe's vision and awareness faded in and out. He realized he could see again when he saw Rhinebolt feeling up Steph. He still couldn't move.

I'm in hell, he thought. *All I get to see is torment.*

Cool warmth shivered down his body, bringing him back to the room. Strength started seeping back in.

Focusing forward, he saw the red light of the projector shining over Stephanie. She had been gagged. White light flashed from the box above her.

Bruce and Steph were right; he's using their method of setting the symbol. That asshole just took a picture of her. Joe started to get angry again. He could feel her rage and terror.

Two gunshots rang out, and the boots staggered back into the range of his vision. He still couldn't move, and time seemed to be skipping a beat.

Stephanie screamed into her gag.

His sense of her concern and fear for another brought his interest back. Joe was kind of gazing at her, but not really seeing her, but he felt her.

Another shot, followed by another, focused him just fine. He saw red puff off of Rhinebolt and he fell to the floor. Someone had shot him.

Yeah baby! Joe silently cheered. *Shoot that bastard again!* Maybe they could save Stephanie. Hope bloomed in him as he felt hope blossom in Stephanie.

Sound came back.

"Yes," Rhinebolt was saying. "Luckily, my previous treatments have made me somewhat immune to simple bullets." Rhinebolt didn't sound very positive as he got up.

"The clock is still ticking, or should I just shoot her now?" Joe could shift his eyes enough to see the guy in tactical boots aiming Stephanie's way. He couldn't get a good enough look to identify him.

No hope, Stephanie had lost hope again and was back to being rage filled and scared at the same time. Tactical boot guy was still with them. Joe couldn't move his whole head yet, just his eyes.

Bang!

Joe must've faded off again because another gunshot brought him back.

"Don't go away yet, old man. I want you to see what happens to your little niece. It's quite the show," Tactical Boots gloated.

Little red hornets were zipping away from above Stephanie to hit Boots. They didn't seem to be hurting him much, but he was muttering.

He discharged his gun again.

Joe strained his eyes to get a better look at Boots. Boot's neck was turning red, and his jacket was starting to smolder. *Yeah babe, you just keep swinging!* Joe silently cheered her on. The little red flits were starting to have an effect.

Boots glanced back toward Stephanie. "Goddamn it, professor, I swear I'm going to just shoot her."

The red hornets had started with a few, but they picked up speed until it looked like a steady stream of them.

Rhinebolt's speaking picked up speed.

"That's it," Joe heard Boots say under his breath and turned to take aim.

Bang!

Boots' head exploded, and his body fell, blocking Joe's view of Stephanie.

"Never turn away 'til their dead, dumbass," Joe heard a whisky voice say. "Sorry, Princess, age caught up to me. I love you."

Goddamn, Joe thought. *It's her uncle. One tough son of a bitch! If he can do it …*" Joe started trying to move. He was breathing better, and he could flop his head a little.

Air pulsed in the room. Joe looked back toward Stephanie. The red hornets were hitting some kind of barrier almost directly over where she lay. "He set the circle," Joe mumbled out loud. The ritual was starting.

Joe started visualizing the things Rhinebolt had done to Stephanie in an effort to get angry. He needed the rage to change. Tony had said the change healed them. "Please Goddess," Joe begged, "hear my prayer. Help me save my Stephanie. Help me change into a bear." He didn't feel any different.

The inside of the circle was red with angry hornets. Joe didn't know what Stephanie had done, but she was still fighting. Rhinebolt was wide-eyed and bleeding, but he still chanted.

Joe was looking right at Rhinebolt when his eyes exploded out of his head. That stopped his chanting.

"You go, girl!" Joe cheered. It could've only been his Stephanie.

Joe struggled harder. He felt himself shift and his arms move. He knew when he shifted his chest because the pain caused him to fade for a moment. He had never, ever hurt this bad. Ends of things were grinding together that shouldn't have been. He was covered in blood, his blood. It wasn't just one area, but all over his body.

Joe faded out again, and when he came back, the chanting had started again.

Joe looked over to see Rhinebolt waving his arms and gesturing.

Stephanie was bucking against the restraints. Her back bowed so far she seemed to lift herself off the floor by her wrists and ankles.

She screamed so hard the gag flew off her face.

Joe struggled forward on his hands and knees. Getting around Boots almost killed him.

He was dragging himself by his one good arm.

The red hornets, he recognized as her dart spell, symbol, whatever, had etched a hole in the barrier, and there was a solid line of them shooting out toward the doorway. The symbols around the circles were lit with their own fire. It was like the power was inching from symbol to symbol, slowly igniting them, first around the little circle, then the symbols of the next circle, and then the inside of the big circle.

Joe lurched forward and screamed when his other wrist shifted, buckling, spilling him to the floor. Using his one good hand, he continued to pull himself along the floor until he ran into the barrier. He clawed at it. "Steph, I'm here. I'm, I'm …" He didn't know what to tell her.

There was a red flash as Rhinebolt's chanting ended.

The symbols ignited like they were on fast forward. Stephanie screamed until her voice broke.

"Ah, first stage, physical transference. Perfect, if only I would have had time to enjoy her womanly form. If she had been taller, she would've been perfect.

The perfect woman." Rhinebolt, if he still had eyes, would have been staring at her naked body. "Now, my injuries will be healed by transferring them to the subject with the first stage." Rhinebolt was talking to himself.

Stephanie's beautiful blue eyes exploded out of her head, just as Rhinebolt's eyes had. A puff of red shot out of her hip and onto the floor as a bullet hole appeared. Twinkling lights were sparkling down Stephanie's body into the symbols and up into Rhinebolt. Joe looked up to see Rhinebolt's eyes regrow. Rhinebolt screamed as well, but not as loud as Stephanie.

Joe clawed like a madman regardless of the pain. "You bastard, leave her alone," Joe yelled, but Rhinebolt didn't seem to hear him.

"Ah, much better. The little, untalented co-ed bitch taking my eyes was unexpected," Rhinebolt breathed out. "Prepare yourself, old boy," Rhinebolt said to himself. "The second stage will ignite, transferring the physical attributes along with mystic attunement." Joe looked up to see Rhinebolt stiffen himself like he was expecting a blow.

Joe looked back at Stephanie as her screaming intensified. Her back arched even more as she gulped breaths to keep screaming. The sparkles were more like flickers of pale blue-green flames washing down her body from feet to head. They passed up into Rhinebolt as well. He didn't yell this time, just gritted his teeth.

Stephanie screamed through all five cycles of the flames. Joe was smashing his clawed, bloody paws against the wall without making the slightest difference. He threw his head back and screamed his frustration. "Goddess," he begged, "please save her. Take me instead."

"Now, stage three, transference of essence." Rhinebolt was almost shouting in anticipation. "This will add years to my life. She is much younger than the others. Oh, and powerful. I can feel it already." Rhinebolt was smiling with shining eyes; he had the lights Joe had seen in Stephanie's eyes.

The entire symbol set exploded in light. Stephanie screamed until she had no air as the black flames started at her feet. As the flames progressed up her body, she started deflating like all the juice was getting sucked out. Stephanie's face was a picture of abject horror. Their connection ended. He couldn't feel her anymore. That warmth was gone.

That's what broke Joe's will. He collapsed, crying, next to the barrier. "No, Steph, no. Goddess please!" he begged.

"Get him away from there," another voice said.

Joe tried to look around as he pointed, "Help her."

Then Rhinebolt screamed much as Stephanie had at first.

Joe's body was broken, because when the men grabbed him, moving him, it caused his vision to tunnel. He turned to see the twinkling, sparkling lights flashing down Rhinebolt's body into the still glowing symbols and then to Stephanie. The very faint image of a blue lady was standing with her hand on Rhinebolt's head and pointing at Stephanie's mummified body.

Joe stared. Rhinebolt was screaming louder and finding it difficult to draw in enough air. There was no pause between stages this time; the sparkling lead straight into the blue-green flames to the black juice-sucking wave. As the effects passed into the symbols, Stephanie's body started re-inflating, growing until she was back to her normal size. But she didn't stop, she kept growing until her hands and feet stuck out beyond the edge of the inner circle and caught fire when they touched the symbols. She finally pulled the bolts out of the floor to escape the tormenting flame and took a fetal position in the inner circle. Her hands and feet were burnt beyond recognition.

Rhinebolt had collapsed to his knees with his hands held up like in prayer as he mummified. A look of abject horror frozen on his eyeless face.

Hands grabbed Joe, causing ends of bones to rub together. The pain was so intense he just let them drag him off to oblivion, knowing he had failed.

He had failed her.

Chapter 28

Stephanie was chained to a hospital bed with her hands and feet bandaged. Her head was strapped into blocks so she couldn't turn it.

She tried to remember how she got here and just couldn't put all the pieces together.

She remembered up to changing the symbols without much problem, not that it was a great thing to remember. Then waves of pain, pain so intense that she passed out from it. There was a brief remembrance of lying naked on the floor with her eye sockets on fire. She remembered the smell, the burnt flesh of her eye sockets, feeling the intense pain and the deep intense need to take a breath.

Then she was here. She almost panicked with the thought, *Does Rhinebolt still have me? Or Nelson? Oh God.* But then a little voice in her head that sounded a lot like Uncle Raymond spoke to her. *You don't have time to wallow. They just kick you more when you're down. Get up.*

No, they can't have me, she reasoned. *Uncle Raymond shot Nelson in the head. But what about Rhinebolt? He wouldn't have me in a bed. Rhinebolt would be raping me. And what about the bandages?* She didn't have any data.

Her body felt okay, as in, not in pain. She could tell she had something on her head, covering her face, at least her eyes. She also had bandages on her hands and feet. *Hospital,* she thought. The only place she had any discomfort was the inside of her right elbow. *They've probably been taking blood*, she decided. *Smells like hospital.*

She could hear people walking around; they swished a lot like their clothes were bulky and nylon. She'd worked in a clean room for micron-level electronics, so she had heard it before. The sounds of different machines, both close to her and far away, made her think, *Monitors, different kinds.*

"Hey, where am I?" she yelled.

"Oh good, she's awake." Someone swished closer. "Where do you hurt?" a male voice asked.

"Where am I? Who are you people? How did I get here? Where's Joe and Bruce?"

No answer, then, "Where do you hurt?"

"Look, tell me where I am, and I'll answer you."

Swishing moved away, then from further away she heard, "She's not cooperating."

Someone else, female this time, came closer. "Where do you hurt? Are you in pain?"

"Where am I? Who are you people?"

It kept going like that; she asked, and they wouldn't answer with anything but a question. They wouldn't answer her questions, so she wouldn't answer theirs.

Something had happened to her eyes. She couldn't see with her eyes, but she could "see" something. People had glowing halos of light around them, some brighter and rose colored. Others dimmer, some dark with angry reds shot or bands through them. She couldn't see the people, but she could see their outlines, contours, and contrasts. *Auras, perhaps?* she thought.

She could also see symbols, well, more like equations, strings of symbols constantly flowing, changing. That part was really fascinating. She was starting to build a library of them in her mind. There was nothing wrong with her mind, if anything, she was sharper and faster than ever before. There were always vague accounts of how blind people's other senses became more acute. That must be it, because, other than her vision, everything was sharper, crisper. She didn't know what it meant yet.

She had no sense of time flow. They came in and drugged her to sleep once, or at least that's what she assumed. Most of her awake time she spent reviewing her known symbols and comparing them to the constant streams of symbols she was seeing. Or ignoring the staff and their one-sided dialogue.

Maybe it was a language, programming language. She had streamed the dart symbol together into a loop. When she got out of here, she and Bruce were going to add this to their study list. She made plans for how she was going to get out.

She woke up when someone stuck another needle in her arm. This time she had had enough and jerked away. "Get away from me. I don't want your treatment," she screamed. "Let me out of here."

She could see the aura of the woman? Yes, a woman. Her colors changed when Stephanie reacted.

A man joined the woman and held Stephanie down so the woman could stick her.

"I have rights, goddamn it!" A spontaneous symbol flashed through her mind like the glowing hand thing. Something happened in the room because the colors in both their auras changed as well as their scent. They left in a hurry.

She studied the flow of symbols again.

"Doctor Blackraven, my staff tells me you are being difficult." The man had a cool, cultured voice. "We are just trying to help you."

"The hell you are. No one will answer my questions. You're studying me. I'm not hurt. I'm the victim."

"Doctor, you were tortured in the worst possible way. You've lost your vision." He moved closer and gently touched her arm. "Your hands and feet were almost burnt beyond recognition."

His aura was dark with red and yellow stripes or hues. They changed and shifted as he spoke to her.

"Bullshit, you're not here to help me. You're here for yourself. Let me go."

"We are here to help you."

"Then why have you strapped my head down and handcuffed me to the bed? Why haven't you let any of my friends come in here? Why won't anyone answer my questions?" She looked around, pushing her aura sight, trying to extend it out. She saw ten other auras, most of them really faint.

"We put the restraints on to keep you from hurting yourself. Burn victims try to move around, because they hurt so much. And none of your friends have come to see you."

"I'm done talking to you. Go away."

"If you keep arguing, we will sedate you, for your own good."

"I'm done with you," was all Stephanie would say.

He kept saying stuff, medical threats really, but she ignored him, and finally, he stepped far enough away.

It was really easy to form the Will, provide the Way, she had already figured out the symbols she was going to use. "Ark-Day." She heard startled cries from the outer room. She wanted it dark to defeat their video monitoring. Very specifically, she visualized the Solomon Circle forming near her and then expanding to a greater diameter. "Ymbol-Say Ash-Flay Orce-Fay Ield-Fay." Stuff started crashing around her and more yelling. She chuckled to herself.

"*Let them try to get to me through that*, she thought as she started studying the Solomon Circle she had set around her bed. The symbols in it were in motion. Fascinating!

She lost track of time again. However, she was getting hungry. "Lock-Unay." The cuffs and everything else holding her to the bed fell away. The bandages on her hands yielded to her teeth and pulling, she took the strap and bandage off her head and the electrodes off her chest and arms as well. Her hands felt fine. She had the right number of fingers and toes. They all worked. Her own aura was a riot of hues and colors. There were symbols running through her hands and arms. Cool. Nothing hurt.

People were talking to her from outside the circle, but she ignored them.

She had eyelids and eyeballs. Releasing the darkness or the symbol holding the light away, she found she could see vague images, but it hurt, so she shut her eyes. *Interesting, I have eyes, but can't see visible light, only auras and symbols.* Another thought struck her. *Lady, hear my prayer*, she silently prayed.

I am with you. The Lady sounded like Rosemary.

"*I am healed, but without vision, are you trying to teach me something?*

Yes. Show you.

Have I seen it yet?

No.

"Crap," she swore. *Lady, I can no longer feel Joe, is he dead?* She dreaded the answer, but had to ask.

No, he is living, but separate for now.

She let her breath out with relief. *Ahhh.* She tried to figure out a diplomatic phrasing for her next question, but couldn't. *Why?*

He too has something to learn.

Oh, well ..." She couldn't figure out any way to ask what he was supposed to be learning without it sounding nosy. So, she turned to her personal problem. *They hold me prisoner here. Will you help me?*

Help is on its way. Be patient.

Sorry to have bothered you.

It is not a bother, you are my priestess. With that comment, Stephanie could tell she was no longer tuned in to the Lady.

"*Interesting,* she thought. *Time to try something else.*

Deductive reasoning told her she had been taken from the crime site. It must've been by the authorities. She was being held here without contact, which suggested government. The FBI had more than likely been clued in about her abduction. So logic would say it was connected to them. Logic also suggested that they were trying to figure out how she did what she did.

"Hey, shut up." She waited until they stopped talking. "I want to talk to a friend. Bring me Bruce Richardson or Joe Bremer."

"Ah, doctor, we were starting to wonder." Mister cultured voice was back.

"I got tired of what you were doing. So here's ..."

He cut her off. "You could be hurting yourself. Please let us help you."

"Shut up." She waited. He didn't say anything else. "Here's how I read this. You guys probably work for the government, and you're trying to figure me out. Stop it. There is a lot going on you don't understand, won't understand, until I explain it, and I'm not going to explain it to you like this. I'm willing to work with the government, but not like this."

"Stephanie," he was trying the personal tact. "You were seriously hurt. It's only been two days. Please let us help you."

"I am fine, healed. See my hands." She held them up and opened her eyes. "See, I have eyes. They don't work yet, but that's because the Lady is trying to show me something."

"The Lady?" He used the special voice reserved for questioning someone's grip on reality. At least that was the voice she used.

"Yes, the goddess that has decided I am to be her high priestess. She has had a lot to do with the symbols I've been able to power." Stephanie sounded like a religious nut to her own ears.

"Oh."

"No, it's not an 'oh' like that. I'm talking religious belief here. Never mind." She shook her head. "I'm ready to leave. Now, we can do this the easy way or the hard way."

"You are trapped in some type of magic circle at a location you are not aware of." He didn't sound like mister helpful now.

"It is science, not magic. I'm not trapped in it. You are held out of it. I can put a lightning storm right down on top of," she turned and pointed to the space with the faintest auras in it. "That room right over there. It will tear this building up, probably start a fire. Oxygen-rich environment, this place will burn like crazy. Haven't you read the reports?"

"You would burn as well."

"I am in a force field; this magic circle will stand up to a great many things, fire only being one." He didn't know she was lying. Was she lying? Hmmmm. "Your call, I'm done talking." She lay back down and started planning how a not-quite-blind person would make her escape.

It didn't take long before she heard, "Hey, Steph, you're looking good."

"Bruce?" She looked over to see a bright aura close to the ground like it was in a chair, wheelchair with another aura close. "You sound tired or strained. You in a wheelchair?"

"It's Bruce. Yeah, I'm in a … How can you … I saw you, ah … Never mind. They let me loose to see you. I've been locked up, too."

Stephanie pointed at the accompanying aura. "You can go now." There was a startled pause and then the other aura retreated.

"Have we all been arrested?" she asked.

"Not you, only your security guys, Joe, and me."

"Is Joe here?" Stephanie's heart sped up.

"Yyeeah."

She didn't like the way he said that. "What's wrong with Joe?"

"It's not life threatening, and you probably don't want all these people with recording equipment to hear it."

"Good point." She stood back up. "Can you come closer?"

"Give me a minute, I'm moving slow." She heard grunts and shuffling. "There seems to be a clear wall in the way."

"Yeah about that, hold on a second." She focused for an instant. "Ield-Shay Ield-Shay Ield-Shay. Are you standing right next to the wall?"

"Yep."

With a thought and gesture, she dropped the circle, stepped forward to pull him toward her, and mumbled, "Ymbol-Say Ash-Flay Orce-Fay Ield-Fay." The circle snapped back into place just as half a dozen little psssts sounded. She hugged him.

"Aaaa, not so hard. Shit! They were going to dart you."

"Yeah, I figured. What's wrong with you?" She could see blotches on his aura in really dark, almost black colors. It seemed to be around his neck, shoulder, and arm.

"Dislocated shoulder, broken arm, messed-up neck, car accident."

"Not my new Suburban?"

Bruce chuckled. "No, it was one of the security groups," he supplied.

"Hold still." She took a moment to focus, really for the audience because she didn't need to anymore. "Eal-Hay. Give it a minute."

"Wow!" There was real wonder in his voice. "You're taller and gorgeous. I mean, you were a looker before, but my God, you're like a giant Barbie doll! Racked and double stacked!"

"Interesting, I wonder why?" It was really good to have Bruce with her. She hugged him more gently.

"It's good to see you, touch you," he whispered. "When I saw your face, as they brought you out, your eyes." His voice broke.

"Shhh, I'm getting better." She opened her eyes for him, "See. I can't really see yet, but I will."

"Ahhhh," he stumbled, speaking like he didn't know what to say. "Do you want me to tell you what I see? Or not?"

"Sure." She didn't show him how scared she really was. Never show weakness was what her uncle had always told her.

"You have beautiful blue eyes." Stephanie let the breath out she didn't realize she had been holding. "They're a little milky, like cataracts, but that's it. You face is very beautiful, with strong cheeks and lush lips." He brushed at her hair. "You know you're taller right?"

"How would I know? I don't have a frame of reference." She stepped away a little and slowly turned in a circle. "Okay, what do you think?"

"Ahh," Bruce was trying not to laugh. "You realize your robe is gaping open in the back, like all the way. You have a great ass." He started chuckling.

Stephanie could feel the heat rising to her face. "That wasn't what I was asking." She swatted at him playfully.

"Steph, if I liked girls … well, never mind. I wasn't kidding when I said you looked like Barbie. Actually, you're better than Barbie. Ah, you've got to be close to six feet tall. No more short-stack jokes for you. Just stacked jokes now." She could tell he stepped to the side.

"Hey, don't look!"

"I'm tying your gown, somebody's coming."

Stephanie focused forward, tilting her head slightly to listen. She heard Mr. Culture.

"She's not cooperating. She also has gotten free of the restraints and put up some type of shield."

"How and the hell did that happen?" The new voice was East Coast and smooth. "Never mind, what did you get before then?"

"Nothing. We can tell you her fingerprints are different, and her DNA has been altered. She would no longer be considered to be Stephanie Blackraven, maybe a sister."

"Great, we may not have her much longer. Did you … ah … alter her?"

"No. I told you we didn't have time."

"Well, let me talk to her, maybe I can work a deal."

Mr. Culture made a "ha" sound, very much like he didn't think that was possible.

"Bruce, did you hear that? My DNA has been altered." She wasn't sure what it meant long term, but it sounded like they could use it to prove she wasn't herself.

"No, I didn't hear anything. Different DNA, huh, after the way you've changed, I would be surprised if it hadn't changed," he whispered back to her.

"Ah," East Coast started as he entered the room. "Ms. Doe, it seems you're giving the medical team …" His aura was dark and swirling with red.

Stephanie cut him off right there with a laugh. "Don't even try it. You know exactly who I am, regardless of what my DNA tells you. Your people took me right out of the site, and they have been using my name, when they deigned to talk at me." She crossed her arms under her breasts.

"He's the FBI guy who was arguing with Agent Farmer," Bruce whispered. "Ah, name, give me a moment. Peace, no Peirce, Agent Peirce."

Agent Peirce started to say something, and she cut him off again. "Look, Agent Peirce, it's real simple; you guys are holding me against my will, illegally. I will start actively defending myself if steps aren't taken real soon to release me. I imagine my lawyers are getting ready to lower the boom here shortly. So, please, get someone here who has a clue, like Agent Farmer."

"Attacking an FBI agent is a federal offense."

"Not if you're defending yourself. I have the right to defend myself. I think I would have an easy time getting a court to agree that I am the victim here."

"I don't think you understand the," he broke off because another aura walked into the room. This one was interesting, pinks, blues, lots of different swirling colors.

"Agent Farmer," Bruce whispered.

"I'll take it from here, Agent Peirce."

"What are … I have jurisdiction in this case."

"Not any more. Pressure has been brought to bear. Facts have surfaced that seem to have changed the deputy director's mind." Agent Farmer sounded pleased with something.

"What pressure? I did …"

The two auras closed, and Agent Farmer whispered, "Pressure has been applied from sources." A cell phone rang. "That is for you."

The auras separated, and she heard, "Agent Peirce. Yes sir, he's, yes sir. … Yes sir. No sir. No sir. Yes sir." He left the room.

"Oh, was he pissed," Bruce whispered. "He looked like he was going to blow a gasket."

"Doctor Blackraven, please allow me to apologize for the Bureau. It seems there was an over zealousness on the part of one group. I assure you, from here on out, things will be different." His aura was really busy. It had symbols shifting and swirling.

"Your, ah … You have the knack," Stephanie blurted out.

"Ah, one moment please. I'm going to go to the outer room, and I'll be right back. Do you need anything?"

"Food, un-drugged."

"Very well, one moment." Agent Farmer went out of the room. "Everyone stand down," Stephanie heard. "Agents return to your other assigned duties. Doctor, you are no longer needed. Leave one competent nurse and clear out. Turn everything off. Release Detective Bremer. Bring good food for four."

The protesting from the doctor was loud and vocally virulent. Agent Farmer finally had another agent remove the doctor.

He came back. "I brought a chair in. Do you mind if I sit? Would you like a chair or two?"

Stephanie frowned, she couldn't quite figure out what the swirling meant. Emotions, maybe, or some variation of the knack, she just didn't have enough data.

"Back to my question, do you have the knack?" Stephanie wasn't letting that go.

"I'm not sure what you mean by knack. I am a practitioner of the mystic arts. I was brought in on this case for that reason. However, this has far outstripped my experience and capabilities."

"Oh, he's a magic user," Bruce chuckled.

"Please, let's keep this on an adult level. But, yes, I can do spells and use incantations. It's not like your symbols. Would you be willing to tell me what happened after you left your grounds yesterday?" Agent Farmer was all business.

"Will you give me your word of honor, sworn by the magic you use, that you will let us go?" Her voice had taken on a reverberation-echo effect as she spoke. She was as surprised as they sounded.

Agent Farmer's aura turned a unique blue-green hue. "That was an oath invocation. You never cease to amaze me. Yes, I swear, you are free to go as soon as the legal action clears."

"What legal action?" Bruce asked.

"Agent Peirce initiated some ill-advised proceeding. Your lawyers were made aware, as due process, and are now making him regret his cleverness."

"Good. I don't like him," Stephanie announced. "He must be a bureaucrat."

"He does spend most of his time behind a desk in Washington, DC." Agent Farmer paused. Stephanie heard the tinkling of glasses and wheels. "Very good," Agent Farmer commented. "Dinner is here. If you don't mind, I will dine with you."

"To show us the food isn't drugged?" Bruce asked.

"Precisely."

"I guess I'm going to have to trust you. Yours is the only aura in the area, I assume there are no more dart rifles aimed at me." She made it as a statement, but really she was asking a question.

"If there are and they fire, I assure you, I will fire back, and it won't be with a dart." There was a brief pause. "You see auras now? You didn't before."

"Okay." She ignored his question. Stephanie gestured, thought a word, and the circle went away. "What's for dinner?"

"Looks like Chinese," Bruce commented.

"Smells like Chinese," Stephanie confirmed. She paused, "Before we start, is Rhinebolt dead?" Stephanie wasn't taking chances.

"Yes." Agent Farmer was very matter-of-fact.

"Did he die hard? Hard meaning painfully, screaming his lungs out?"

"That would be a good approximation, only take it times ten. I observed the process." He didn't sound happy.

"You got to watch? What did you see?" Stephanie had to know.

"Steph, is that a good idea?" Bruce whispered to her.

"I have to know." She thought about the pain and then shook her head. "I have to know."

Agent Farmer hummed for a moment, like he was undecided. "When I got into the room, you were naked and bolted down to the floor. You were in intense pain, or so I assume, by the way you were screaming and had lifted yourself off the floor by your wrists and ankles. Detective Bremer was pounding on an invisible barrier. Your eyes were already missing. As I watched, you deflated and Rhinebolt shimmered with a sparkling luminescence. His expression was the exact opposite of yours.

"As your desiccated body dropped to the floor, the luminescence reversed. It started flowing off him and into you. He started screaming and deflating. You inflated. It seemed to overinflate you. Your hands and feet extended beyond the original circle. They got burnt. Ahh ... Hmmm ... Caught on fire. It reached a point where you wrenched the bolts out of the floor and rolled into a fetal position.

"Rhinebolt screamed until he had no more air and just continued deflating. It looked extremely painful. However, something was holding him in his circle. His final appearance was even worse than Andrew Stone's, he was kneeling with his hands ... you don't need to hear the rest.

"At that point, the containment flashed and was gone. The flash destroyed the box hanging above the area and the computer it was connected to." Agent Farmer crossed his legs and waited.

"Wow," Stephanie breathlessly exclaimed. "I'm glad I wasn't awake. So, he died hard?"

Agent Farmer agreed, "Hard."

"Well, in that case, grab a couple of chairs and let's eat." Stephanie added a cheerful lilt to her tone. "I want to hear what you know about our departure from the grounds first." She was definitely not going to show them how much she was shaken by his description.

Agent Farmer grabbed two more chairs and served dinner.

"At 2110 hours, vehicles started leaving your compound." Agent Farmer was in his matter-of-fact delivery mode.

Stephanie leaned toward Bruce and playfully whispered, "Does he have his little notebook out?"

Bruce snorted and blew food as he laughed. "How can you find this funny? And yes, he does."

"I don't know. I guess dying by being sucked through a straw and being brought back to life just seems to have changed my perspective."

There was stunned silence for a moment.

"Is that what it was like?" Agent Farmer asked quietly.

"Actually, the pain had knocked me out by then. My eyes exploding will be a special memory." She was trying for funny, but it didn't come out that way.

Bruce gagged and then gulped some fluid.

"Sorry," she added sheepishly. "I thought that would be funny."

"Back to my narrative," Agent Farmer stepped in. "At 2235, plus or minus ten minutes, gun shots, wolves howling, and other roaring animals were heard at Soaring Eagle Regional Park on the east side of Redmond. The gunshots escalated to automatic weapon fire and then a freak lightning storm struck. The storm destroyed forest and a nearby waste-processing facility. Eleven wolves and three gang members of the Lobo gang were found dead. I have assumed the wolves were actually werewolves. I would like your confirmation." Stephanie nodded to him.

"At 2250, a high-speed chase was reported passing through Redmond and ending in a multicar crash on the north side of Highway 520 near an industrial park.

"A massive bear was reported by police, being released to run rampaging through the park, killing ten men, all of whom had automatic weapons. There was even a TOW missile reported onsite under a truck.

"That led to the ritual chamber and three dead. A very strange scene, indeed, with some type of automatic dart spell and the ritual in progress. Detective Bremer was found beating on the ritual circle enclosure. It took six agents to pull him away. He damaged three of them."

"You said three dead?" Hope blossomed in her heart.

"Yes. Nelson, one of his accomplices, and Professor Rhinebolt," Agent Farmer stated questioningly.

"Are you pressing charges against Joe for attacking federal agents?" Stephanie asked quietly.

"No." Agent Farmer sounded surprised. "No, if anything, he is the hero of the hour. By all accounts, it was he who led your people to the site. He was broken and still struggling to get to you."

"Broken?" she asked, but was almost afraid to hear the answer.

"Arms, fingers on both hands, five ribs, pelvis, shoulder, bones broken. That doesn't count all the bleeding wounds."

"Broken bones?" Stephanie blurted out. "How did he get broken bones? People were shooting at him."

"Bullets break bones," Agent Farmer stated quietly.

That gave Stephanie pause. She rallied quickly. "Bruce tells me that he is fine, physically?"

"All of his injuries have healed." Agent Farmer was back to his briefing tone. "All of his injuries had healed before we got him to this facility."

"Bruce?" she asked.

"For some reason, he feels he failed you," Bruce quietly told her while reaching out to touch her hand.

"What?" Stephanie wasn't sure she had heard that right. "He what?"

Bruce cleared his throat. "He said he wasn't good enough for you. He failed you."

Agent Farmer's aura flared and she thought he looked away briefly. "Detective Bremer was released and asked to be taken from this facility. He didn't want to see you."

It was Stephanie's turn to look away. It hurt, and then a different part asserted itself. "That idiot, what the hell is he thinking? Was he thinking at all?"

Bruce chuckled weakly. She even got a different aura flare from Agent Farmer.

She and Bruce told their story. She left out the details about Rhinebolt's master symbol and the changes she made, other than to tell him she had changed it, with the Lady's help. She emphasized the Lady's help and influence.

After sipping more pop, she asked, "So, what was Rhinebolt doing? He was a pompous ass, but he was also pretty smart. He had to be after something."

Agent Farmer looked up from his notebook. "I don't know. I haven't gotten access to his files yet. My assumption is that he was stealing his victim's ability to work magic. Of the few victims we have been able to collect in-depth data on, they all had the 'knack' as you put it. Also, an assumption, I think our government, through many cutouts, was involved, thus Nelson's backing and resources."

"Now what?" Bruce asked.

"Now," Agent Farmer said, "we go on. I would like you two to join the government resource pool for working these types of items."

"Not going to happen," Stephanie stated. "At least not as direct hires. Maybe consult or through some type of organization, but not directly."

"I'm with her," Bruce added. "Politicians are assholes and they seem to get to call the shots."

Chapter 29

"Young lady, it's time for you to take a break." Rosemary sounded very firm from the door. Stephanie could see her green and blue aura coming toward her.

Stephanie was in her favorite room, the library. It smelled just right, and generally, no one else visited.

"I just had a break. I had lunch with you and Bruce."

"That is not the kind I'm talking about. You have been going nonstop for the last month, ever since ..." Rosemary always stumbled over that part. She had a bad scar on her lower back. She had let Stephanie touch it, but wouldn't let her do her healing symbol to heal it. There was also the psychological damage from Chris being gunned down in front of her, and of course, being charmed to be a sex slave. "You know, since the event."

"Rosemary, I've a lot to do. With the establishing of the foundation, the FBI reports, the local police, the appearances in court and my personal studies, I just can't take off."

"Stephanie." Rosemary sounded just like a mother. "You know you need some down time, to let things ..." Stephanie knew she was waving her hands vaguely in the air, it's what she did, "Settle. Let yourself deal with the changes."

"I can deal fine. Anyway, I'm doing Bruce's Zen meditations to center my wa." She couldn't quite keep the cynicism out of her voice. "As much as I hate to admit it, it is helping me to understand the changes."

"Stephanie, you can't see. You are going to have to take steps to restore your vision."

"I can't see visible light. I can see other things, and I'm learning to control it." She carefully got up from her desk and moved over the space set up between bookcases she used as her meditation site. "The Lady said she was trying to teach me something. Anyway, between the auras and other heightened senses and awareness, I'm getting along okay."

"She also said you need your protector, Joe."

Stephanie felt a sudden pain and anger. "He doesn't want me. You remember the text he sent me, the blind lady, saying we were breaking up." She turned away as she said it. When she had finally tracked him down to confront him, they had had a terrible fight through a closed door. He wouldn't face her in person.

Maybe she did have a smart mouth; she certainly let him hear it, all of it. "And, frankly I don't know what it was I saw in him. I'll be damned if I'll crawl to get him back."

"He's carrying his own psychological wounds. He should've died from the wounds he received. If the Goddess hadn't enriched and filled him with her power, he would've died. And he did fail in the mission set before him." Compassion filled her voice. "He had to watch you ... ah ... change. Anyway, Bruce told me Joe seems to be coming to grips with it all and is really sorry for how he treated you."

"Bruce told you; when did he see Joe?"

"Ahh," Rosemary made her quibbling noises.

"No, no, no, no, you started this. Now when did he see Joe?"

"At the inquiry, the courthouse. Joe's hearing was this week."

"What hearing, what courthouse? What is going on?"

Stephanie heard Rosemary take a deep breath and let it out as she moved closer. "There was a closed door hearing about whether Joe was in control of his bear form. After the event last month and the special circumstances, the judge wanted to see for himself. The lawyers . . ." Rosemary didn't like them much. She had a special tone in her voice when she talked about them. "Had Joe transform in front of the court and then he was questioned. Apparently, it was quite the show. Joe was acquitted, released from all charges, with records sealed. He's a free man."

"And no one thought to tell me about this? Why?" Tears started leaking. She hated crying, showing weakness, but just couldn't help herself. Her emotions had been all over the place since her change. Stephanie was suddenly feeling very hurt and alone.

"Honey, no one wanted to hurt you. You've been through so much." Rosemary was holding her hand now.

Stephanie slowly pulled her hand away and herself together. She needed some time. "I'm going to meditate now. We'll talk more later."

"Okay, honey, you call if you need anything." Rosemary sounded a little hurt, but her aura was swirling a different hue.

Stephanie would never admit it to Bruce, but the mediation helped. It allowed her time to study herself, her new gifts. Bruce had created a biofeedback set that used sound instead of lights to indicate the brain wave patterns she was trying to induce. It used flutes, harps, and woodwinds to represent the proper patterns. She was getting pretty good at it.

She fumbled a little getting the headset on. Her aura vision, or third eye, as some of the mystic texts referred to it, didn't allow her to "see" inanimate objects very well. She settled herself on the floor mat and drew in the first deep breath, the settling breath. It triggered a peaceful feeling, sweeping from her chest out to her extremities. She let her mind float as she "felt" her fingers one at a time then her toes, slowly moving one muscle at a time. Then she went through her senses, skipping sight, or at least visible sight. Her hearing was especially acute. She could hear things from rooms away, little things like a heartbeat, if she concentrated. The harp was playing, indicating she had achieved the correct mindset.

"Ilense-Say." She enacted the symbol of quiet around herself, so the other noises wouldn't bother or distract her. Then she closed her third eye, shutting off the aura vision. It was the hardest thing she did, since it left her blind, really blind. Drawing out her Bone Knife, she laid it before her. She opened her symbol vision and only the vision of symbols to study it. The crisp sharp lines jumped out at her. She studied it as she had before, then closed it off, and looked with the aura vision. The knife had swirls and whirls in it of color, muted dark colors, but colors. *How can a knife have an aura?* she thought. *Maybe it isn't an aura, per se, perhaps it's energy, collected energy.* That thought stumbled her a bit. She assumed it was life auras she saw, but if it was energy, then maybe it was electron flow, like electricity. She looked over at the biofeedback unit. Nothing. *A new type of energy?* she mused. *I guess we'll call it magic for now. Hmm, so this aura vision lets me see auras in people, which equate to emotional states, health, and the knack. It also lets me see magic energy"* She huffed out loud. *I can't call it magic, so M energy.* She looked up from her knife and noticed some of her books also had swirling M energy in them. *Interesting!*

She almost strangled herself with the biofeedback headset, as she lurched up to pull the books down, but got untangled before pulling anything over. She had three books that swirled with M energy. In her current state, she couldn't read them.

"*Now you are ready.* The Lady's voice came to her.

What?

He is ready. You are ready. Go to your protector.

He told me he didn't want me. A deep sense of loss and longing settled on her. She was alone. There was no one for her.

Go to him.

Stephanie couldn't help herself. "He doesn't want me!" she shouted. Quietly, she added, "He told me he wouldn't hurt me." The sense of being alone was crushing. She just broke down sobbing, her will washing away with the tears. Then she couldn't see anything, no symbols, no auras, nothing, darkness.

"I'm blind, I can't see!" she screamed. That's when she really lost it. Everything from the past several weeks crashed in on her. Panic happened, deep sobs, she crashed around as she tried to move. People moved in to help, but she wasn't consolable. No rational thought, finally, she slumped into a lump on the floor and cried until she slept.

Stephanie woke up in a bed, which smelled like her bed, but she still couldn't see. A noise woke her. Her hearing was still extra sharp. There was extra breathing across the room. She pulled the pistol from under her pillow. *Bless* Agnes. She aimed at the rustle of cloth and a silenced breath.

"Princess, don't yell. I don't want to have to subdue Agnes." Only one person called her that. "Don't shoot me. I've been sent to help."

"Uncle Raymond's dead, who the hell are you?" It really pissed her off to think someone was trying to impersonate her great uncle.

"No, you fixed it so I didn't die. You gave me to your goddess. This is all on you."

"What!? I did not give you up. I healed you or at least tried to. A couple times." She started to feel hope. They didn't recover Uncle Raymond's body at the scene. No one admitted to knowing anything about him. Who shot Nelson was a mystery.

"There was a price. Don't get your panties in a twist. I had a choice." The pistol was snatched from her hands. "It seems you aren't the only last-of-your-kind around, Princess." She felt weight settle on the bed. He smelled of tobacco, whisky, gun oil, and leather just as he always had.

"What the hell … You know North American Indians don't have princesses."

"Incas did."

"What?"

"Oh, you figure it out, you're so damn smart. I should've let the orphanage keep you."

That's what he said whenever she started getting on his nerves. She launched herself at his voice, to hug him. "Please tell me you're real. Please tell me you're real." The tears were leaking again.

His big hand settled on her back. "Yeah, I'm real, older, but real. Hell, I'm in the best shape I've been in for fifty years."

"I'm not alone," she whispered into his neck.

"How and the hell can you think you're alone. Christ, there's a whole house full of people here for you. I had a hell of a time sneaking in here."

"I don't have anyone to love me." She gave a little sob.

"What the hell happened to the big guy that was so hot to court you, Joe?"

"He doesn't want me now." She was talking through her sobs. "Not since the … the … scene."

"Christ, why not? He waded through at least twelve guys. Got his ass shot off. He was one big badass bear. He kicked ass and took names, fought all the way to the ritual room. He cleared the path for me to get in there. I've seen some shit, and let me tell you, I've never seen anything like that. You know he flipped a truck over on some guys rigging a TOW missile. It was glorious." That sounded like Uncle Raymond.

"Well," she got herself under control. "Apparently, he decided I wasn't good enough."

"What?"

She had heard that tone before as well. "Don't you go hurt him!" She was worried for Joe now.

"This guy some kind of moron or something? You two are linked through the Great Spirit. It's not like he gets to walk away."

"Uncle Raymond …" She was trying to warn him.

"You go fix this, or a month from now, I'll take Moron Boy out to the woodshed and make him see reason. Nobody spurns my Princess. Nobody." The last statement was cold and pitiless. He pried her hands loose, and she felt his weight leave the bed. "A month."

"Why do I have to fix it? He's the one …" she stopped herself when she realized if she didn't, Uncle Raymond wouldn't wait a month. "Okay."

"Another thing, there are those in our government that now know I'm not really gone. So you shouldn't be getting any more shit from that side. They'll play fair. The rest of Nelson's team … retired."

"Retired? You mean dead?"

"Yeah. That's what I used to send the message to our government." He was sounding colder than normal. No remorse.

"Okay, well, the government and I kind of worked it out already. I too have learned how to bring down the rain, so to speak. I've started a foundation for studying symbols. They're investing in it."

"Yeah, good idea, makes them feel like they have control, even when they don't. You take care of Moron Boy, one month. I gotta go. I'll be around, but you probably won't see me. I'm dead, remember?"

"I love you."

"Right back at you, Princess."

She heard a rustling, and then a door slammed open.

"Mum, you all right?" It was a worried Agnes and at least three others.

"I'm fine. I had a visitor." Stephanie wiped her face with her sheet. "He's gone now, and I'm still very blind."

People she couldn't identify moved through her room. "We should move you to the safe room, mum. Why is your pistol disassembled?"

"I think he got ticked when I pointed it at him."

"Hunh, I used to know ..." her voice trailed off. Stephanie could almost hear her thinking. "Well, we should be a move'n you, mum."

She let Agnes bundle her up and walk her to another room; they used the lift since stairs were problematic. She tried praying to the Lady, who took the call, but didn't really help or tell her anything. Very frustrating!

Breakfast the next day was interesting, as well as dressing. Before, she had seen all sorts of symbols and aura shadows to kind of provide her with information, clues of what things were and where they were located. All that was gone; she couldn't summon the vision. Being blind had some real drawbacks. There was a skill set needed to navigate as a blind person, and she didn't have it yet.

Rosemary showed up at about the time Stephanie launched another sausage off her plate while trying to stab it with a fork. "Today is a holiday," Rosemary started without preamble. "The winter solstice. We will go for a drive to get you out of this house for a while."

"Rosemary, I don't," Stephanie whined.

"I tried to warn you yesterday what would come of your actions, and you wouldn't listen. So, stop your whining, wipe the egg off your chin, and let's go." Rosemary was all professor today, no arguments.

No one was listening to Stephanie's complaints. Agnes just bundled her off to change. Bruce made shooing noises. Stephanie decided to just buck up and let it ride.

The circus mounted up or at least that's what it sounded like with all the guards and transport. Stephanie wasn't sure who all went, and she was in no position to argue with anyone because no one would listen to her.

Well, she had a few choice words for Bruce, about Joe, when she got near him, but nothing for her security. Agnes gave her sunglasses and a jacket complete with scarf, so she wouldn't catch the weather or something like that and a new female guard named Tessa. Tessa sounded younger, didn't have Agnes' built-in cynicism.

Stephanie just didn't feel like fighting. She let Rosemary drag her along.

Apparently, Lawrence, the super butler, had imported security from the UK. Her detail was much larger, she couldn't see them, but she could hear and smell them. She started identifying them by those traits. It was harder to get an accurate sense of them. Tessa smelled of heather and rose.

Rosemary put her foot down about driving and won. So it was Rosemary, Stephanie, and Tessa in the car with the others following or leading or whatever. They drove for a while, with Rosemary making small talk about the history of the winter solstice.

"So, today is a big day for the Lady?" Stephanie finally butted in. "Why did she decide to shit on me today then?"

"Young lady that is no way to talk about the Lady!"

"Bite me!" Stephanie blurted out. "We both know humans are like finger puppets to her. She has a use for us now, but when she's done, so are we."

"Stephanie Marguerite Rachael Macgregor Stuart Blackraven, you can't talk of her like that!" Rosemary appeared truly shocked.

Tessa gave a startled gasp from the backseat. "Macgregor! Stuart!?!" She must have been really shocked because she was all-Scottish with the accent.

The vehicle swerved as Rosemary got it off the road. Stephanie heard rustling just before Rosemary's hands grabbed her shoulders. "Please." Real concern was in Rosemary's voice, "Don't every talk about her like that again. Lesser servants could get away with it, but not you. You are her High Priestess, and even when she doesn't appear to be listening to you, she is. She learns from you, just as you learn from her. Please, don't teach her that we don't matter."

"No problems," Stephanie heard Tessa say from the back, still with the thick accent. "Apparently, the Priestess and High Priestess are arguing religion." She was really rolling her r's and cutting off words.

Stephanie could feel Rosemary stiffen through her hands as Rosemary turned toward the backseat. "I said you could ride with us if you didn't talk. Commenting is talking."

"But she's a bloody bonny Stuart?" Tessa blurted out. "That would make her . . ."

"I said no talking." Rosemary was fierce. "You say another word, you go back to Scotland."

Stephanie moved her hands up to Rosemary's face by gentle touching until she pressed her palms to Rosemary's cheeks. She gently turned her face back toward her. "Rosemary, on me. Look at me." Rosemary allowed her head to be turned. Stephanie smiled. "How did you know my whole name? I didn't even know what it was until all this crap started."

"I needed to," Rosemary sounded aloof, "so she provided."

"Why?" Stephanie asked. "Why do you need to know?"

Rosemary shook her head in the negative without talking.

Stephanie took a breath to steady herself. "Okay, I will try to give the Lady the respect she is due, but right now, I'm having a little trouble adjusting. I'm not feeling too charitable toward the Lady right now since I'm blind, and I'm pretty sure it's her fault and on purpose."

"Tessa," Stephanie kept her hands on Rosemary's face, but shifted her attention to the voice in the back. "If you told her you wouldn't talk, then don't." A cool puff of air seemed to whiff through the car. "That Lady is with us, so don't attract her attention."

"Yes m'lady." Stephanie heard a serious, soft lilting voice from the back, accompanied by increased heart rate and the smell of fear sweat.

"Stephanie, the Lady's compassion has already been felt by your people. She learned that compassion from you." Rosemary's voice had a strange quiver to it. "Stoneman, Frank, and two other of your guards were infected with lycanthropy during the fight in the park. The Lady has brought them over just as she did Tony. Through her efforts, they have all transitioned through the full moon and become guardians instead of animals."

"Aw shit!" Stephanie exclaimed. "I'm stuck with Stoneman. Damn, I was hoping he would move to another job."

Rosemary snorted and shook her head. "Child, you have no idea the devotion that just falls your way." Rosemary patted Stephanie's cheek and then moved back over to drive.

"What does that mean?" Stephanie asked.

Rosemary laughed with aged humor in her voice. "You'll figure it out. You are a clever one."

"That's the same thing ... ah ..." Stephanie couldn't finish that sentence. "And since when did I get people?" Stephanie was really puzzled by that.

Rosemary evaded questions and provided trivia as they drove on. It was Rosemary's way.

It didn't matter if Stephanie talked because Rosemary just carried on as if she hadn't.

It was good. They were back to normal. Finally, they stopped for coffee.

Stephanie had no idea where they were, except that it smelled of pine and was close to a highway, as she could hear the cars and trucks whizzing by. Little bells tinkled as the door was opened. The shop smelled of coffee, cinnamon, yeast, and other yummy things. As they moved carefully to a table, she got a whiff of Old Spice. Suddenly, she knew he was close.

"Stephanie," a female, almost familiar, voice called out. She heard someone approach in haste.

"Friend," Rosemary called off her security as Stephanie heard them start rustling forward. "All of you out of the shop. I've got this." Rosemary's voice was very forceful. Even odder, it seemed to work.

"Abby." A seismic event occurred. "She won't recognize you. She's blind." Joe sounded tired, worn, and really unhappy. "Mom, this is a … this is ... cheating," he finally wound down.

"Stop talking, Joseph, you're embarrassing us." It was a strong voice that sounded a great deal like Abby's. "Well, what a surprise! Priestess Stein, fair greeting to you."

"Well, isn't it just." Stephanie could tell Rosemary was pleased with herself. "The blessing of the Goddess on you, Initiate Bremer."

Stephanie held her hand out, "Abby?" The gesture and the name seemed to convey her intent. Someone gently took her hand. Stephanie pulled her into a hug. "It so good to see … ah, well … ah whatever."

"I get it. It's good to see you, too. Like wow, you are hot! The hair ... figure ... taller, too. Wow, I'm jealous. The news was, like all over it, but I didn't believe it. Wow, you look really good. Sorry about the eyes thing."

Stephanie laughed. Abby was young. "Yeah, it sucks, but I'm hoping for it to improve here soon."

"Abigail," that mother's voice again. "Don't pester her." Abby released the hug and stepped away. "Joseph, you should greet her with a hug. You are courting her, after all."

"Mom," Joe sighed. "You just … can't … I'm not good enough for her," he finally mumbled.

Stephanie could hear the sigh from his mother and Rosemary.

"Is it so hard, Joe?" Her voice wavered against her will as she held out her hand toward his voice. "It's just a hug. Please, I've been worried."

She felt him come closer. No emotion, no "sense" of him, just the size of him moving. "Wow, you are taller." There was wonder in his whisper. "You look really good, Steph, really good." His voice broke.

As soon as she felt his hand on her arm, she launched herself into him, grabbing on hard, pulling herself into him. He smelled good, solid, right.

It was like an explosion of color. Pain lanced through her eyes. It took her breath away for a moment. Tears ran down her face. "Why didn't you come back to me?" she whispered into his neck. "I needed you. I need you." She could "feel" him again: the worry, concern for her, and anger. Along with it came a warmth that spread out from her middle. She wasn't alone anymore.

"I failed you when it really counted. I couldn't bear to see what I'd done to you. You were naked, bolted down. My God, they took your eyes. You deflated to ... I couldn't get ..." Joe was fighting not to cry. "I failed you."

"No you didn't, you didn't fail me. You're my hero, my champion. You led everyone to me. That's how I got saved. You saved me." She blinked and could see. She closed her eyes, flipping the little switch in her head, and the auras and symbols were back. She had to concentrate a little to shut them off. "Oh my."

"What's wrong, Steph?" Joe was worried now. His head came up as he looked for an enemy.

She could "feel" it from him.

"Perhaps you two would like our table in the back corner? It's a little more private." Stephanie looked over at an older Abby, a little grey, maybe a little more padded, but the same blond hair and eyes, maybe an older Viking woman ready to burn and pillage. She dressed like Rosemary. She had Joe's nose.

Stephanie pushed away from Joe and wiped her eyes. "Oh, I'm sorry, Mrs. Bremer. So rude of me. I didn't mean …"

"Pish posh," She was smiling from ear to ear with tears in her eyes as well. "You two have had a tough go of it lately. One of you dumber than the other, I think, probably made it tougher." She gave Joe a piercing look.

Stephanie stepped forward and surprised her with a hug. "I'm Stephanie Blackraven; may I date your son?" she whispered.

She got hugged back with a little laugh. "I'm Charlotte. He's not a bad boy, just gets confused. You'll straighten him out. And yes, you may."

Rosemary grabbed Stephanie's arm as she released Charlotte and turned her. "Steph, your eyes?" Rosemary was openly weeping and smiling at the same time, as she gently removed the sunglasses to look at Stephanie's eyes.

Stephanie blinked at the light and gave a little laugh. "I can see fine." She had to sniffle a little. "It came back as soon as Joe hugged me. That's what the Lady wanted me to see. I need him."

"Steph, your eyes?" Joe looked terrible. Face gaunt, beard stubble, black rings under his eyes, his clothes were hanging on him like he'd lost weight. He had a haunted look. "You can see? Are you okay?"

"I am now." She grabbed his arm. "You don't get to go away again."

"Steph …" he started. "I'm not good …"

"No," she cut him off, "Mr. Bremer, you stop that. You didn't do anything wrong. We are going to talk about this right now. I said some … harsh things to you, about you, that were unfair. I need, … no, we need to talk things through. You go back to the table. I need to go freshen up and I'll be right there." She turned to the women present. "Don't you let him run."

They all laughed.

"Did he just fix her vision?" Abby asked her mother.

"It's a miracle, that's what it is, child." Rosemary answered. "The Goddess moves …"

"And if we're not fast enough, we get swept away," Stephanie finished for her, smiling.

Charlotte gave a big laugh. "Yes, dear it seems that way sometimes. We serve her, not the other way around. You run along and powder your noise, not that you need to. You are a pretty thing. We'll keep him from escaping."

Stephanie gave her a little head nod and headed to the ladies room.

A thin, wiry, college-looking guy nursing a coffee stepped over in front of her. "Doctor Blackraven? Doctor Stephanie Blackraven?"

She stopped, frowning, trying to determine friend or foe. "Yes?" she agreed carefully.

"I'm a huge fan." He smiled. "I'm thinking of transferring to Bosh – Gates. Could I get your autograph? Wow, you're really pretty …" He stopped talking and stared at her with his mouth hanging open. He was holding out a notebook opened to a blank page.

"Who should I make it to?"

"Ah ... what? Oh, to Justin," he mumbled. "Are you teaching next semester?" His mouth was still hanging open.

"I don't think so." She placed her hand above the page, the Will, the Way, "Ite-Wray." Flowing letters and script appeared on the page.

"Magic, hot damn!"

Stephanie held up a finger and announced with force, "Not magic, science!"

Made in the USA
Charleston, SC
16 August 2015